THE MISFIT MAGE
AND

HIS DASHING DEVIL

MN Bennet

THE MISFIT MAGE AND HIS DASHING DEVIL

DIABOLIC ROMANCE BOOK ONE

MN BENNET

Paperback ISBN: 979-8-9872532-5-0
Ebook ISBN: 979-8-9872532-4-3

Edited by Charlie Knight (CKnightWrites.com)
Cover art by Miblart (miblart.com)

www.mnbennet.com/

DEDICATION

To everyone who likes a little humor with their carnage and a bit of wickedness in their romance.
May the devil and his mage bring you joy.

AUTHOR'S NOTE

Thank you so much for considering *The Misfit Mage and His Dashing Devil*! I'm delighted to share Wally and Bez's journey. There's so much to enjoy about this wonderful world of magic such as the banter, gallows humor, and the fun romance that sneaks right up on you. That said, there are some elements I want to make readers aware of before diving in. For those interested, I've included a list of content warnings on the following page.

This book contains the following elements:

Foul language
Graphic violence and gore
Blood
Bullying
Torture both mental and physical
Murder [some brutal]
There are several open door, descriptive sex scenes between adults
Depression and anxiety
Gaslighting

1

Walter

"You need to slide back onto it. Otherwise—"

"I know." I gulped. This wasn't a big deal. I'd done this plenty of times before. In fact, I'd been doing this a lot longer than Ian, yet somehow, he'd gained far more experience.

"Come on, Wally." Ian's breath licked my ear, sweet and soft. His hand gripped my hip, pulling me closer to his waist, and I willingly slid toward him because the idea of my back pressed to his chest sent a quiver through my body. This entire thing was exciting. Well, nerve-racking, but in a wonderfully distracting sort of way. "It won't hurt. Promise."

"I'm not worried about that." My ears burned. Okay, I was a little worried about the pain—something which often made me hesitate— but mostly, my calves ached from holding this straddled position. "It's just I don't want someone walking down the trail and catching us."

"No one ever walks down these trails." Ian moved his hand, sliding it from my hip and planting it firmly on my abdomen. "Besides, you shouldn't be embarrassed. All anyone would see is a rockstar with some amazing moves."

My stomach clenched, and I buried the rush fluttering from that simple touch that evoked so much curiosity. "You're not helping."

Ian shushed himself, clicking his tongue against the roof of his mouth as if to mimic locking his lips. I ignored the urge to ensure no one was wandering down the nearby trails to soak in the beautiful luminescent lights radiating off each portal in the Dimensional Atrium. I loved it here, the way everything, even the blades of grass, bounced the lights like endless mirrors casting serene warmth.

Doorways linked here to every magical location throughout the state, allowing mages and Mythics alike quick access—as long as they had clearance. Fae magics stirred in this pocket realm, illuminated by a dimly pink and orange sun and rainbow-painted moon. They were each frozen here, high above the purplish-blue sky, with the lights of various portals bouncing off them to brighten everything in enchanted colors.

The calming comfort of this place pushed away my jitters, and I focused.

"That's it. Now, get a firm grip and—"

"I vaguely remember showing *you* how saturation works." My toes curled, anxious and uncertain, as I held the wooden broom we straddled, imbuing it with mana until the sigils covering the stick glowed.

I hated flying. I'd often either fail to lift off or fall flat on my face, and either way, it was embarrassing. Almost as embarrassing as Ian assisting me with practice for an exam I'd failed more times than I could count. Ian had never attended an academy yet impressed everyone during his apprenticeship and aced the practitioner exam on his first attempt. Meanwhile, I hadn't mastered one single magic.

When Ian offered to help me practice for the exam, it seemed like a great idea. A real win-win situation. I'd known him for a while and really enjoyed his company; he liked hanging out with me. Maybe. Probably. Most likely. It wasn't like he knew too many people in Seattle and even fewer mages or Mythics when he'd arrived. Still, I wanted to figure out if his nice nature and touchy-feely assistance were how he acted with everyone or if there was a spark there.

"You'll want to steady that charge."

"Huh?"

Ian stroked the broom handle, evenly distributing the saturation of mana I'd imbued. Come on! That was clearly suggestive as fuck. Or I'd done what I always did—overanalyzed every tiny detail searching for any cue that led to the answer I wanted.

My breathing hitched, but I stabilized my mana. I hadn't quite lifted off and had already screwed up a core fundamental of imbuing mage tools—which meant taking the magical residue within myself coursing as mana and saturating the sigils with a proper charge. Too much in one or too little in another would cause the mana to erupt in unexpected ways. With a broom, it usually involved getting bucked off like riding a raging bull.

I wobbled, legs dangling, and very much wanted to quit before I made an even bigger fool out of myself. Ian kept a hand on the broom and arm wrapped around me as we lifted off the ground.

"Come on," Ian whispered. "I want you to show me all the best views here in the Atrium."

"You probably have more time to visit this place than me." Between work and working after hours and avoiding practicing for an exam I'd fail again, I rarely made my way to the Atrium anymore. It was more of a headache finding the time to visit, but as a professional practitioner in the sentinel regiment, Ian made use of the portals daily for work.

I shook away the self-doubt, self-loathing, self-what-the-fuck-ever, because I wanted to make the most of this practice. We floated high above the Sigillaria trees lining the trail, their trunks glittering with lights all the way to their forked branches and majestic leaves. It was hard to know if these looked anything like the actual extinct trees, but every plant and animal dwelling in the Dimensional Atrium came from a species long lost, forgotten, or eradicated by humanity. The Fae preserved them here. They preserved everything in their many vast realms. It was nice having access to this little pocket reality they shared with mages.

Sticking to the woodland trails, I jerked and weaved around branches. My broom sputtered, zipping quickly and then halting because my saturation continued faltering.

"Sorry. Having a bit of trouble."

"Relax." Ian rested his chin on my shoulder, pressing his cheek to mine to guide my line of vision. "Enjoy the view and try not to overthink the magic."

I turned willingly, assuming he wanted to glimpse the Fae patrolling this territory, something I had tried doing for years. Occasionally, I'd see one in the corner of my eye, but they were nothing more than a glare in my glasses since they refused to be observed, determined to remain the observers. But it wasn't the Fae that piqued his interest.

A herd of Pyrenean ibex grazed at the edges of rocky terrain, their horns coated in gold and silver, which didn't look anything like the species in recorded history.

"Not sure if the Fae modified them through recreation magic or a mix of doppelgänger cloning," I explained, "but the Pyrenean ibex don't actually gather in those patterns. And while their fur is likely altered due to the discoloration here, they had much shorter coats. Their horns also—obviously—don't shimmer with metallic sheen, but it's the odd curvatures that really make it apparent how much the Fae decided what they liked about the original species versus what they sought to alter."

Wind whistling in my ear was the only sound as I took a breath, pausing my over-explanation of what Ian likely found to be cute, goat-like critters. I preferred the truth of things, studying the historical relevance and understanding the ins and outs of how something worked, which might've been off-putting. Okay, definitely off-putting.

"Wally!"

Ian's shout startled my attention back to our course, where we were about to collide with an oncoming tree. No, not oncoming. That'd involve the tree moving.

No.

We were the ones moving. *Me*.

I was the one directing this crashing flight as we descended lower on the trail toward a cluster of trees too thick to avoid.

Pouring mana into the broom with saturation only sped our impending collision because the sigils' fueling speed, instead of lifting, glowed brighter, and once again, I'd proven I couldn't do anything right.

Ian wrapped his fingers over mine, yanking the broom back and altering our direction. A gust of wind burst—very much not a natural anomaly but a sign of Ian's precision over elemental magic, even though he was a clear water sign—which helped push us up and over the thorny bristles of long-forgotten trees.

"I'm sorry." I trembled, unable to shake away the dread. "I suck at this. I suck at everything."

"Chill." Ian steered the broom to the ground from behind me. I was too frazzled to concentrate, so I let him take over since he had a knack for what I never did. "You don't suck."

"I do. I suck a lot."

Ian snorted as we descended. "Are you beating yourself up or bragging?"

"Huh? What do you mean?" I slid forward off the broom, finding my footing with shaky legs.

"Think about it."

I huffed. "Not what I meant."

"Too bad." Ian winked.

That was a sign. Or debris from our flight caught in his eye, forcing a one-eyed blink to remove the obstruction, which was totally feasible and far more likely than him flirting with me during a practice flight in which I almost crashed. Still, his bright blue eyes and long lashes were worth staring at for investigative purposes. He stretched his back, arching until his tight black tee lifted slightly, revealing his abdomen. I turned.

"You've got to get out of your own head," he said. "You know more about magic than anyone I've ever met."

That was true. Not in a braggart way. I knew literally everything there was to know. What I didn't know, I studied, learned, and taught to anyone willing to listen. A relatively short list, which mainly involved the Magus who only kept me employed since I comprehended the theory of magic, mana, and Mythics better than most. If only I could apply theory to practice, I wouldn't be outdone by a guy like Ian, who didn't come from a mage lineage. Ian didn't learn about the Mythic world until he was twenty-five when he witnessed magic in use and retained the memories after sentinels failed to glamour away the event.

We were the same age, yet he'd adapted quickly to mage society, rose through the ranks, and went from apprentice to practitioner in an official regiment well within a year of training. Ian was practically chosen for greatness, stumbling onto his destiny, while I couldn't manifest mine despite years of effort. Further proof that what a person knew mattered significantly less than how they applied that understanding. I'd had my entire life to practice and study, yet remained an apprentice for the archivist regiment. It all boiled down to filing practitioner's findings instead of being permitted to go explore and research my own.

I fidgeted, searching for the right thing to say to Ian. A thank you for his time, for saving me, for believing in me even if I had an annoying tendency to whine. Instead, I remained silent, absorbing Dolen's Crossing, where all the portals in the vast Dimensional Atrium converged.

Not only had Ian steadied my mana and avoided crashing, but he'd also taken us back to the entryway. Portals glowed, and practitioner mages utilized the doorways to skirt through quickly from one place to the next, walking over the constructed stone pathways, none savoring the beauty of this realm. It was day-to-day for them, and so few explored the many facets this pocket reality offered. Ironic considering Dolen meant wanderer.

All I wanted was to wander and study everything about the Mythic world up close, which I could only truly do with a practitioner title. Go on excavations for magical artifacts, immerse myself in Mythic society, unravel the secrets of Diabolics—something few knew because while they lingered near our world, it was rare that they tore the dimension separating us asunder. To say I held a fascination for everything magical was an understatement.

"You okay?" Ian nudged my shoulder with his, another comforting sensation that sent every synapse firing off wild ideas.

"Fine. Just realizing my lunch break is almost over, and I have to get back to work." I headed toward the portals before I made a bigger fool out of myself. "Thank you again. I'll have to pay you back sometime. For your time."

"Wait." Ian moved in close. *Too close.*

His lips practically touched mine, and the entire Dimensional Atrium faded away. The carefully cultivated aromas the Fae kept well despite all the foliage and fauna cohabitating in this dwelling were washed away beneath the powerful citrus cologne Ian wore. It held a strong musk of sweetness and spice that left me entranced. His Adam's apple bulged as he swallowed, his eyes locked on mine, and his lip quivered ever so until he smiled.

"Y-yes?"

"Sorry." Ian backstepped, boyish and nervous and almost as fidgety as me. "I've been trying to play it cool for weeks now. Casual when I see you in the museum—which almost never happens. But then you needed a study buddy, and I thought it'd be a great chance to hang out…but now you're off to the repository again."

Where I spent almost all my time. That or locked away in my room studying for an exam I never passed.

"Why apologize?" I did my best to keep my face from making any frantic or curious or shocked responses, fighting to not appear hopeful because I could very well be misinterpreting where I thought this discussion was heading. Something I did too often.

"I've sort of been dropping hints, hoping you'd ask me out. Not that you need to ask me out—I can very much do the asking. Just wasn't sure if you were interested. And then you needed help with the exam, and it felt weird asking, like 'hey, I'll help you, but only if you go out with me,' which is slightly creepy and not the vibe I wanted. But I sort of…I don't know." Ian's lips pulled into a tight smile. "I wanted to ask. Unless this is a platonic vibe, and I've gone and ruined it with a crush."

Crush.

He said crush. Ian had been thinking about me as much—or close to—as I'd thought about him. And he *had* dropped cues.

"Not entirely platonic or creepy at all." I cleared my throat, desperate to buy time in my response and bury any rambling words that wanted to find their way out of my mouth. "I hadn't really given it much thought because I've been so behind on work—seriously, the Magus has us processing a thousand different artifacts a month these days, which is like ten times the usual workload—and then I've been focused on the exam. It's coming up soon, and the next one is three months away, which I know because I've already signed up for that one too, in case I fail this one, which is a terrible way to prepare for success, always planning on the contingency of failure, I know, but I try to think of it as proactive. Which is why I haven't given you much thought. I mean, I have. Thought. Think. About you. In a normal amount of ways that are both platonic and non-platonic."

Why couldn't I shut up? This was me tragically attempting to play it cool. Not working. If a Diabolic could just leap through one of these portals and rip my tongue out of my mouth so I'd stop making an utter fool out of myself, that'd be wonderful. A blessing. And yet… I had the overpowering desire to clarify what really didn't need more clarification.

"I've thought about you, but sometimes I overthink things, which you might've noticed or recall me mentioning multiple times because I have this tendency to properly and thoroughly and fully explain—"

"Would you like to go on a date?" Ian interjected, his voice steady and confident, leaving my entire body ready to collapse into a puddle of insecurity. "It'd be a group setting. A few sentinels I work with are heading to this Mythic bar. Apparently, it's really fun. Plus, even though they have hired mages working to handle any humans who waltz in and glimpse magic, I've heard a lot of the patron practitioners assist with glamouring. We could drink, chat, and practice our magic."

"A win-win-win situation." Because my glamouring was even worse than my saturation.

"Exactly." Ian rubbed the back of his head, tousling his shaggy brown hair. "Which, to clarify, was how I intended on leading this discussion, but then you bolted off and got all ramble-y."

My entire body vibrated. I resisted the urge to say the same thing because if he could overlook my babbling, I would gladly not remind him of it. "So, a group date?"

"That was the intention. Casually ask you, hang out with some other folks…maybe break away from the group and see how things go."

"That sounds like a fun, casual, cool, pleasant time." My cheeks twitched as I forced a smile and held back a dozen other comparative words. "When were you thinking?"

"Tonight."

"Tonight?" I gulped.

"Unless you plan on locking yourself in that repository all night."

"No. I'm very much leaving on time today. Six o'clock." I often worked extra hours to help the archivist practitioners catalog their findings, handing out free labor in hopes it'd offer some advantage. After three years in the repository department, the only advantage it'd given me was back pain, exhaustion, and a dirty apartment I lacked the energy to clean.

"Perfect. That gives you plenty of time to meet us at seven." Ian strolled toward a glittering green portal, a definite swagger in his step. "In the meantime, I'd say we both went over on our lunch break. You think I can blame traffic, or do these things pretty much nullify that excuse?"

He scanned his badge and hopped through the portal.

"Wait—" He never said where to meet him.

My pocket buzzed.

I approached a crimson portal leading back to the Magus Estate, beaming at the text message and attempting something polite in response. I reached into my pocket to fish out my badge and…

Dread consumed me. It was missing. Shit.

I patted myself down. An open portal wouldn't take a person anywhere without the proper clearance thanks to how everything magical became so entwined with technology adding extra measures in security—a truly amazing thing that I loved, but I'd lost the only thing offering me access to the repository.

It could be anywhere in the Dimensional Atrium, which would take hours to search. The Magus would kill me. Searching every pocket three times over, I finally felt it tucked inside my back pocket and took a calming breath.

Weird. I must've been so frazzled meeting with Ian, I stuffed it in my back pocket. So outside my routine. But all of this was outside my routine. That was the point. Become a practitioner so I could escape the mundane routine of filing amazing work and join the archivist regiment to actually find my own. And if this date with Ian led to dating, which turned into something potentially romantically awesome, that'd be a cool change in routine too.

2

Beelzebub

An irritating off-rhythm buzz had joined the flicker from the light on the ceiling nearest my prison. Orb. Whatever. A tiny little ball in a huge room.

For two solid weeks, that damn bulb had blinked erratically, slowly dying…like myself. Only when it died, I'd have a reprieve from the glare of brightly colored incantation symbols warding every lackluster artifact in this sterile white room.

What I wouldn't give to rip apart everything in here, feel it all crumble to dust in my grasp. Ah, to feel again. To taste. Even smell. It was hard to know if my smell was intact or if I'd simply grown numb to this sterilized environment. I still possessed sight and hearing—two senses I'd gladly surrender because of that incessant goddamn lightbulb.

I sighed, perhaps. Not like I could feel, let alone fathom any reactions my own body gave as a discombobulated fraction of my former self. I couldn't do anything trapped inside this orb, placed above the artifacts high on a mantle inside this repository. Unable to cover my ears or close my eyes, I suffered alone, observing everything, always aware yet with nothing to do.

The door beeped, and Worthless Walter, my daily companion, returned from his lunch. Shockingly, his bleach-marked blue polo didn't have any new condiment stains. His clumsiness was truly tragic. Oh, how I enjoyed his presence this time of year. It was one of the few times his misery became so deeply entrenched in his being that every little thing filled him with trepidation. Such truly entertaining meltdowns.

But he whistled some offkey tune, and a cheery pep in his step made his curly blond hair bounce. The fuck?

No, no, no.

Walter had a practitioner exam coming up. I was sure of it. He'd complained ceaselessly since his form was approved. It was practically a sign of the changing of seasons. Summer had very much ended, and with fall settling in, Walter should be in full-blown dismay.

Every three months, he'd attempt that practitioner exam like clockwork, and every three months, he'd be defeated by it, unable to master any of the five Pentacles of Power all mages possessed. It left him devastated. Utterly destroyed. Emotionally eviscerated.

It became one of my few delights to look forward to in this hellscape. Perhaps it stemmed from the whole misery loves company mantra, but I took solace in Walter's pointless plight. How had he gone and found a way to ruin what little happiness I cherished?

"Okay," he said loudly, craning his neck to ensure no one else was in the repository. Few archivist practitioners lingered here if they could avoid it. "I've got exactly four hours and fifty-six minutes to finish today's agenda."

Ugh. Walter and his auditory whatever. He'd explained it before—as with every single thing he did day-to-day—because it allowed him to process learning better. Of course, it annoyed the actual archivists who worked in the repository, so when they were around, he settled for mumbles. But he found himself alone this afternoon. Perhaps that was where this hollow joy came from.

"I have to restock the basilisk eyes and harpy feathers, check to make sure the vanguards returned those brooms on loan. Oh, there were some sigils that needed double-checking. Then I need to finish filing Chancellor Alden's finding on the Fae rift. She'll be pissed if I push that back another day." Walter tilted his head, his glasses slipping down the bridge of his nose and his hazel eyes trained on me. "But believe it or not, Bez, I plan on getting this all done in a timely fashion. That's right, I won't be spending my entire Friday night with you."

Thank the gods for tiny mercies. The only thing worse than his need to verbalize all his work was this insufferable desire to make conversation with me during his twelve-hour days like I actually fucking heard a word he said. I mean, I did, but he had no reason to believe that. Plus, he rarely shut up, so I never kept up with his terrible discussions. Or lessons. Fuck, he loved to teach me things I either already understood or had no desire to learn.

Another beep at the door, and Walter quieted.

"And who are you talking to, Wally?" My jailer, Magus Remington, hobbled into the repository. The wrinkles on his face deepened and spread like webbed crevices. He looked nothing like the mage nearly fifty years ago who helped bind me within this orb. I took small pleasure in knowing I'd outlive him. I'd outlive everything, eternally bound to this horrid orb. However, given the time Remington recently dedicated to cataloging and moving so many artifacts in and out and elsewhere, I might luck out and get to watch the old bastard keel over and die in here.

"Huh?" Walter's thick brows raised, adding to the worry lines on his crinkling forehead. "Was I talking? Probably just thinking out loud."

The tips of his ears reddened, accentuated by the black rims of his glasses. He gained such satisfaction by sharing his findings in complete detail, step-by-step. Like me, he had no one to share his thoughts with. No one who cared. Unlike me, he could change that loneliness. Pathetic.

"You were talking to that devil again."

"It's mostly an auditory learning thing, which is for my benefit." Walter shrugged, an aloof gesture he saved for whenever someone expressed displeasure for something he enjoyed. A weakness his body revealed to show he didn't care much about it either, but he did. "Making conversation with Bez doesn't hurt anyone, and it helps me work faster. Plus, I think he likes it."

I hated it.

"Don't nickname Beelzebub. It is a devil, contained for a reason."

"I-I know."

"I don't keep this in the repository as a trinket for idle gossip or chitchat."

No. The old prick kept me here, high out of reach and on full display, so the many mages and Mythics permitted in this dwelling could observe how he grew to power. His little climb from a pathetic chancellor of the archivist to Magus came from his victory over me. A battlefield of carnage and corpses and the skittish practitioner I'd overlooked contained me in a damn artifact.

I'd replayed that day too many times, only my thoughts and failures to keep me company. There had been so much blood and fire and magic in the air that day. I should've double-checked the bodies. It was a brutal battle of countless mages, and I got sloppy.

Now, I remained here as a trophy of Magus Remington's success. He was the sole survivor against the devil Beelzebub, preventing me from summoning an army of demons to invade their world. I scoffed. As if I'd ever open a doorway to bring more demons to this shithole of a world. But the tale grew with popularity, it seemed, and Magus Remington rode that wave.

"I didn't mean anything by it, Magus." Walter's tremble was a familiar one. "Talking to Bez…to the devil. Sort of just a habit, I guess."

"It's fine, Wally." Magus Remington smiled, which stretched his face. "But it can't hear you in there. Once contained inside a devil's orb, they're stripped of all tangible and intangible forms. It's simply raw energy."

Screw you, old man.

"Well, we can't know for sure," Walter said because so many of his little side projects involved researching all he knew about the Diabolic realms. My realms. A pathetic attempt to research something no one else ever had. Something about leaving his mark on history. He'd barely scratched the surface since his studies were limited to this repository, and no one else cared about Diabolics aside from noting the various dangers of demons and their superior devils.

"We've done extensive studies. It's merely Diabolic energy— thankfully contained and not harming anyone."

Yeah, one of those studies should involve releasing a devil from these fucking orbs so I could give you a piece of my mind and express how inaccurate all your studies have been. Of course, right after I gutted Magus Remington like the worm he was. And then Walter for three years of endless prattling. It was worse than years of being ignored.

"I didn't come here for a philosophic discussion on the semantics of Diabolics." Magus Remington's tone had shifted, light and filled with velvety charm. Something he had lacked when he was a whimpering young man coated in the blood of his fellows. How he'd grown since our encounter. "I was hoping you could retrieve an artifact from the vault for me."

"The vault?" Walter practically squealed, scanning the still-empty repository like someone had magically arrived. "You want me to retrieve something by myself?"

Oh hell, he'd go on about this for weeks. Walter rarely had permission to go into the vault, and every time he went with an escort or alone, he returned with a thousand unsolicited stories about artifacts I didn't want to learn about. This was worse than any Hell.

"I'd like you to bring Agatha's Heart out and properly compile our findings here in the repository."

"You want it in the repository for loan?" Walter asked, hesitant but craving clarification. Always needing to understand something entirely before making a move. "I thought witch relics weren't supposed to be offered as support tools."

Yes, so many artifacts stored in the repository by the archivist regiment were loaned out to aid other mage regiments like the vanguard and sentinels in their battles to maintain peace. Yet Walter should realize with my presence, many of these artifacts were merely meant to evoke an air of presence to add to Remington's prestige.

"We won't be loaning or displaying Agatha's Heart," Remington explained. "I've been in contact with a coven of her descendants who would like it returned to their care."

"Of course," Walter said. "You've been offering a lot of artifacts back to the Mythics lately."

"It's a good way to maintain a steady alliance with the Mythic Council," Remington said. "Something not all Magi do. If it's within my power, I will gladly empty our vault to ensure a brighter future for us all."

Blah, blah, blah-biddy, blah. And Asshole Remington went on one of his tangents, discussing the importance of mages being ambivalent, maintaining peace with human and Mythic societies, all while respecting the unique cultures of each. Yada yada with a cherry on top of the garbage.

What was the reality of this peace? The Mythic and mage communities' solution to humanity: hide the truth, never allowing the world to become aware of magic again. 'Lest we return to the past, where Mythics were feared as monsters and mages were revered as gods' or some shit. These decisions about secrecy came before my time, and I had a lot of centuries of living under my belt. Most of which were spent in this insufferable human realm.

Mages spoke highly of being the neutral power in the Mythic world yet did so by maintaining absolute authority. Not very neutral, in my opinion.

"When do you need Agatha's Heart fully compiled?" Walter asked.

"I'd like it completed by tonight."

"Tonight?" Walter gulped. "Does it need to be tonight?"

"Yes, but don't concern yourself with anything else in your current queue. You can still leave on time." Remington withdrew a pen from his suit pocket, writing symbols in the air. "And I'd be delighted if you joined me at the ceremony when it's returned to the coven."

"That would be incredible." Walter's eyes lit, half from the sheer delight of accompanying the Magus and half as he studied the old man's easily formed incantation.

Remington handed the swiftly crafted incantation to Walter. Words conjured into the air through mana and pure will of thought, which now sat carefully on Walter's palm containing a code to the vault only the Magus possessed. Walter scurried away, which left me a few hours of peace since he'd linger in the vault, exploring for hours.

Magus Remington studied his life's work, a repository he hoped to empty. Though I held only a limited purview, I could see that the old man's concern weighed heavily in his gaze. Something threatened this peace he'd carved in the state, the safe borders he'd cultivated. Perhaps in his decrepit condition, he worried that, whoever his successor was, they'd undo his nearly fifty years of toiling efforts. He should thank me more often. No one would've listened to an idealistic brat like him had he not gotten lucky and sealed me in here.

It explained why he'd entrusted this task to his dutiful little archivist apprentice. Most of the practitioners of this regiment were busy finding new artifacts to fill the repository to the brim; their sole purpose was to find, store, and preserve those magical riches. Also, it gave the archivist regiment power over the other regiments, loaning out ancient Mythic tools on a whim. Possessing total authority on powers only their regiment could fully utilize.

The bulb's flicker drew Remington's attention, and he approached. "Work orders have been so sluggish as of late. I do hope it hasn't bothered you too much, Beelzebub."

Irksome old bastard. If I could grind my teeth, I'd sink them in his jugular this instant.

"Not to worry, though. I intend to have you tucked in the deepest depths of the vault soon enough. Maybe your eternal slumber there will be more peaceful." Remington turned for the exit. "More than a Diabolic as deceitful as yourself deserves."

He knew nothing about me. Nothing about Diabolics, from the demons who served to the devils who reigned. Yet such was life. I was vilified in the carefully crafted narrative mages and Mythics painted.

3

Walter

Everything in the vault held such captivating intrigue. Dim lights maintained perfect illumination for all the hidden treasures placed on aisles that stretched for miles. Glittering rocky walls created an illusion of a room in this infinitely endless space conjured through Fae magics. I could spend the entire night here. The entire weekend. Week. Month.

Nope. I had exactly five minutes to retrieve Agatha's Heart—which I'd done thanks to the instant transportation sigils along the entryway of the vault—and make my way back to the repository. Honestly, though, I wouldn't want to call forth these artifacts one by one. I'd prefer trekking through the silent corridors of this endless storage facility. Averting my gaze, I ignored all the unstudied tomes, barely touched relics, and forgotten tools of the past. There would be another day to indulge in all of them. In fact, Magus Remington entrusting me to assist in handling the return of this witch relic was a sign of positive things to come.

Not that I valued superstition, despite understanding the ins and outs of all forms of magic, but there was an expression of good things happening in threes and sevens. Ian had asked me on a date, which I couldn't miss. Magus Remington had asked for my expertise, which I couldn't screw up. The third potential good thing in my future—the practitioner exam. This was the one. Practically destined to succeed. Even if there wasn't magical merit behind this stuff, for once, it was nice to have my head in the clouds looking for something brighter as opposed to studying the storms on the horizon.

Once outside the vault, I stood in the archive's basement, awaiting the metallic door to seal itself, keeping everything contained in a room about the size of a closet. Fae had always been the most valued among the Mythics due to their innate ability to conjure trans-dimensional spaces. Too bad I had to push off Chancellor Alden's research on Fae rifts and their portal magic; it sounded so fascinating and in-depth.

I frowned. She'd lecture me on prioritizing a social life over completing… No. Magus Remington explicitly said to ignore everything else and focus on Agatha's Heart. For once, I wouldn't overextend myself.

I made my way to the exit where Harley stood, ready to scan my person.

"Ha. Figured you'd be in there for hours."

"Not today," I said, holding up the case containing Agatha's Heart.

As the posted sentinel mage working the vault, she held the responsibility to ensure I didn't retrieve more than Magus Remington permitted. Not that I'd ever take anything from the vaults. But I definitely understood the appeal. Most of the artifacts weren't inherently dangerous yet remained hidden for preservation. I could find a hundred uses for Agatha's Heart, which I'd document in my report. The sentinel regiment served as security throughout the state anywhere magic dwelled, from guarding buildings to serving as protective detail for chancellors and escorts for Mythic ambassadors.

"How's your day?" I asked as Harley scanned the relic case.

"Boring, mostly. You're sadly the highlight of my shift." Harley finished the scan. "I thought working at the Magus Estate would be exciting. It's a lot of empty hours."

Harley was young, bubbly, and chatty. Twenty-two and freshly graduated from the academy, she talked a lot about work and nonwork-related things, like regretting her choice in picking the sentinel regiment instead of something with more travel. Occasionally, she'd pry me for details on applications and transfers into the archivist regiment, but I really didn't think she had the personality for research. Travel, yes. Adventure, probably. Long, isolated hours of study? Doubtful. So, like now, I nodded as she spoke and skirted the topic.

After Harley scanned my relic, and my person, she let me pass. Normally, with the entire night to catch up on my workload, I'd linger in the Magus Estate, absorbing the fine portraits displayed on the walls or studying the craftsmanship of the golems who'd made the marble floors. Instead, I quickly skirted into the foyer of the West Wing, where several portals served as a miniature version of Dolen's Crossing, allowing the Magus quick access around the massive manor, a convenience I very much enjoyed. I scanned my badge, opening a glittering golden portal to the archives located in the East Wing, and stepped through. Gold flecks clung to my glasses as I exited the portal. I resisted every urge to clean them, knowing the magic would fade but the smudges would stay.

"Hmm. Figured you'd be roaming through that vault all night, given the free pass you had." Carl, another underworked sentinel, licked his thumb, flipping the page to the latest noir novel he'd picked up. "Another late night planned?"

"Nope." I scanned my badge to the repository. "I'll be out by six. Guaranteed."

"Unlikely, kid," Carl chuckled, half his gaze on me, the other half on the book, and none of his attention on the cameras at his desk.

Carl was an older former vanguard and panacea regiment who moved into a sentinel position later in life. Unlike Harley, he probably enjoyed the easy desk job at the estate. Most shifts, he'd read a book, watch shows, or dabble in a new hobby his wife dragged him into. He'd even crocheted me mittens once. Ugly, itchy things, but it was nice.

"You'll see. I'll be out before you finish that book."

He wore the standard blue blazer of a sentinel, yet I found myself drawn to the three regiment emblems pinned to his chest as he spoke. Each badge was polished and proof of the excellent service he'd shown among multiple regiments over decades.

"Uh-huh." Carl flipped another page, likely speed reading just so he could finish before I clocked out.

I rolled my eyes, entering the repository. As an apprentice, I didn't receive an emblem or blazer despite years of work in the repository. I sighed. Not a huge deal, given the archivist colors. I didn't look great in orange anyway.

"Yes, yes, I know, Bez. You weren't expecting me for hours. Maybe not even until tomorrow." My fascinations were a running joke in the estate, but I wouldn't let a little thing like compiling the findings on Agatha's Heart keep me from an early departure.

Black and crimson mist swirled inside the orb perched high in the repository. Sure, Magus Remington stated there was nothing sentient within, merely Diabolic magic flowing in a fractured state. He'd know best, truly. But we'd never know for certain. And yes, devils were awful murderous leaders of tiny Hell dimensions reigning over armies of demons desperate to plunge their way into our world—or so many among the Mythic communities claimed—but if Bez was aware in there, he was probably lonely. I would be. I was. Here almost all day, every day. No one to go home to or visit. My own fault for isolating myself until I reached my practitioner goals, which always fell just out of grasp.

I shook it away. The point was, talking to Bez was a win-win situation. He definitely enjoyed the conversation. Who wouldn't? And I had someone to share all my findings with.

"Hmm. That sort of makes you a captive, or captured, audience, doesn't it?" I went to open the case containing Agatha's Heart. "Never mind, Bez. Ignore me. My mind's everywhere today."

It was stunning. Agatha's Heart sat atop a small pedestal. With the tissue completely drained of blood, the organ appeared white. It didn't pump, yet the faintest echo of a thump drummed deep inside.

"It's said Agatha Hollow's magic was so powerful she could amplify anyone's latent ability," I explained as I went to the computer to pull all the information catalogs from the archives. This particular artifact had been found two decades ago and placed in the vault without much added study. I read over what little information other archivists had done, but there wasn't much to share with the coven upon return. "Looks like this'll be a small report to file. Or I could go the extra step, quickly, of course, and compile a bit more for Magus Remington."

I walked toward the Archivist Nexus Grimoire, which connected to every source of lore mages had acquired. Not merely here but across the world. The chains of connection even linked across to Mythic servers. Sort of like a magical library database for easy access when researching. So long as the person knew what to look for using keywords and phrases.

"Agatha's Heart, Hollow coven, witch," I said, opening the leather cover.

Blank pages with a yellow tint etched words into long-spanning paragraphs and traced faint images into highly detailed portraits. Lore surrounding Agatha's Heart stretched back hundreds of years. I read through the pages, detailing fact from fiction, which would hopefully help in writing up an amazing report. Time disappeared while I compiled the information. This was the best part of the job, investigating and rooting out the Mythic truth hidden in the old legends. Plus, Magus Remington would be impressed, and hopefully, the witches would be too.

Agatha's death dated back to a time before the Mythic Council when Mythics openly fought for territories. Witches harbored a lot of disdain and distrust for mages. We were inherently human, not Mythic like them, yet our bodies absorbed the magical residue leftover from Mythic casting that lingered in the atmosphere and offered us access to the Pentacles of Power.

The petrified heart had a low echo with an alluring rhythmic thump. Licking my lips, I was surprised this had been placed in the vault as opposed to added to our vast catalog of items loaned to the vanguard regiment. It was Mythic, but that didn't always stop mages from finding roundabout ways to add them as support tools.

Despite years of training and full understanding of how the five mage magics worked—from incantations, saturation, glamouring, all the way to elemental sway and creating a familiar bond—I still botched each and every demonstration during the exams. Usually, tenfold worse than my brief practice flight with Ian.

"This artifact would all but ensure I aced the practitioner exam." I shuddered at the idea, contemplating even for a fraction of a second using this preserved heart as a catalyst to amplify my magic and finally escape life as a lowly apprentice. I stared at the display where Magus Remington had already conjured to seal the heart behind an invisible protective barrier of his magic. Beside his incantation sat a wand to assist me in enacting his wards. A practitioner would easily activate Magus Remington's incantation without a wand, but since my incantations floundered, I always had to use a tool to achieve the same goal. "Guess that defeats the purpose of proving I can sufficiently use my magic."

I continued typing up my report until I stumbled upon a passage written by an archivist in London. She surmised Agatha's Heart magnified mana and magic potential while simultaneously intensifying the user's emotional state, swaying users into an erratic frenzy to achieve their heart's greatest longing.

I gulped. There were no shortcuts to skill.

"Since it amplifies magic and emotional desire, it's definitely not safe to use." I detailed this in my report. "Hopefully, the witches read the risk factors of using this artifact because it looks like Agatha wasn't fond of having her heart ripped out and used to empower others. It's kind of poetic or tragic or both."

I grabbed the pedestal, carefully carrying Agatha's Heart to an empty spot on the mantle for display. Ignoring the wand, I reached for the incantation of words on parchment. It was an easy thing to do, which I'd done a thousand times before—granted with a wand to redirect the symbols. All I needed to do was feel for the threads of his magic and pour my own will of thought into their placement around the artifact. Closing my eyes, I searched for the slightest tug of resistance, the words that wanted to stay on the page. My chest warmed, and my fingertips pinched.

A short whoosh hit the air, and a satisfying collection of clinks cemented the incantation. I opened my eyes. All twelve symbols glowed blue, surrounding Agatha's Heart with a barrier, then they faded away, hidden from the eye but fully active.

"I did it." I hopped—actually, jumped in the air. "Bez, tell me you saw that. Oh my gods, even if I don't pass my practitioner exam, which is statistically very possible, I just adjusted Magus Remington's sealing ward without a tool. At this rate, I'll never need a support tool for setting the wards in place, and I'll never have to ignore the snickers of practitioners as I request a wand for a simple incantation activation. Eat your hearts out, archivists; I am making progress."

Did I shimmy? Bet my scrawny ass I did. I'd never managed to enact Magus Remington's wards before. Yes, all the work was done, conjured, prepared, and only needed a literal last step to properly seal an artifact. But I always screwed that up.

"It's seamless," I proudly boasted. Oh, dang. I hoped this wasn't the third good thing I had to look forward to because I'd love to finally ace the practitioner exam. All I needed was to show mastery over three of the five Pentacles of Power. Saturation, check-ish. Incantation, check-sort of. Glamouring, to be determined. In very unlikely circumstances, maybe I'd reach seven positive signs in short succession. Not that I needed it—three was a better fortune than expected. Superstition included. "Oh, Bez. I wish I had someone to tell other than you. Not that I don't love sharing news with you, which you probably, maybe, kind of, sort of enjoy, but I think I'm actually getting my shit together. Literally organizing all the chaos in here."

I ran my fingers along my head, a soothing sensation that likely further messed up my curly locks.

My phone buzzed.

Ian: Hope the other sentinels r keeping u entertained.

Dammit. I'd lost track of time.

Ian: Sorry. Late. Always late. Last minute work thing.

I told myself not to forget. What was wrong with me? Wait. I took a deep breath. He wasn't there yet, also distracted by work. We could laugh about this. Tell funny, witty, cute jokes about it.

Ian: Tell me ur not still working. 😔

Me: Nope. Already here.

What was wrong with me? I lied. Well, my fingers lied. Clearly, they had a will of their own, saving me from screwing up the first date I'd had in four years.

Ian: Good. 😊 Thought u were chillin at the estate.

He added a gif of someone stating it was time to 'leave the mansion,' which I assumed was the closest he'd found for 'leave the estate.' Something I needed to do. Mainly because I'd told him I already had. Which I'd planned. And failed at. Always failing. Shit.

Me: Absolutely not. I can wait.
Here. At the bar. With the other sentinels.
(Who I haven't talked to at all because I'm waiting on you.)

I added a 'strumming fingers of annoyance' gif.

Yikes. Too forward. Too formal. Rude. Why was I lying? Also, I should've added a better gif and taken the time to scroll past the first page of choices. The guy in the image looked very displeased, and I wasn't displeased at the bar. Mostly because I wasn't there yet. This was why I didn't do fun. I didn't know how. It involved something I lacked.

My heart lurched. He'd ignored the barrage of nonsense.

I groaned. That was the furthest thing from smooth or sexy. He'd probably cancel before I even stepped out of the Magus Estate, which I should've done twenty-six minutes ago, according to my watch.

I blushed at the shirtless men he dropped in quick succession by gif-spamming. Slightly cringey and definitely not the direction I'd take a first date, but I admired the enthusiasm. Maybe he was like me, awkwardly finding the right online thing to set a proper mood.

I stuffed my phone in my pocket, ignoring the buzzing because I needed to leave the Magus Estate and get downtown before it was too late. Thank goodness for portal transports.

"Time to go," I double-checked the wards surrounding Agatha's Heart, preferring to have a chance to triple-check them, maybe have someone else finetune the magic I'd applied, but there wasn't time. "It's fine."

The bulb closest to Bez's mantle flickered, which I ignored considering I'd already placed three polite, highly detailed tickets for repairs that no one deemed essential. I squinted when the flashing intensified, lights blinking rapidly. This wasn't the bulb but one of the glyphs in the repository.

"Nooooooo." I read over the prompts Magus Remington had left six times over, reciting them verbatim. Everything went exactly accordingly to his simple commands. There was no way this should be glitching. How'd I fuck this up?

Deep breath. I could quickly fix this screw-up before someone noticed and reach the club before Ian realized I'd lied. What was wrong with me? I tugged my hair until the pain settled my anxiety.

"Okay, I need to retrace my steps." I eyed Bez's orb. The symbols holding the artifact in place flickered red, illuminating the barrier, then vanished. One by one, the symbols cast by Magus Remington's incantation magic glowed, blinked, then faded away. "No, no, no, no, no."

This wasn't me. Even if I'd messed up the incantation sealing Agatha's Heart, none of the other seals should be affected. A glitch at this level was beyond my capability to fix. I needed a practitioner. No. I needed Magus Remington now. What happened to his incantations?

I exited the repository, quickly approaching the glittering golden portal.

"Well, I'll be. 6:35," Carl snorted.

"Huh?" I scanned my badge.

"It's not on time, but a record for you, kid. Figured I'd clock out before you."

"I'm not leaving just yet." I scanned my badge again. Instead of a beep inviting me access, it buzzed. "I need to find the magus real quick."

"Ha. So much for an early night."

"What is wrong with this damn thing?" I scanned the badge again.

BUZZ.

BUZZ.

BUZZ.

I stepped into the portal, and nothing. Glittery liquid clung close to my skin, vibrating a magical hum, yet it wouldn't transport me without proper authorization. Of all the times for a system-wide glitch. Of course everything would crash the one night I tried to leave early.

I could simply walk through the manor and make my way to the North Wing with the central living quarters. Magus Remington would likely be there in his study. He needed to be informed before any of the artifacts were damaged from exposure.

"Is there any way you can override this?" I asked, stepping toward Carl's desk. "The wards are glitching, and I need to speak with Magus Remington. It's probably something I screwed up in the repository, but if the archives end up needing an entire overhaul, I might as well just cancel my date."

"Date? Look at you, breaking out of that little shell." Carl gripped his desk, pushing himself up with a beleaguered breath.

"It's not that shocking."

Carl meandered to the portal, scanned his badge, and received the same error buzz I'd gotten. He huffed, more annoyed than stressed. Reaching into his pocket, he fished out his keys to unlock the panel. "System might be doing an update. Usually needs a hard reset when that happens, but nothing's scheduled."

The golden doorway rippled, and two people materialized instantly. A hooded man wielding a blade coated in sapphire symbols, adding to the silvery shimmer, and a masked woman whose fanged teeth glistened.

My entire body tensed. A vampire. These Mythics rarely had permission inside the Magus Estate; they were merely tolerated to maintain peace. I'd only met a few Mythics when I attended the academy. The only vampires I'd encountered came from textbooks and research.

"How did you—"

The hooded man slashed Carl's throat. I slapped a hand over my mouth, stifling a scream.

"Such a waste," the woman said, eyeing Carl, who collapsed onto the floor. His eyes were wide with shock, hand clutched to his bleeding throat. His free hand slipped on the slick, wet marble as he dragged himself forward. The vampire strutted by a dying Carl, gaze raised toward me. "Hmm. You look rather tasty."

"You're not here to feed." The man—the mage—ran his hand over his blade. The glowing symbols shrugged the blood away based on some intricate incantation he'd enacted. "Kill him so we can move on."

Carl gurgled. I quivered. I needed to do something. Help. But how?

He slammed his hand into the floor. Cracks along the marble spread like a forest fire, ripping and unleashing the stone beneath. I shook from his elemental control. The entire manor quaked—a last desperate act to serve the sentinel regiment and alert everyone of the infiltration. The cracks created a chasm between the vampire and me.

I needed to escape. Find help. There were over thirty sentinels patrolling the estate. Why would these two break in? How'd they hack the portals?

I fled as fast as my legs would carry me back inside the repository.

4

Beelzebub

Something fascinating had happened. All the wards holding me in place had broken away, and for the first time in nearly fifty years, the air around me held a magical sensation. I was so close to the actual freedom I craved.

The residue of Mythic magic hummed, vibrating against my orb. I couldn't move, couldn't reach it, but I felt everything. Such an intoxicating embrace. After so long held captive with mere phantom recollections of feeling, it was within my grasp. I had to act. Capitalize on this glitch before Magus Remington locked me up again.

A delightful tremor knocked half the artifacts in the repository off their pedestals. Nicked, broken, or simply freed. I wriggled and writhed inside the orb, hoping to knock it off the mantle. Shatter it to pieces. It didn't budge.

"I have to call someone." Worthless Walter scrambled into the repository, face terror-stricken, talking aloud again. His tedious need for auditory processing. Blegh. His expression, though… That held such intrigue. Perhaps this glitch with the wards held more ramifications than my limited perspective allowed me to see.

He reached for his phone, scrolling through it. "Carl is dead. We're being attacked. I can't confirm that. What can…wh-what can I…" He clutched the phone close to his chest, hyperventilating. "What do I know? The estate's been infiltrated. All the wards are broken. Shit. So much is damaged."

Well, well, well. An interesting turn of events, indeed. I slithered silently inside my orb, eager for Walter's words now.

He scurried toward a stone tablet. The corner snapped right off, and Walter's breathing slowed as he sank into sorrow for whatever lost history had crumbled to dust. "Portals are down. A sentinel is dead. People have invaded—a vampire and mage, witch maybe. Incantation is the only magic I saw, so variables both can use. They'll follow me into the archives. I need a plan."

This was turning into the best day of my eternity. Best day so far. Even if I didn't escape, the idea of attackers striking the heart of the mage territory, the Magus Estate itself, filled me with a rush that practically made my broken bits of flesh trapped inside this orb warm with delight. The political climate Remington ran had gotten worse than I could've ever guessed.

I cackled—and it held sound, too. My voice boomed, reverberating against the walls of the repository. The wards casting the barrier which divided me from the world had faded.

Walter's eyes quirked, frantically studying the empty room. He lowered the tablet delicately, as though that would do any good. He heard me…but would he listen? Hmmm.

"Hey, Walter. Can you hear me?"

He backed against the wall, scanning all the artifacts. His complexion had turned ghostly, and he looked about a second away from hurling all the trepidation which consumed him. I wanted to linger in this moment, savor every second of acknowledgment, yet time was short.

"Answer me."

"Who's there?" He grabbed the wand he often relied on for manipulating already conjured incantations, a true bauble among the trove of treasures in the repository. "I should warn you, I'm a skilled practitioner who has full understanding of every item in this room, so you're—"

"Oh, shut the fuck up, Walter. No one's buying it. Especially not me."

A wispy breath escaped his lips, and his entire body convulsed as his gaze met the orb high on the mantle. "Bez?"

"Yes." Having him beneath me, awestruck and frightened, was a pleasant sight after so long being ignored and overlooked.

"You're talking, which means you're aware."

"Always have been," I growled.

"Always?" He gulped, perhaps evaluating all the conversations he'd shared—I use the term loosely—in the three years since he'd landed a position in the repository. "That's...that's awful. But if I can hear you now, that means all the wards are down and—"

"You already know this. You literally just expressed this. Keep up with your frantic little beehive of a mind, Walter." I shifted within the orb, coiling my discombobulated form round and round, which drew the little mage's attention. "Tell me. How do you plan on escaping these invaders?"

"I have to call someone. Alert the magus. The sentinels. Send for the vanguard."

"Pretty sure everyone knows something's up."

"Right. Carl... He used elemental magic before he...before he died." He choked on the word, tears building behind his glasses. "Such force."

Walter scanned the busted artifacts strewn about. His somber expression was a perplexing sight. Was he sad about this mage or the state of his favorite room in the entire world?

An adventitious opportunity had presented itself, and I needed to carefully cultivate the right way to manipulate Walter. Something that'd convince him here and now I was his only chance of survival.

The door rattled, and I snickered. I might very well be his only hope of survival.

"No one will reach you in time. But if you release me, I'll take care of the threat."

"You've got to be joking."

Of course he wouldn't agree. That kind of suggestion required more time than either of us had.

"You're going to die. This threat will take all of five seconds to slaughter you, the lowly apprentice who can't master one magic."

Walter squirmed. My conversation skills had gotten rusty, and they weren't the best to begin with.

He jumped at the pounding of the door. Walter clammed up, eyeing the secured door. Not that it'd do him much good. Clearly these attackers didn't require clearance to move about freely. Such delectable ambition, yet it interfered with my immediate goals, so these interlopers could wait their damn turn.

"I'll just ask your friends after they kill you." I fidgeted, still pathetically attempting to shake this orb off the ledge.

The door flung open, and in came two attackers.

"There wasn't supposed to be anyone in the repository," the mage said. Definitely a mage with how the magic residue clung to his flesh, as opposed to the Mythic woman, whose pores seeped with magic from head to toe. A Mythic who required blood sustenance, given the metallic taste wafting off her. The fangs weren't quite vampiric, though.

"It wasn't supposed to be this trashed either." The woman kicked an artifact, strutting toward a frightened Walter.

He held the wand up like it possessed any actual ability to assist with his casting. That wand had one setting saturated into it: it moved incantations from spot A to spot B. Walter, in his dreadful dismay, had no incantations cast, no time or skill to conjure them, and absolutely no use for that limp wand.

"Please." She lunged forward in a blur, unamused and unthreatened by Walter.

Such an amateur. He could've gouged an eye out with the wand at the very least. Instead, he clutched it tight, resisting the ghoul's grip. And she was definitely a ghoul. Not much stronger than wimpy Walter either. Vampires weren't all that quick but stronger than most mortals. Ghouls were quite possibly the fastest of Mythic beings, but everything about a ghoul moved in an accelerated way, including the rot taking over their necrotic flash. That explained the mask and the fully adorned leather getup from head to toe. Bet her teeth were prosthetics too.

"Stop toying with him." The mage checked his watch.

Walter shouted, struggling beneath the force of the ghoul, and dropped to his knees. Quite a pleasing position to catch him in before his untimely death. My only regret was that I couldn't wring his scrawny neck myself. Plus, these two very rude intruders would probably be even less inclined to assist in releasing me than poor, soon-to-be-dead, Walter. Taking the wand, he aimed it at the mage's sword.

"Well, well, well," I mused. "Not as incompetent as I thought."

He ignored me. Rude.

Latching onto the incantations, he ripped them off the blade and flung them at the ghoul. Six symbols sprang to life, hacking into her back and unleashing fire and ice, cleaning away the blood all at the same time.

What a bizarre collection of incantations the invading mage had placed upon his blade. I chuckled at the cleanliness this mage took for his murderous endeavors. Death *should* be messy.

The ghoul screeched. An intolerable and grating sound, yet it flowed deep within my discombobulated form. I'd been stuck behind a barrier of protective wards so long, I hadn't realized everything had held a hollow echo like listening beneath a pool of water. Her crisp wails were refreshing in that sense. It must've hurt.

Oh, how I'd missed pain. Any sensation of living. Truly relishing each breath of life.

"You little bastard." The mage stormed toward Walter.

Whether from the shock of the collapsed ghoul, the excitement inside the repository, the momentary badassery he'd managed using someone else's incantations against a threat, or a thousand other variables he attempted to process in an instant, Walter froze. He should've aimed the wand at the still churning incantations ripping through the ghoul and flung them at the mage. Burned him alive. Cut off his head. Something. Anything.

Instead, he remained doe-eyed as the mage punched Walter across the jaw. Quick and brutal. Then again. And again. And a few more times for good measure. Geez. Walter wheezed and cried. His face was red with fresh welts and bloody, glasses cracked and half knocked off. It was painful to watch, though silly with his dazed expression. Yes, Walter had many irksome qualities and was an utterly pathetic individual, but surely he could've overpowered this tiny, angry tyrant. The mage didn't even cast magic, simply unleashed furious blows in swift succession. Walter had height and weight on him. He was a lanky little thing, far too slender for a full-grown mortal lacking muscle, but still. He could've countered a few of those strikes.

Walter was weak-willed, but the obnoxious fire of belief should've mustered some fighting spirit. Nothing. Each blow a crack against his frail head. Beating my little companion seemed to be the only highlight of this incursion I'd find, bound yet so close to freedom.

So much for being quick about it. This mage on a schedule took his sweet time beating Walter. After pummeling him, the enraged mage took a breath, releasing his incantations and offering his ghoul partner a reprieve. She shuddered on the floor while Walter dragged himself away, pathetically crawling past artifacts.

Some might've helped. Most would, at the very least, make for a good blunt object to chuck.

"Fight back you weakling," I snapped.

Walter ignored me. His loss. I had a thousand solid suggestions for him.

The mage scanned the room for the source of my voice, the veins on his forehead bulging. Returning to his prey, he waved a hand, creating a powerful gust of wind that hurled Walter against the wall. I shook. The impact cracked Walter's back, sending a cascading shiver through me.

No. This wasn't a shiver or shake, but wobble. That filthy, angry mage had slammed Walter into the wall beneath me. My orb tipped ever so.

More. More. More.

Then it rolled back into place on the mantle. Dammit. So close.

"Please, stop." Walter wheezed, each breath adding to his pained, bloody expression.

"Stop?" The mage's eyes held a petty impetuous hatred. "I'm just getting started."

Again, he flung Walter, the gust fueled by reckless short-sighted rage. Whatever plan this mage held had vanished once he sank into fury. Tsk. But this time, it worked in my favor. In Walter's too, perhaps. At least I'd offer him a quick death.

The orb containing me rolled off the mantle.

"Finally," I cackled, drawing this interloper's attention. "Thank you."

"No." Walter stretched his arms, attempting to prevent my escape. Grimy little dying worm had the audacity.

It didn't matter. Glass clinked between his palms, crisp and enveloping. Shattering shards had never held such a perfect symphony. I'd relive this vibrance over and over, every single day given a second chance. Oh, and I'd never forget how a sliver sank deep into Walter's palm. He winced.

"No good deed," I roared, erupting from the smashed orb. Exploded. A thousand whipping tendrils of broken, misty flesh stitched together purely by ethereal Diabolic energy. It'd take weeks, perhaps months, for my flesh and bone to properly manifest, heal, and become whole once more. Until then, I'd simply have to borrow someone else's.

Worthless Walter shriveled into a fetal position, clutching the fresh injury to his hand, ignoring the dozens of forming bruises and open cuts along his bloody face. Frantically, his eyes searched the repository as I leapt about, relishing in my freedom and smashing what remained of many artifacts. Such an expression of horror from the little mage, probably terrified I'd come for his soul. As if I'd whet my appetite on such a pathetic host when someone far more appealing lumbered here, still incapable of ascertaining the situation.

The enraged mage turned his fury toward my cumbersome tendrils, channeling fire. As if such a thing would ever harm a Diabolic. "What the f—"

"Don't mind me, friend." Reeling my spreading cells back together, I lunged ahead. "I'd like to thank you."

The mage's eyes grew wide as every piece of my being invaded his body. Only possession would ensure I escaped now. My broken flesh and blood and cartilage squirmed inside every orifice, drowning this mage. He flailed, gasping at air he'd never taste again.

Deep within the abyss of the subconscious, the soul lingered in darkness. I sank into this hollow place, allowing the comfort of flesh to envelop me. Outside, the mage struggled, coughing and choking up bits of my essence, gagging in protest of my arrival.

Tens of thousands of memories floated throughout this space which I had no interest in exploring, so I brushed them away and pulled the mage's ever-present consciousness toward the dark.

"Riley Hamilton," I said. "Awful name."

"What are you? Where are you?" He spun in the blackness of his mind, no certainty or skill to navigate his own headspace. Mortals. Naïve even when they had the universe at the tips of their fingers thanks to magical residue cascading off Mythics.

I conjured a book. Forming into a manifesto of memories, I skimmed a few light reflections which led him to the estate this evening. A heist. A coup. An invasion. "Cute plan from what I can suss out. I'll probably have to scrap most of these memories to make room for myself, but I wanted to properly thank you."

He stalked toward my voice, merely an echo thrown about this infinite space for the sake of misdirection. Not sake. Pleasure. I could drag this out for hours. Days. Weeks. Something intoxicating to savor as I snuffed his very existence out of this world. But at this very second, his body recoiled, resisting my invasion, and I had no time or desire to share.

"I'll be making this quick." I dragged my claws along his spine, relishing the twitch of terror. How he spun in horror, searching for me, desperate and frail and frightened beyond belief. He wouldn't find me in the darkness because in here, I *was* darkness, only capable of tiny tangible moments. But he'd help mend that. Mend my body. I so missed this sensation. All sensation. "Consider your ending a kindness. One you arrogantly denied poor pathetic Walter."

Riley quivered, running away in the abyss like his plodding steps weren't the easiest thing to follow. Mortals. Such tragic things.

"Not to worry. I'll make his death almost as fast as yours."

With a snap of my fingers, everything about Riley Hamilton crumbled to ashes, sinking into the chasm of infinite darkness every mind synced to at one point or another.

Such a quick and boring death. Not nearly the satisfying first kill I deserved after so much patience. This manor had plenty of mages, quite a few who didn't belong in the Magus Estate, so there'd be time to indulge. However, there was one mage I had to find first. A debt of death I owed an old friend.

All of Riley Hamilton's thoughts vanished. All the magic residue clinging to his soul faded. My Diabolic essence settled in nicely. A cozy, comforting embrace deep inside his flesh after so long bound and broken inside a now destroyed orb. I chucked the book, which held the few moments of what remained of Riley Hamilton, into the depths of darkness, everything about him left behind in pieces I'd stitched together. Nothing about this coup caught my interest. Perhaps I'd sort it later if time or curiosity allotted such fancy. What I wanted was to swim above the sea of emptiness and embrace the world again.

I took a deep breath through lungs that weren't mine. Well, they were now. Air had never tasted so delicious. The sweet aroma of Walter's blood mixed with the stench of the ghoul. Scanning the bright lights of the repository, I settled my gaze on the flickering bulb. With a wave of my hand, I telekinetically shattered that damned light. Now, I had to decide who to kill first: the ghoul or Walter. Not much of a choice. A trail of blood led to the exit of the repository.

"Well, well, well. You've still got a bit of fire in you, Worthless Walter." I cracked my neck. Such a pleasant feeling. Bones and meat and insides all brimming. The former mage's sword lay embedded in the ghoul's chest. I lightly kicked her, testing the waters for a trace of life. Dead as dead was dead. "Good for him."

I squeezed a hand against my jaw, the mage's jaw. Mine. Mine. Mine for the time being. Such a forgotten experience to feel again. It ached. Pain coursed through my face, spreading along the nerves to my tender ribs. It was like this host body went through several rounds as a Walter punching bag instead of the opposite. Stretching my jaw helped alleviate the throbbing, distracting me with new pin prickles of shooting jabs. Fuck. I knelt, grabbing a large chunk of reflective glass from my former broken prison. Of course, this repository didn't house any actual mirrors. Not even a mirrored artifact. Bits of my essence and filmy, pink flesh oozed off the glass. I licked it off, lapping it up and rejoining the last bits of my being. With the makeshift mirror cleaned, I properly examined this host.

The mage's face appeared intact. No bruising or blood. So either I'd already begun the healing process or simply forgotten the limited resistance of a host body. Gross. At least this one possessed nice aesthetics. Good face. Sharp jaw. That ridiculous stubble which I'd in no way keep up with, no patience for perfect wispy hairs which only grated on flesh. Annoying yet aesthetically enjoyable. I didn't fully grasp it. His blue eyes popped with a vibrance along the broken red blood vessels of white until my Diabolic nature took hold, shifting the irises a dark crimson and the sclera a soft pink.

Lustful. Luxurious. Luscious.

"Dashing as always." I smirked. A perfect specimen even in the most inferior of beings. Not that I could talk. Horrid, hollow, and hellish that I was.

Chucking the glass, I looked forward to fully examining these new threads, every aspect and fiber of the being, but first, I needed to search the manor. Escape was my priority. A necessity. Though leaving a trail of bodies in my wake held such excitement.

I wiggled my fingers simply for the sheer sake of movement. A soothing sense. The muscles pulled, resisting death, adapting to their new rule. My rule. A law of life this vessel would obey. Staving off rigor mortis, I rejuvenated a wealth of health into this body. My life. Stiffening of death took the body a couple hours. Surely, it hadn't taken me that long to conquer the former Riley Hamilton.

I could leave, quick and quiet, silent as the night was deadly— this chaotic invasion made for the perfect distraction. However, a splashy return would make for a hell of a hello to Seattle.

I raced out of the repository. Each inhale brought a taste of carnage. Fresh death permeated every corner of this manor. The aromas of blood and mana and magic slicked my throat, settling deep within my chest. I wanted to savor every satiating scent. I wanted to indulge in all the returning sensations as my essence rooted through every single nerve ending of this new host body. I quaked, obsessed by simply feeling. How I longed to return to my true form, yet this would do as an appetizer to life renewed.

I paused in a hallway, stretching my limbs, cracking every joint of this fresh vessel, and groaned. It'd been so long since I possessed a body, had the freedom to do so, I suppose I'd gotten rusty. The steep learning curve was worth all I'd be able to achieve now. So many things to accomplish…

Taking a deep breath, I sniffed out Magus Remington's scent amidst the surge of blood and mana bombarding my senses. A few Mythic aromas dwelled among the mages, too. Pathetic dying wretches.

Dead. Inhale. Dead. Inhale. Dead. Inhale.

Each breath helped pinpoint Remington. Deep and filling these lungs entirely, something the former owner never achieved given the thick black tar rotting and coating the thin tissue of these organs. I groaned. It'd been so long since I'd possessed a body. Enjoyed it. Fixed it. Conquered it.

Walter's conversations held some benefit. I replayed his nauseating descriptions of his leisurely tours through the estate when he needed to stretch his legs before another night of long-winded studies. All the obnoxious oddities he'd stumble upon during his trip helped me navigate this labyrinth. Golem-created marble floors. Mythic aristocracy lined the wall leading out of the East Wing. A dragon-scale armored suit at the entryway of the central estate. Leaping above the staircase, too impatient to bide my time, I rushed ahead. I knew I needed to pause, though, slow my desire, my craving.

Arrogance had led to my downfall before; I wouldn't make the same mistake this eve. Once I reached Remington, I'd gut him quick and brutal. Enough to break him yet allow me to savor his death.

He needed to feel the same pain I endured. The same devastation and heartbreak. Destruction and death without dying. He wouldn't die tonight. He wouldn't die for a long time.

I panted outside the study centrally located in the living quarters of the North Wing, exactly as picturesque as Walter described it a dozen times over. Minus the busted, bloody walls, broken trinkets, and the dead bodies. So many freshly snuffed-out lives.

My entire being quivered in excitement. Remington dwelled within. Frightened, perhaps. Shocked and confused, maybe. Bound by the lingering mage magics singing in the air. I'd have to check on him for clarification. How I hoped to find him squirming and in agony.

Stepping over corpses of sentinel mages and infiltrating Mythics, I tightened my core, preparing to unleash a furious and deadly opening blow. I'd hurt him tenfold.

"You, old bastard." I unflexed, releasing unnecessary energy rather than wasting a shocking surprise strike I no longer required.

No wonder his scent rose above such heated death. Magus Abraham Remington sat in his chair behind his desk, book dropped onto the floor, blood soaking into the open pages. Here he was, impaled by a half dozen blades, dead as a fucking doornail. Even the soft expression in his blank stare seemed peaceful. He'd likely died the instant the blades struck.

"Fuck you, Abe."

A convergence of superfluous events had offered me a taste of freedom, a chance for our ill-fated reunion, yet he'd found a way to ruin it. He'd ruined everything. I hated him. Every single thing about this magus. A disgusting monster.

I sniffed, ignoring revulsion. Pain. Memories. History. None of it mattered. I withdrew a blood-soaked blade from Remington's chest.

No hilt to hold, but the sharp steel didn't cut through this flesh imbued with my power.

"What did I wish to taste most of all? Your death. You just had to die before I arrived, didn't you? Worthless bastard."

I kicked his chair over, letting his limp body and the remaining blades crash onto the hardwood floor.

"Alas, perhaps I can find a few of your loyal regime wandering the halls." I grinned, though I'd need to make this quick. A scaled attack such as this would only last so long before the regiments serving the former magus gathered to investigate. "I will squash everything you valued. All that you loved. I'll rip it to shreds."

5

Walter

I held the railing, slowly taking the steps down the East Wing. The estate had never been this empty, this dark. I stopped walking to catch my breath because every part of my body ached. My face throbbed from the beating. I gripped the railing too hard and winced. Blood trickled out of my palm. I'd sliced it open trying and failing to catch Beelzebub's orb.

A literal devil had been unleashed in the estate. I needed to find Magus Remington and other sentinels, but I hadn't seen anyone since fleeing the repository. Thankfully the devil's possession took time because I'd blacked out after the assault. When I came to, he was still in the process of claiming the body.

I should've done something. He was a devil, though. Nothing could kill a devil. Even if he'd been a simple demon, what was I going to do? I couldn't think of one artifact in the archives capable of containing a devil.

A blade whooshed past me, nearly slashing me as I reached the last step, and I gasped. Before I turned something—someone— slammed into me. A tackle that sent me tumbling down the step, head smacking against the hard floor. A heavy pressure pinned against my back. I squirmed beneath, stuck on my stomach, and too exhausted to break free.

"You look like absolute shit, Walter." The raspy voice of the mage who'd attacked me held a faint echo. An echo belonging to the devil who'd possessed him. "Given the beating you've taken, that face of yours is already looking better. I can fix that, though."

Pressure lifted off my shoulder blade. I sucked in a shaky breath from the momentary relief, but then the heel of a boot pressed against my cheek. Heavy and sticky. Was Bez standing on my back? My skull throbbed. I screamed. He was a moment from crushing my head.

"What do you want?" I shouted.

"Relax. I was just saying hi." He lifted his boot. "You're so emotional."

The loll in his voice was sadistic. Droplets of fresh blood dripped onto my cheek, running over the dried blood on my face that pulled and itched at my skin. Someone else he crushed beneath his heel or maybe he had stepped in one of the pools of puddling blood across the estate.

He plopped down. Literally fell to his ass, landing on my back like he thudded onto a couch. "Crushing your skull would be satisfying, but way too quick and boring."

"Get off of me."

Bez sucked his teeth with some grating, contemplative whistling. "No."

"You can kill me, but you can't—"

"You're right, I can kill you. And I will. However, there's literally nothing I can't do. Except get that awful song you were humming earlier out of my head. How's it go again?" He hummed. "It'd help if you could hold a tune or offered some lyrics."

He continued humming the song I'd had stuck in my head earlier. Something simple and sweet and silly when my evening was supposed to end early with a date.

Ian. My chest tightened, partly from the pressure of Bez on my back but also in fear for Ian's safety. He wasn't here, but he would be soon. All the mage regiments would arrive once they realized the magus was in danger. Would it be enough to stop a devil? A devil that killed over three hundred mages before Magus Remington detained him inside the orb. I shuddered. Everything happened so fast, and I let it shatter between my hands. I couldn't do anything right.

"Kind of ironic. The one night you're happy, the whole world goes to shit." Bez cackled. "Maybe not irony. A sign for sure. Worthless Walter's joy brings doom upon the world."

I squirmed beneath him, attempting to lift myself up and knock him off my back. Too exhausted, I collapsed back onto the floor. Besides, I had no plan for if I got free. Run? From a devil? Very unlikely. Fight? Given how even the best mages with access to all five Pentacles of Power would waver in the face of a devil, I didn't like my odds.

"Back pain?" he asked.

"What?"

"I feel you there," Bez said, jabbing his finger dead center into my upper back where his feet had collided with me a moment ago.

I twitched, grinding my teeth. He wouldn't have the satisfaction of a scream. He walked his fingers along my spine, playful, and sinister. I waited for the cruelty as two fingers walked over sensitive skin, likely already bruising. He poked me again, and I yelped.

"Yeah, right there. I've got the same gnawing ache in my back, too. Not sure if it's because it's been so long since I possessed a body or if this mage simply had shitty posture. Either way, it's like a pinched nerve. So annoying. Not as annoying as you, but you know."

My teeth chattered.

"We can be bruise buddies." Bez slapped my back, making me yelp again. "Well, you've got a lot more bruises."

"What do you want?"

"I'm bored." Bez adjusted, fidgeting around on top of me, crisscrossing his legs. "I've done a quality lap around the entire estate. Everyone's dead. Corpses everywhere. Mostly your mage fellows, but they took out a few of the intruders. Seemed like a big, very calculated strike."

"Everyone's dead?" My breathing hastened. My eyes watered. Everyone? No. Surely someone else had lived. Escaped. The portals were down but…

I looked to the closed foyer doors leading out of the estate. Had no one gotten this far? Had no alert been signaled for help?

"Everyone. Even that insufferable magus."

"Did you ki…kill…" I panted, terrified for an answer and whatever came next while trapped beneath Bez.

"Kill Magus Remington? I wish," Bez huffed, a grumbling irritation. "I would've liked to kill some of the sentinels too, but alas, all dead. Would've even settled for killing a Mythic or misfit mage, but they're gone. Well, the ones who aren't dead."

He meant like the mage he possessed. Misfit mages were known for offering their services freely, breaking away from tradition and serving their own needs. A light term for mages who indulged in chaos for profit. Murdering the magus, the estate, and killing so many in a full-scale attack was bigger than some hired mages.

Bez hopped off my back, and I rolled over, taking a deep breath. Standing above me was a devil in human flesh. His Diabolic nature had fully rooted inside the host body—red eyes with pink filling the whites, his veins slithered, bulging and black, filled with Diabolic essence, worming inside the cells of the human host.

"Get up, Walter." He nudged me with his foot.

"No. You're gonna kill me. Just get it over with already." I couldn't even muster bravery in the hollow words. I didn't want to die. Didn't want to suffer at his hands. But what could I do? Nothing. At least I could refuse his rude request.

"Die like a man, a mage, a mortal with some pride. Stand up." Bez snapped his fingers, the blade he'd hurled twirling in the air and then reaching his grip with a telekinetic pull. Diabolic magics had a vast array of capabilities. If he wanted me dead, literally this second, he could do so in about a hundred different ways. "You really want to die like that ghoul you impaled?"

"What?" I scrunched my face. Was he screwing with me? I barely dragged myself out of the repository when I came to. I assumed he'd stabbed her when taking possession over the mage's body.

So many questions I'd had for Bez, for Beelzebub, surfaced. He was a devil reigning over a Diabolic realm filled with an army of demons. Each devil was a construct of infinite darkness, born of strife, malice, and hatred. Supposedly, every time a new devil tore itself from the seams of universe, a new Hell dimension was created, demons born, and in that world, the devil ruled. Rarely did they come to our world.

There were so many things about Diabolics I wanted to understand. If they had the ability to rip through dimensional planes like the Fae, why didn't they? Why had Bez come to our world? Why hadn't he brought an army of demons with him? Why had none come for him? Questions to things the Nexus Grimoire held no answers to and thoughts I never believed would be satiated because I didn't believe I'd actually come face to face with a devil.

He leaned close, smirking, and tapped my forehead with the sharp blade. "Thinking. Always thinking, aren't you? Here you are, lying on the floor at a devil's feet, and your mind is probably buzzing with a thousand thoughts. Annoying questions. Trembling curiosity on how you managed to be the last living person in the Magus Estate.

Frightened musings on how badly I'm going to eviscerate you."

I closed my eyes, refusing to look at his face, the wicked, gloating grin.

"I'll take that as my cue to begin."

The blade lifted from my face, and Beelzebub roared. A loud howl which boomed from the acoustics in this room. I trembled, awaiting the first of what'd be many agonizing blows. The tip of the blade pricked my stomach, stopping short of impaling me. I grimaced.

"Hmm. Perhaps that'd be too quick."

The blade lifted. Bez's feet bounced beside me, the sticky thud of the boots tapping against the floor and lifting repeatedly. Was he fidgeting? Antsy? Nope. I kept my eyes closed.

He shouted again. This time the blade pinched the inside of my thigh, and yet again stopped shy of piercing my flesh. My legs quaked and my flesh quivered against the sharp tip.

"No. I need to be cautious of those arteries. Don't want you bleeding out too fast. Won't be fun then."

"Dammit, just do something," I snapped. Somehow his difficulty in deciding how best to torture me was an even more brutal agony than the beating I took earlier.

"Don't rush me. You're my first kill in half a century. Possession aside—doesn't count. I want a real kill." Bez strolled around me, circling like a vulture. "It needs to be just right. It's been a while, and I'm rusty." He stopped moving, feet bouncing again, working himself up. "Bad enough you're not my first choice. But beggars can't be choosers, and the choices are slim at this point."

I opened one of my eyes. "Are you seriously talking about killing me like it's some two in the morning bar hookup?"

"Absolutely not. It's far more intimate than screwing." Bez slapped his forehead with the flat end of the blade. "Intimacy is what we're missing. Sorry. It's been so long. Not at all like riding a biker."

He hurled the blade again, swinging it into a powerful clank as it drove into a stone load bearing pillar. Dropping to his knees, Bez crawled toward me on all fours. Slinking like a beast, teeth bared, and eyeing each of my limbs before resting on my stomach. No, no, no. I backed away, using my elbows to carry me swiftly from his clutches until I could roll over and scramble to my feet. I didn't want to die. And like he said—he was rusty. I'd outrun him. Or die trying. Definitely going to die.

"Where you going?"

Fuck this devil!

I raced toward the foyer doors, grabbing the handle with my bloody palm. It burned, sending pin needles surging up my arm. Ignoring it, I pulled the door open. Once outside I could…well, running was really all that came to mind despite a thousand ways it'd all go wrong.

Bez appeared next to me in a flash, slamming his shoulder against the door, shutting it. He then popped his hip against mine. Either by the will of telekinesis or the sheer overwhelming physical strength a devil possessed, the light collision of our hips sent me flying across the room. I crashed onto a sofa, a hard thud which knocked the couch into a wall. The stiff cushions did little to soften the landing. Bez appeared again, instantaneous and before I had my bearings, standing in front of me one second and then straddling my waist the next. His body moved mystifyingly fast.

His touch started warm and gentle, but it quickly became less gentle and more invasive. Prodding my face, licking dried blood, tugging my hair. Only when he stopped to sniff me did the blurring movements cease.

"There it is. Under the fear, the dread, the weakness…it'd seem there's a bit of courage buried deep inside, Worthless Walter." Bez's teeth chattered. Each rattling clack wormed itself into my eardrums. The weight of his body pressed down onto my thighs, pinning me to the couch. "Even a bit of mana seeped down in your core. Too bad you'll never learn to use it."

"You don't know me." I shoved my hands against his chest. The muscles were firm like steel; pushing against him was like moving a boulder. Impossible. Unless… Magic might be the very thing I needed to level this fight. At least long enough to escape.

"I know you too well." He ran his hands over my face, pressing along the bruises. It hurt, and he smirked. Slowly, he traced his fingertips down my neck, resting a hand on my throat. "Part of why I'll take some small satisfaction in snuffing out your life."

Tilting his head quizzically, I figured he was contemplating if strangling me would offer the satisfaction he craved. He shook his head. Clearly, me gasping for breath wouldn't be fun for him. Delicately, carefully, he slid his fingertips along my chest, resting on my stomach. He poked at my flesh in different places like he was testing the waters.

Fuck. He wanted to make sure he didn't hit an organ. This sick bastard was going to torture me for hours. Days. Or until someone arrived. *If* someone arrived. For all I knew, the attack on the estate was a preamble. This group, organization, whatever they were could've struck the Regiment Headquarters too. Our outpost facilities. They could've killed the leaders of the six regiments and worked their way through the Mythic Council. For all I knew, outside this manor, the entire city of Seattle could be on fire. If it wasn't, it would be soon since I allowed a devil to escape.

I didn't have anything to write down an incantation, and my verse on chanting incantations sucked too so spells weren't an option either way. Saturation was a possibility, yet the only thing in my grasp to pour mana into was couch cushions. Not sure a pillow fight would break Bez's grasp. Glamours rarely affected those with access and understanding of magic, and usually required a level of expertise I lacked. I'd never established a familiar bond before, and I'd rather not start by summoning an animal to face its death against a Diabolic. The only slightly viable magic I had to access from the Pentacles of Power was elemental magic.

Taking a deep breath because who cared at this point, I channeled wind. Bez paused, staring directly into my soul. I unleashed what air I could muster in a single shot, and Bez leaned back. He gripped my shoulders, refusing to release them. I failed to knock him off.

As the gust settled and his ruffled hair fell back in place, he leaned forward and headbutted me. I shouted, and he winced, hiding it with a chuckle.

"That's the good ole college try." Bez patted my chest. "But then, you failed at college. Or might as well have. A legacy with all the advantages in the world, and you're what? A seventh-year apprentice? Eighth? Do you even bother tracking the number of years anymore, or is it a sore spot?"

It was. Made worse by Bez poking me in my actually sore ribs. When he jabbed at my tender torso, his convulsed in unison.

"Let's get started, shall we?" Bez reeled his arm back, holding all his fingers close together and coating them with a sheen black energy like a metallic blade replacing his hand entirely.

Cackling, he thrusted his hand forward to stab my stomach.

6

Beelzebub

I froze. A fraction of an inch from the flabby tender spot below Walter's liver. Cracking my knuckles which refused to work, I pulled my arm back a second time prepared to impale him. Or was this a third or fourth? I shook my head. Earlier with the blade didn't count. The mood was off, lacking. This was the perfect setting. He squeezed his eyes shut. Legs jittering beneath me. Such intoxicating terror, defeated resilience, and all mine. Everything I wanted in a fresh kill. Especially since, while I wouldn't tell him, there was something incredibly satisfying about plucking the idealistic, too soft for his station, Walter from this world.

"Dammit," I snapped.

Twice now. I brushed the slightest tip of my Diabolic claws against his skin, the only thing between him and me was a thin layer of cotton, yet I choked again. I should be choking Walter instead of hesitating. Why was I hesitating? I wanted him dead. I wanted every mage in this horrid city dead. Hell, I'd slaughter the Mythics for principal sake. Wrapping my hands around Walter's throat, I figured quick and boring would suffice. All I needed to do now was squeeze.

His pulse pounded against my palm, life literally in my hands. Mine for the taking. All I had to do was snatch it. Rip him to shreds. Eviscerate him to the core, begging for a death I'd gladly give once gratified by his suffering. My fingers trembled, refusing to clench. To tighten. To break his feeble mortal neck.

"Why?" I released him, pressing my forehead against his.

Walter's breaths were faint. He was exhausted from the beating earlier, the running, the casting magic he had no finesse for. Funny how this body had no problem pummeling him yet now, even with the former host removed, it disobeyed my commands. Why?

His annoying words drummed in the back of my head. Thousands of one-sided chats we'd had over three long insufferable years whispered. The light lilt of his voice and nosy curiosity and gentle lectures. As much as I hated to admit it, I enjoyed his conversations. His delusions of grandeur. His absurd kindness to the most worthless people. Still, none of that should stop me. I'd killed those closest to me out of necessity. Surely, some mage who barely landed on my radar could die out of a whim. Besides, all mages were treacherous and deserved what they got.

Despite draining himself, my prey continued channeling mana he lacked for magics he hadn't mastered. Outside the orb, observing it in action, I finally understood where it floundered. He didn't have much space in his body for Mythic residue. That weakness coupled with the fact he conjured too much in a strike, compensating for his inferiority, made his spells fizzle out. Abe had that problem way back when. Tragic. Not a surprise such a selfish prick never shared his little tricks for balancing those shortcomings.

"Just fucking get it over with," Walter growled. "Do it already."

Bold, shaky words, from a little boy who kept his eyes tightly shut. The grit in his voice was alluring, though.

"That's my problem." I chuckled. "You're in my head. Overthinking Walter, most annoying of his name, can't make a single move without considering sixteen steps. No more thinking. Primal. Acting. Action."

I plunged my fist forward, ready to gut him. Who cared if I savored the seconds? I simply needed this finished. My knuckles quaked against the tip of his jaw, a slight crimson glow peeking out at the ready to defend him.

"Son of a bitch." I leapt off Walter. "You little thief."

"Huh?" His eyes widened like I'd buy that doe-eyed vulnerability. He knew exactly what he'd done.

How had I allowed myself to contemplate, even for seconds, that I enjoyed his nauseating company? Here I was, deluding myself into thinking such drivel because of this absurd urge to rationalize the reasoning behind my hesitation. Another awful side effect of too much time spent listening to Walter.

I grabbed his wrist and dragged him off the couch. Holding him close, I sniffed his jaw where the thievery revealed itself by guarding against my strike. Nothing. Working my way down his neck, nothing. I clutched his soaked polo and took an inhale. Sweat and fear and unintentional primal excitement swirled together with faint traces of mana. I had no desire to explore or unpack those issues.

"Where the hell, literal Hell, is it?" I snatched his hand, staring at his sliced palm. "There it is, you crafty, sneaky weasel."

I squeezed the open cut, and my entire body vibrated, compelling me to stop. Painful for each of us yet not life threatening. My palm had a slight itch, burning throb, which undoubtedly measured about a fraction of the ache in Walter's hand. I hated the instinctual resistance to stop, but it worked.

"Stop," Walter shouted.

"Shut up." I pressed my thumb deep into the open wound, waiting.

Crimson tendrils leapt from his cut and slashed my hand to ribbons. They were darker than blood, sheen with Diabolic essence, and lined in faint traces of black. I released him, letting him fall to his knees in shock and confusion while I dealt with this little betrayal. My hand quickly healed itself.

"What the hell was that?" He frantically scurried backward watching the Diabolic energy root itself inside his wound again, slowly stitching it back together, but the essence likely prioritized on the facial, chest, and internal injuries he'd suffered.

"Gods, you're loud," I said. "It's my essence, which you stole."

"W-what?"

"Yeah, you stole a piece of me."

But when? How? I'd never shared my essence, the very fiber of my soul, with anyone. I strummed my fingers along his shaky head, contemplating the possibilities. I'd resisted relinquishing it to the most brutish enemies, yet he'd snapped up a piece for himself. How?

"Your essence?" He had that annoying contemplative realization look on, which would result in too much talking. "Everything I've read says devils don't break apart. That doesn't make any—"

I slapped a hand over his face, palm smooshed against his soft lips, silencing him because the literal last thing I needed was a Walteresque level lecture.

I thought back to our interactions. Not the last three years, but this eve. When could he have done it? Perhaps when I was possessing this host? Running my fingers through his soft hair, I shook his head then mine. That didn't add up. Walter was many things, but successful wasn't one of them. Also, lying he couldn't do. His pasty little ears would've given him away. And a dozen other signals. For one, he wouldn't have fled. He'd have been arrogant about it. He did cockily attempt to cast against me, after all. No. Fight or flight, perhaps. Desperate last act of rebellion. A 'fuck it' mentality, maybe?

Walter wasn't brave though. Well, except when he took that little beating and tried… I craned my neck. That was it.

"Clearly, my time in the orb had an effect. Obviously, when you failed to stop my release—a running trend for you—a sliver of the orb holding my essence crept inside you."

"Meaning, what?"

I released his hand, though I wanted to clutch it until I snapped the limb off. It'd make no difference since my essence circulated through every cell of his body, defending him from my wrath and any other minor threats he'd face. "It means you need to return it. Give it back, and I promise to make your death quick and entirely painless."

"Yeah, fuck you. That's not happening."

I grimaced. My sales pitch was lacking. Still, he could've countered. That kind of language was going to get us nowhere.

"This is a Diabolic binding," Walter clarified more to himself than me; I knew because he had that thinking-out-loud glimmer in his eyes. Slightly less nauseating given his cracked glasses, split lip, and the blood caked on his face. "I've heard of mages taking a demon's essence, forcing them to do their bidding. I didn't realize it worked on devils, too."

I rolled my eyes. It didn't. That was a conversation we definitely weren't having, though.

"From what I've heard—"

"Yes, yes, you're the most informed little nerd mage the world has ever seen. You grasp what a Diabolic binding is. Congratu-fucking-lations. But do you know why they're so dangerous?"

"Yes, I do. It's because—"

"So, then you know I'm going to make your life miserable the second it fades, making you regret every second you refuse to return my essence. If you'd like a quick death then you better—"

"You better!" Walter snarled. "Better stop interrupting me."

"Or what?" I invaded his space, inching closer and closer until he backstepped against the wall. Gods, how I'd love to pin him to it. Break him apart. Maybe bring out more of that snarling rage which crept out of him little by little. I placed my hands on the wall behind him, enclosing him from either side.

"Back up."

"No." My chest pressed against his; his heart pounded furiously as he wormed his way around me.

"Back up. That's a command."

I backstepped—not from the silly demand, but the burst of laughter that erupted from me. "Oh, you really thought you knew something."

"It worked, didn't it?"

Stifling a snort, I returned, taunting him. He commanded me a second time. I didn't budge. A third. I smirked. After a shaky, confused fourth command for me to back away, I batted my lashes and watched the confusion in his eyes swirl round and round. A Diabolic binding required so much more than he realized.

"Mages who take Diabolic essence into themselves risk two possibilities," I said. "First, too much, and it'll rip their very being to shreds, killing them. Second, too little, and it'll fade fast, releasing the demon, or in my case, devil."

"Well, it's not too much because I feel fine." His queasy expression said otherwise.

"Walter, I think we can agree your problem has always been too little." I remained invasive, much to his dislike. "When my essence fades on its own, which it will, I'll be released. Do you know what usually happens to mages who force obedience through a Diabolic binding?"

He gulped. "I'll just have to find a way to seal you away before that happens."

That wouldn't be happening. I'd gained a second chance at freedom, and nothing would take it from me again. Thankfully, Walter knew many things, but not the necessary steps to invoke a command.

"New plan." I grabbed him by the waist and slung him over my shoulder. Ignoring his protests and feeble strikes at my back, I carried him out of the estate.

I couldn't let Walter come to harm while my essence coursed inside him. While only a fraction of pain he endured would affect me, the last thing I needed was for Worthless Walter getting himself killed. Once the Diabolic binding released, then I could kill him.

Fresh air had never smelled so good. The lawn of the Magus Estate wafted with Mythic residue. Unlike the aroma inside, this was untainted by the corpses.

Suddenly, that delicious smell radiated, accompanied by elemental magics crashing from all around. Lightning overhead. Flames before us. Ice springing up behind. A half dozen earth minerals lunging from beneath. I conjured a black barrier from my own Diabolic essence, absorbing the brunt of this onslaught. Weaving around the attacks, I carefully ensured Walter didn't get struck. Lightning popped against my chest, singeing my shirt, but my skin remained unfazed.

"Hey, assholes! You realize I've got a hostage, right? Are you trying to kill him?"

Walter fumbled about, wriggling loose as if it'd do him any good.

A horde of Collective mages appeared, half from the sentinels posted nearby—the shield emblem on their blue blazers made that apparent. I'd seen enough of them escorting mages into the repository over the years. The other half came from the vanguard wearing dark red blazers with an emblem of a sword and dagger crossed over each other. Clearly, they'd come to instill order here at the Magus Estate. Too little, too late since just about everyone, including their Magus, had fallen.

"He won't let me get harmed," Walter shouted. "He's—"

I threw him to the ground, pressing the heel of my boot against his throat. Not enough to harm him, oh how I wished I could, but enough to shut his mouth.

"You stay right here, my little damsel." Conjuring black tendrils from the pores of my skin, I coated my forearms in sleek, black blades. Overlapping tendrils wrapped tightly along the skin of this body, enhancing the durability where summoned, but with the significant drawback that the flesh elsewhere would be a bit more vulnerable. It didn't matter. Maybe fifty practitioners surrounded us, so I'd make quick work of them. Kill a dozen or so, injure the rest, and take Walter before they had an opportunity to regroup.

I didn't know how much of my essence he'd absorbed. It couldn't have been much from a sliver of glass. Still, I needed a few days, a few weeks if I were truly unfortunate—which, given this situation, clearly Walter's horrid luck had rubbed off on me.

Vanguards drew blades of steel and iron they'd coated in saturated mana. It wouldn't endure. Sentinels opened grimoires, writing incantations they wouldn't finish. I'd lop off their hands first.

Cackling, I raced forward. Half the eyes barely widened in shock by the time I reached my first set of vanguard mages. I struck the blades from their hands, and their bodies moved on instinct too slowly in comparison to each swift step I took. They hadn't registered what I'd done, where I was, how I blurred across the battlefield. Most scanned for essence they couldn't track, some reached for a lost weapon, and none had any idea how exposed they'd left themselves.

Slashing my way across the courtyard, I relished the bloodshed sprinkling the battlefield. No deaths yet, though. Still too many mages preparing an attack in the distance. I needed to quell their magic before a single one had a chance to strike. Needed to ensure Walter didn't blurt out the most obvious weakness I held.

For his sake and mine, I'd have to finish this and fall back quickly.

Earth erupted in front of me, blocking my strike against a frantic-faced mage. I reeled my arm back. Not only earth. The elemental shield collected metal minerals in the exact spot my blade struck, absorbing the blow. Ignoring the relieved sentinel, I scanned the field of broken bodies and mages preparing attacks. Where did the actual counter come from?

From above, an overpowering and familiar scent struck. Despite the strong citrusy cologne he saturated with mana meant to obscure it, I still recognized it. A mage with piercing blue eyes and black hair rode a broom directly toward me, channeling lightning in a single palm and speeding faster than this support tool saturated with mana should offer. This man held a different level of strength compared to the others who'd arrived. I leapt from his attack, ignoring the sentinel emblem on his blazer. Defensive guard—yeah, right. He moved with more veracity and ruthlessness than most of the vanguard warriors.

Wind gushed, shifting my balance and leaving me open. A second bolt hit me, cutting my skin. My blood splattered the grass, sizzling with an acidic burn—a Diabolic last line of defense when the body we held became injured. That, and proof our very existence was toxic to everything in this realm. Everything in every realm. Even our own.

Burying my irritation, I syphoned my essence back within and lunged at this arrogant prick. But each time I threw myself at him, he either evaded or created quick, breakable barriers through incantation or elemental power. I'd outlast him in a fight.

"Ian, stop!" Walter raced toward us, a slow-moving object on a field filled with magical projectiles.

Unleashing a blitz of erratic energy, I fired off defenses, each aimed to navigate the field and protect Walter while offering me enough contained force to withstand and finish off this Ian character. I didn't know and didn't care who he was to Walter; he was in my path and the best way out of the Magus Estate grounds was likely by cutting through this single opponent.

As expected, his movements became sluggish, worn, lazy even as he buffered with barriers and rock in tandem, unable to manifest either to take the brute force of my punches. It took time. Precious wasted seconds of my freedom I wouldn't get back. But I'd have an eternity to enjoy it once I punched a hole through this guy and escaped.

"Beelzebub, stop!" Walter screamed, desperate, in a frenzy. His heart thumped so frantically, it created an echo in my chest and a lump in my throat. "Please."

He dropped to his knees, unable to do a thing in this battle. He knew that much. Yet, the anguish in his voice commanded ferocious power.

I stopped, frozen with my fist a hairline from smashing this crummy sentinel's head in. Dammit. Walter was in my head, literally tethered to my being, and for whatever reason, almost killing this guy evoked an emotional order—a hold he had no idea how to activate yet triggered through sheer fear.

"Stop. Just please…stop fighting." Walter's command coursed through my veins like acid, eating away my desire until I considered it.

"Fuck me." I backed away, dropping my arms as Diabolic energy simmered, lowering my guard entirely.

Vanguard mages took the opportunity to summon chains through chanted incantations, each muttering their spell in unison. Cold metal coiled around my torso, tightening and binding me in place as sentinels saturated the chains with mana, strengthening them to detain me.

I glared at Walter who struggled to make sense of everything, curious eyes fluttering a hundred different directions, assessing the situation. So much for my freedom. I'd escaped that orb only to end up bound to the worst guy on the planet.

7

Walter

Bez listened. Why'd he listen? There was a trick to Diabolic binding I had no idea how to trigger. He was an instant from decapitating Ian, and my insides erupted. Bez's essence ignited within me, every muscle of his body linked and connected with mine. A fiery primal urge resonated, and I wanted to feel every sensation his devil body possessed. Not the host body he'd crammed himself inside, but his actual true body which represented him in his entirety.

More than anything, though, I wanted him to stop. Willed it. His actions became my actions. My desires became his desires.

I sulked, lying on the floor of a cell. The room was small and bare aside from the lumpy mattress on a twin frame which was more uncomfortable than the smooth, cool floor. It'd be a lot easier to investigate this binding, the ins and outs, duration, longevity of commands, their extension, and how to activate them, if the Magus

Estate hadn't gone into complete lockdown mode once they detained Bez.

After explaining everything I knew, which was very limited, a vanguard unit checked me over. They said my wounds weren't extreme—hence why they didn't bother having an actual healer check my injuries—yet held skeptical gazes. I thought I'd die several times over tonight, and now everything moved like a blur. A thorough debrief, followed by the laziest of vital checks, and then the unit quickly ushered me to the Regiment Headquarters. They escorted me to a holding cell and sealed the door with a solid stone slab reinforced by incantations while they sorted through the evening's events. What was there to sort? I'd told them about the Mythics who attacked and the mages they'd brought. When they examined the bodies, maybe they'd find leads. There was so much I needed to know, but no one answered my questions, and now I was alone staring at this stone door. Why such a delayed response? How'd they know Bez was a danger the moment they arrived? What were they going to do with me?

I gulped. Once they realized the very true threat my link to Beelzebub possessed, who could say how they'd react. I should've kept my mouth shut. My ears burned at the thought of lying. Even lying by omission. The vanguard needed all the information I had, the most accurate accounting. Even if my overly detailed rambles— yes, I understood that nothing I told them made complete sense— helped one person, it mattered. Lives were at stake, and one withheld word could kill someone. Someone else.

My stomach churned, thinking back to Carl's anguished face. A man with a thousand hobbies and one step from retiring, sticking it out to ensure his kids had what they needed. And carefree Harley, who wanted to be anywhere with an adventure so she could explore the world, but she died with everyone else in the estate. Magus Remington, who only wanted to strengthen the bonds between the

Mythic and mage communities to help all of us thrive in the human world. All dead. Everyone dead. Too many people I'd glossed over every day at work, refusing to give a second look because I had goals. Thoughts. Dreams. I was busy. Life was busy. I couldn't be responsible for more death.

"Wally, are you okay?" Ian asked from behind the door.

I leapt to my feet and rushed to the door, wishing I could see him. Make sure he was okay. Even though Bez hadn't slaughtered anyone, he'd slashed up all the vanguard and sentinels in his path, toying with them, taunting them with a cascade of blurring speed. That was what he liked—taking his time with kills because he was a fucking monster. A Diabolic. A devil accustomed to his own realm where he clearly ruled cruelly.

"Are you okay? I asked. "What's happening out there?"

"I'm fine. The panacea regiment works wonders with their incantation. Just a few light scratches now."

Our healers were the best of the best when it came to mixing magic and science, but even they couldn't undo the death inside the Magus Estate.

"As far as what's happening…" He paused, and his tongue clicked against the roof of his mouth. I couldn't picture the carefree smirk he usually had when giving the double click. This was one hollow sound, practically instinctual, and something I thought he immediately regretted. "I'm not supposed to talk about it. Not with you."

"What?" I pressed my fingertips against the stone door, wanting nothing more than to tear down the barrier constructed through elemental magic. "Why?"

"I can't say." His breathing hitched, voice faint, muttering perhaps.

I pressed my ear to the door, desperate for him to continue. It was selfish, rude, and entitled, but I needed to talk with someone. I was a goddamn Alden. That should've carried some weight. Should've afforded me some answers. Should've allowed someone to speak with me, for me. It didn't. I was… I didn't even know how to finish that thought.

"They're worried about your Diabolic binding," Ian said, his breath released so freely, I imagined the minty sigh he made every time I told him I had to go back to the archives. The smell didn't cut through the stone stab between us; I considered it fortunate his voice did, but I still enjoyed the memory of his fresh breath. Strong cologne. Sweet smile. Kind words. Consideration. The same caring that brought him down here to check on me despite everything.

"It wasn't intentional. I sort of screwed up trying to help." A running gag in my life. "What happened with Bez—er, Beelzebub?"

Ian didn't respond. His fingers strummed against something. Maybe a phone in his pocket? The hilt of a weapon? I wanted to see him, his reaction, his hesitation. It'd help all this paranoia and doubt and regret running through my mind.

"He's detained," Ian finally said. "Hasn't moved, spoken, or resisted since being chained. But the vanguard are pretty adamant about reinforcing the chains and barriers surrounding his cell."

"Makes sense." Maybe my command kept him confined. Something told me the precautions and magics to detain him played little in locking him down. "Do you know how long they plan on keeping me here?"

"Very much above my station."

"I suppose this does count as watching the door." The light lilt of Sarai's voice echoed in the hallway chamber outside. "Though I believe you were told not to interact until a full debrief could be accounted for."

"S-sorry." Ian's voice trembled.

"Sorry, Sarai," I added, drawing on everything we had once upon a time. Childhood memories. Friendship. A sordid awkward middle school romance. A horrible coming out rejection to avoid a sexual advance. Fake enthusiasm for her success. Regret I'd let it drive a wedge between us. Regret I'd let my failures wedge out a lot of people in my life. Of course, Sarai would be the first of the chancellors to arrive.

Light shimmered beneath the door, revealing and unraveling the barrier they'd put in place. I gulped as the stone door opened. Footsteps shuffled away before it opened, and given the silence in conversation, I gathered Ian had been shooed off to stand watch elsewhere. They really didn't trust me.

I had no choice. I couldn't keep the accidental Diabolic binding a secret, especially when disclosing it would help the Collective understand that it happened when I attempted to stop Bez's release. And as awful as it turned out, I could assist in containing him before he harmed someone. Someone else. Thank the gods he hadn't killed anyone…yet.

Sarai stepped inside the cell holding a duffle bag. Her long curls were draped around her round face, framing her features perfectly. Subtle makeup highlighted her big, brown eyes, thin eyebrows, and small, sloped nose. She wore a whitecoat with the winged heart emblem, nothing like the modern caduceus symbol most modern medicine had adapted into a sign of health. The caduceus, a staff with two entwined serpents and wings at the top had an old allure to it, yet only dated back to the early nineteenth century when the US military adopted it. Ironically, they chose a symbol from Greek mythology which had nothing to do with medicine but missed our very ancient healer symbol which the mages had used for centuries. Suppose it had to do with glamouring away truths from humanity. I shook my head. Here I was, detained and prioritizing obscure historical facts that wouldn't help.

"You look well, despite all you've endured this night," Sarai said, ever present cadence in her voice unwilling to harm anyone with a cross word or a withheld one.

She fell somewhere between a lack of honesty could hurt the soul and too much could break it. As the head of the panacea regiment, she meant to mend the injured emotionally, physically, and spiritually, not break them.

"I'm doing okay." I fidgeted as she swooped in close, examining my bloody face and arms. "Thanks for checking on me, Chancellor Russo."

"You don't need the formality, Wally."

"*You* don't need the formality, Chancellor Russo." I very much did. I understood my place among the hierarchy as an apprentice to a regiment I'd likely never join now, standing alone in a cell with a practitioner chancellor, third youngest to ever reach the rank of leading an entire regiment in our collective of mages.

I'd barely graduated with my apprenticeship intact three years ago, and Sarai moved from being an elite practitioner among the panacea regiment to running it by twenty-two. Her touch was soothing, casting waves of saturated healing mana meant to mend injuries I didn't think existed anymore. And they didn't—Bez's bizarre connection had healed them. So her advanced healing strengthened my tired muscles, fueling me with buzzing energy that'd keep me up for days. Not that I could sleep. Not after all the death. All the horror. Everything that bound me to Beelzebub.

"Relax." Sarai sat on the lumpy mattress, motioning for me to join her.

"What's going on?"

"Right now?" She continued working. "I'm examining you, the extent of your Diabolic binding, and making sure there isn't something deeper ailing you."

"I didn't perform a binding. Wouldn't even know how." My face heated. "Well, I've read about them. A little complex from my understanding, but easy enough. Still, with everything that happened, I didn't have time. Not that I'd make time for a binding ritual. It just sort of happened by accident."

Sarai smiled, continuing to channel her mana through me, rooting through my insides and searching for answers the most detailed MRI would miss. "I'm not here to question you, doubt you, or judge you, Wally."

Maybe. But someone surely was. Otherwise, why else would they detain me?

"So, how's work been in the repository?" Sarai grimaced. "Sorry. My small talk is lacking. Usually, I keep it simple and distracting while doing a scan of vitals before moving into the more invasive checks."

"Invasive?"

"Yeah, getting the patient talking, comfortable, maybe even a bit chatty. Then"—she reached into her white coat, withdrawing a syringe—"when we get to the blood draw portion, it's easier."

"It's fine. After everything, a needle doesn't seem all that scary." I turned away because while I knew the prick of the needle wouldn't hurt nearly as badly as the beating I'd taken, the slicing of my hand, and the brash encounter with Bez, I still didn't want to see the needle go in.

Sarai swabbed my arm. "Here we go."

"You're not supposed to tell someone when you stab them." I winced, preparing for the inevitable jab.

"That wasn't so bad now, was it?"

I blinked. Wow.

Sarai tucked three vials of blood into her coat pocket. I hadn't felt a thing. Also, the crimson tendrils didn't reach out or stop the needle. I couldn't believe I'd forgotten about them. What if they'd reacted? Struck Sarai? Made my Diabolic binding all the more terrifying?

"Why hadn't they?" I asked.

"Huh?" Sarai raised a brow, then quickly recovered and grinned. She'd grown accustomed to my need to think aloud.

"There were these tendrils that appeared when Bez tried to stab me," I explained as I'd also done to the vanguard. Which should've made it clear his intentions were as malicious toward me as every mage in the city. State. World. "Maybe they only react when he attacks me. No, then they would've stopped him from tackling me down the stairs."

"Good thing you're not concussed," Sarai interrupted. Her exam would've revealed any injuries, so many already healed by the Diabolic essence inside me.

Maybe the tendrils reacted when it was something life threatening. They'd intercepted every serious strike Bez attempted. It might only have prevented him from harming me, or it might have acted on more serious threats from anyone. I had a hypothesis, but it'd require testing if I wanted it to carry any weight.

"Could you stab me?"

"Whoa. Um, no?"

"Not like in the chest. Well, maybe. Something that'd be semi life threatening but not like actually threatening."

"No."

"It won't hurt much. Probably," I said. "Plus, I'll heal fast. Maybe. Most likely."

"I'm not stabbing you."

"Come on! Haven't you wanted to at least once?" My cheeks pinched as I forced the quirky puppy dog smile I hadn't broken out on Sarai since high school. "Could I stab myself?"

"No."

"I just wanna—"

"This isn't some game, Wally." Sarai's entire demeanor shifted. "There are serious implications being discussed right now. What happened at the Magus Estate. Magus Remington's death. Everyone who was killed. And a devil unleashed with no true way of being contained again."

"There might be something in the vault. I'd have to explore it, but—"

"But nothing. You won't be exploring anything." Chancellor Russo stood, waving her hand. It released a small gust, which carried the duffle bag toward me. "They'll send someone to bring you a meal later. In the meantime, let's get you cleaned up."

She unzipped the bag, revealing a change of clothes, cloths, and a bottle of water. She dabbed a cloth with water. Taking off my broken glasses, she set them aside and brushed a damp cloth against my face. It tugged. Not painful but bothersome as she scrubbed dried blood away. Silently, I let her work. Three rags later and with flecks of blood on my ruined shirt, Sarai had finished. Afterward, she grabbed my glasses, chanting a soft incantation to mend the cracked lens. Symbols glittered across the glass, settling at the rims and fading once they were repaired.

"Thanks."

"I hope everything works out, Wally."

"Have you spoken to my parents?" With everything happening, I hadn't considered until this moment how it'd affect them. My siblings. Everyone. The Alden name carried a lot of weight, but even they couldn't fix suspicion that I'd actively made a Diabolic binding.

"Just your mother. She was opinionated."

I grimaced. "Of course."

Sarai left. The stone door closed behind her, a glow beneath confirming the barrier was intact again.

I wiped away what grime I could with the remaining cloths. Not exactly the shower I wanted, the shower I needed, after getting a quick whiff of my pits. Guess my deodorant wasn't run-for-your-life-and-try-not-to-die proof. Still, this gave me a task. Something I controlled.

I changed into the loose-fitting black sweatpants, tightening the draw string as much as possible. They were still saggy. The white shirt was tight and itchy. I emptied my pockets, realizing they'd taken my card key but left my wallet and phone. Not that either did me much good here. My phone had zero bars.

Pacing the room didn't alleviate my nerves, fears, or wandering mind during the hours of silent contemplation.

The barrier glowed again, and the stone door opened. Maybe whoever came to bring me food would be open to a little conversation. Two older sentinels entered the room wearing stern expressions and carrying shackles in their hands. I doubted this would lead to a funny chat.

"Put your arms forward, hands open, and facing up," the first one said.

"What's going on?" I asked, which the sentinel ignored. "Is this part of the protocol?"

Again, my question was ignored. This must be standard practice. That was all. They'd acknowledge me otherwise.

I took an uneasy breath and obeyed the directive, allowing the first sentinel to cuff my wrists, while the second kept a careful eye on my hands like he worried I'd attempt casting. Clearly, neither had been briefed on my talentless exploits. Honestly, the magically imbued cuffs were overkill, but the Collective had endless rules and policies, so I just needed to go along with it until they'd sorted all this out.

There was no reason to panic over formal procedures, especially when I'd done nothing wrong. Once I spoke with someone in charge, they'd realize this was a big misunderstanding, an accident, and everything would be fine.

"This way." The first nudged me toward the door.

I walked side-by-side with the sentinels down the dark stone hallway. There were few holding cells. Maybe. It was difficult to discern the doors from the walls in this dim lighting. Occasionally, the glossy sheen of a barrier made a door pop out. This place was a lot bleaker than I'd imagined, and I'd always figured the prison system for misfit mages was pretty awful.

We walked up a staircase. The boost of Sarai's healing magic helped make the trudge easier, but after seven flights, I wanted to reach an end or for them to use the elevator I'd arrived in. The Regiment Headquarters was a vast building, holding layouts for each of the six regiments to do business independently or collaboratively if the need arose. The building was firmly planted as a front for some conglomerate, which kept out prying eyes, and the close proximity to the Mythic Council and Magus Estate made this a key location to maintaining order. Not that it did any good for Magus Remington or everyone else assigned to the estate.

We passed the windowless, armored walls of the civil courthouse, where lesser crimes were handled. I didn't frequent this area much, aside from the occasional Alden business, but there should've been others here. The open area was completely empty, silent except for our footsteps. We reached the end of the hall where huge iron doors spanned wide and reached high to the ceiling. It required two sentinels to saturate the crank in tandem to draw the daunting door open.

I tensed while standing in front of the Tribunal Courtroom entrance. My chest tightened, and I struggled to breathe, but I continued rationalizing my paranoia away because I'd be fine.

There were no chairs inside. No tables. No audience. I was escorted to a single podium in the center of the room placed below high benches that stretched along the wall. All six Regiment Chancellors were seated at their individual bench. The Magi seat remained vacant.

A decorative white tapestry with a golden symbol of the panacea regiment hung on the wall behind Chancellor Russo. Sarai's kind smile was a small comfort. Seated next to Sarai was Chancellor Driscoll, an elderly man who'd served as the head of the vanguard regiment longer than any of the others had served. He was actually supposed to be the next magus once upon a time, but his feats paled in comparison to Remington's. Driscoll scowled. Avoiding his gaze, I stared at the dark red emblem of the sword crossed with a dagger. The craftsmanship behind these tapestries was lovely. I would've enjoyed learning if they were simply stitched or if perhaps some wonderful magic had been at play. This was not how I wanted my first viewing to go.

Chancellor Belmont cleared his throat, drawing my attention. Heath. A nice gentleman who encouraged the change in my degree. The archivist symbol of an orange tome highlighted his fiery red hair. It'd gotten a bit wispier since the last time we'd seen each other.

This was mortifying. Facing every chancellor, the head of the regiments, for who knew what. Okay, I had a pretty good idea what.

On the opposite side of the Magi seat sat Chancellor Ambrose. An elderly woman and second longest sitting chancellor. The hammer and nail emblem hung proudly behind her, added with a bit of extra flourish than the other tapestries, highlighting how the artisan regiment handled all the creation and currency within the mage and Mythic world. It even had a brighter glow to it than the violet crown banner behind the empty Magi seat.

Next came the infiltration regiment responsible for keeping everything about the world of magic hidden from humanity. The misty indigo cloaked figure served as their emblem. Quite fitting considering Chancellor Strome wore a hood, hiding his face.

My lip quivered. I struggled to turn my eyes to face the final chancellor. I tugged at the cuffs which suddenly felt too tightly clasped around my wrists. The sapphire shield emblem held such haunting prestige. A regiment I was meant to join. A regiment my family had proudly served for countless generations. The pillars of protection, ensuring the safety of every mage, Mythic, and human from the dangers of magic.

My eyes landed on Chancellor Alden. Her scornful stare held more contempt than when I'd told her I wanted to change regiment majors. The wrinkles around her eyes had deepened more than when I'd told her I failed my first practitioner exam. The roll in her eyes held the same aloof indifference she'd shown at the last family dinner when I'd shared my plans for taking the practitioner exam for the fifteenth time. Her eyes studied me, seeking out every weakness. My mother's disappointment was the most suffocating thing in this room.

My posture was wrong. I probably lacked a dignified stance at this podium. I scratched my wrist, trying to find relief from the cuffs, which she immediately scoffed at. Somehow, I even did shackles wrong.

"Walter Alden," she said, no acknowledgement to the similarity in our names or the fact that she'd picked my name. Walter meant 'commander of the army,' but the only thing I commanded was failure and embarrassment for the Alden line. "You've been brought here today on accusations of treason, inciting insurgency, and assassinating Magus Remington and thirty-two serving sentinels."

"What?" My throat tightened, voice cracking. "I had nothing to do—"

A cackle roared from behind me, bellowing throughout the Tribunal Courtroom. I ground my teeth. Bez.

Close to twenty vanguard and sentinel mages surrounded the chained devil they'd strapped to a dolly to wheel into the room. Magic permeated the air, keeping him confined. At least a dozen spells were at the ready, blades drawn, elements circulating, and the chains rattling. They didn't shake from his resistance but the unhinged laughter he released since he didn't put up a fight as they ushered him into the chamber.

"They think you're behind the coup." He panted, attempting and failing to stifle his laughter. "Too funny."

I clenched my clammy fists. Why would they think I was behind this? Glaring at the annoying devil, it hit me. He did this. Some perverse attempt to turn the chancellors against me.

"You can't believe a thing he says," I pleaded. "I know it looks like I did a Diabolic binding, and I guess technically, I sort of did. Maybe subconsciously, though I'm not entirely sure how that'd work, but I had no part in his escape…except for the not being able to stop it part. But I tried! And I definitely didn't have anything to do with what happened to Magus Remington or anyone else there."

"This has nothing to do with your Diabolic binding," Chancellor Alden said, clearing her throat in a way that meant my shutting up was overdue.

I slumped in defeat.

"Though I'd say it's high on the list of charges we've compiled," Chancellor Driscoll said, sneering at my mother, then at me.

He probably found her presence biased, which it was, but never in my favor.

"I'm telling you, whatever Beelzebub said—"

"I haven't said anything about you, Worthless Walter," Bez interjected, continuing his snickers. "Other than how pathetic and incompetent you are, naturally."

Jerk.

Chancellor Driscoll slammed a fist, quelling Bez. "The evidence of your involvement in this attack has little to do with this devil."

"Evidence?" My knees trembled. They had evidence? How? For what?

8

Beelzebub

They wheeled me to the opposite side of the room, every mage at the ready with what I assumed were their most effective assault and defensive spells. Irksome. Useless, too. Unless Walter invoked a command a second time. I couldn't risk it. Not yet at least.

That little prick stood at the podium, queasy, like he was a moment from shitting his pants. It'd be funnier if I didn't have to prioritize his safety. And if I wasn't chained. The orb lacked sensation, but these shackles were heavy and cold, imbued with magic which kept tightening every time I flexed this body's muscles.

The desire this vessel had to breathe didn't help. An unnecessary sensor in the respiratory center of the brain, one I hadn't had the opportunity to alter. I didn't need oxygen. Didn't need much of anything to exist. Part of why I loved mortal hosts. The Diabolic sensations were denser and hardly reacted in this bland reality. Everything was obscured and simplistic. The mortal lens allowed me to pick and choose which senses to favor, which flavors to delight in, and which habits I didn't want to add to the humble routine of existing.

"Given the severity of Walter's involvement in these crimes, I'd like to recuse myself," the woman in front of the sentinel flag said. I didn't know her name, any of their names. Didn't want to. Their regiment was as close to understanding these old fools as I wanted to get.

She wasn't as old as the one to her right with the artisan regiment flag. Lots of senior citizens close to Remington's age sat at the highest level of authority in their mage structure. Bet they all came from the best families, too. Except the husky panacea chancellor. She looked quite young and ample.

"I think that is wise, Chancellor Alden," the old grumpy vanguard chancellor said. "Let's avoid any discrepancies during such a dire time."

I raised my brows. No. Fucking. Way.

"Psst. Psst. Psst," I called out in a loud hush. "Walter. Earth to Walter."

He ignored me, keeping his eyes locked on the chancellors, shaking like a leaf about to be swept into a hurricane.

"Is that your mommy? Damn. No wonder you're so gloomy all the time. You mentioned your failures a lot, but I didn't realize exactly how big of a legacy failure you were."

He ground his teeth, tension so tight in his clamped jaw, I felt the slightest pressure in my molars. My chest heated. Ugh. It was bad enough feeling faint traces of his injuries, I didn't need his physical reactions as well.

"Let us commence the tribunal on Walter Alden's involvement in the attack on Magus Remington and the Magus Estate as well as the diplomatic integrity of our council," the artisan chancellor said.

"A reminder: we cannot draw hasty conclusions. I would

personally like to hear from Wally before we throw out swift judgments," the archivist chancellor said. He was an older man, a bit rounder in the middle and with thinner hair than the last time I'd seen him. Guess as the leader of the archives, he didn't prioritize spending much time in them. At least not the repository. In fact, once Walter started, this chancellor never came back around. Still, he had kind words and a creepy—I suppose some would say sincere—smile when looking at the shaky mage.

"I concur," the panacea chancellor said. "Most of these allegations seem circumstantial, and I'd like—"

"Of course, you'd like to give your academy pal a pass," the grouchy old vanguard chancellor interjected. "You shouldn't even be in this hearing."

Based on the calm composure of the young healing chancellor, I gathered the vanguard had showed off an arrogant need to talk over her on more than one occasion.

I chuckled. What a shitshow this tribunal was turning into. "Pardon, oh great and wise mages, best of your regiments and most suited for circle jerks, but can you get this started? The sooner you're done, the sooner I can commence my newfound freedom."

Vanguard practitioners on either side of me surged with mana, like they were flexing their feeble muscles to intimidate me.

"Or are we waiting on Walter's representation to arrive?"

"That's not how our tribunals work," the archivist chancellor said, creepy smile intact.

"We are the authority here," Chancellor Mommy Dearest explained. "It is Walter's responsibility to explain his actions, his role."

"I didn't have a role. I don't know anything."

If this were a Mythic hearing, Walter would have a real opportunity to explain his case, justify these claims. But mages only ever wanted things tucked into neat black and white packages.

"Well, I'm not a mage. And I sure as hell don't acknowledge your authority—"

"You are a Diabolic *thing*; you have no voice in this hearing," the vanguard chancellor said, utter disdain in his tone and a fiery glare in his eyes. I could've glared back, acknowledged how much I despised mages who dehumanized and devalued me by only calling me a thing, a monster, but no matter how sharp witted or cruel my comment, it'd only encourage him. So, I puckered my lips and blew him a kiss. The discomfort and disgust in his wrinkled old face was mildly satisfying. A threat would've been more enjoyable. Live and learn. "Why is this thing even in here?"

"We didn't have a choice in its presence," the artisan crone answered, "given Walter's actions."

Ah yes, Worthless Walter and our Diabolic bond. It forced our close proximity. During my elevator trip to this tribunal, the tether yanked the entire ride up. Thought I'd collapse through the bottom every single floor up. Walter reminded me of that expression 'can't live without him, can't kill him until my essence left his system.' I also couldn't let this tribunal of regiment chancellor clowns kill him either. This long drawn back and forth really all came down to that.

"Walter Alden," the vanguard chancellor began, "we have reason to believe you hacked into the Magus Estate systems. This turned off all early detection protocols, jammed alert signals, and sealed all portals in and out of the estate."

Walter trembled, biting his lip as he listened to these outlandish accusations. It was what he did whenever he realized his thought process was best left internal, one of the few times he caught his need to speak his thoughts. It made him look like a weird squirrel, but it made for quiet working hours. Okay, minutes. It was Walter; he was allergic to silence.

"In killing Magus Remington, you also undid the protection wards across the estate."

Yeah, since Remington arrogantly used his mana and magic as the catalyst to activate and seal all the artifacts, making him the key to his little archives. Narcissistic much? Pride goeth before the fall, or in this case, directly after. Good riddance.

I squinted because none of these details added up unless Walter had hidden his true intentions that night, and quite frankly, over the last three years. "Worthless Walter couldn't have killed the Magus. He was with me when the wards failed."

Also, he was too weak-willed to kill. Too weak in general to succeed.

"It's our belief the Mythics and fellow misfit mages acquired in this conspiracy targeted the former magus while Walter raided the vaults."

"I-I-I'd never."

"It was your card key used to embed the virus into our system."

"Virus?" Walter squirmed at the podium. "What virus?"

"The one you laced within an intricate incantation so you could raid the archives," the vanguard chancellor said. "Many of the artifacts stolen were either personally handled by you, or we found logs of you snooping and researching these stored possessions despite you having no access or privileges."

"Are you joking?" I snapped. "He's an overworking know-it-all nerd who spends all day and night researching useless drivel. Of course, Walter looked up the artifacts he wasn't supposed to. He likes jerking it to knowledge."

"Someone silence that thing," the vanguard chancellor said.

A vanguard practitioner approached, materializing an iron mouth gag to bar between my teeth.

"Try it, and I'll kill you."

"He won't." Walter grabbed the podium, pleading. "He hasn't. He hasn't killed anyone. Well, not since his accidental release from the orb. Except the mage he's possessing. But he was one of them who infiltrated the Magus Estate. Not that I'm condoning the death, any death—no one should die. Ever. That said, Bez…eelabub hasn't harmed anyone aligned with our Collective. I won't let him. I promise."

Ah, fuck me. Had he realized how to trigger commands? I searched his pasty face, unable to find a hint of pink or reddened skin. He wasn't lying, so either he'd figured out how to control me, or he truly believed he could and would stop me by any means.

"Please step away from the devil." The archivist chancellor raised a hand, waving the eager vanguard back. I bit the air, a not-so-subtle reminder of what I'd do if he attempted to silence me. After a half century with no voice, I refused to allow anyone to confine me to silent isolation again. "The allegations against Mr. Alden are severe, and I understand Chancellor Driscoll's desire to resolve this devastating attack, but I'd like to raise the question on how we handle this devil."

"Simple," the vanguard chancellor Driscoll—more like Dickhole—said. "We seal it once more."

"With what artifact?" the archivist chancellor asked.

Right. Their vault had been raided. I doubted they even possessed any other relics powerful enough to contain a Diabolic.

"Walter's Diabolic binding presents us a unique opportunity," the archivist chancellor continued. "We've never had the chance to speak with or learn from lesser demon Diabolics, let alone hear from a devil itself. This could offer us more knowledge than—"

The artisan chancellor dismissed the archivist with a curt gesture. "Out of the question. If we cannot contain it, we should kill it."

"Devils don't die," the youngest of the chancellors said. "And we wouldn't know the risks to Wally… Mr. Alden."

"Devils don't die from what we know," the last of the chancellors said, a cloaked man who led the infiltration regiment. Those who spied on everyone. Humans who learned too much. Mythics who didn't abide by neutrality. Mages who didn't toe the line of the system in place. Diabolics who dared to enter this world. They were a regiment of whispers and stalking and death. "I've found many misfit mages similar to the one before us who've bonded with a demon. When the misfit mage is slain, the demon in question shares the death."

Walter, a misfit mage? They'd do anything to sell their reasoning. I flexed my biceps, testing the limitations of the chains wrapped around me from head to toe.

"We can't seriously be having this conversation. We're not executing Wally." The panacea chancellor stood, slamming her palms on her bench revealing her close connection to Walter.

"We can't very well allow a devil to roam freely," the sentinel chancellor rebutted. So much for recusing herself. "I believe Chancellor Strome makes a valid point. We need to consider all the options. Our magus is dead. There is a group who has waged a war against us, and we have no idea who they are, what they want, or what move they'll make next. And now, we have a devil in our midst."

"I'd like a private conversation with Walter Alden about this organization before any further discussion on whether the execution is necessary. If granted, I may find those answers." The infiltration chancellor eyed the trembling Walter, his gaze hidden by a hood, but the change in his stance spoke of an intent to have more than words with my worried mage. "As you said, the fuse to a war has been lit, and I'd like to know who ignited it."

That was likely the thing grating his nerves most here. All of them, in fact. Each of these regiments held their dignity based on the roles they served. The vanguard eliminated violence by hunting it down. The sentinels protected the 'innocent' against enemy attacks. The infiltration snuffed out threats before they ever became dangerous. These three in particular had utterly failed in their duties.

As such, Walter became their scapegoat. Nothing he said or didn't say would change that fact. None of this was in his control because the six most powerful mages in this region had to save face and prove their authority. Killing a devil would help make a strong impression.

But I wouldn't be dragged further into mage politics. Whether Walter understood how to command me or not, he had to realize staying meant certain death.

There were eighteen vanguard practitioners and sixteen sentinel practitioners surrounding me. Six chancellors who each exemplified the highest level of expertise in their regiment, though, it was debatable how much skill in practice they held versus politics. Either way, four were well past their prime: vanguard, sentinel, artisan, archivist. The panacea chancellor was young, so either she possessed exceptional casting skills, or she'd navigated the mage world well. The only real threat came from the infiltration chancellor. They were the deadliest regiment, ruthlessly slaughtering anything opposing the mage and Mythic alliance or the hierarchy mages had sat themselves atop.

I unleashed my Diabolic wings and tail to assist in shattering these chains. The pale gray of my tail caught the eye of several mages who I tripped before they could cast. My wings were thinner than normal, dark gray and naked without feathers. I groaned. Unfortunately, my body hadn't fully healed.

I couldn't risk unleashing my other Diabolic features either. Too much and this host body might split apart, and since my true form remained mostly broken after so long trapped inside that orb, I couldn't risk losing this meatsuit.

"Contain Beelzebub!"

Walter turned, doe-eyed little fool, mouth already moving. Everything stilled. Mana. Magic. Spells. I wouldn't be able to maintain this hyper flexed speed long given the energy I'd need to break through that fortified iron door. Leaping around a half dozen magical strikes, I evaded the frenzy and lunged on top of Walter.

He tumbled back, taking me with him to the floor. "Bez, sto—"

"Shut the hell up." I slapped a hand over his mouth. Couldn't have him uttering some accidental command that'd get us both killed.

With a hand firmly pressed across his face, squeezing his cheeks tightly, I lifted him off the floor and spun him around. The fall had slowed my speed, which gave the mages a chance to strike. I kept my wings shielded over Walter, his back pressed against my torso. He squirmed the entire time. Little dick even stomped on my foot a few times as I guided us to the iron door.

"You could make this a bit easier," I whispered. "They're planning on killing you in an effort to kill me. Now, I don't know if a devil bound to a mortal would die if that tether snapped, but I'd rather not find out. Would you?"

His body stiffened, no longer resistant, which made one obstacle easier.

"Not a hypothesis Worthless Walter wants to test?" I chuckled.

He mouthed something, biting my palm in the process, but he kept backstepping with me.

"Good boy." I grinned, reaching the door. He gnawed harder. "Naughty."

"Aff-hol," he attempted to say.

I turned around, using my wings to buffer a barrage of magic and blades. Slamming a fist into the iron door did nothing. I sighed. "One tiny break."

An onslaught of spells continued shredding my wings. I circulated Diabolic energy into them, but if it continued, it'd take flying out of the equation. Damn. I missed the sky, too.

I reeled back a fist coated in Diabolic essence. This was strong enough to rupture a Fae dimensional portal, so if it didn't break this door, I'd have to somehow manage to kill every single mage in this room while keeping Walter safe and muzzled.

The door cracked. Walter's shoulders tightened, adding to the tension in my own body. His eyes were wide and searching for the mages I kept at bay with my tail. My poor tail. Unable to look, I had to rely on reflex and instinct. Thank the gods I'd had centuries of thrashing about to avoid a punishing blow.

"Relax." I guided Walter's head, showing him the Diabolic energy seeping into the cracks, poisoning the magic saturated in this door and eroding it from within. "Time to go."

I tackled the door, bursting through into an empty open area. No time to observe. There weren't enemies awaiting, so I bolted away from the threat behind us. Walter's heart pattered swiftly, almost as swiftly as my steps, which accelerated my heartbeat and the adrenaline coursing through me. And then I crashed into a goddamn wall.

"Stop doing that."

"Ooing wat?"

"Stop panicking." I climbed out of the rubble and darted down a hallway before the vanguard caught us. "It's irritating."

We raced toward the glass-panel double doors. I had no intention of crashing through something else, so with a bit of telekinesis, I shattered them so we could leap outside.

My eyes bulged. "Gah! What hot hell is this?"

Streetlights ate away the night sky, devouring each star and obscuring the moon herself. Cars. I'd forgotten how awful they were, and there were so many more on outstretched roads, which lacked the room to carry this jammed traffic.

Noise everywhere. So much louder than I'd remembered. Not simply the sound of vehicles, but everything. The tippity tappity of devices I'd grown accustomed to from my time with Walter and every insufferable mage glued to their cellular devices, but also the devices in their ears as they strolled down crowded streets blasted. It stung my ears, a symphony of chaotic beats from a thousand horrid places, so loud it practically buried the heavy footsteps of our mage pursuers.

I swallowed hard.

Ugh. The taste. I dropped to my knees, releasing Walter and gagging. Odors had grown foul in the air, casting a thick sludge which sat on the roof of my mouth when I tried to swallow. What had mortals done to their realm? Such suffocating air.

I took a deep inhale, dulling my senses, limiting my perception. I couldn't work at full capacity. Not in this hellhole they called a city.

"Are…are you okay?" Walter pressed his hand onto my shoulder. The last extreme sensation I had before dimming the world.

"I'm fine." I shrugged him off, then snatched him back into my grasp, mouth covered because I didn't need or want his commands.

"Lend me your strength so I can end this devil!" The vanguard chancellor bolted forward in a haze. He muttered a mix of elemental lightning and incantations, amplified by the saturation his squad of practitioners imbued him with.

Shit. Dimming my senses added a sluggish reaction to my surroundings. I couldn't undo it. Not until I adjusted to the horrid world mortals had created. But I couldn't remain idle either.

Casting a barrier, I blocked the chancellor's strike.

"I don't think so!" The frail artisan chancellor wielded a massive hammer twice her size with ease. One smash with that crafted tool, and my barrier crumbled.

No time to dodge. Especially not with Walter in my grasp. Once the barrier collapsed, she fell back and let the vanguard chancellor move ahead. Oh, him I'd gladly slaughter before making a break for it. I pulled back a fist, preparing to punch a hole right through the old man's head.

A pain seared through my fingers where they covered Walter's mouth. I groaned, releasing him.

"Don't kill anyone!" His command circulated through every fiber of my being, and in the last second before colliding with the chancellor's skull, my arm twisted, missing him by an inch.

Dammit. I stood exposed. Countless mages were running forward, and I had no ability to defend myself. Again. Walter was going to get us killed.

The shocked chancellor recovered quickly, conjuring blades from thin air.

Wait.

Walter said not to kill anyone.

I smirked at the chancellor, backhanding him and throwing him into the artisan chancellor, a light strike which caused mild injury but wasn't death. Not the satisfaction I craved. Oh, well. It'd do. May their brittle bones break atop each other.

I glared at Walter, covering his mouth again because his need to care for others would be the end of me. His index and middle finger were swollen, turning black and blue, already swirling with crimson healing to aid in his recovery. Had he broken them to loosen my grip over his mouth? Had he studied and learned that quickly how the tether connecting our bodies worked? How I hated this little nerd.

I didn't care. Didn't have time to care. Unveiling my wings with Walter in my grasp, I flew high into the sky. The infiltration chancellor zipped behind, chasing us on a broom with fire conjured in his free hand. I turned around, creating my own black flames from the tip of my tail.

"You're not the only one who can summon elements, mage." I hurled a blaze onto the streets below. Fiery black cinders cascaded everywhere, though none were strong enough to stick to cars or mortals or the earth itself. It was a superficial strike falling within Walter's absurd command, but it forced the chancellor to turn back and assist in helping civilians all before glamouring them to forget that magic they'd seen on full display.

Flapping furiously, I carried Walter away into the night sky, searching through the memories I'd kept of the former host for a direction because this world had changed so much in the half century since I'd been contained. Hundreds of years dwelling in it with slow, subtle shifts, and the moment I turned away, it seemed the entire board flipped over into something new.

9

Walter

I'd never flown so high. Every muscle in my body quaked, and the only thing keeping me from plunging to my death was Bez. He had a tight grip around my waist with one arm, his tail coiled around my legs, and his damn hand slapped over my mouth. The hold made it impossible to suck in a desperately needed deep breath.

Flying in Bez's grasp was nothing like flying alongside Ian in the Dimensional Atrium. As much as I wanted to struggle, I worried Bez would drop me. No. He might die if I did. Or so he said. So much had been said. Done. My mind struggled to make sense of the charges thrown at me.

This was Bez's fault. What the chancellor's said didn't add up because there was no way I could've done that. Well, I could've. Hacking the systems wouldn't be all that difficult for someone who knew the right people in the sentinel regiment. It'd also require an expertise in magic and technology, which theoretically, I had. But I definitely didn't have the saturation skillset to manipulate the magic imbued in our systems.

We soared miles over the city, the drop to Columbia Center a terrifying sight, yet the bustling streets and nightlights made for the most enchanting view. Bez whipped between buildings, taking faster and sharper turns than any mage I'd ever seen fly; somehow, we'd zipped past Rainier Square Tower and circled the Space Needle in a flash.

"Where's that stupid street?" Bez muttered, pausing midair. His wings flapped, creating a gust which held us in place. "Do you see Moray Avenue?"

I scanned the roads below. Of course, I didn't see the street sign. Everything looked like a blob this far up. I shook my head.

"You're so useless, Walter." Bez, the dick, continued flying in circles, searching for Moray Avenue. When he'd finally found the street, he zipped low.

He dived too close toward the road, nearly letting my legs hit the roof of a SUV. "Ooo kose," I shouted.

Whether he heard me or not, in an instant, he whipped back up into the air and lunged directly toward an apartment building. Every floor up was like those awful theme park rides that lift you up in the air before plunging back toward the ground. One. Two. Three. Each story he passed was a dizzying experience. Seven. Eight. Nine. I closed my eyes instinctively when Bez stopped, awaiting the plunge.

He dropped me, and I immediately thudded against a concrete balcony onto my knees. "What's your problem?"

"Shut up," he said.

"I won't. I demand—"

"Try that command thing, and I'll rip your tongue out," Bez interjected, his features furious, wearing the same scowl as the mage who assaulted me. The mage he possessed. "I'll be fine without it, but I bet it'd hurt like hell for you."

I stiffened. Bez approached the sliding glass door.

"What are you doing?"

"Laying low for a bit."

"You can't just break into someone's apartment." I quieted, then shook my head. No. I wouldn't let him intimidate me. "What if they're home?"

Bez slid the glass door open. It was unlocked. "Riley never locked this because, apparently, he was terrible at remembering his keys."

"It's the tenth floor." I glanced over the railing at the daunting drop.

"Not everyone sucks at flying a broom. Just you."

I ground my teeth. "Asshole."

"Dick."

I considered speaking out, but his frown frightened me. Not Bez's face. Riley's face, the face of the misfit mage who'd killed Carl and attacked me, the one Bez chose to possess.

Bez smirked, soft and friendly, nothing like the wickedness I'd experienced thus far. "Sorry. I'm exhausted. This is the most action I've had in a while, and you're a fucking headache."

That was the worst apology I'd ever heard. But considering he was a devil and he'd already tried murdering me, I guess he didn't really do apologies.

Hesitantly, I stepped inside with Bez since it didn't seem like I had any other options. The walls of the mage's apartment were covered in cloaking incantations, highly intricate and nearly on par with what the sentinel regiment used.

"It's not entirely you," I said. "The face."

"Oh?" He raised an eyebrow. "Too dashing for you?"

"Sure." I scoffed, then eyed the messy apartment which smelled like I'd walked back into my frat boy phase. Well, not *my* frat boy phase. More like my misguided interest in douchebags with confidence.

"Whatever. I need a shower." Bez stripped off his shirt, and I turned away. "Don't try running, Walter. I'll feel the tug of the tether linking us. The last thing you want is a naked, soaped up devil chasing you down the hallway."

I snorted. As terrifying as that was, it was sort of ridiculously hilarious in the worst way. "Maybe I'll fly away."

"Yeah, riiiiight." He stepped into the bathroom by the tiny hallway connecting the living room, kitchen, and bedroom. I plopped onto the couch. Screw Bez.

Turning on the TV, I flipped channels until I reached a news station. Not that it'd make a difference. No magic accountings ever reached the media thanks to the highly efficient infiltration regiment. The news did note the traffic jam on Heyward, caused by Bez's reckless flames, but the reporter blamed a gas fire. Thank goodness for quick and effective glamouring.

He shouldn't have been able to nearly harm so many people. I commanded him not to.

I sank into the dirty couch cushions, sadly the most comfort I'd had since this ordeal began. I didn't tell him not to hurt anyone. The first time, I commanded him to stop. The second time, I said not to kill anyone. I slapped my forehead. "Of course. The commands are literal in their interpretation. But that begs the question how specific I can get with the commands before the time limit runs out. Assuming there is a time limit."

Perhaps I could create an indefinite command, something highly thorough and detailed enough to consider every potential outcome. "Would clauses work on a devil?"

I eyed the bathroom door. Water blasted, but I bit my lower lip. I couldn't chance Bez hearing me. I also had to wonder how long a command lasted. My first command held for hours, from the estate all the way to the tribunal. Then again, Bez might've been biding his time. I couldn't ask him outright. Not unless I made answering honestly a command. Not that I knew exactly how to issue one. Strong emotion? Succinct clarity? Straightforward request? Something unambiguous in nature.

I ran my fingers through my hair, tugging my grimy curls. None of this mattered. Not really. I needed to prioritize the accusations the chancellors made. They wanted me dead for the Diabolic binding and my role in the attack on the Magus Estate. Something I could never do. In theory, maybe. But no. This level of cooperation and coordination and cunning required more than even my best hypothetical potential.

Still, they had evidence, which suggested my key card was used to embed the virus into the system. I mean, I understood the basic framework to creating a virus. Viruses replicated by creating their own files on an infected system, attaching themselves to a legitimate program, tricking processes, which further infected the computer's boot processes and corrupted user documents, protocols, updates, and a whole plethora of systems.

But the framework and sophistication of the Magus Estate was built on multiple servers. An independent server specifically for the dimensional portals, and one for the archives, which split into separate ones for the repository and vault. Neither of which I knew the location of. I suppose, since it was all tech based, I wouldn't need the physical location. Not if the virus was complex enough, which it'd need to be to account for over a dozen private networks and the magical layers entwined in each server. Plus, only the sentinel regiment had access to the servers. And only the highest ranked sentinel practitioners had that type of clearance. I might be the child to the sentinel chancellor, but she'd never explained how any of it worked.

The shower turned off, drawing me from complex conspiracies I lacked answers for.

"Don't you just love feeling squeaky clean from top to bottom?"

Bez stormed out of the bathroom. "Especially, the bottom. You mortals sweat in the worst places."

The first thing I saw was his shaggy jet-black hair, no longer matted, and the roots a vibrant neon orange. The next place my eyes instinctually fell to was Bez's cock because he'd strode into the living room stark naked, shaking his hips. I turned, closing my eyes. Still, in that fraction of a second, I got a very clear look at his appendage, which was clearly a shower, not a grower.

I swallowed hard. "Put some clothes on."

"Yes, yes. But I prefer to air dry."

He was the worst. The literal worst. That said, my curiosity itched. "How'd you change your hair?"

"Hmm? Oh, a glamour." Bez's clean musk wafted close, too close. Even with my eyes closed, I could feel the heat of his body near mine, warm and radiant. Almost inviting. I ground my teeth. He invaded my space in the same way he had last time in some attempt to annoy and frustrate me. I ignored it. "What can I say? I love Halloween."

"Diabolics can also glamour things?" I raised a brow, keeping my eyes firmly closed. None of that had been recorded in anything I'd read. Not that the Nexus Grimoire had much on Diabolics or their realms, aside from the differences between devils and demons.

"Those inside the right host body can. If a bit of the Mythic residue still resides inside the former tenant."

Not that I cared much for the former host, the man responsible for cutting Carl's throat and pummeling me half to death, but guilt still crept up. "Did you have to kill him when possessing him?"

"Yes. I'm an only child so I hate sharing."

"You prefer stealing."

The room grew silent as Bez ignored my comment, which pretty much summed up the entirety of our exchanges over the last three years. I sat silently, bouncing my knee and agitated by the quiet. I wanted to ask something. Open my eyes. But I didn't want a full view of Bez. My ears burned. I didn't want to want it.

"There. Better?" A snap, like from a waistband, followed Bez's question.

I ignored him.

"Open your eyes, you prude."

Having finished air drying, he strutted back into the living room wearing very small, form-fitting powder blue boxer briefs which left little to the imagination. Especially since my imagination had seen the entire beast tucked inside those silk undies.

Drawing my gaze up his firmly sculpted body, I met his eyes. The irises remained red, the whites fully pink, but they'd gotten bigger and were slightly further apart than before. Everything about his face had changed. The black veins had lessened, faded, and no longer bulged across his face. He had higher, more prominent cheekbones, a larger nose with a bit of a bump, and fuller lips. Even his forehead had become further arched. The only thing resembling the face of the former host was the sharp jawline. It was like looking at an entirely different person.

Had he changed his appearance because it left me unsettled? How? And why?

I leaned forward. "How'd you change your face?"

"I didn't, weirdo." Bez strolled toward the kitchen and opened the fridge.

"It's different. Very different. Did you change everything? Is it another glamour? It's so intricate." I found myself standing, eyeing his *assets* as he bent over to search the contents of the refrigerator. I gulped. There'd be no way to know if he'd changed the entire body from head to toe.

"Huh?" He stood, a pickle stuffed in his mouth and a hand deep in the jar. He crunched down, swallowing half in a single bite. "Oh, you mean the composite."

"What?"

"Yeah, it's something Diabolics do when possessing mortals." Bez ate three more pickles, swallowing them whole, then guzzled half the juice down and belched. I widened my eyes. Once he had his fill, he returned to the fridge for more…food? "Right now, my form is all kinds of jacked up, but it's settling in here, shaping to the constraints of this mortal mold. Some of my features will end up reshaping the host to better fit my body. Right now, I've changed about—I don't know—eighty percent. Well, those changes a mortal body can contain."

"Meaning?"

Bez held a spray can of cheese whiz and whip cream to his mouth, releasing both simultaneously. I gagged. Oh, gods.

"What?" he asked, mouth stuffed with a mushy mash of fluffy white and goopy yellow. My stomach churned. "It comes from the same cow. Well, not the *same* cow. Though, everything here tastes so much of carbon, I'm not sure any of it came from an animal."

"What do you mean what the mortal body can contain?" I snapped because I had to know. Wanted to. Desperately. And his disgusting cravings made me nauseous.

"Chill out, Walter." He chucked the empty cans back into the fridge and pulled out a box of pizza.

"Are you seriously still eating?"

He lifted the lid and sniffed with a sour expression. "No. It's got pineapple on it. Gross."

"Well?" I slammed the fridge closed, ignoring the tightening of Bez's biceps, shoulders, chest, and abdomen, which could've been a defensive beat-the-crap-out of me instinct or simply his way of bragging. Who needed that many well-defined muscles?

"It's the way we conform. We pick a body, preferably one with a physique we want, but y'all have such limited forms. It's quite boring." Bez shoulder bumped me as he sauntered out of the kitchen toward the bedroom. I followed. "Point is, it's my body now. So, I'm making a few renovations to update the accommodations. Obviously, I can't adapt all my features without risking ripping this balloon apart, though. Horns, claws, tails, wings, extra appendages."

"What extra appendages?"

"Wouldn't you like to know?" He winked.

Bez opened the closet door, flinging shirts onto the bed and carpet. "Boring. Ugly. Tacky. Uh, maybe—no. Itchy. Who would ever wear this? Yuck. Bland. Blasé."

He'd emptied half the wardrobe before his eyes lit up, a smile filling his face as he caressed the single dress suit pushed to the back of the closet. Immediately, Bez threw on the frayed, navy-blue suit which probably came out for every major social event from weddings to funerals. He rolled the sleeves of the dress shirt and jacket up to his elbows, and the slacks cut off at his calf like dressy capri pants. Wait a second.

"Have you gotten taller?" I asked.

"Gods yes. I'm fine being a tiny tyrant, since most mortals hardly reach six feet, but I refuse to have to look up to everyone I make conversation with."

It was amazing how much possession changed the host body. Really, it was less of a possession and more of a transformation. Fascinating.

"So, you ready to go?"

"What?" I froze. "Where?"

"Anywhere but here. They want me dead. They want you dead, too. I'm not sticking around."

"I'm not leaving." I crossed my arms.

"Oh, you sure about that?"

The fact was, Bez could force my hand a lot more assuredly than I could his. What I needed was something mutually beneficial. The only problem was all Bez wanted was to murder mages.

"I want to clear my name."

"You still have a Diabolic binding, which will make you a target." Bez rummaged through the sock drawer, pulling out rolled up ties and holding them to his chest. "It also makes me a target by association."

"How long will it last?" I asked, which was a waste of time because Bez would only lie.

"Not sure." He shrugged. "A few weeks maybe. A few days if I'm lucky. I didn't see how much of me you took."

I had no idea either. I stared at my palm, a light pink scar almost completely faded now, but that single cut had turned my entire world upside down.

"Does it feel good?" Bez folded his collar up, wrapping a bright blue tie around and adjusting it.

"What?"

"Having me inside you? Do you quiver with delight? Quake in anticipation?"

"You're insufferable." I sucked my teeth, taking a tense inhale because as murderous and aloof and innuendo-y as Bez was, I needed him. "I'd like to make a proposal."

"For marriage? Pass."

"For mutual assistance."

"Handies?" He rocked his head side-to-side considering. "You'd just talk the entire time. Pass."

My cheeks burned. "This is serious. I'd like to find the real culprits behind this attack."

"To clear your name?"

"Yes. And then we can wait out the bond. You can leave."

"Not sure I see the mutual assistance part of this."

"You get your freedom, I get a cleared name, and we stop this war on the Collective."

"Mages and Mythics and whoever the hell else fighting among

each other makes my lowkey life easier. Let them be distracted."

"But, and hear me out, a Diabolic has never helped the Collective before."

"Untrue."

"Well, never in recorded history," I clarified, which seemed pointless if he just made things up. If a Diabolic had actually done anything other than slaughter innocents, there would definitely be an accounting of it. "If you help solve this, expose the real agenda and people behind it, everyone will remember the devil who prevented a war…"

Bez's expression turned quizzical, lips pouted and eyes rolling toward the ceiling in contemplation but definitely not listening to anything still coming out of my mouth. Honestly, I wasn't entirely certain what I was saying anymore, lost in his irksome expressions. "And you want to make a deal with a devil?"

"Not particularly since you'll probably kill me once the bond is lifted anyway." But one problem at a time. I could find a way to seal Bez before that happened. In the meantime, he was my best bet at solving this conspiracy and clearing my name.

"Nonsense. A devil never breaks a deal." He extended his hand. "Consider me in."

"Wait. Just like that?"

"Sure."

"Why?" I inched closer like it'd somehow give me a better understanding of his minxy smirk.

"Perhaps an instinctual compulsion or boredom coupled with curiosity."

"Instinctual what?" Was that connected to the vocal commands? I mused it over. Not that he'd tell me.

"A few ground rules first." Bez wiggled his already extended hand, and I reached out to shake it.

"Fine." I tensed my hand, ignoring the tight squeeze of his grip.

"No killing people."

"Okay. No more commands."

I nodded. Not that I knew how to properly invoke them anyway. Bez released my hand. "So, what's your big plan?"

"I figure there has to be intel in your host's memories."

"Not the person pulling the strings. Maybe some other low-level players, but I'd have to search through them. Honestly, I chucked most of the garbage memories."

"You can do that?" Each facet revealed another layer of curiosity.

"To make room for mine, yes, I can."

"We'll follow one lead at a time," I said, repressing the urge to study Bez and Diabolics further. "Once you've sorted those memories and found intel on those low-level associates, we can follow up on them. Maybe we'll get lucky."

"Walter, you've never once in your life been lucky." He crossed his arms, glaring. After a small pause, his lips curled into a wicked smirk. "Fine. Watching you royally screw this up will be deliciously entertaining. I'll start looking inward through boring memories."

"Good." I plopped back onto the couch, watching Bez close his eyes, press his palms together, and pretend to meditate. He was definitely faking because he moaned instead of the soft *om* humming for contemplation.

My pocket buzzed. Oh, no. My phone was vibrating. I checked it. "Unknown caller." I bit my lip. Could they be tracking me? Us? "No. Not a chance. They wouldn't call if they were."

"Walter, your voice is disrupting my meditation."

"Sorry. I'm getting a phone call."

"Ignore it. I've observed you actively avoid answering it for three years. Mostly with anxious dread as it glows and vibrates."

Not true. Okay, a little true. Still, this could be important…or a trap. Screw it. How much worse could my life get?

I clicked accept. "Hello?"

Bez shook his head disapprovingly. "Don't answer the telephone."

"Wally, are you safe?"

My heart pounded. "Al?"

"Who?" Bez asked.

"I'm sorry for everything that happened," Al said. "I can't believe Mom."

"Who is it?" Bez asked, pressing his ear against the phone.

"Stop," I said.

"Are you okay?" Al's deep voice held the same protective urgency it always had. I was certain me taking off with a devil after a tribunal accused me of treason and conspiracy sent his whole head spinning round and round.

"I'm fine. Is this…" I bit my lip. "Are you calling because you're concerned, or is this a trick?"

"I wouldn't trick you, Wally. Not ever." He sighed into the phone, the sigh he usually let out when he wanted to lighten a mood, tell a joke, say something uncouth during one of our mother's banquets. He couldn't exactly lighten these events, though. "I'd like to meet you."

"I can't. It's not safe for either of us."

"I have information that might help clear your name. Guessing the fact you answered means you must have command over that devil, which will also help."

"Not command," I said, ignoring Bez's piercing stare and him mouthing profanities while eavesdropping. "We sort of talked it out."

Al laughed. "You always could talk anyone into anything, Wally."

"If that were true, I wouldn't be in this situation."

"You're still the only apprentice I know who talked his way into working in the archives repository and the only Alden to convince Mom the sentinel regiment wasn't in the plan."

I sank into the cushions. Neither of those had anything to do with my persuasive skills.

"What does he want?" Bez hissed.

"Tell your devil I'd like to meet. I'd like to share my findings, get both of your help."

"Where?" I asked, though still uncertain if meeting was wise.

I needed more information about the virus used on the Magus Estate, the one which supposedly came from my card key. If anyone had intel on that, it'd be Al since he held the second highest rank in the sentinel regiment.

"I was thinking—"

"Wait." Bez grabbed the phone, covering the speaker. "We pick the location. Safer that way."

"I wouldn't even know where it'd be safe." I shrugged. "We'll need someplace crowded, magic friendly but not Collective friendly."

"I've got the perfect place in mind," Bez said, mischievous grin growing on his face.

"How would someone who hasn't been in the city for fifty years have the perfect place?"

"Let's just say Riley frequented one of my favorite hotspots, and from what I can tell, it hasn't changed much."

I gestured for him to return my phone. "Okay. We're doing this then."

10

Beelzebub

What a disastrous idea. Between my recent release, buzzing adrenaline in a new body, and Walter's absurd plan to meet with his brother, I'd spent the entire night wide awake. When he'd finally dozed off—willing himself to stay awake, paranoid I'd renege on our deal—I should've gone back on this ridiculous bargain, snatched him away, and left this gods-forsaken city. Instead, I upheld my deal, watching the little mage catch some z's, while contemplating what drove me to follow his plan. None of this benefitted me. It'd be simpler to lock him away until our bond faded, kill him, then do literally whatever I wanted anywhere but here.

"Okay, there's Elena's Emporium, which means we need to go left." Walter guided us through Mercury's Marketplace, the veiled magical place of commerce, a secret collection of shops and businesses catering to all those in the Mythic and mage communities. I'd allowed him to lead because of his annoyingly detailed itinerary, which he pestered me about the entire morning, even declaring we didn't have time to walk through Pike Park Market, the mortal neighborhood where the main entrance to Mercury's could be found.

I'd always enjoyed the delightful collection of food vendors flooding Pike Park, with so many wonderful flavors to mix and match and devour. Unfortunately, since my time in the orb, they'd built a field called a Lumen, where mortals infested and bellowed beyond reason to the point my dimmed senses could still hear the faintest echoes of their roars from miles away and behind the glamoured wall of Mercury's Marketplace.

I adjusted my sunglasses, keeping my presence discreet in Mercury's, which meant no Diabolic features on display. Not that many would notice on this bustling dirt street cluttered with cumbersome crowds of people. Many Mythics had their own unique features, from the winged harpies' offering patrons a sample of their perfumes, to the gorgon soliciting passersby palm readings at her small shop, all the way to the shouting centaur selling kabobs. All the stores were cramped and crowded, built too close to or on top of each other. It made me grateful I'd turned off my brain receptors for air since there was no room to breathe.

Which was also why I demanded Walter and I meet his brother here. According to Riley's tucked away memories, both the mage Collective and Mythic Council struggled to reinforce full order in this hidden territory, far from the reach of humans. Mercury's Marketplace proved an easy place to get lost or disappear. Something we'd need when Walter's plan backfired.

"Looks like he's not there yet, so we should stay out of sight." Walter snatched my hand, dragging me behind him through the crowd and into an alleyway. Sure, his grip was firm, but his skin was so soft.

"Why are we hiding?" I whispered in his ear. The sensation tickled the back of mine, so I knew it left little Walter flustered.

"We can't just stand out in the open waiting on Al."

"Ah, yes, Alistair, your eldest brother who's agreed to assist us because he loves you."

"No. I mean, yes. Obviously, he loves me, but he agreed to assist because I explained to him the situation, how I wanted to help, and he knows I'd never do anything the tribunal accused me of."

"Except for the Diabolic binding." I rolled my eyes. "If he's anything like your mother, this is a trap."

"It's not a trap."

"We should be following other leads."

"Do you have other leads?" Walter's voice had an edge to it, an angry attitude I'd never heard before. It made it difficult not to smirk.

"Not yet," I grumbled. Riley's memories had been utterly useless. He had more on trivia and pop culture than insight on the plot to raid the Magus Estate.

"Until you do, this is the plan."

I huffed. "When this goes bad, which it will, I'll gladly get us out of here so you don't have to add 'falling into an obvious trap' to your long list of failures."

"It's not a trap." Walter kept his gaze on everyone making their way past the Depot, among which were many sentinels, easily identified by their blue blazers and shield emblems as they cut through the crowd. "There's only a tiny probability Al would lie, especially if the chancellors put pressure on him."

"See. Trap."

"Shut up."

The second this turned bad, I'd snatch Walter away and take him someplace safe. Someplace far. Someplace he couldn't cause me trouble. Why didn't I do that to begin with? It'd be so easy to tie him up and lock him away. Still, my heart pattered in a rhythmic beat for his success. Was it my heartbeat or his?

He had his fidgety anxious expression on, studying something he lacked the variables for, which often made him uneasy. Walter preferred planning for everything. It was this damn binding casting the desire to see this through. Nothing more. Once my essence had been relinquished from him, I'd be free to be myself again.

Sentinels cut through the crowd, surveying the sea of patrons swarming about, then they crossed to our side of the street. I positioned myself on the corner as some of them plastered posters on market store windows.

"Shit." Walter poked his head further out, chin brushing against my shoulder.

Other sentinels handed out flyers with our pictures. I'd shifted this host enough to go unnoticed, but Worthless Walter would stand out the second any of the Mythics or mages here caught a glimpse of him. I could glamour his features. It'd take time, probably more mana residue than I currently had stored, too. Shit.

A sentinel turned and stared right at us. I backstepped past Walter as the sentinel conferred with another, then nodded in our direction.

I spun Walter around.

"Stop," he whispered. "If we run, we'll look suspicious."

"And if those two get a good look at you, we'll look even more suspicious because they're looking for us."

He had a point, though. The second I bolted, they'd give chase. I had no way to know how many sentinels were currently in Mercury's Marketplace. Walter wouldn't make any commands, assuming he kept his end of the bargain, but I still couldn't kill anyone until his last command fizzled out. I huffed.

"I just need a second to think." Walter gulped. "Maybe you can glamour my face or let me borrow your sunglasses. No, that'll leave your very Diabolic eyes exposed. Plus, sunglasses are super suspicious. I mean, I'd wager a lot of people wear like—"

"I got a plan." I smirked.

Since I only had a second to devise a way to avoid nosy sentinels,

I developed the quickest plan to pop into my mind. It had the bonus of being delectably entertaining and messing with Walter's head.

"Follow my lead." I pushed Walter against the brick wall of the alley, running my hands along his quivering torso.

His entire body heated, confusion swirling in his eyes, yet there wasn't even a faint hint of resistance when my lips met his. I slid my tongue into his mouth, the sweet taste enticing me further as I guided him. Whether from instinct, desire, or just playing along, Walter's hands lifted, and he ran them up my shoulders. His fingertips sent a rousing shudder down my spine as he traced them up my neck, running his fingers through my hair as he tilted his head.

The sentinel cleared her throat, biting back an embarrassed *whoops*, but we kept our lips locked and faces turned. Seconds passed as the sentinel lingered. I panted, breaking away momentarily.

Walter's eyes drifted toward the sentinel, so I kissed him again. Rougher. More passionately. I held his hips, though part of me wanted to grip the back of his thighs and lift him off the ground. That'd surely make it clear the sentinel needed to offer us a bit of privacy.

Heat spread through my chest, blood coursing faster everywhere. Distracted by the fruity taste of Walter's lip balm, I almost missed the retreating feet of the sentinel who came to investigate two lovers cozying up.

I could end this. No need for such a diversion anymore. Yet the gentle caress of fingers in my hair coupled with the subtle thrust of his hips I held in place made it difficult to break away. This was his lust, clearly. I was simply caught in my own game. Pushing my thigh between his legs, I considered a hundred more possibilities for us, all of which would be more entertaining than walking into a trap.

"You know, Wally, if you were looking for a boyfriend, there's better ways to go about it than a Diabolic binding." A broad, well-built blond perched against the alley corner. He kept his arms crossed, which didn't cover the sentinel emblem on his blue jacket. It was the playful smile he wore that I found baffling.

Walter pulled away, wide-eyed and slack jawed. "Alistair. This isn't…wasn't… It was a cover." His voice creaked. "Right? Yes. Emergency. Your sentinels were…"

Mildly disappointed by the break from my entertainment, I lowered my thigh which was still firmly positioned between his legs. "Not exactly the head I planned on messing with," I whispered.

Walter's entire face burned bright red, blood changing direction, but not enough to lessen the bulge I noticed tucked uncomfortably in his jeans.

"Making out with a devil." Alistair shook his head. "What would Mom say?"

I shrugged. "I begged him to stop."

"Bet you did." Alistair's smile turned sour when he shifted his gaze from his little brother to me. Alistair appeared a polar opposite to Walter in demeanor and appearance. A tall, muscular mortal who held himself confidently, his features were sharper, too, yet softened by the playful smirk. Even his blond curls had a shaggy swoosh whereas Walter's were as chaotic and untamed as the many tangents his beehive of a mind explored.

"Why are your sentinels here?" I asked.

"They're always here to secure Mercury's Marketplace," Walter said, adjusting his tight black shirt which had ridden up thanks to my assistance. "But there are a lot more than you said there'd be, Al."

"Mom is attempting to secure her position after your escape," Alistair said. "And as her dutiful son, I assured her I would do my very best by securing the misfit mage behind the massacre at the Magus Estate."

I nudged a shaky Walter. "I told you it was a trap."

"Trap?" Alistair burst into laughter. "Please. If I wanted to take you in, I would've grabbed you at the apartment last night."

"You knew we were there?" Walter asked. "But I kept the call short, and the place was covered in incantations."

"And it belonged to Riley Hamilton, who your devil possessed, so I figured staking out the place would be a good call." Alistair approached. "Turns out, it was good I went and let Chancellor Driscoll know no one had come in or out."

Alistair was too friendly, too helpful, too unlike his chatty little brother who was a yarn ball of anxiety and depression one small cat bap away from unraveling.

"I want to know who's behind this, why they set you up of all the mages working in the estate, and what their next move is."

"That's exactly what I want to know," Walter said. "I think if I understood how the virus was actually used on the security systems, I may be able to figure out who really did it."

"Let's talk more privately." Alistair reached into his pocket.

"Not happening." I glared, crossing between Walter and his brother.

"Well, we look a bit conspicuous talking in an alleyway." He offered a ring to Walter. "It's saturated with my mana and has a glamour enacted."

"Thanks." Walter put it on.

"No problem. Figured you wouldn't think of doing it." His smile became grating to my eyes. Too much delight in an Alden mage. "Or be able to."

I rolled my eyes. "I could've done that."

"Made one for you too, devil. But I see you've got it covered."

"How do I look?" Walter looked up at me.

"The same." Which he did. Nervous grin, curly blond hair, hazel eyes frantically searching my expression for tone or sarcasm. Nothing had changed in his features either. Same dimpled cheeks, small nose, and jutted chin.

"Diabolics and their resistance to the Pentacles of Power."

Alistair chuckled. "It's fine. Should work on everyone else."

True, but a practitioner could easily see through deceptive glamours. Would this glamour Alistair provided oh so conveniently be enough to trick his fellows? I wasn't convinced.

"Let's discuss this over a meal," Alistair said. "There's a lovely elven cuisine around the corner. Outdoor seating which will offer a bit of distance for private conversation and public enough to hide in plain sight."

This was the first thing that'd come out of Alistair's mouth I didn't immediately distrust.

"I could go for some food," I said.

The high-ranked sentinel practitioner led Walter and me out of the alley and down the crowded street.

Walter pulled me aside, leaning in so close the lavender body wash he'd used became the only scent in this swarm of scrambling shoppers. "W-why'd you kiss me back there?"

"Huh? Oh. That. Yeah. Hmm." I grinned, minxy, intimidating, and frazzling Walter long enough to contemplate my reasoning. "I was simply abiding by your rules."

"What?"

"Your rambles are deadly. Those poor unsuspecting sentinels had no idea what they were walking in on."

"Talking doesn't kill people," he hissed, gritting his teeth.

"Trust me, your voice holds a violence unlike any I've heard before." I gestured. "See, you've still got that whole contrived over-complicated explanation face—yikes. I simply worried you'd talk the sentinels to death as a diversion. Since you're so opposed to murder, I didn't want you breaking your own rule."

"Jerk."

I winked.

He stormed ahead, joining his brother for our little investigative meeting which would likely lead to nothing. Staying back a bit, I searched more recesses of the memories I'd kept, skimming for names, locations, or anything that'd actually uncover this conspiracy and lead back to Worthless Walter. Their choice in making him a patsy was a bizarre one, indeed.

I craned my neck, sniffing the air. Whether Walter's brother intended on leading us into a trap remained unknown, but darkness clustered in the air, a delicate thread of crimson-black fibers thinner than hair and stronger than steel unseen by all in Mercury's Marketplace other than myself. Carefully crafted webs stalked our movements toward the restaurant.

I huffed. Guess I'd have to determine if she'd come as a friend or foe. Of course, I couldn't allow Walter to realize or he'd pester me with a thousand questions. He'd question me even more if we walked into a demon's trap. As if the Collective wasn't enough of a hassle— I really didn't have time for Diabolic drama, too.

11

Walter

Bez ordered half the menu when we arrived. The elven server had brought him three appetizers, four mimosas, and his second entrée before she brought my only ordered dish. Bez shoveled food in his mouth in the most obscene manner. I should've been listening to Al or ignoring Bez. Instead, my mind wandered back to that kiss. Most of what Al said came down to idle chit chat anyway while we'd ordered, flirting with the server or joking about Bez's appetite.

Why had Bez kissed me? My ears burned. Why couldn't I get it out of my head? His lips were soft and aggressive. His tongue was invasive, the worst type of kiss, and yet… I bit my lower lip, worried I'd debate it out loud at the table. He did it as a diversion because he claimed my slight talkativeness would be…NO.

There was a passion in his touch. I couldn't get his hands out of my head. The way they caressed me, touching every part of my body as his lips consumed me. How his panted breaths synced with mine and time simply stopped. Fear. Anxiety. Dread. It all washed away in those short seconds. Was that all an act, too?

My body vibrated at the memory. Was it purely out of distraction? It worked, totally throwing off the sentinels. But was he interested in me? He had straddled my waist but that was in an effort to murder me. Was it that strange instinctual compulsion he'd vaguely referenced? He had flaunted his very naked body last night.

I shook my head. No. Watching him eat the bratwurst he'd insisted on substituting for the maple sausage links, he clearly wanted to get a rise out of me. What better way than to mess with my head? Bez knew all about my guy problems, my lack of dates, my awkward inability to talk to anybody except for him the past three years, mainly because he never answered back.

He was a Diabolic, which wouldn't be a bad thing—it wasn't as if they could all be cruel, murderous beings—except Bez had already attempted to murder me, a chancellor, and several mages including Ian.

Ian. I sighed. He was who I should be thinking about, not Bez the manipulative vengeful Diabolic devil.

"Can you stop doing that?" I muttered, glaring as Bez sucked the syrup off his bratwurst.

"What?" He grinned. "I like to lick off all the sticky sweet parts before enjoying the *thick* meat."

I huffed and pressed my hand to my bouncing knee. He wouldn't get a reaction out of me. He wouldn't trick me. I refused to play his mind games. I was mature, intelligent, and saw right through whatever weird agenda he had planned.

"Can you both pay attention?" Al asked with his stern expression— a face he rarely brought out, and something ingrained from following our mother's teachings on how to command an audience.

"Sir, yes sir." Bez swallowed the brat in one gulp. "I do love that assertiveness the Alden's possess. Well, some."

Ugh. If Al had accidentally formed a Diabolic binding—which he'd never do, because he was the golden boy—he'd have figured out how commands worked. Hell, he'd probably have convinced the chancellors during the tribunal meeting that Bez would make a great addition to the Collective. The two of them would likely hit the town every night, cruising for dates and succeeding on every mission that came their way. That was Al, though. He did everything right.

"I am listening." I hunched, averting my gaze from either of them, poking my runny scrambled eggs. I'd asked for sunny side up. It seemed no one took what I said or asked for seriously, not even our server.

"It's my belief Chancellor Driscoll had a hand in this."

"Why?" I asked.

"Before the attack on the Magus Estate, my squad was issued an order to investigate a strange disturbance in the Dimensional Atrium. An ill convenience since we're the closest responding sentinel squad outside those within the estate."

They were also the fastest and strongest sentinel squad. Mother ensured Al had the best team at all times so he'd rise to the top of the ranks. Not that he needed assistance. He ranked second only to her in the sentinel regiment and that came despite him fighting against his place at the top. But at the end of the day, no one really defied Chancellor Alden and her plans for the family legacy. Well, no one who wanted to be successful.

"What infiltrated the Atrium?" I asked, wondering if perhaps this Mythic and misfit mage attack had more to do with the restrictions on the Dimensional Atrium than the Magus Estate. So much power came from the Fae realms, and they shared only the slightest bit of it with the Collective. Aside from Mercury's Marketplace, the Mythic Council headquarters, and a few select mage-appointed locations, there were few spots Mythics had magical reign in. Most weren't even allowed inside the Atrium; only those with clearance from the Fae and Collective could enter the Dimensional Atrium.

"It was a baby goblin that'd somehow slipped security," Al said.

"Adorable," Bez said.

"It's believed the portal was triggered by the Mythic signature of the goblin, and his lack of magic didn't register a need to block access."

It didn't explain why Al suspected the vanguard chancellor.

"I mean, anyone could've wrangled a baby goblin out of the Atrium." Al gestured toward me. "Even um…other apprentices would've managed."

"I don't see how that makes Driscoll a suspect." I spooned the soupy eggs. Yuck. I grabbed the extra crunchy toast instead which, of course, spilled crumbs all over my shirt.

"It does when Driscoll practically forced Mom's hand to get me away from my outpost and into the Atrium where the portals connected to the estate suddenly went on the fritz."

"Since when does she take orders from Chancellor Driscoll?"

"Since Remington explained their inability to play nice was affecting the Collective." Al bit down on his sloppy, extra thick meat sandwich without so much as a drop of grease smudging his cheek. Gah—he even ate better than everyone else. "Ironically, had Mom ignored Remington's suggestion, he might still be alive."

"Well, one point for mommy dearest." Bez raised a mimosa. "Maybe there's something to like about her, after all."

"Okay." I shrugged, ignoring Bez's antics because, quite honestly, that was the only way I'd survive being bound to him. "Say Driscoll had a role in this. Why set *me* up?"

"No idea, but I think it's meant to hurt our mother."

"More like help her," I scoffed. "Sorry. Just not seeing the great Chancellor Alden all that upset by this outcome."

"It hurt her standing among the other chancellors, with an Alden under suspicion."

"Great." I took one of Bez's mimosas.

"Hey!"

I downed it, paying his protests of thievery no attention. If I somehow managed to survive the regiments' pursuit, the charges of treason, and the devil latched to my side, I'd have to contend with my mother's rage for years. She'd hold whatever social standing lost because I'd 'allowed myself to be framed.' I sighed. I could hear the cutting comments during family events already.

"Point is," Al said, "Chancellor Driscoll's pledge for interim magus went unchallenged."

"Not to be rude," Bez said. "Correction: full intention of being rude. Your theory simply sounds like typical mage hierarchy bullshit. Not a conspiracy."

"He's not wrong." I reached for a second mimosa because I very much wanted a buzz to continue this conversation.

Bez bopped my hand. "Get your own."

"I asked for a refill on my water five of your cocktails ago." I rattled the ice in my empty glass and snatched a second flute of orangey champagne.

"There's more," Al said. "His elite vanguard squad was the first to respond."

"Ooooh," Bez interjected. I glanced at him, assuming he held some curiosity for the mages responsible for detaining him.

Nope.

Of course, it wasn't the potentially nefarious plot underfoot. He was giddy because the server had brought his triple chocolate banana raspberry waffles smothered in cool whip and a side of tabasco sauce with pickles soaked in the dish. I cringed, knowing he'd probably put the spicy pickles on his waffles.

"Enjoy." Our server brushed a lock of hair behind her pointed ear, smiling at Bez.

"Thank you so much for your excellent service," Bez said with a sultry rasp in his voice.

I rolled my eyes.

"I would like to note, however, that you brought the wrong eggs."

Our server's vibrant purple eyes widened. "Pretty sure you ordered poached."

"Not me, darling." Bez chuckled. "My annoying friend. Well, friend is a strong word. *Ass*ociate. Heavy on the ass."

Bez and our server giggled in unison.

"It's fine. It's not a big deal," I said.

"I've got a few tables to cover, but I'll be back to check on you."

Bez grabbed her wrist and cocked his head. His sunglasses slid ever so, revealing his dark red eyes surrounded by pink.

"Bez," I hissed, scanning each of the nearby tables in case someone noticed.

"Actually, I'm going to insist you rectify this oversight." Bez's smile vanished. "He's barely touched his meal, and I can't have my associate underfed."

Everything went silent. The chatter of nearby tables. The bustle inside the restaurant. The busy street beside us. All of it vanished aside from a subtle ringing accompanied by a slithering sound. It was sticky and grimy, and everyone seemed locked into the ticking seconds, unfazed by this tremendously terrifying presence. I turned, eyeing those nearby. They moved like molasses.

A faint screech wailed in the distance, growing louder and louder until the elf's teeth chattered and her entire body trembled. Her screech turned into an agonizing shriek, and then the world went completely silent. Nothing for several seconds until every noise in and outside the restaurant bustled again. I shook at the sudden onslaught.

"Let me get this order fixed." She grabbed my plate, simultaneously snatching a pitcher from a nearby station to refill my water before disappearing.

I widened my eyes, stretching them so far, my eyebrows brushed my curly bangs. "What'd you do?"

"Diabolic dreams," Al said, unimpressed by the loss of time. "One of your many abilities, correct?"

"I asked her politely first." Bez shrugged.

I'd read about those, literal living nightmares cast on the person with a simple gaze. I shuddered. There were so many Diabolic abilities I needed to review, to understand better. I squirmed, counting on my fingers all the powers I'd read and comparing them to things I'd witnessed.

His advanced recovery. His augmented strength and speed. The way he could unleash parts of his devil form at will. Telekinesis. The black barrier he'd conjured for protection. There was also Diabolic control over the elements, which was nothing like mages or witches who synced with nature. Diabolics perverted it, bent it to their control—hence the black flames.

"A thank you would be appreciated."

Thank you? That was the most extreme and unnecessary response ever...even if the gesture might've been well meaning. Like all things with Bez, it was impossible to decipher.

I ground my teeth in response, turning my attention back to my brother. "All of this seems coincidental or circumstantial at best. I'd like to study the virus used to infect the systems. I'm not the biggest expert, but if I had some resources, I think—"

"Wally, this isn't the repository," Al interrupted. "Everything you're doing, will do...hopefully, it'll be under the radar."

"So, why are we here?" Bez asked. "What assistance could you need from Worthless Walter and a devil?"

I slammed a fist on the table, drawing more attention than I wanted. "Stop calling me that."

"So sensitive."

"Asshole," I whispered.

"The goblin I mentioned earlier had an incantation branded on his back, similar to the incantation on Wally's card key."

"That sounds like evidence to me," Bez said, which I begrudgingly agreed with. "Present this to your tribunal. Why send us to investigate?"

"We handed the goblin to the panacea regiment for healing. The incantation was gone by the time they finished their examination—something I didn't think much of until I saw the evidence presented against Wally. Namely, the card key. Add to that fact, one of Chancellor Driscoll's elite vanguard members deciphered the hack in mere seconds." Al straightened his shoulders, broadening his chest. Two physical actions of clear intimidation which he rarely did when encountering someone else's magic. I began to wonder how much of this was about me and how much was about his pride. "It's my belief this particular member and his fellows released the goblin into the Atrium, had my squad sent on a goose chase—"

"Goblin chase," Bez interrupted with a gleeful smile because, of course, he fucking did. "Completely different. Geese are far more difficult to chase and much more aggressive when you catch them."

Statistically speaking, Bez wasn't incorrect. Goblins were sweet, despite what the average human thought or the superior mage believed. They were gentle. Geese on the other hand, were cruel overlords who thrived in the chaos of nature. I didn't believe that simply based on the number of times they'd decided to block the road when I drove by, chased me by the lake, or stolen snacks out of my bag when reading at the park—I had statistics on my side. Geese were monsters.

But I trembled with fury. Bez hadn't interrupted on some pretense of accuracy. He did it to frustrate me. Everything he did was in some effort to irritate me. He couldn't kill me, so he decided the best way to rid himself of me was to annoy me to death.

"Can you stop for two seconds?" I snapped. "We're discussing something life or death."

"I'm all about life or death." Yeah, his life, my death. Bez craned his neck, looking behind me, then smirking. "Pardon. Please, arrange our investigative adventure. I need to use the little Diabolics' room. Too many mimosas."

"Good." I crossed my arms as Bez strutted away, nodding politely at our server who scurried all the quicker with my correct order.

Everything had been changed. Sunnyside eggs. The toast was already buttered, soft yet the perfect crunch. Three pieces of bacon, and the third piece was extra burnt in the worst and most delicious way. Crispy hashbrowns with the cheese already melted between the softest parts. Did Bez tell her to do all this? How'd he know this was what I'd wanted to ask for when I arrived?

I licked my lips. Coincidence? Three years of listening to my rambles? I never talked about breakfast. Did I? Perhaps some connection from the Diabolic bond. Maybe his instinctual compulsion to me, whatever that meant. I had ideas, but there was too much to make sense of. "And not with Al here."

"Are you done hyper fixating on whatever theories are running through your head?"

I took a bite of the hashbrowns and nodded.

"Wise to let your devil wander off?"

"He won't go far." He couldn't. Not with the bond.

"Vanguard Corvine is the one I'd like you and your devil to question."

"Question him?" I asked. Did he seriously expect Bez and me to capture and question a member of the elite vanguard? "Why us?"

I should've followed up with how, where, and maybe a not-so-friendly reminder that the entire frickin Collective was looking for us.

"You're an anomaly, an unexpected outlier. Whoever framed you likely predicted you'd die during the attack. Just another casualty in the assault on the estate." Al sipped his coffee. "You didn't, though.

In fact, you did the impossible. You released a devil and formed a Diabolic bond. That makes you an unforeseen threat and an adventitious element of surprise."

"You want us to cut through the bureaucratic tape you can't." I sulked. Al didn't need to further explain. An investigation like this would ruffle a lot of feathers, especially when they already had a prime suspect, namely me, so Al wanted Bez and I to work behind the scenes—illegally obtaining information that'd clear my name. "What do you need us to find from this Vanguard Corvine?"

"His grimoire. It might hold all the incantations linking him as a suspect."

"Or he removed them."

"Let's hope not." Al tapped the table, drawing my wandering attention. "And when this is done, once we've proven you didn't have a part in this attack, I'll deal with the chancellors and their fears over this Diabolic bond. I don't know how to handle Beelzebub, but I will seal him away again. By the time the bond fades, I'll ensure you have your old life back and that monster is locked away once and for all."

I stared at my breakfast, perfect even under such imperfect circumstances. How I desperately wanted my old, boring routine of a life back. All the times I'd craved adventure and purpose, only to find out after a single day I couldn't hack it.

A strange guilt crept inside me too, though. Bez and I had struck a deal. A deal I considered double-crossing him on the moment I made it because I worried about the harm he'd bring to the world. But what harm had he brought so far? All the horror happening was from the mages and Mythics.

Then again, the only thing holding Bez in check was our Diabolic bond. Unleashed onto the world, he could and likely would hurt so many. But knowing he had awareness for nearly fifty years inside that orb, alone, no one to share his thoughts with… Did he deserve that again?

My heart thumped. A strange sensation. Not the beat of my heart, but the light tug with each pump of blood coursing through my body like a string tied to my chest, reeling me toward the devil which created such curiosity and insecurity and too much confusion. "I should find Bez."

12

Beelzebub

I strolled inside the restaurant, scanning for an old acquaintance who'd crossed my path. Everything about Alistair's plan bored me and wouldn't result in clearing Walter's name. It'd only add to the confusion of mage politics. Walter wouldn't want to hear that, though, and I had no desire to explain it to the simple little apprentice. Instead, I continued my pursuit. Everyone dining held a Mythic or mortal scent. Mostly elves and mages here. However, a faint trace of Diabolic energy wafted between the delicious aromas coming from the kitchen. I weaved between tables, brushing past servers, and burst into the back kitchen.

"Well, well, well, if it isn't the worst devil in all the realms." Mora slurped a cherry red smoothie. "Still my favorite, which isn't saying much."

I leapt forward in a blur, stopping short of snatching her by the throat. Partially compelled because of her aloof attitude after five decades of silence, another part concerned her behavior would oust my presence. Only at the last second, right as my fingertips reached her neck, did the faint black aura appear in the corner of my eyes.

A dust cloud of Diabolic energy quelled her words, making any conversation fall silent in the presence of those working in the kitchen. Mora's control for veiling her actions had improved tenfold. Better than mine. She'd improved so much since last we spoke. Here she was spilling Diabolic phrases in front of Mythic fry cooks all carefree because none of them registered the words due to the cloud of confusion she'd cast. I needed to work on mine. It'd been so long since I'd used any magics. Each fiber of my being creaked, rusted over from a half-century of that discombobulated state. I needed to practice, work on the finesse every Diabolic required when walking in the mortal realm.

Subtilty had often been my downfall. Devils were supposed to be bold, cunning, and ruthless. They weren't supposed to hide in shadows because they were the shadows.

"You look as stunning in this form as your last." I eyed her new body—or newest body.

Unlike me, Mora enjoyed embracing whichever appearance she inherited when picking a new host body, doing little to alter the form through composite shifting. Personally, I hated staring at a new mortal face and needed to resemble myself as much as *humanly* possible. Mora had never held value in her demon body or her Diabolic life. A tilt of her head allowed her long, wavy chestnut locks to drape and frame her face. Porcelain pale skin, so white, most probably mistook her for a specter more than Diabolic. Even her eyes were a bland blue, no real sparkle behind them, lacking the Diabolic pink pigment in her sclera. All her demon features remained hidden, with the exception of her pointed ears.

"Do you work at this elven business? Blending?"

She preferred blending among Mythics and mortals, didn't relish the violence which came so naturally to our kind, yet knew when and how to indulge in it for necessity.

"Absolutely not. But always hiding in plain sight, darling." Mora stepped closer, placing her neck within my grasp.

It'd be easy to squeeze. I could strangle the life out of her faster than the haze she'd cast would fade. Kill her long before a single soul noticed.

"Why are you stalking me, Mora?" I lowered my hand, clenching my fist.

"When the long-lost devil Beelzebub reemerges right on the cusp of a coup attempting to overthrow the Collective, it piques interest."

"Yours?"

"Certainly." She brushed the back of her hand along my cheek. "I've missed you, Bezzy."

"Don't call me that."

"How'd you escape?"

"What do you care?" My blood pumped, coursing with unchecked energy as emotions took hold. Mora never revealed her hand, always cautious and playful. Nearly fifty years inside that orb. Part of me wanted to rip her still-beating heart out of her chest, tearing out all the Diabolic tendrils woven into this host body, too. Another part of me wished to hug her after so much time apart.

Mora was the only demon I'd met since arriving in the mortal realm who I hadn't outright despised or killed for the sake of convenience. The only one I'd ever toyed with the idea of trusting. No. The only Diabolic I actually trusted, considered a friend. A mistake. Mora had taught me better. Trust was a tool used to gauge motivations and achieve mutual benefits, nothing more. A lesson learned when I stumbled upon her as a young, naïve, and lost Diabolic so many centuries ago. It was because of her I learned to blend among the mortals to avoid their ire. Kill the mages who chased me. Feed from Mythics to maintain my strength. And build the legend of Beelzebub so I'd never fear the shadows again.

I quelled the bubbling rage, resigning not to allow the primitive desire to snuff out her life win out. Yet. Had it been because I missed a familiar face? No. No one mattered in the grand scheme of things. Not even myself. All I wanted was a break. Perhaps it was Walter's goddamned command still circulating inside my core.

Mora had invited me to this city, the best place for a Diabolic to blend. Our aura was hard to detect or track, making us almost invisible to mages or Mythics. However, fellow demons or devils could always sniff out their own. Neither Mora nor I cared for other Diabolics, so Seattle seemed the best place. Honestly, the entire northwest region was flooded with more Mythics than most territories. In a sea of so many different magical scents, a Diabolic could disappear if they desired. Mora did. She kept her profile low, fell in love with some witch, and made me believe in the simplicity of it all.

Then I met Abe, the young archivist prodigy on track to be a chancellor. Abraham Remington had the friendliest smile and kindest attitude toward the unknown aspects of Diabolics. A friend with a dream so big it swept me away into believing mages could truly see me for something more than a nightmarish devil. The worst mistake of my life.

"There was nothing I could've done for you after you ambitiously attacked the Collective single-handedly," Mora said. "It was a foolish thing, Bez."

"It wasn't supposed to be single-handedly." I ground my teeth.

It wasn't supposed to be an attack, either. Liberation. Something to free the scattered Mythics under the reign of a cruel Magus. A man bent on outdated policies which divided mages, Mythics, and mortals of all kinds. I was only meant to help remove one enemy to all. Abe painted such delusional lies as truth, craftier than even Mora herself, I fell right into thinking I'd absolve a past of murders with one singular righteous kill. This region would hail me a hero. No such thing, though. Abe penned the perfect patsy in exposing my villainous actions, all while leading the charge against me. Still, I'd rather slaughter a thousand than suffer at the hands of one. Not that it worked. Abe bound me away and created the peaceful co-existence he'd always wanted, all while ensuring the mages and Mythics had a mutual enemy—the devil who came to massacre them. Interesting how someone deep within the recesses of this city had the same vision as Magus Remington when establishing a new narrative; however, they'd picked Walter Alden as their villain—a poor choice.

"You've been here this entire time?" I asked after mulling over past miseries for too long. Mora kept quiet, studying me, likely gauging how best to broach her next words.

"Kell loves the city, the seasons, and hopes to one day reunite with…" Mora paused. "I don't have the heart to say covens don't undo banishments. Especially when forbidden magics are used. I swear, witches are worse about shunning their own than mages. Probably why mages supersede them—a better consensus."

A consensus that made Walter a target and scapegoat to cover someone else's agenda. "Mages also have more numbers considering they can recruit when enrollment is scarce."

Witches were a bloodline. Stronger magics, although it did little when the mages outnumbered them a hundred to one.

"I must say, Mora. Surprised your witch mate is still alive and kicking." I snickered. "Kell must creak like old floorboards at this point."

"My essence and the bond we've created allows Kell a much slower decay than the average mortal." Mora giggled—her lips curled into a twisted smirk I'd seen far too many times, which meant she'd lost herself in her own humor. "It'll be centuries before the crow's feet creep in."

"So, the Diabolic bond offers longevity?"

"What's immortality if one can't share it with those precious to them?"

"You've willingly submitted to several Diabolic bonds."

"Yes?"

"How do you break one?"

In the three centuries I'd known Mora, she'd had a new partner every time our paths crossed. The next great love of her life. Following her heart in this realm often left her heartbroken with a body to bury and a new host body to find in order to maintain that low profile she loved. Sometimes even a village for us to burn. Surely, she'd had to sever a romance with a bond still active.

"You can't break a bond." Mora shrugged. "Well, I can't. But I'm usually careful never to offer too much. Never know how long forever lasts."

"Keeping your mortal on a tight leash for monthly restoration."

"No. In the past, perhaps. Kell and I perform the ceremony maybe once a year. It's the longest contract I can offer." Mora sipped her drink, studying me. "Why are you so curious about Diabolic bonds?"

"Simply nice to see you making your affections last," I said flatly, hiding my curiosity with disinterest. When I came to Seattle, she claimed Kell was the one. Something she'd professed at least a hundred times. It was somewhat comforting to know she'd made it work. "Half a century, you really are settling down."

"The heart wants what the heart wants."

"I'd still gamble on finding Kell's chest ripped open, heart discarded, and you soaked in blood before you hit the hundred-year marker."

"Bitter, jaded, nonbeliever." Mora waved me away dismissively. "You'll eat those words and whichever lovely cake I serve on our hundredth." Mora licked her lips, eyes rolled high, savoring some delectable memory. "Oh, my goddess. It reminds me… We had the most decadent molten lava cake on our fifty-second. Chocolate made by these wonderful nymphs. Unicorn dust sprinkled on top. Yum."

"Sounds delicious and very mortal." I grabbed her cherry

smoothie, sniffing the mana and blood laced in this sweet treat. "I see some things haven't changed."

"Low profile doesn't mean a girl should abstain. Abstinence leads to binging and depression." Mora pushed the bottom of the glass, inching it closer to my face. "It's all about moderation, Bezzy. If you knew it, you'd have just as much fun without so many folks chasing you. You'd be happier."

"Devils are never happy, dear. You'd know that if you knew more of them."

"I've met enough devils to know I've had my fill." Fluffing her hair, Mora shook away the memory of her forgotten Hell realm ruled by the boring Bael, one of the laziest, unchanging devils our many worlds held. Every time a glint of her past crept into her mind, she had the same faint expression, loss for words, and swift recovery. Pouty lips, primped locks, and some god-awful comment to follow. "I have one suggestion for you, darling. Get out of the city. Out of the state. Three away to be safe. Hell, cross a border or two. Someplace where the mages aren't so empowered."

Was that concern? With no biting comment, either. Mora had changed. Or perhaps I'd forgotten with so much time apart.

"Worried for little ole me?"

"Worried you'll cause more trouble. Things are stirring here, dangerous things. Deadly. The Collective won't lose; they never do. But I imagine a lot of Mythic factions are going to leap at this false sense of weakness, which means more enforcement from mages."

"I can keep a low profile."

"Your nose is growing."

I set her drink down, walked to the backdoor, and nodded to take this conversation someplace a bit more private. Mora kept her shroud veiling our presence but a hand in her pocketbook. A weapon, perhaps.

"Such distrust," I whispered in her ear as she brushed past me.

"I've killed for less, and so have you."

"I hold no grudges," I said, slamming the metal door behind us.

Mora shuddered. I smirked at the satisfying startle it caused. Her black shroud thundered, defensive and channeling elements momentarily before quelling the instinctual defense.

This alleyway offered her three quick exits if necessary.

"Why do you care if I linger in Seattle?"

"You cause trouble, *Beelzebub*," she said the name with cutting disdain. "I hoped you'd outgrown it when I invited you here, having kept quiet for the better part of a century."

The 1800s were droll and tedious. I'd slept through most of it.

"Then I caused a mage massacre."

"That you did," Mora said. "I never thought you'd see this world again, but I'd hoped if you did, your time away would solidify why it's important for Diabolics to keep a low profile."

"Demons, perhaps."

"There are worse things than dying. You know that." Mora eyed the sunlight peeking into the alleyway. "Remington is dead. Everyone who's wronged you is long since gone. With the mages in disarray, you should leave."

"It's more complicated than that."

"Who are you?" Walter asked, entranced by the veil hazed throughout the alleyway, shrouding Mora and myself.

Shit. Speak of the devil—well, the complication. Of course, he'd remained immune to its ability, given my essence squirming inside him. Mora tilted her head, widening those bland blue eyes of hers. Intensifying her illusions for privacy, she studied Walter's expressions as he watched the sparkle of the shroud in the darkness. I ground my teeth.

"Well, well, well. Kell will be stunned when I share that our favorite devil went and formed a Diabolic binding." Mora sauntered past me, heels clicking along the pavement and playfully curtsying to Walter. "See you around, Bezzy."

Turning the corner, Mora's Diabolic shroud vanished along with her presence. Clearly, teleporting before I or anyone else had the chance to pursue her. No matter, if I needed to, I'd track her instant transportation based on her faint signature that dwelled. By announcing herself, it'd made it so much easier to find my dear old friend.

"Bezzy?" Walter's eyes practically ballooned as he stared.

"Call me that, and I'll rip your tongue out."

"Who was she?" he asked. "How'd you know her? She looks young, which means she's likely very old since—well, you haven't been around in a while. A Mythic? A contact of your former host? No. That doesn't add up since she wouldn't recognize him after all the changes you made to his body. A witch, maybe. So Mythic. But I've never seen magic used like that. Teleportation through an incantation, sure. Advanced and massively complex. The cloudy haze, though…" He adjusted his glasses, studying the air where the Diabolic haze had lingered, searching for every answer to every conceivable question his frustrating mind could come up with. "It's like everything vibrated and froze and bam: gone. How'd she do that?"

"Shut up." Honestly, I'd hop into Mora's Diabolic network to get as far from Walter as possible if it weren't for the damn tether from our connection.

"Just tell me. Who was she? What was she? What'd she want?" He stalked close, continuing his incessant prattling into a hundred various half-explored rambles before launching into a new tangent. "Well? She can't be Mythic, right? They hate Diabolics more than mages."

Yes, yes. Everyone hated us. Humans feared us on a biblical proportion. Mages despised us for our actions. Mythics hated us because we perverted their magic in this realm. Sure, when a mage used the magical residue in the atmosphere, they got put on a fucking pedestal. When a Diabolic did it, we were called monsters.

"Was she another Diabolic? Her eyes were so normal, though."

"My eyes are normal, asshole."

"I didn't mean it like that. I just meant hers weren't as noticeable." Walter's face turned red, his hands fidgety, curiosity swelling along with his puffed chest. "Just tell me who she was."

"She's a purveyor of dreams, seamstress of desires, patron of carnal devotion."

"Tell me the truth!" His voice rattled inside my skull, vibrating through my very core.

Persistence and yearning and craving to know any little detail all burst at the seams of my very being. A surge of electricity flooded my veins.

"Her name is Mora—Morax. The only demon I've ever trusted and still trust." The tether connecting us snatched me forcefully, drawing a confession. "A former demon king who ruled among the hierarchy of demon lords in another Hell realm, one she abandoned long ago when escaping to this world. Goddammit. We set rules."

"What?!"

"You broke a rule. The only rule I'd set." I shoved him. "You issued a command."

"Not on purpose." He backstepped, frazzled and confused, his eyes already studying the implications of how he'd triggered the command.

"You still broke a rule."

Motherfucker. He wanted to find a way to control the Diabolic binding, always studying everything he could down to the deepest core of truth. An annoying trait of his I'd learned to read from the subtlest shift in his quizzical expressions. The arch in his brow, probably asking himself if his tone played a part. The way his fingers tapped his chin while biting his lower lip. Whatever thought had appeared, he'd doubted it. Fingers strumming his chin always meant he wanted to cross off the potential hypothesis but hadn't found a better solution yet. I growled.

His anxiety ate away at me, stirring my insides. I hated it. Couldn't decide if it was this bond we shared or three unbearable years of observations, but I had such an acute sense of his inner thoughts and irritating quirks.

"Just spit out whatever you're thinking, you insufferable bastard."

"It's nothing." He feigned a weak smile.

"Say it, Walter."

"I'm not sure how commands work, so how can I abide by the rule without accidentally invoking them? You know? And I'd ask you, but you'd likely yell or lie or both because you'd be worried I'd use said knowledge against you. In reality, I'd have more clarity on how to prevent this from happening in the future."

"You want to know how to avoid commands?" I stepped in close, my chest nearly pressed to his.

His heart thumped faster, and his body warmed from my swift approach. The sensation crept beneath my flesh like a rotted infection of feeling.

"Let's just find those vanguards your brother suspects and get this over with." I adjusted my tie, tightening the knot around my neck, hoping to suffocate anything considerate or helpful or kind or equally curious that might accidentally spill out in conversation.

Whether intentional or not, Walter had already broken our deal. Which meant he'd break it again. More likely, he wouldn't hold it up to begin with. Little wormy mage was probably already conspiring ways to handle me after our bond broke because, as the Diabolic, I was the real threat here. It wasn't like I'd get anything from this deal we'd established anyway. The only certainty it'd offer was clearing Walter's name. The only thing he offered was a guarantee to wait out our bond so I could leave in peace and a chance for mages and Mythics to see Diabolics in a positive light. Why'd I even entertain the idea it'd help prove Diabolics weren't the enemy? Twice in my long centuries, I'd roamed this realm and attempted to show I wasn't the enemy, the threat. Twice, I'd failed, and I was despised for my efforts. I wouldn't allow for a third.

I couldn't trust him. I wouldn't trust him. Not any mage. Not again. I made that mistake with Abe and ended up dragged into a battle I wanted no part in, where all the blame fell to my feet.

"Hurry up." I brushed past him, nudging his shoulder.

Why'd I always get dragged into fucking mage politics?

13

Walter

Bez grumbled as we stepped off the bus, complaining the entire trek downtown. Ignoring him, I used the GPS to track the outpost where Vanguard Corvine was stationed. This part of the city had a relatively low mage presence, considering the Mythic Council favored the profits and popularity downtown tourism had to offer. The major caveat being all magic had to maintain a low profile.

"What are you doing?" I snapped as Bez stretched, uncoiling his sleek-shorthaired gray tail. Grabbing it, I half expected it to be soft and fluffy. The fur was coarse and muscles firm. I tried to stuff it back into his pants, but within two seconds of gripping the tail, it'd lifted me off my feet and thrown me against a trash can. "Asshole."

"Says the guy touching me without consent. Rude." Bez wiggled his tail, shaking his shoulders loose. I half-expected him to release his wings and hold up a sign. "That bus was awful. Unbearable. I hated it. So confining."

"You spent the better half of a century inside an orb, and you're complaining the bus was cramped?"

"It was. Too many mortals. Touching. Talking. Smelling weird." Bez took off his sunglasses, revealing the heavy mascara and eyeliner, which only intensified his crimson irises and the pinks of his eyes. He huffed on the lens, rubbing a smudge and making it worse. "It would've been quicker if we'd flown."

"And be detected?"

"No one can track my essence."

"It's broad daylight," I grumbled, brushing gravel off. "Can you put your tail away?"

Bez blinked at my response. Not quite a glare but still dissatisfied. Maybe that had to do more with the red glint of his eyes. Unlikely. He was mad about my command before, which I had no understanding of controlling. I hoped asking instead of issuing the statement would make a difference. Based on his displeased expression, it didn't matter.

I'd invaded his privacy, learning he knew the demon Morax, who I'd heard rumors about. Not as a demon, though, but a dark witch, Mora Mayfaire, who preyed upon the desperate, conjuring deals and offering discreet services. I might've studied a lot of different ways to fast-track my failures into successes during my years at the academy. Not that my weak research on the witch who was actually a demon turned up anything.

"We have to maintain a low profile, or do you…" I bit my lip. Asking if he wanted to fight his way through downtown, even sarcastically, would likely encourage him.

"I am keeping a low profile." He adjusted his blazer as the tail slithered back into his backside just above his butt. There wasn't a hole in his blazer or pantsuit, and his shirt was tucked in, so maybe a small rip in the dress shirt. "Stop studying me, nerd."

"I'm just making an observation." I hadn't noted when he'd

unleashed them during our escape or when we'd arrived at the apartment for the night. There was a lot of processing going on. Still… "Do your Diabolic features rip through your clothes?"

"Duh."

"I'm only asking because werewolves and shapeshifters have these enchanted wardrobes, so their transformations don't leave them naked."

"Do I look naked?" He smirked.

My ears burned, reminded of his very bold strut after his shower. "Can we just go?"

"You're so boring." Bez made a pouty face, putting his sunglasses on. "Let's go."

We walked to the vanguard outpost. The plan was simple. Stake out the place, identify Vanguard Corvine, grab his grimoire, and leave. If done right, we wouldn't have to actually interact with any of the mages inside. We had the advantage of Bez's Diabolic presence being difficult to track and my lack of mana making me a literal blip on the radar in this sea of magic downtown.

"Where's this vanguard outpost?"

I scanned the towering building. "It's in the suite at the top."

Bez eyed the empty street, then stepped in close, chest pressed against mine. I backstepped, but he grabbed my wrist.

"Relax."

I lacked words. Okay—I had a million words, but thankfully I didn't blurt them.

His body burned away the chilled fall weather. Every other time he'd stood this close, I'd never noticed his warm presence. Granted, those times involved attempting to murder me, kidnapping me, and kissing me. It was like his Diabolic nature radiated hellish heat. He leaned in closer, his chin grazing mine. Was he going to kiss me again? I turned. No sentinels or vanguard or anybody around. This wasn't some ploy. Or was it? Definitely. He wanted to get a rise out of me. Mess with me somehow. His head rested on my shoulder while one hand wrapped around my lower back, and his other squeezed the back of my thigh.

"W-wh-what are you doing?"

"Try not to scream." He snickered into my ear.

"What?"

"I'm not taking a bus to the rooftop, that's for sure."

"That's not how that works—"

Bez unveiled his wings. Gray feathers filled my line of vision, and in an instant, we soared directly up. I held onto Bez's shoulders tightly, legs swaying, with only his grip keeping me steady as I took heavy breaths into his chest while avoiding looking down.

My feet dangled above solid ground, and my butt plopped hard onto the gravel rooftop before I'd found my footing. "Dick."

"So, what's the plan? Break and enter? Hope the vanguard in question has this grimoire? Hope yet again it holds evidence Alistair requires? Hope yet just a bit more that the chancellors see your actions as helpful and clear your name?"

"The plan is to get the grimoire—discreetly, while avoiding the vanguard. Then, determine if it has anything useful, and hand it off to Alistair."

"Fine." Bez crossed his arms, practically brooding a stealthy mission which meant he couldn't pummel mages. "Let us commence your useless mission."

"It's not useless. Al believes it'll benefit—"

"Blah, blah, blah-biddy, blah. I get it."

I huffed, muttering a few breathy profanities until Bez removed his sunglasses, grinning. I hated his angst. His cavalier attitude. His everything.

But I trusted Al. He'd always looked out for my best interests even when it'd have been easier to look away. I didn't trust Al's intentions with Bez, though. It was something I needed to mention to

Bez. He was such a loose cannon and unpredictable. Same thing, I guess.

No. It was untrue. Bez had upheld everything between our arrangement, gone out of his way to save me, and agreed to my deal even though it'd have been so much easier not to.

Yes, it was the Diabolic bond. Had to be. Still, maybe if I proved I could be trusted, he wouldn't…well, he wouldn't change. Maybe if we did this together. Did it right. He'd realize his freedom didn't have to involve murdering everyone who crossed his path. He had a Diabolic friend. Morax. A demon who'd lived in the shadows of Seattle for decades without brutality. He trusted her with his life, said so himself. Maybe Bez could learn the same.

"Now that we're here, I'd like you to do a hawk's eye observation spell."

"A what?" Bez leaned forward, tilting his head like he was actually listening intently, but in reality, he wanted to invade my space and make me anxious. It wouldn't work. I backstepped, avoiding his warm touch.

"It's a sophisticated incantation." One far too complex for me to handle. "It'll be an easy show-off moment for you."

"Can't."

"Yes, you can." I gestured to his shaggy black hair and vibrant neon orange roots, along with the additional piercings he'd glamoured—well, maybe he'd stolen them from some shop when I wasn't paying attention. He was a devil. But he definitely didn't have two pierced studs in his ears before or the industrial bar on his left. His hair, piercings, and sunglasses screamed rock 'n roll, but his suit said strictly business. Then there was his actual personality which roared 'insufferable.' "I'll walk you through it."

"I don't have much magical residue stored and currently using what remains sparingly," Bez bemoaned like he'd endured such a travesty at having to prioritize what remained. Prioritize it over superficial, glamoured bullshit. "If you want this simple little incantation performed, you'll have to do it yourself."

"It's not a simple spell. It's a complex collection of several incantations collided together to make one massively powerful stealth spell. This *simple*, as you put it, incantation has to be precisely stacked on top of one another, or the whole thing will implode."

"But you know how this works. All the words. What you need to do is get out of your dumb little head and use your annoying big brain to perform." Bez thumped my forehead. "Or I can just bust in, break some bones, retrieve the book, and we can be on our way."

I glared. He wanted that: Me to admit I was too weak to perform this and give him permission to loudly break inside. It'd be best to attempt it myself and fail—as the most predictable outcome—than to give Bez free rein into infiltrating a vanguard outpost. I'd seen him hold his own surrounded by over thirty mages. The half-dozen living in this suite would be eviscerated if he went inside.

I visualized the sigils in my mind, attempting to draw them through a mental image. This would be easier with a wand. It'd be easier with parchment to trace them out. It'd be possible if someone conjured the magic, and the only step which remained was the activation. I'd done that plenty while working in the repository.

Bez brushed up behind me. I shuddered despite how warm he was, how soothing his touch felt.

"Relax," he whispered. Soft and raspy. "You know the words. Pull the mana up from your core and release the magic."

Easier said than done. I muttered the first word, holding the blue, glowing sigil of magic between my hands. This simple incantation would cloak the spell. Now came the hard part. Keeping a grip on the sigil, I whispered the second word. A faint pink sigil rested atop the first, combining the extended vision I'd need to see beyond the walls within the suite. Stacking sigils of different natures was difficult. They resisted my grip like magnets possessing the same poles of attraction. Ironic since these two sigils held no similarities. That was what made the hawk's eye observation spell so advanced. Even skilled practitioners struggled to combine incompatible incantations.

"Next." Bez's gravelly voice sent a chill through me.

Was he taunting me? False encouragement meant to build me up only to cackle when I screwed up the stacking factor. I clenched my jaw, growling the next incantation. I wouldn't give him the satisfaction. One after another, I placed differing sigils atop each other.

"Don't drop 'em," Bez teased.

"Shut up," I snapped, almost releasing the stacked sigils.

Shit. I took a deep breath. To keep them together, I had to have a level head. This wasn't combat. There was nothing to knock me off my emotional center—except for Bez. Pressing my palms as tightly together as possible, I whispered a repetitive chant for each incantation until the sigils threaded. Glowing little strings tethering these opposite spells together the same way the Diabolic essence had forced Bez and me together.

I opened my palms, releasing a golden silhouetted hawk. It soared high, observing the suite and linking to my vision. The rooftop appeared translucent beneath my feet. I trembled. Not out of fear but delight. I wanted to shout. Jump. Flip off every person who'd ever laughed at me for messing up a simple incantation. I'd literally performed a top-tier incantation on my own. Burying my excitement, I sent the hawk through the building walls in search of the grimoire, navigating through the corridors and avoiding the nearby mages. I smiled. It was so easy—I'd never been this successful before with a simple spell, let alone something this advanced.

Vanguard Corvine's grimoire lay alone on a table. A thick black book with silver lining and a matching lock. Not something easily accessible, but Al would find a way. There were a dozen intricate incantations that would override the failsafe. Carefully avoiding

Corvine's gaze, I instructed the spelled hawk to grab the grimoire, imbuing it with gold so it cloaked the spell book. I skirted it through the suite up toward the ceiling.

"Shit." I bit my lip. I forgot the intangibility overlay sigil, so there'd be no way to carry the grimoire through the door.

"What?" Bez asked.

"I forgot to cast a sigil. The hawk has intangibility, but without the overlay, it won't transfer to held items, which means I failed, and you get to grab the damn grimoire."

"Chill, little overthinker." Bez patted my stomach.

"What're you doing?" I tensed.

"You don't need mana to make an alteration."

I felt Bez inside me.

Gross. Phrasing.

Not Bez, *Bez*, but his essence, pulling at my core, needling my stomach. It worked. The incantation altered, even so distant, and I sighed. Such a relief yet a simultaneous reminder I lacked any talent. This great feat of success had nothing to do with me. Obviously, the only reason the stacked incantations worked was because of the Diabolic essence within me. I was still useless when it came to casting.

The grimoire phased through the rooftop and landed in my hand. I unraveled my mana over the hawk's eye incantation, releasing the magic.

"Good job, Worthless Walter." Bez snickered. "You're almost like a real mage now."

I didn't have the energy for a quippy retort. Between the mana required to cast such a complex spell and the realization I hadn't really done much, I simply clutched the grimoire and stayed silent.

"You should be giddy or some shit. You were elated when you sealed that artifact, and that turned out to be a botched job. Or the invasion of the manor. Point is, why aren't you perkier?"

"It wasn't me. You know that."

Bez raised a single, questioning eyebrow. "And how is that?"

"It was your essence." I rolled my eyes up so I didn't tear up. "Just mock me already, gloat that I can't do anything, and burst my bubble. I know it was you, not me."

"Walter, if I wanted to gloat, I would've done so." Bez grinned. "I don't have to time my insults to your tragic self-esteem. This was all y—"

"You filthy misfit mage," someone shouted. "Think that pathetic glamour would fool the elite vanguard?"

I whirled around. Six vanguard mages hovered on brooms, glowing incantations already circulating them as they surrounded us from all sides.

"Detain the traitor and his damned devil!"

Bez wrapped an arm over my shoulder. My face burned, and his warmth enveloped me as he leaned close; his stubble tickled my ear.

"Looks like I get to have a little fun, after all."

No. No. No.

I didn't want the vanguard to get us, but I couldn't allow Bez to have whatever his version of *fun* was.

14

Beelzebub

I pushed Walter to his knees, figuring he'd cause less interference scrambling on the ground than running away. Six mages. Not very sporting. I strutted forward, adjusting my loosened left sleeve, which had rolled down a bit. A fireball hurled in my direction. I tilted my head, not bothering to block or counter. Seriously. This was an elite vanguard squad?

"So impulsive."

They closed their ranks, hovering above the rooftop but safe from a dropping point. Good.

"No killing," Walter yammered.

"Yeah, yeah." I waved a dismissive hand.

I knew the arrangement. Besides, it'd be far more entertaining to make them live through the hell I had planned. They'd tell the horror stories to their kin for generations. The tale of how the devil ripped into their soul, shredding the fibers of their being and exposing their deepest fears on a platter.

A collection of incantations released a flurry of swift-moving elemental magic along with enhancing the ferocity of their spells. I conjured a black barrier. The blows wouldn't faze me, yet the cascading debris might hit Walter. Couldn't have that. Taking off my sunglasses, I tucked them into my blazer pocket.

Minimizing the barrier, I cloaked my hindrance in a semi-transparent black veil. Not that the mages bothered to target him. Oh, no. They sent their futile casts directly at me. I weaved around them in a hazy blur, dodging fire, ice, and lightning. Six mages circled me, each saturating their broom for faster flight with one hand while casting incantations or elemental magic with their second. These coordinated strikes were timed to push me into a second or even third blow. It was only my speed which evaded the elements or explosive sigils when my foot tapped it. I sheathed my talons, coating my hands in black Diabolic energy to amplify this mortal host body.

Dread crept inside me. I groaned. Walter was getting inside my head again with his doubts and fears and concern over life. Releasing the energy, I waved my hands. Each mage and magic flung about thanks to my well-timed and heavily applied telekinesis. I couldn't play defensively, though. I needed to end this quickly and succinctly.

A mage rushed in close, attempting to stab me with an enchanted sword. Our eyes locked. I smirked. That was all I needed. I leapt back and danced across the rooftop, sweeping in close to each pursuer and meeting their eyes with my own.

Having locked contact with each mage for at least a moment, I had a thin thread of Diabolic energy linked to their visual cortex. I quickly channeled illusions, rooting through their nightmares, regrets, and biggest failures. Each unveiled in seconds. Quickly, I manifested those fears, syncing them to the vision, worming deep into the brains, and allowing them to destroy themselves.

One after another, the vanguard mages hollered in horror. I chuckled. They gripped their heads, pulling at their hair in some tragic attempt to rattle the images away. No such luck. Mortal insecurity was the easiest thing to prey upon. The first, a stout man with such succinct control over his incantations, wobbled on his broom. He collapsed to the rooftop, writhing in agony. Two and three shortly followed. Their elemental compatibility showed promise, but I wouldn't consider them elite in anything. Four ground her teeth so hard I thought she might crush them to dust in some sad attempt to break free. Alas, she passed out before I could find out. Five held out, screeching like a child. His voice had an annoying squawk to it. I was grateful when he fell face-first into the gravel.

"Not very sporting." I brushed my hands.

"Die, you Diabolic trash!" The sixth, Vanguard Corvine, flew directly toward me, flaming sword in hand.

I craned my neck. The nightmares circulated as they had with the others. A web of hellish history infested his mind, yet he grinned. An angry scowl of a smile, which considering the nightmares of his past, it made sense. This was a mage who'd acquired a lot of power and indulged in exerting his cruelty on those beneath his station. This was a man who swam in nightmares to satiate his passions. The things he'd done to acquire power would make the most vicious Diabolic blush. Diabolic dreams wouldn't affect him. Not this quickly. And I didn't have the time or interest in finding what made this sadist tick.

I lunged forward, intercepting this vanguard mage and snatching him by the throat. He squirmed and struggled. His magic floundered as my grip tightened. My blood pumped, thrilled by his anguished expression. A look he himself had seen all too many times based on the brief history of favorite memories he savored, which deceived me into believing they were his nightmares. My heartbeat quickened. I cracked my neck. Walter.

"Relax," I said, quelling his anxiety which funneled through me, ruining this moment.

"B-Bez, we got the grimoire. Let's go."

"Sure thing." I hurled Vanguard Corvine across the rooftop and over the edge.

"What the fuck," Walter shouted.

"Oops." I snorted. "Gotta make it sporting."

I picked up the fallen broom and chucked it over the edge too.

"You did that on purpose." Walter ran at me, shoving me with his feeble little push.

I cackled at how he knocked himself backward trying to bulldoze me. Weak and wiry. Practically adorable.

"You did that to spite me," he snapped.

"I have no idea what you're talking about, Worthless Walter."

"Stop calling me that." He shoved me again, grimacing at the ache it gave his wrists.

My stance was solid, my flesh denser than steel when desired. He'd only hurt himself, but not too much.

"It's because I broke the rules on accident, so you…you killed him!"

"I threw him off the roof because he's a prick, not because of your violation." I blocked Walter's next awful attempt to strike me with a soft backhand.

He winced, gripping his bruised knuckles. "Killing someone is way worse than invoking a command."

"I beg to differ." I waltzed toward the edge of the rooftop since Vanguard Douchebag's shouts had grown fainter. "I just threw him. Plus, I gave him his little broom. No rules broken."

"I said *not* to kill anybody."

"I didn't kill him."

"A fall like that kills people."

"No. It's the landing that'll kill him."

Corvine splattered onto the ground in a delectable bloody smear. I missed the explosive sound, which barely reached us. My teeth chattered at the thrill. I enhanced my senses so I could savor the visual of his broken bones and frantic face, along with the scent of death.

"Yep." I laughed. "Definitely didn't stick the landing."

Walter's body shook with such unfathomable fury. He swung a fist. Knuckles cracked against my jaw, and I grinned. He hit me so hard, the bones in my fingers throbbed.

I playfully offered him a second shot, knowing he'd realize his error, but instead, he screamed a full-blown feral shout and ran at me.

In a swift blur, I dodged his tackle. He hit the gravel, groaning.

"Are you done yet?" I asked.

"Shut up." Walter stood.

"You must realize how futile these attempts are." I shrugged. "I mean, even a competent mage would struggle against a devil."

"I am competent."

"Are you, though?" I tilted my head.

Walter's hazel eyes widened, bloodshot and pissed. I'd never seen him so enraged. My veins bulged and constricted in sync with his fury. The little nerd finally had his last straw and snapped. I evaded his pathetic swings, lightly smacking him. Cheeks. Ribs. Gut. Soft and vulnerable spots without invoking the Diabolic protection. Nothing fatal. Nothing deadly. Just enough to remind him he stood no match.

He panted, struggling to stand as his rage consumed him. Was this an effect of the Diabolic bonding? I continued recoiling over his neurotic emotions enveloping me, had mine finally infested his heart? I smirked.

"Stop fucking smiling." Walter swung a fist.

I dodged. Honestly, my muscles and joints ached more from his failed fighting than his successful blows.

"Can we quit this?" I asked, resting my elbow on his shoulder.

He spun around, swinging furiously. I zipped away, backstepping faster than his eyes could follow. Still, he chased, predicting where I'd land. Impressive. A fist landed on my bicep, aimed for my torso, but I admired the valiant effort. His body trembled from his exhaustion.

No. This had nothing to do with me and so much to do with years of repressed rage. I loved it. Loved his outburst. Had he had more of these moments in the repository, I probably wouldn't have wanted him dead so much.

"Enough," Walter shouted.

Fire surrounded me.

"Looky there, when you get out of your own little head, the magic just pours out."

Walter had a bewildered expression. He stared at his hands, then the flames, and shook his head doubtingly. The fire spiraled and intensified. I snarled. Something sweet wafted in the air, covering something foul. I'd caught this scent before. I turned. In the distance, a mage flew closer on a broomstick, controlling the flames and muttering something. Beneath the fire, faint sigils glimmered. Dammit. The elemental attack was merely a distraction. The mage darted over me and snatched Walter into the air. I leapt forward but not fast enough. Metal sprang up, enclosing me from every direction in a circular container.

"This won't hold me," I growled, punching the hot metal.

My chest ached. The Diabolic tether linking me to Walter yanked at my core, knocking my footing off. It'd be quicker to punch my way through the rooftop than this magical wall, but I found myself pinned to it. Every muscle of my body was drawn to the fleeting Walter. I channeled essence, coating my hands in sheen, black talons. I shredded through layer after layer of metal walling.

"Get back here!"

15

Walter

Wind whooshed across my face. My chest tightened, a light tug reeling back to Bez. I quaked, clutching the fabric of a sweater tightly while sitting on a broomstick twirling through the sky.

"Ian?" I held him as he zipped further from the devil bound to me. My legs intertwined with his, and I clamped my thighs around his waist, certain I'd plummet otherwise.

I wouldn't, though. Ian had a hand firmly planted on the small of my back. Mana saturated the broom, and the glowing sigils offered extra support and comfort in this swift ride. We'd cleared several blocks, perhaps a whole mile, as I gained my bearings. What was Ian doing? How'd he find me? Soon, we slowed, descending toward a rooftop with a beautiful waterside view of Elliot Bay which meant we might've still been downtown.

Sunlight trickled through the thin clouds casting a rainbow shimmer on the water's surface. The merfolk, who remained glamoured to humans, created a dazzling array of glittering colors from their fins and aquatic magics. I could stare at this all day. All night too, given the way their magics created firework vibrance under the moon's light, the sun tended to obscure. Unlike mages or witches or most Mythics, in fact, they displayed their magics daily for entertainment and beauty and joy. How wonderful to live beneath the sea.

"What are you doing here?" I slid off the broom, just as anxious and confused as the last time I'd shared a ride with Ian.

"You know"—Ian brushed his finger through my hair—"you look pretty good with brown eyes and hair. But I prefer the curls to this shaggy style."

I clutched the grimoire from Vanguard Corvine. My ring clinked against the lock, sealing the spell book. Of course, Al's glamoured ring. I twirled it with my thumb pressed against my ring finger. It changed my appearance but must've had a secondary tracking feature.

"Did Al send you?"

Why would he send Ian to grab me? Was this some plan to separate me from Bez? To what end? Did Al not trust me to handle this? Was he worried for my safety? I'd never seen him and Ian interact. Their sentinel squads certainly didn't work the same districts or caseloads. Everything must be all hands on deck with the attack on the Magus Estate, though, and the roaming devil with his misfit mage, namely me. I gulped.

"I'm glad we got away from that devil," Ian said in a way that conveyed his relief.

"We haven't." I pressed a hand to my chest. It was the lightest pull, like a string wrapped around my ribs guiding me toward Bez. He must've felt something similar. "You need to go."

"It's enough distance for what comes next." Ian smiled.

"Are you planning something?" Had Alistair found a way to

contain the devil? Good. Bez couldn't be trusted, clearly. I wanted him to have a chance, but he'd only use freedom to slaughter anyone and everyone on whatever Diabolic whims motivated him.

"I want you to know I tried so hard to ensure the blame didn't fall on you."

"What?" My head swirled into a hundred paranoid what-ifs on Ian's meaning of blame, but as per usual, I had to be overthinking this.

"It had to be you, though. We needed access to the repository, to the vault. But I tried to give you every opportunity to get out early. Even offered you an alibi." Ian brushed a hand along my cheek, kind and comforting, like he really cared about me. He didn't, though. Ian shrugged. "Pretty sure the chancellors would've still blamed you, given the chancellor in charge wanted to find a way to pin everything on an Alden mage."

Chancellor Driscoll. Al was right.

Ian playfully patted my shoulder as I pieced together this revelation. No. Not playfully—the gesture itself, the expression on his face, the words pouring out of his mouth all had a patronizing tone.

"Lay all the blame at your feet to feed some bullshit mage political agenda when clamoring for power." Ian chuckled, tracing sigils in the air with his fingertips, and I shrank into myself, finding such expert-leveled skill intimidating, impossible to match. The air buzzed with his saturated mana and hummed to the tune of his incantation. "When I first sought you out, I didn't care much for the spoiled incompetent guy who couldn't control any of the Pentacles of Power."

"Sought me out?"

"But the more I got to know you, the more I liked what you represented."

"What I represented?" I squeezed the grimoire, furious he'd

played me, used me, framed me, but mostly hurt because that gnawing insecurity whispering in the back of my head was absolutely right—someone like Ian would never find someone as worthless as me interesting.

"Still, I'm not interested in the Collective's agenda for controlling the magic of this world or the Mythic Council demanding the importance behind secrecy. I want free magic for everyone. You understood that, which was why I liked you. You wanted to share the wealth of knowledge hidden in the archives with the world. Not like Remington, a decrepit relic himself, attempting to right his own wrongs. I don't think he chose to give back because he cared. I think he knew, felt, the tides turning against him, and hoped to shore up some allegiances." Ian laughed, running a hand through his black hair, ruffling it. "A lot of good it did the old fool."

"You attacked the Magus Estate. You killed Magus Remington and everyone else. How'd you—"

"I embedded the virus to hack the system into your key card. That's why I didn't want you there. At the very least, they might've suspected someone else set you up. Could've bought you time until the next phase. We could've been so happy."

"Why?"

"I went my entire life without magic, only blessed for a privileged invitation because of a chance encounter and the skill I hold." Ian continued looping sigils together. "Imagine how much magic could offer the world if we stopped hiding it away. Why is it fair the masses only gain insight into this beautiful world through chance, luck, and extreme talent?"

The sigils glowed brighter. Based on the formation and symbols used, this was some type of summoning incantation. It'd instantly transport anything the spellcaster desired. Was he planning on teleporting me far away from Bez? Too far for the tether to follow? How far would that be?

"The Collective and the Mythic Council have tried co-existence. It only leads to worse things," I said calmly, fighting so hard to remain composed.

"Does it, though?" Ian cocked his head. "Or is that some Collective-Mythic propaganda to keep infinite resources contained to a very tiny population. Personally, I think they just like the power. Can't blame them. I enjoy the power, too. Just not the politics."

"You're a misfit mage," I said with a creak.

"You're the only misfit mage here. Killing our magus. Plotting with radical Mythics. Unleashing a Diabolic." He shook his head, clicking his tongue with a mocking tsk.

"Whoever you're working with, other Mythics and mages, you can't seriously think Driscoll or any chancellors would allow this. You're being played."

"Oh, I understand that. But my part in this has opened so many doors and given me two of the best things from the vault. The first being Agatha's Heart to further enhance my magic, which will ensure I avoid my co-conspirator's plans for tying up loose ends like me. Like you, Wally, I always plan ten moves ahead. Unlike you, I don't doubt myself in the process because I know I'm better. Destined. Filled with purpose."

Agatha's Heart. That explained his behavior. It held a dangerous side effect of souring the mind to achieve the heart's desire. But he wouldn't have felt that effect when first attacking the estate. He did that of his own volition. The artifact simply made it possible for Ian to hold his own against Bez here and back during their battle at the estate. No. He'd always had superior skills. Had he been chosen and influenced from the very start? To what extent? Provoke a war? A change in policy?

"Now that I'm inside, I'm going to tear the whole thing down. Starting with you."

"I thought you didn't want to frame me."

"I didn't." A tiny white portal opened, and Ian stuck his hand inside, retrieving a dagger covered in mysterious symbols. I faintly recognized them. "If you'd left like I'd asked, you'd be fine. But no. You stayed, bound yourself to that Diabolic. A devil, no less. I tried to save you in the repository. I killed that ghoul before she'd recovered. I wanted to kill that Diabolic while still possessing poor, pathetic Riley, but they say devils don't die. I watched that essence worm inside you, changing you, protecting you, so I did what I'd learned from you. I researched and found this lovely blade inside the vault."

Ian walked toward me.

"The Demon's Demise." I slipped the glamoured ring off my finger. I needed time to think, to plan.

"Ridiculous name." He waved the dagger. "But powerful enough to help rid the world of that thing leeching itself to you."

"It won't work on a devil." I turned to run with no idea where I'd go, how I'd get off this rooftop, but I needed to get away from Ian until Bez found me. The tether snagged; he was approaching. I had to buy time.

"Not gonna use it on the devil." Ian appeared in front of me amidst shimmering sigils, blade in his hand moving closer. "God, I love magic. Instant transportation. Not as fast or filled with as much range as the Fae, but still enough to catch you."

I coughed, splattering blood onto Ian's somber face. Blood. Where'd blood come from?

My knees quaked, and Ian gripped my arm, steadying me. Everything started to ache, starting with a sharp sensation in my chest that spread through my body with each heavy breath. Looking down, I saw the blade buried deep into my chest. I wanted to scream. Cry. Run. I couldn't do any of that, though, only breathe, which became more and more exhausting with each wispy inhale. Every breath became a chore. I wheezed, struggling to pull in the faintest bit of air. Everything hurt, and standing became too much.

I wobbled backward, but Ian held me in a kind embrace, delicately lowering me to the ground.

My insides wriggled, and crimson weaved out of my chest, lunging for Ian's arm.

The Diabolic essence. It chased him momentarily, ignoring the blade embedded in my chest. Once he'd stepped away, it dove back into my chest, and I ground my teeth, feeling the muscles literally ripping and stitching and closing around the blade.

"They say the Demon's Demise is saturated in ancient magic. Some artifact which Diabolic energy can't repel or register." Ian approached, retrieving the dagger. I sighed, embracing the relief from the pain with the blade pulled out for but a second as warm, sticky liquid weighed heavy on my chest, pinning me to the ground and leaving me gasping for air my lungs couldn't hold. "Seems to have worked. I'm sorry, Wally. If there were another way, I'd have taken it. In order to keep my place, achieve what I need, Chancellor… No. You should die with some peace."

Ian brushed my bangs out of my eyes as they slipped under my glasses. It did little to help my hazy vision.

Bez roared, his voice an echoing shutter that reverberated through every cell of my body. Everything grew fuzzy. The flap of his wings drew my gaze, but he was a blob among the bright daylight.

"I'm glad you're here, Beelzebub," Ian said, faintly or not. I struggled to determine where his voice came from as everything felt like a far cry in a deep well. "To be the first mage, first recorded person to end a devil. You've given me infamy, and I'll use it wisely."

"Shut the fuck up." Bez raged. His very being cast a shadow on the bright world.

Ian shouted.

I wondered if Bez killed him. He'd come so close last time, yet I stopped him. Now, here I was, regretting it with my dying breaths.

Bez knelt over me. His face blocked out the sun, expression dark and sour. Pained, maybe. Exhausted, perhaps. The link affected him, too. "Oh, Worthless Walter."

I shuddered as the world grew dark. Desperately, I tried to speak. Beg. Anything.

"S-s-save…" I stopped, recalling the last time I'd willed a command unintentionally. If I didn't, though, I'd die. We could both die. Would Bez let that happen?

"What the hell am I going to do with you?" Bez pushed an arm under my back, lifting me closer to him, panting.

16

Beelzebub

Each breath ached. Every single movement of my body. I nearly buckled and collapsed atop Walter. I'd hurled the mage holding the faint scent of death off the roof with a powerful blast of telekinesis. The same death I caught beneath his cologne outside the estate. The same death which wafted inside of Magus Remington's study. This pathetic nobody killed my rival. My enemy. My betrayer. Now, he'd nearly gone and killed me, too.

"I'm not done with you, devil." This malcontent mage hovered in the air through the force of elemental magic while drawing his discarded broom to his side.

"Fucking mages," I grumbled.

He chanted incantations while his eyes grew black like a witch channeling too much power.

How I wanted to rip out his entrails and stuff them down his mouthy throat, but I lacked the strength for a battle. Not with Walter this severely injured. Not with my own body ready to crumble any second. Sigils glowed around the mage, conjuring complex spells even the most talented practitioners struggled to muster independently. Only one choice.

I grabbed Walter and blinked. Our bodies vanished into black mist, traveling across the thin webs of Diabolic essence Mora had laced throughout the city of Seattle ages ago, the same ones she used to find me at Mercury's Marketplace before disappearing back through them. Perhaps she believed I'd forgotten how the signature of her pathways worked. Maybe she still trusted me enough not to change them. Point was, zipping through the ether of her essence was the only way to get far away and fast—flying at a speed nothing could match, each step through the shadows like walking on clouds. Diabolics couldn't teleport. Not really, but inhabiting a terrain long enough allowed us to layer it with our essence. Mine had faded and fallen away after nearly fifty years of confinement. Thank the gods Mora stuck around.

The city was a blur of lights and noise and reeked of magic and mortality. I needed someplace safe. Somewhere to fix Walter. Fix myself.

"*Beelzebub,*" Mora called out, feeling my presence.

Her voice vibrated along every web I traveled, and I searched endlessly for her. She'd have a solution. Black tendrils weaved inside this vacant reality, snatching at my misty form.

I hit the hardwood floor of a living room with a thud, Walter's broken, shuddering body resting on top of my chest. Searing pain coursed through this host body; every ounce of my essence shredded the internal organs, repairing them, and breaking them apart again in search of this phantom injury. An injury housed inside Walter's unconscious body.

"What happened?" Mora stood half-dressed in an oversized sweater, her pale legs exposed.

"He's dying. I'm dying." I sat up, cradling Walter and checking for his faint, irregular breaths. They'd become so shallow, his pulse nearly nonexistent. He'd die in a moment and drag me with him to his grave.

"We don't know that," Mora said, poorly hiding her frantic fear. "Diabolic bonds are as unique as fingerprints. Trust me, I've had some close mortal calls."

"I can't chance it," I snapped. "Get your witch to heal him."

"Kell's not here and not a witch who specializes in healing." Mora kneeled beside me. "Sort of what makes us work so well. I do the healing and immortality, along with a few dozen other tricks."

"Mora, I can't die like this." My voice cracked, hollow and lacking my natural bass. It was happening. My hold on this host was fading away because I was fading away. "This mage has my essence."

"I know. I thought it was cute. You said you'd never settle down and—"

"Dammit, Mora."

"Sorry." She pulled a comforter off her couch and pressed it to Walter's chest. Like it'd do any good considering his blood already soaked into my clothes and pooled on the floor.

"What do I do?"

"You could give more of your essence. That'd fix him up."

"Shit." I groaned. "Beats dying, but I'm not sure I can bear another second with him."

"If that's true, I have another possibility." Mora planted her hand on my shoulder, squeezing to draw my attention as I stared vacantly at Walter's anguished face. "Take your essence back."

"I can't."

"You can. Right now, what little remains is fighting to keep this mortal alive." Mora leaned in, blocking Walter's face and filling my vision. "All you have to do is dig your hand in there and rip it out. It won't resist. Too preoccupied with your dying mage."

"You're sure?" I asked.

"Positive. I've rescinded my essence from a few mortals in my long life." Mora half-smiled the way she'd done a thousand times when she hid the twinkle in her eyes and the agenda on her lips. "If you want him dead and your freedom intact, I suggest you act quickly."

Mora stood and sauntered out of the living room.

My eyes watered. I growled, then rolled them up to the ceiling until the blurry mess disappeared. Tears caused by the pain created in my shared burden of Walter's pain. I lifted his body. His eyes fluttered, long lashes sticking to each other between sweat and tears. My essence deep inside him did everything it could, triggering every muscle until his body convulsed. He really had such a small amount of my essence. Another few days, and it would've burned out.

"I never wanted to meet you, Walter." I cracked a knuckle against my thumb. "Not really. Yes, I endured your presence at the repository, but I never wanted to meet you." I cracked a second knuckle. "When fate smiled on me for what felt like the first time in centuries, I didn't want to meet you in the manor." I cracked a third knuckle. "I was so angry with Remington. Abe, the old prick. Mages in general, I suppose. I knew what'd happen if our paths crossed. The same thing that happened every time I encountered a mage, a mortal, a conflict I didn't like." I cracked a fourth knuckle, wiggling my pinky afterward as it'd gone numb with the rest of my body. "How you must be in such agony. Don't worry. It'll all end soon."

I dug my hand into his warm, bloody chest. He gasped and screamed as I invaded the wound in search of my essence. I shushed him, then covered his mouth with my other hand as I wormed my way deeper. There it was. The puncture in his heart. The last droplets of my essence circling the drain of a dying mortal. As I scooped them into my palm, my own heart began to stitch itself together. I might actually be released from this pathetic nothing of a mage. He could die untethered to me. Die from a betrayal which burned deep in his core. Die from the onslaught of charges his Collective threw at him. Die from trusting the wrong person. People. He'd trusted me. Such a foolish mistake.

I'd made foolish mistakes, too. Mistakes in a dimension of damned demons seeking salvation they'd never be gifted because our world didn't offer compassion. Mistakes I'd made when entering this realm, believing compassion came so freely here. Those errors nearly cost me everything too many misfortunate times, until one day the mistake actually cost me my freedom. But none of them cost my life. Not like Worthless Walter lying near dead in my grasp. He'd lose his life for his naivete.

"It really could end this easily." I brushed a hand over the damp curls along his forehead. The phantom sensation I'd carried lingered, ruffling my shaggy bangs. Or perhaps it was a delusion of these days bound together.

I squeezed my hand embedded in his chest into a fist until my nails punctured my palm. Blood oozed into him, taking with it traces of essence. Walter had stopped fighting as he seemed to have thankfully gone unconscious again. Tiny crimson tendrils leapt to defend his exposed chest, stabbing at my forearm. Pinpricks which didn't faze my mostly numb and exhausted body, much like Walter's broken form.

He couldn't die. Shouldn't die. I needed the essence to grow stronger and faster, so I lifted my other hand, coating it in sheer black talons and slashed my arm. Blood gushed into Walter's chest. The Diabolic essence boomed inside him. Tendrils thicker than my biceps sprang out in defense and hurled me away. I slid across the living room floor into the kitchen, smiling.

He began healing quickly. Nothing could harm him with that much essence; then again, given the severe injuries he had and how close to death he'd been, most would fade. Each restorative breath Walter took consumed my essence, absorbing it and replacing the energy with life. His life. There'd still be essence remaining once he'd fully healed, which would be burdensome, but at least this time, I'd go with my original plan. Detain him until the essence faded naturally, then part ways. He didn't need to die for being foolish. Neither of us did.

"You picked life?" Mora asked, holding two plastic cups. "Odd."

"I didn't have a choice." I extended a bloody hand, which she ignored because she was the worst, so I helped myself up, brushing my tattered and blood-soaked blazer to look half presentable. Honestly, the wrinkles made me look so garish.

"You had a choice, sweetheart. I presented you with two options."

"No. I've never removed essence before. It's like those movies with the wires and bombs and the dying if the wrong blue one—because they're always blue—is cut. I couldn't risk blowing up," I explained. "It was purely pragmatic."

"Hmm. Sure, that sounds honest." Mora slid a plastic cup across her dining room table as an offering. Dining room. This was her dining, kitchen, and possibly greeting area. How quaint.

"You also had that wicked grin you get when keeping information," I said, grabbing the cup. "Couldn't chance you were deceiving me."

"Never, Bezzy. I was merely curious what'd you do when given the opportunity." Mora cast shadows on the wall with delicate movements of her fingers, stick figures meant to represent shapeless worthless mortals surrounding a Diabolic shadow. It came with wings, horns, and tails. Even the shadow itself held a crimson hue. Gods, she'd planned to bore me with some fable tale of my life. Mora truly was the worst being I'd endured. "The Beelzebub I know cuts ties and runs whenever forced to confront his feelings. Hacking down anyone he deems guilty of wronging him." The shitty shadow interpretation of me ripped apart the other shadows and flapped its wings, flying along the wall until it reached the dark recess above the refrigerator. "I knew you were infatuated with this mortal. I could smell the lust wafting off each of you."

"That's quite a gift you have," I scoffed. "But it's lacking. *His* lust, perhaps. Walter, like most mortals, is a fool for aesthetics, and I've always been quite pleasing to look at."

"I've got two millennia of perceiving body language and sniffing out pheromones; I'm hardly ever wrong. Still, quite shocking to see my favorite lonely devil choose someone over himself."

"Especially since the last time I put someone else's needs above my own, I ended up locked away, betrayed, abandoned, and left to rot for far too long."

"Precisely. You're quite enamored." She pursed her lips in the direction of the sleeping Walter, ignoring my scowl and enraged comment. "He must be quite entertaining. The awkward, wordy mortals are often filled with all sorts of surprises once you unwrap them."

I glared. Mora had met Walter all of five seconds before vanishing, which meant she'd kept a close watch, studying us. Irksome. "It's this damn emotional connection. He's infected me with his feelings because of the bond. It's made me make careless choices. This one was not, though. I kept him alive. Now we can lock him up in your hovel. Honestly, all these centuries, and you live in a tiny apartment?"

"Kell enjoys the atmosphere, and I've grown to enjoy living modestly."

I raised a brow. "How do you bear the noise?"

Cities were exhausting even when dimming our senses, but to live inside an apartment building with the scuffling sounds of a thousand mortals. Disgusting.

"Neighbors? Oh, I kill them." Mora sipped her drink. "I limit myself to one indiscretion a month for the sake of maintaining a low profile, but truthfully, if you're gonna blast music at two in the morning because you believe your ears deserve to drown in the acoustics of bad sounds, you deserve to die."

"Quite the opinion."

"I won't be kept awake because of someone else's poor life choices."

"So you take their life." I drank the fruity concoction she'd offered. It sizzled on my tongue with the faintest acidic trace. "Mmm. What is this?"

"Unicorn. Hard to get but worth every drop."

"Delicious. I could get used to this humble place for a time."

"You can't stay here, sweetheart. I adore your presence—despite your curt attitude—but you're on everyone's radar, and it's unlikely I'll be able to shake the attention away like I did before."

I glowered, taking a big gulp of the wonderful drink. It was like swallowing rainbows. Sweet and sour and sharp all at once. Gods, I'd love to devour some good unicorn meat.

"However, you're welcome to stay until your mortal lover recovers or until Kell returns to the city. Gives you a week."

"Two things." I held up my fingers because, between the toxins of the drink blurring my vision and the blood loss to heal Walter, I felt woozy. "First, he's not my lover. That's the Diabolic bond. Already explained that which, if you'd listened, you'd know. Two—second, after first... How is Kell out of the city? How are you functioning with your bond yanking at your host body?"

"Three things, my dearest, darling, dashing Bezzy. One, you've got to learn to hold your drinks." She finished her cup. "Two, the emotional connection conjured through a Diabolic bond doesn't exist. Loyalty is forced by commands. It compels the body. Not the heart or mind. Lie to yourself if you wish, but you're not fooling me."

I prepared to interrupt, but my jaw dropped, and I remained speechless. Mora had ranted about how every bond she'd gone into had made her and her mortals closer, implying the bond itself held some emotional tether. That was what this had to be. I was ready to kill Worthless Walter. It was the bond that prevented that. It was the bond that made me agree to his asinine plan. It was the bond that made me save his life. My heart raced. That was all this was. A Diabolic connection out of my control. Either of our control.

"Third, and this one's important." Mora stood, smiling. "The leash that holds you two is dictated by the Diabolic. You're only forced to remain at his side because you wish it. I've got enough slack and comfort to let Kell cross an ocean before I feel the reel of our tether."

"That makes sense," I interjected, ignoring her second comment, which I lacked a response to. "Subconsciously, I know Walter is utterly incompetent and would die the instant I lost track of him. Hence him literally almost dying, so clearly, that's why the leash is so tight."

"Or, like a good puppy, you want to stay close by." She patted my head like a dog until I bared my teeth. "Angry puppy. Come along. I'll make you something else to drink with less of a kick. I've got pixie kidneys. Blend them with a bit of orca blubber, and you've got a divine, tame cocktail."

"I'll take another glass of the unicorn, thank you."

I very much needed to wash the thoughts out of my head. Mora's illuminating revelry made it seem like I had actual feelings for Walter. Feelings that kept us close. Feelings that motivated my decisions. Feelings that… NO. None of that made sense. I hated him. Hated all mages. Granted, he was better than most. Considerate in the most insufferable ways. Thoughtful in the most overthinking manner. Polite in the weakest way possible, where everyone walked all over him.

Everything about him was worthless and vexing. A living, breathing reminder of the man I wanted to be centuries ago when I deluded myself into believing I could be a man in this world. Before mages reminded me that all I'd ever be was a Diabolic stain on the fabric of this dimension. I'd contemplated mortal friendship, lust, love—all the foolish things those finite beings deceive themselves into. Every time it'd been a failed experiment. The last time ended with imprisonment. I'd never allow such trickery again.

17

Walter

Everything hurt. Something kneaded my insides. Not something. Bez. His Diabolic essence. It saved me after Ian… After he'd stabbed me. Why? Some ploy involving Chancellor Driscoll to incite a war between the Collective and displeased Mythics, along with misfit mages like Ian who wanted to what…? Liberate magic to the masses.

I sank deep into the cushiony mattress I found myself in, unable to pull myself up. Unable to open my eyes. The moment I opened them, all of this would be real. Permanent. I'd walked right into a trap and couldn't accept the open world around me until I comprehended at least a fraction of it. My eyes bounced back and forth beneath my closed lids, avoiding the sunlight which pierced into this room. I bit my lower lip and pulled the comforter covering me over my head. I wanted to sleep forever. Or until I had a solution—which might as well be forever.

Ian wanted free magic, which in theory always sounded lovely, yet mass introduction to magic, mages, and Mythics was something that'd been experimented with a hundred times over. Dating back thousands of years, the Collective and Mythic Councils had entertained the concept. It led to all sorts of unproductive societal reactions.

There were too many examples of attempting to co-exist that proved fallible by those with magic abusing it and those without craving it. Simpler to keep the worlds apart. Something Ian would understand if he'd been raised in mage society, grown up with the teachings from the Collective, as opposed to stumbling onto his fate later in life. Maybe that was his misguided reasoning. No. He made his choice. He knew so much more than I realized possible.

He conspired. Murdered. Framed. Defamed. And who knew what else he had planned with Chancellor Driscoll. Two opposing forces, which made no sense unless the two kept their agendas very secretive. Not that Driscoll could. The chancellor had hated Mythics his entire life, part of what prevented him from rising to the role of magus. Which meant Ian was playing Driscoll, helping him light the fuse to a war that would lead to exposure.

Still, to what end? And although Ian might've grabbed a few relics and even gathered a small army of loyalists, it wouldn't be enough. What made the Collective a force unlike any other was that all mage territories united when things like this occurred. If the chancellors couldn't quell Ian's rebellion, then soon, the mages across the world would send their most elite to lay waste.

A solution that would cost the city of Seattle. Maybe even the state. Anytime magic razed destruction upon the land, mortals paid the price, and mother nature became the scapegoat. I empathized, considering how I'd found myself in the role of the wrongfully blamed.

I huffed, needing to understand, find a solution through the few variables I knew about.

"Are you going to lay there pretending to sleep all day?" Bez asked. A crisp page flipped.

My chest warmed, and my heart hastened. He was in my room. Not my room. Whatever room he'd brought me to. There was so much I needed to resolve and understand about the events which led me here, and thinking about him was definitely last on my list. Especially considering… I pulled the blanket tighter over my face like it'd somehow erase my presence or his awareness of me.

One of my favorite things was lying in bed, ignoring everything in the world while simultaneously planning for every outcome. What made it ideal was I was also forgotten by the world. But not with Bez nearby.

His mere presence made my skin vibrate and itch. I lifted the plain white shirt I'd been put in, ignoring the fact all my clothes had been changed while I was unconscious, and stared at my chest. Pale. Hairless. Soft. Not very defined. Most of all, there was no scar. Not even a tiny nick where the blade had carved its way inside me. I felt it. The blade. The pressure against… my heart? Bones? Everything? Now it was like it'd never happened. I pulled my shirt down, remaining hidden beneath the covers. That was Bez's doing. His essence. It saved me. Even after he…

"Wow. Really gonna pretend like I'm not even here," Bez said, loudly licking his finger and flipping another page of some book. "Rude. Truly. Precisely. This is why I can't stand you. Not even for a second."

Excuse me? I tossed the covers off and sprang forward. "Then why'd you save me?"

"Oh, looky. Prince Uncharming has awoken. Thought I was pulling a total Worthless Walter and talking aloud to myself." Bez held his book high, poorly hiding his wide grin.

"You didn't answer me." I gritted my teeth. Bez had this annoying aversion to answering questions. I'd actually found it more difficult to get a direct answer from him now that he'd been released from the orb than three years of silent conversation.

"I didn't." Bez returned to his book. "You're just lucky so much of my essence remained inside you. Otherwise, you surely would've died. Should've, in fact, considering how pathetic and naïve and tragic and—"

"Shut up!" I growled, fury in my veins. His body was a fuzzy outline, so I searched for my glasses. There on the nightstand, tucked beneath a cloth, yet the lenses weren't smudged.

I put them on, fully taking Bez in. He widened his eyes, the pink faded slightly, but the dark red was as sharp as ever.

Bez. The Diabolic who'd saved my life more times in the few days I'd known him than any other person in my life combined. Bez. The devil who gambled on my wellbeing for… I didn't know. Bez. The one who pulled me out of death's grip and slashed his arm to pour his essence into me when he thought I'd died or passed out or both. Why lie about it now?

"Chill." Bez closed his smutty romance book, tossing it on the bed. My ears burned. I'd read that one to him once before. Well, not him. Okay, him before I realized he could hear every word I said. If I'd known, I would've read the actual scenes in the book instead of reliving the steamy scenes alone and aloud in the repository.

"How long have I been out?" I asked, averting my eyes from the cover.

"Seven weeks, three days, and fourteen minutes." He looked at his bare wrist, pretending to count. "And thirty-two, thirty-three, thirty-four seconds."

"What?" I leapt out of the bed, legs shaky on the hardwood floors. How'd I slept that long? Coma? Mystical? What'd happened to everyone? "Is Ian still out there? Does anyone know about him working with Chancellor Driscoll? Have the chancellors subdued the culprits? Have they contacted The Global Collective? Shit. What's happening?"

"Relax. I was lying. It's what I do." Bez cackled. "It's been two days, which is kind of dramatic considering my essence healed you in minutes. Basically, you're milking the bedtime, but whatever."

"What's your problem?" I stomped toward him.

With him sitting, I towered over him for once, but he just stared up, smirking like the smug bastard he was.

"Nothing." Bez stood, reaffirming his height. Had he gotten taller? Had I shrunk? I arched my back and squared my shoulders, breathing harder and invading his space because his gloating grin infuriated me to the point where my chest almost touched his. "I do find it funny the first thing you ask about is that mage who tried to kill you. Ian, was it?"

"I'm trying to prevent him from…" What was I trying to stop him from? Aside from framing me, which fell more to the Collective's willingness to accept, did I care? I did. He'd used me. Set me up for Driscoll. I was just an easy Alden mark. The pathetic washout they could use to hurt the people in my family that mattered.

"I just think it's funny, is all. You thought this attractive, powerful mage was interested in you." Bez spoke with such venom in his words, they practically stung as they poured out of his mouth. "He's the date night boy, right? The one you were swooning over. The one you stopped me from killing. Oh, the minute your command struck me, I felt your pathetic pining."

"Stop it." I trembled.

"You actually believed he liked you? Worthless Walter, the most tragic apprentice, all too neurotic, landing a catch like him? Obvious scheme."

"I said stop." I shoved Bez back into the wall. Rage consumed me, and mana funneled through my veins. I wanted to eviscerate him. Destroy him. Not because of what he'd said but because he was right. I was worthless. "I'm sorry. I shouldn't have pushed you."

I backstepped and plopped onto the end of the mattress.

"No, you're fine." Bez leaned forward, exposing his chin and sharp jawline. "Strike me. Take out all that rage, Walter. I won't even dodge. It's not like someone of your caliber could harm me anyway."

"No." I shook my head.

"Go for it. It's cathartic. Though, the walls might be softer on your knuckles."

"Why are you doing this?"

"Because you're boring and tragic, and at least provoking you could offer a brief second of entertainment."

"That's not it." I bit my lip because all I wanted was to call him out for saving me. He'd had the chance to get rid of me. Kill me. Let me die from my own mistakes. He didn't, though. And he didn't want credit. He wanted to vilify himself. "You saved my life. I saw it. I felt it. Felt you hollow out the last fragments of your essence, death right there, and you gave me the power to keep breathing."

"I had an epiphany. You'd make a better hostage than corpse. That's all."

"Liar."

He was infuriating, always intentionally provoking me. I wished he'd shut up and let me think. Figure out why he was… That was it. I could play his games, too.

Not games. Bez enjoyed picking and jabbing at me and knew how to do it because he knew me. He studied me. For three years, he'd observed me. Listened to my droning about anything and everything. He claimed to hate it. To hate me. Yet he knew the most minute things about me. He'd memorized them, down to my favorite breakfast I might've mentioned offhandedly once or twice. Not enough for me to recall the discussion. And I remembered too many times I'd lectured Bez on the histories of things I'd studied. Or embarrassing desires or dreams. He knew me and attacked because, perhaps for a Diabolic, the idea of feeling something frightened him. No. He had Mora. She had love. Right?

"Your fear of feeling is very mortal, Bez," I said, settling all the quivering muscles in my body.

"What?" He chuckled, the hollow laughter of someone deflecting. "I fear nothing. And I am certainly nothing like you mortals."

My body tensed and shook like electricity and endorphins and excitement all erupted at once inside me. I wanted to be bold. Honest. Passionate.

"Fuck it." I grabbed the collar of his shirt and pulled him into a kiss. His body collided with mine as we fell back onto the bed.

His eyes were wide in shock, but his lips never left mine. Every muscle of his was firm and stronger than metal, yet the skin I touched was smooth and delicate. His lips were soft and full. Also, forceful and biting. Our teeth and tongues touched and nibbled and licked. None of it should've worked. It did, though. I panted between long winding kisses as he lay on top of me. Bez's hands found their way under my shirt, gently caressing me. I lost track of his arousing touch because I was lost in his intoxicating taste. His mouth was sweet and bitter, and something on his tongue burned ever so slightly in the most delicious way.

"Stop. What are you doing?" Bez pulled away, lifting himself off me and rolling over.

The warmth of his touch faded, and I craved it. Craved him.

"What's it matter? It's all games to you, right?" I rolled on top of him, straddling his waist. I planted a hand on his chest, forcefully keeping him pinned to the bed. I muttered, stopping myself from saying what I thought. I couldn't hold him down. He willingly lay beneath me because he desired this as much as I did. Maybe. Probably. Yes. I hoped.

Every part of me yearned to explore these sensations. These urges. This hate which had blossomed instantaneously into passion. Not love. Not sure it was like either. Dammit.

Bez turned his head, given time to react or think between all my internal contemplation. That was my problem. Bez saw it, knew it, felt it. I wanted to plan for everything, which made me hesitate to live for anything. It was a weakness. Sure, he mocked it, but I could see in the way he studied me. He liked it. Liked me.

I leaned in close, pressing my forehead against his. The heat of his body only further excited me. It was his reluctance that gave me pause. Everything gave me pause. My body tensed, nervous, doubtful, always hesitant.

"I don't play these games." Bez sat upright, hand holding the small of my back. His eyes looked so soft and somber this close.

"I'm not messing with you. Maybe I am. Maybe I'm fucked. Well, that's a certainty. My life is up in flames right now, and you've helped me bear through it." I kissed his neck. Not as forcefully as I wanted. Merely a sign of affection. I hoped he saw it that way. "You were a prick the entire time." I kissed a bit lower. "A real jerk. Even tried to murder me." I unbuttoned his shirt and kissed his chest. As my lips met his pecs, he lay back on the bed. Bez guided my head with a gentle hand as he descended back onto the mattress. "You didn't murder me, though." I continued unbuttoning his dress shirt, lightly kissing his torso and working my way down his stomach. "You've gone out of your way to help me. Save me. Do things the way I wanted because you knew it made me feel safe in this unsafe world."

"No. I just…" Bez paused, eyes on me as I slid off the bed with my body between his thighs. "It was the emotional bond linking us."

"Not a thing, according to Mora." I unfastened his belt.

"You heard that, too? Impossible. You were out cold."

"Your essence coursed through me," I said through gritted teeth pulling his belt off. Bez had revealed himself to me, whether through trust or insecurity or a million other factors I'd gladly explore. It didn't matter. I wanted this moment to be honest and real. "I could feel your words. Your actions. Your everything. It echoed inside me."

That was true. It took me time to clear my head and push everything out to make sense of his stirring thoughts.

"Then you should stop and wait for the essence to pass. You are a kind mortal. An insufferable and annoying mortal, but still." Bez lifted my chin with a hand. "I'm a wicked Diabolic who wants nothing but destruction. Trust me. It might sound fun for a night, but you'll regret this."

I bit his hand lightly, then pulled his pants down past his knees.

"Walter, you're making a bold move."

"Didn't think I made those, did you?" I licked his hip where the cut of his abs was, then kissed the muscles of his abdomen, savoring the sweet taste of his skin and the firmness of his body; each continued kiss led lower as I followed the trail of hair leading to his cock. "Guess you don't know me as well as you thought."

Before he could say one more thing, I wrapped my lips around his tip. Bez stiffened. My jaw tightened as I swallowed deeper. He ran his fingers through my curls, playfully caressing them. Every time I went a bit further, he clutched my hair but didn't push down. I pulled back momentarily, rotating my tongue around his tip until he quivered. Bez's hips thrust forward, then stopped.

A polite devil.

I didn't want to be coddled.

Wrapping my hands around his, I guided a more forceful approach as I swallowed the entirety of his cock. My eyes watered, and my throat ached. Bez groaned, squeezing my hair and thrusting quickly. I had an involuntary shudder, then unfastened the tight string to the loose pants I wore. My body burned with excitement, and Bez's warm Diabolic touch sent a surge through every cell of my body.

He released my head, and I pulled back instinctively. I didn't want to, but I couldn't breathe. Panting, I wiped some of the spit off my jaw. Bez stood above me, fully erect. His wings had sprouted. Huge dark gray wings with more feathers than I could count and such a wide span they blocked all the light out in the room. His hands were sleek and black, covered in Diabolic energy, yet their touch had been so soothing. Could he alter the feeling from pain to pleasure merely by will or desire?

I wanted to know it all. Know everything about him.

"Get over here," Bez instructed.

His tail came out of nowhere, wrapping around my neck and lifting me. I rose with guidance, embracing him. Bez ran his hands over my shirt, ripping it open instead of taking it off. I vibrated. His lips kissed my chest, licking my left nipple, while his hands slid down the sides of my torso. They reached my hips and pulled my pants to my ankles. In an instant, Bez was on his knees, hands cupped around my butt and mouth enveloping all of me. I moaned, biting my knuckle.

He moved with his blurred speed. One second, I'd feel his tongue on the most sensitive places; the next, he'd nibble the back of my neck; after that, he'd return to his knees but be lost the second I blinked. I groaned only to find his tongue invading my mouth and hand gripping my cock. I couldn't keep up with all the sensations.

"Wait, I'm going to…" My breathing hitched. "Stop."

"Don't worry if you finish first." Bez licked my neck and bit down. It hurt in the best way. I dug my nails into his back, sliding down until I reached the joints of his wings. "I've got a long night planned for you, Wally."

My cheeks burned when he called me that.

Bez tossed me onto the bed. I watched him crawl at the edge toward me. One of his tails opened the nightstand drawer and fished out a bottle of lube. As he got closer, I rolled onto my stomach, following the instruction of his hands as he positioned me.

18

Beelzebub

Walter remained obedient as I moved his legs to a wider stance, guiding his hips to a proper level. Running my claws down his back, he abided my instruction to arch further. I spit into my palm, adding to my already slick dick. Walter didn't move. His shoulders tensed, bracing for what came next, but his muscles remained calm as I pushed my way inside him. The tight warmth made me growl. I leaned forward, pressing my weight down on him slowly, allowing him to adjust to the feeling as I slid deeper inside him. He was completely submissive in his desire—no surprise. The euphoric sound of his moans made me thrust faster, deeper.

When he whimpered, I paused, hesitant. A hand on his waist, another pressed deep into the mattress above his shoulder. Walter might've craved a dominant partner, but he didn't simply lie there awaiting my next move. He wrapped his hands around my arm next to him, kissing my fingers and licking my claws. All the while, he pushed back on me, demanding satisfaction.

"Aren't you a feisty one?" I pulled my arm away from his grasp and smacked his ass.

He wanted me. He saw through my façade. He saw through what even I couldn't make sense of. What I still needed to understand. All the same, I found myself obeying the desires of his body, relishing every sound which escaped his lips, and pounding away harder and harder. This unfathomable desire to serve, to please him. I obeyed this stirring sensation, taking powerful strokes and burying myself all the way inside Walter. When he buried his head in the bed, I jerked him by the hair, pulling him closer. His back arched, muscles stretched. I wanted to hear every unfiltered sound. I wanted his primal guidance for my next move.

Walter turned, his lips searching for relief. His glasses had gone crooked between burying his head and getting pounded. Still, he ignored them, reaching out for me. I kissed his nape, taking my time, and adjusted his glasses. With each kiss, I thrust, watching him moan and then purse his lips for a kiss. I nibbled on his neck, just below his jaw. I wanted him to beg for it. Beg for the satisfaction of my kiss.

"Bez," he whined, and I craved everything.

I yanked his hair back, a pleasure we both enjoyed. As he moaned, I kissed him, swallowing his sound. He wrapped his tongue around mine. The way he gripped my hip, pulling me closer, it encouraged me to heighten my pace, thrusting harder. Just as he felt he'd buckle, I'd ease, draw him close. My sweaty chest pressed to his back. Our sticky flesh held us together. His lungs swelled with my arms wrapped around his chest, panting with pleasure.

It'd been so long, and I came close, but I wanted to savor this sensation, this fleeting moment. When it was over, he might regret lying with a devil. Walter would want his life back. He, above all the mages I'd known, deserved to have his happy, normal little magic life. I'd help him achieve it, even if it meant we parted.

I pulled out of him and flipped him onto his back. In the meantime, I'd indulge and enjoy every second he offered. I drove myself into Walter, wings flapping so fiercely it conjured a gust in the room.

He stared at me, and I cherished every expression as I fucked him.

After a quarter of an hour, he quivered, body jerking, unable to contain himself as he climaxed. His satisfied exhale rang through me, pure ecstasy, sending a surge that sparked my appetites. I continued, eliciting a panting, pained pleasure from Walter as I pounded him. My muscles tightened, cock throbbing, and I came. It didn't stop me, I remained buried deep inside him, enveloped by the warmth. Every nerve ending tingled, alert and delighted. I kissed his neck, licking his sweet sweat and relished the rhythmic sensation of my hips slapping against his skin.

Our climax led to little rest, and we continued exploring each other's bodies throughout the day and well into the night. As the moon's light shone through the window, we took a break.

"That was something." Walter took heavy breaths, desperate for air but more desperate for me. I was his oxygen. Even if only for this moment, it was a nice feeling.

"We could go again," I teased, nestling into his chest as he wrapped an arm around my back.

"I wish. No. I definitely do not. Not sure my ass could handle another round given we went, um, well, I sort of lost track between the two of us." He pulled me in tightly, hugging me against his sticky body.

How I'd like to walk away from all of this, simply enjoying these moments. Walter looked into my devilish eyes without hesitation. I ran my claws along his soft chest, and he pulled them into his hand and then kissed them. I'd retracted my wings because snuggling in a mortal position and bed really wasn't suited for my wings. Still, he'd enjoyed the sight of them. Between his lust for me and his curious eyes searching for answers, I found myself hard again, pressing on his thigh.

Walter giggled. "I can't believe we…you know. It's like… Wow."

"So, what comes next?" I asked, rubbing my erection against him.

"Sleep, maybe? I'm kind of exhausted."

"You slept for two days."

"But this is after being impaled."

I kissed his shoulder, snickering. "I'd hardly say I impaled you."

"Not what I was referring to. Although, you kind of did." Walter's muscles were like jelly. His physical fatigue was likely the only thing that curbed my salacious appetite to continue.

"What comes next in this pursuit of clearing your name?"

"I don't know." Walter pushed himself back, sitting up with his back against the splintered bed frame.

I didn't recall breaking it. Guess that explained the cracking sound somewhere between the second and third rounds.

"We should find that treacherous mage and murder him."

"No. But I do need to tell Al, maybe my mother, too." Walter sighed, releasing so much toxic dread once the term 'mother' left his lips. "I doubt she'd believe me. If I had that grimoire, maybe it'd hold some evidence of Chancellor Driscoll's involvement, of his connection with Ian. It'd explain why he arrived when he did."

Walter's lips twisted as his face scrunched into quizzical thought. My little overthinking mage had a point. Ian surely had other opportunities to kill Walter; however, he didn't attack until we'd obtained the book.

I hopped off the bed, strutting across the bedroom in the nude. Peeking with my peripheral, I hoped to see his ears burn, but alas, Walter had seen, touched, and licked nearly every inch of my body. Doubtful he'd blush at the sight of my naked ass now. Suppose I'd have to find new ways to embarrass him. I picked the grimoire up from the corner of the bedroom and trotted back to the bed.

"You grabbed it!" Walter's eyes widened, a full smile on his face. "That's impressive."

"I didn't do anything." Which was true. It merely ended swept into our travels when I fled from Ian, the grimy mage I'd kill one way or another.

Walter examined the lock mechanism, then searched the nightstand for something. He slipped on his pair of lime green briefs, covering himself, before stepping off the bed and further investigating the room.

"What are you searching for?"

"Pencil, pen maybe, paper, parchment preferably." Walter rifled through drawers stuffed with trinkets and spare clothing Mora had acquired. "Could you help?"

"I've got plenty out here," Mora said loudly from the other side of the door, knocking like it made a difference as she whipped the door wide open.

I put my hands on my hips, holding no shame, while she blatantly studied my mortal physique. It didn't appear too aesthetically different from the last time she'd seen it fully exposed, but each host body did have a few slight variable changes depending on how it merged with my composite. Walter slapped his hands over his bare chest and small stomach. Not where Mora's eyes landed anyway.

"Didn't want to interrupt," she teased. "But it sounded like you'd finished."

"Just give us a moment to get dressed." Walter's face burned bright red as he hid himself behind the bed, scrambling to pull pants on while lying on the floor. He grabbed his tattered shirt and frowned. I supposed I could've simply taken it off him.

I grabbed another from the drawer of spares Mora had in this guest room and found a personal favorite for Walter to wear.

"Are there any others?" he asked.

"None your size." I batted my lashes.

"This is definitely not my size." He wriggled into the bright pink shirt.

The tight cut framed his slender, muscular body well. The deep V-cut and short sleeves exposed his pale skin, while the short cut at the bottom revealed the fuzz of hair on his belly leading to his crotch.

"Come and join me." Mora extended a hand to Walter. "I've made tea. We can discuss Bezzy while he dresses."

"It's not like either of you hasn't already seen everything." I grinned. "I'm fine as is."

"Manners, Bezzy."

"Stop calling me that."

"Put your cock away, and I'll consider it."

I rolled my eyes and dressed. Stepping into the kitchen, Mora pulled a cup of tea from Walter as it neared his lips.

"No, no, dear. Mortal tea is on the kettle," she explained, handing me the hot glass. "I'll fetch it. It's one of Kell's favorites. Pistachio Lime Yerba Mate."

Walter scrunched his nose at the offering. I, on the other hand, thought it sounded delectable. More than the whiff of diluted troll wafting from the steam in mine and Mora's cups.

"What's in the other tea?" he asked, eyeing her cup opposite him like he half expected a severed finger to float up.

"Baby organs." I smirked as Walter shuddered.

"Ignore him," Mora said, handing Walter his tea. "Babies are far too gummy to make into a good tea."

Walter spit his drink, eyes bouncing between us, likely gauging if Mora jested or rather made light of murderous Diabolic tendencies.

"I'm kidding. Everyone knows mortals taste better once they're ripe." Mora twirled her fingers, telekinetically bringing a collection of pens and pencils with various papers and parchment for Walter.

"So, dear. What do you intend to jot down?"

"Oh, um…" He gulped, so flustered and struggling to shrug off Mora's sick humor. Not all humor—we did feed upon whatever seemed most palatable in the moment. "Well, since the grimoire has a lock, I thought I'd start with a divination decryption incantation. They're both fairly low-level, and I've used them lots with my work in the archives."

"Why don't you perform a release incantation?" I asked.

"That's too high-level for me." He lowered his head shamefully, something he'd done far too many times working in the repository when scolded by his *betters*. This technique perfected his humility by averting his gaze and letting his long curls drape over the tops of his rims. He'd performed a collection of sophisticated incantations to retrieve this grimoire, yet still believed it'd been my Diabolic essence that had assisted in the feat. We'd have to sit and discuss this matter. Diabolic essence didn't enhance a mage or Mythic's power. In fact, too much of it, and it'd devour the individual's mana to thrive in the higher capacity of a host body. Hence why the mana in this body had nearly been depleted.

"We can discuss your self-worth issues another time," I said, stepping toward the table. "For now, let's put a pin in the introspection and open this damn book."

"W-what are you doing?"

"Speeding up the process." Coating my hand in Diabolic essence, unveiling my true sleek black talons, I pierced the lock and opened the grimoire.

"Quick, which for you, Bezzy, isn't surprising."

"Eat me," I said. "If you knew Walter, you'd know he'll spend hours examining every intricate detail about the locking mechanism, going on superfluous tangents from the color variation, metals used based on the Mythic era, incantations tied to each gear within, and a thousand other tiny details nobody finds interesting."

"Hey," Walter whined. "I find it interesting."

"Which is tragic but forgivable." I flipped the leather binding open to the grimoire and slid it toward him.

His studies were among the most thorough I'd encountered during my containment in the repository. Of everyone, he had such a learned nature, joyfully sharing everything he'd gained, like offering the gift of knowledge to all those around him. Never the type to squander or horde such things. That was his downfall. It led him to this path, a path that pushed us together in a misfortunate culmination of events. So many exploited Walter during his years in the repository, something undoubtedly this Ian mage took full advantage of too. If Walter planned on clearing his name and regaining his life, we'd have to fix that fatal flaw before parting.

I'd tasted the pleasure that came with embracing Walter and feeling again. It wasn't something meant for me, a devil despised by this entire realm, yet I'd indulge those feelings for a time before releasing him. He was too kind for such things. Too kindhearted for me.

"Whoa." He flipped through the grimoire, jotting notes while simultaneously adjusting his glasses.

I huffed. He had his full-blown entranced nerd mode going on. "Mora, care for a stroll? He's got his research cap on."

"Oooh." She sipped her tea. "I love research."

"It's less glamorous than you think," I said. "Plus, given that fidgety 'I have to write and read and think and plan face' he has, it'll be several hours. We should go. Unless you wish to linger and listen to a thousand half-uttered mutterings."

"This is an Atlantean sigil which shouldn't be recorded in any grimoire since merfolk magic is sacred, never disclosed to outsiders. Not to mention, they use a very different method of recording their… Hey!" Walter glared. "I don't talk in half-uttered mutterings."

I raised a brow, making a judgy face.

"Much." He returned to scrawling illegible notes in the half-concocted shorthand scribbles he called words, which only he ever understood. In the repository, he'd have to translate and rewrite them to make it presentable for the archivist practitioners who'd take full credit for his findings. A benefit to finding himself on the outside; he wouldn't need to take such extra measures.

"So many of these come from different Mythic spell works. Some of these aren't even incantations, rather framework designs on how their anatomies interact with the physical world when they delve from one pocket realm to the next."

"Huh?" Mora tilted her head. "Could you elaborate?"

"Don't," I attempted to interject as Walter lifted his head, eyes filled with delight. Fuck me. Well, not literally. Walter knew how to pin me down with rambling words until he rode me into submission.

I plopped in a chair, accepting my fate, and did my best to listen attentively. Such hard work.

"Okay, to explain… Most Mythics live in our realm full time." Walter beamed. He did look so pretty when he smiled sincerely, as opposed to the nervous, slightly cute grin he made when forced. "However, even those who dwell here have pocket realities conjured by the Fae. It's all dealt through the Fae alliances, their hierarchy meant to establish their superiority to all other beings, which, obviously, not the discussion now—but…"

He rambled on, and I mouthed his brief mentions of his dissertation before winding his way back to the topic at hand. Somehow, I'd memorized his tangents.

"These were put in place eons ago. Dramatic—not eons, but a long time ago. I think even before the Diabolics came into being. Or before they came here."

Mora smirked at me, and I rolled my eyes. Wrong on both counts, but a discussion for another day. If we opened that box, he'd spend the whole time investigating answers instead of finishing his explanation.

"The purpose, of course, being to provide outs for Mythics not wishing to inhabit or entertain the human realm. That said, these realms aren't meant for permanent housing. Well, maybe they are. It's not discussed among the Collective. At least not to apprentices." Walter took a deep inhale and a slow exhale. "Anyway, Corvine's grimoire holds spells belonging primarily to Mythics. It's like he has a book of skeleton keys."

"So, he definitely acted on Driscoll's command and is working within this coup. Or was, before I righteously killed him." I nodded. Corvine's mind made much more sense now. The cruel depictions he savored deep in his subconscious. They weren't merely fantasies but recollections of acts of stealing and torturing Mythics to acquire their knowledge. Fucking mages.

"I'm not sure any of this proves Al's suspicions."

"Alistair Alden?" Mora asked.

"You know my brother?"

"No." Mora coughed; cheeks flushed a bit. "Merely heard the name in passing."

"Dirty girl," I said in Gaelic, one of the few languages I knew Walter had no ear for since most of his linguistics came from Mythic tongues and a few mortal ones. "What would Kell think of you banging an Alden?"

"You thought you were the first?" Mora retorted in the same tongue. "Besides, Kell invited him up. I must say, I didn't piece it all together, but those Alden boys have quite the assets."

"I know you're both talking about me. I heard Alden, but I'm going to ignore you."

"Pourquoi si sensible?" Mora asked.

"He speaks French," I replied.

"Mon ami. Tu as choisis un sacré Alden," Mora said. "Je suis curieux de goûter."

"Anyway, Diabolic mean girls' shenanigans aside, I think I have a plan," Walter said, biting back an exasperated exhale. "It's gonna take time to enact."

"Time?" I cocked my head, curiouser and curiouser over the Alden mage attached to me.

19

Walter

I grabbed the steaks Bez tossed into the basket and placed them back on the grocery shelf with all the other meat products. He whined, as he had down nearly every aisle because I'd said no to most of what he wanted to buy, which was practically everything in the store. We only needed a few essentials. Mostly, I planned on using the cashback option at the checkout to pay for our motel since Mora made it abundantly clear we'd overstayed our welcome after my recovery. Not that I blamed her, given how everyone pursued us. As the alleged misfit mage behind the attack, I was on the Collective's radar.

I stared at the dye in my basket, wishing I'd kept Al's glamouring ring, but I couldn't trust it wouldn't be tracked again. If that was how Ian actually found me. Had to be. Maybe. There was a chance he'd simply kept close tabs on Vanguard Corvine, too. Or Ian had mastered divination incantations and could locate me at any time. I tugged at the strap of the backpack Mora had given me. There was a chance Ian was tracking the grimoire inside it, ensuring he recovered it before it exposed him. Al believed it held secrets, but I had doubts. I swallowed, burying the concern of him lurking around every corner, ready to kill me, kill Bez, frame us, and destroy the Collective.

Bez picked up the steaks again.

"No," I said firmly. "I'm already getting you two bags of candy. Besides, you don't even need to eat."

"It's not about needing. You don't need that attitude, yet you choose it." Bez pointed. "She doesn't need that flamboyant dress, yet here she is. He doesn't need all those tattoos, yet he's inked himself in them again and again. Those children don't need to screech down the aisles, yet imitating banshees clearly offers them delight. It's never about needs, Walter. It's about wants. Desires. Cravings. Satisfaction. And what I want is my steaks."

"Fine." I offered my basket for him to place them. "Then I'm putting your candy back unless your wants come with helping pay at checkout."

"You can't put the candy back." Bez pouted. "What am I supposed to season the steaks with?"

"Gross." I bit back the urge to gag, imagining all the Twizzlers, Starbursts, and Jolly Ranchers mashed or melted on top of his steaks.

"Your mortal palette is weak. Everyone knows sweetmeats are the best."

"You realize we won't have a grill or stove or oven of any type. Not even sure the motel I picked comes with a mini fridge." I'd specifically looked for the cheapest, cash offer, no ID checks, pay by the day or hour place. And based on the terrible reviews, it'd offer the most anonymity—something we desperately needed, especially with Bez strutting around the store, tilting his sunglasses, and exposing his Diabolic eyes.

"It's better without all the cooking, anyway." Bez further rolled up the sleeves of the suit Mora had offered him. The pants didn't cut off at his calves like the last pair.

"You're going to eat it raw?" I gagged, unable to hold it back this time.

"Not all of us like to cook out the flavor." Bez opened his mouth wide, sticking out his tongue and jabbing it with his finger, mocking my disgust with his own.

"Well done is a perfectly valid way to cook and eat a steak."

"Your tastebuds are criminal."

"Whatever. You've got your steak and candy. Wants fulfilled. That's all you're getting because you don't need to eat." And I did, so I had to make certain I had enough money to buy food for myself too. The Collective might not have frozen my accounts, but after years of poor pay, I wasn't exactly swimming in cash. Especially since my mother had taken back my trust fund when I changed regiment pathways from the sentinels to the archivists. "Why are you obsessed with food? How does it even work? I was under the impression Diabolics didn't require anything to survive."

I walked close to Bez, ignoring my doubts, regrets, and anxiety and replacing it with curiosity for how Bez worked both physically, magically, and maybe one day mentally—that'd be a much harder thing to gain a grasp on. His personality was scary and annoying but also intriguing and considerate. Bez masked himself in such contradictory layers.

"Unlike mortals, I don't require nutrient sustenance. But food makes me happy, so I sometimes alter my anatomy when in host bodies to accommodate for more of it."

"That's pretty mortal, eating more than you need and making room for even more."

"There are so many flavors, and I want them all."

"All at once, apparently."

"Yum." Bez snapped his teeth like biting the air itself. The act highlighted the sharpness of his jawline and made one of the veins along his neck bulge momentarily, turning black before settling into a normal human appearance.

"But do you actually need anything to survive?" I asked, grabbing a few things from the produce aisle. "Or is it more of a 'you think, therefore you are' kind of situation?"

"My essence feeds on the Mythic residue in the atmosphere and energy exerted and lost in the ether by the living. It's not something I require, as my essence will also restore itself in time, but this helps speed up the process as well as offering a few additional skill sets that aren't inherent to my kind."

"Like how you accessed the Pentacles of Power by glamouring your hair," I said, fascinated by the whole process. "Theoretically, you could access any unique magics or abilities by any mage or Mythic if you devoured their essence or energy?"

"Yes and no. The energy is more muscular. It's something everything in this world gives off through basic function, which I transform into my own physical form or the physical form I'm inhabiting. The Mythic residue can only translate into my own natural abilities or those of the host body I possess."

"Let's put a pin in that because I have lots of questions," I said, reaching the register.

After checking out, I convinced Bez to walk the half mile to the motel. He preferred flying, but it was close enough to walk, and we needed to maintain a low profile. Plus, I had to focus on a plan. What came next. Something increasingly more difficult when soaring through the sky wrapped around Bez.

The grimoire weighed heavy on my back, along with the overfilled plastic bags of groceries Bez refused to help carry. I had to find a way to fully decipher and connect this grimoire to Ian. If there was a connection. There were so many signs and seals and symbols within this book that dealt with protocol magic. Spells and keys designed to unlock security measures. Things that shouldn't exist. Things only the best of the best in the infiltration regiment would know about—yet Corvine worked inside the vanguard regiment. These skeleton keys definitely helped him rise in the ranks, making vanguard cases easier for him to pursue without the limitations of seeking aid from other regiments. Still, none of that tied to Ian, who was part of the sentinel regiment. Unless he assisted in acquiring them. Doubtful, since this grimoire was years old and filled to the brim with secrets. I needed to talk to Al about this.

First, I had to develop preventive measures. Then I had to find a way to prove Ian's involvement. Also, I needed to locate him. Not in his sentinel post but among the Mythics and misfit mages he worked with when attacking the Magus Estate. He claimed to have big plans, and I believed if we found a lead, the sentinel regiment could use it to catch him in the act. It'd make a huge difference. It'd be easier finding something on Ian if Bez hadn't tossed half the essential memories in his host body out. Nothing he searched held viable leads. Or so he said. It wasn't that I doubted him. Well, I did. I bit my lip. But I also trusted him. More than anyone in my life right now.

I also found it difficult to plan for anything because Bez filled my every thought. His body. His touch. Our sex. We hadn't exactly mentioned it since. Part of me wanted to attribute that to Mora's presence, my recovery, and the outlandish idea that under that gruff attitude, Bez was partially a gentleman about it. I practically snorted. Not a chance. Still, he hadn't brought it up, and I was too timid to mention that we'd screwed.

Did he enjoy it? Was it bad? Was it a one-time thing? Or I supposed, multiple times, one sensation thing? My chest warmed. I hoped not. After every second spent pleasing Bez, tasting his body, allowing him to explore and control mine, it created this calm, collective satisfaction. Clarity I hadn't had in… Well, ever.

It was just difficult to know what this meant for us. Bez was a

Diabolic who happened to relish in eliminating anyone who crossed him. Not sure he'd change. He was pretty murderous. Something I definitely couldn't do. My breathing hitched with each step toward the motel, tightening my throat similarly to the way I'd choked after being stabbed in the chest. Ian did that. Acted without a moment of hesitation. With Bez at my side, it'd be so easy to track him down and return the favor. Bleed him dry, the way I nearly bled to death on that rooftop. Then on Mora's floor. It was only thanks to Bez I survived. And his essence ensured I wouldn't have a scar. The same essence currently circulating through my veins at that very moment. I wanted to blame the Diabolic bond for the vengeful thoughts bubbling when Ian came to mind, but that was me. Maybe…

"You're awfully quiet, Walter." Bez spun around, walking backward with his hands tucked behind his head. The muscles of his biceps flexed, stretching the tight fabric of his suit jacket.

"I've got a lot on my mind." Sweat pooled in the wrinkles of my brow, sliding down the nose pads of my glasses. I wanted to wipe it away, adjust my glasses, or both. Instead, I trudged ahead, carrying the bags of groceries.

"You always have something buzzing about that beehive you call a mind. No, no. There's a reason you're being quiet." Bez pouted his lips, crinkling his chin in the process.

I lifted the grocery bags, frowning. Bez rolled his eyes.

"Hmm. I suppose I can offer my assistance." Bez grabbed the bags of groceries, and I flexed my fingers until the red along my knuckles lessened.

We continued until we reached the motel. I had Bez wait outside while I checked us in at the lobby. The woman working behind the counter had made it clear on the phone that the cost for two guests went well above my budget, but I had to ensure we had a safe, discreet place to rest for at least a week. Maybe longer. There was so much I still wanted to line up. What I had planned… a lot of it fell to chance. Luck. Fortuitous alignment. Stuff that never really happened to me. The only thing which ever really lined up in my life was misfortune and failure.

"Key." The woman slid a cardkey across the chipped countertop.

I stuffed it in my pocket and led Bez down to the end of the motel close to the overgrown wooded area beneath an interstate bridge.

The room had a dark green shag carpet and matching comforter. It smelled stale and rotten. The hiss of the AC unit did little to wash away the humidity inside and probably added to the foul scent. At least I hoped it came from the ripe fluids inside the rusted AC unit and not something else. Bez set the groceries on top of the single large table in the room where a box television with rabbit ear antenna sat. I didn't know those still existed. The box TV. It was so bulky and inconveniently located since it was positioned in front of the full-size bed, but the table was lower to the floor, more like a coffee table. There were no chairs in the room, only the mattress for sitting, so if I wanted to watch television, I'd have to crane my neck to see it. The single dresser would've made a better spot for the TV. It was higher and perfectly sized for the box television.

"Though, I suppose most people don't come here to watch TV," I muttered.

"Huh?" Bez raised his eyebrows, scanning the room.

"Nothing. Just thinking aloud."

"This is by far the worst accommodations I've been forced to endure. And I lived in a Hell realm, a tiny orb, and a London prison during the plague."

"You did?"

"I suppose it makes sense," Bez continued, ignoring my curiosity about the prison story. "We need a low profile. Scary. Manhunt. Or mage hunt? Devil hunt? Point is, they're hunting us, and no one would think of checking these shabby accommodations."

"Well, actually, I'm sure they would. I'm hoping they won't."

Bez plopped on the squeaky mattress. I ground my teeth at the piercing screech of rusted coils.

"The single bed. Nice angle. They'd most certainly search rooms with two guests. Clever little Alden." Bez lay back on the bed, untying his tie. "But did you provide us with this one small bed to keep a low profile or so you could cozy up to me late in the night?"

"I got one bed because it was cheaper, and I don't have a savings, and all my auto payments are going to cause my overdraft to go over, which means even if I manage to get my life back, I'll be in debt and homeless. Definitely unemployed. Doubt they'd rehire the guy who bound himself to the one artifact holding a devil inside."

"Good. You're better than that job, scrounging around answering everyone else's questions and filing their work and surrendering your credit for what? Their egos? I say let the archivists suffer without your presence. They can use those pennies they paid you to buy drinks to drown their sorrows."

"No one's missing me from the archives." I chuckled, hiding the twinge of self-doubt because no one *would* miss me. It wasn't like I offered much to the repository or the archivist regiment other than serving as a glorified notetaker. "Once they have the Magus Estate up and running again, I'm sure they'll be fine without me there."

"Unlikely." Bez sat up, legs crisscrossed, hands on his knees. "You were the most talented person I'd seen in the repository. And I had nearly fifty years to observe the comings and goings of mages."

My face burned, and I smiled.

"You were also the most annoying person in the repository. Possibly the world. Which is also saying something since I've been here for centuries."

I grimaced. I searched the grocery bags to settle my rumbling stomach. The apples and fresh berries were certainly a healthy option, or the protein bars I'd bought. Instead, I snatched the bag of Cheetos Bez not-so-subtly tossed onto the conveyor belt when we checked out.

"Those are mine." He hopped off the bed, puffing his chest.

"Pretty sure I bought these." I opened the bag and ate a handful.

"Bah. Currency." He waved a hand. "Worst evil in this dimension."

I crunched on the Cheetos, savoring the powdery cheese sticking to my gums and the irritation it gave Bez until he opened his candy and began stacking it on top of his raw steaks.

"Okay. You win." I set the chips down and grabbed the grocery bag with some basic essentials.

Bez crumbled the remaining Cheetos on top of his candy-covered steak. "It's a garnish."

"It's disgusting." I went to the bathroom, realizing I'd bought toothpaste but not the toothbrush. Sighing, I squeezed toothpaste into my mouth, turned the sink on, splashed some water into my mouth, then furiously squished the cheesy puff crumbs away with my tongue and gargled.

Spitting, I didn't bother cleaning the bits of toothpaste or Cheeto crumbs that clung to the dark rings of the grimy sink. Okay. Bez had a point. This place was awful. The shower curtain had a brown shadow of filth, and I really didn't want to peer inside the tiny claw tub.

I pulled out the hair dye, preparing to change my blond curls to a pretty chestnut. It wasn't much of a change but hopefully would do the trick for some eyes. I'd also keep my glasses off in most cases. Wish I could've gotten some contacts. Actually, no, I didn't. I shivered at the idea of jabbing my eyeballs.

"What are you doing?" Bez waltzed into the bathroom, practically inviting himself without so much as a knock.

"Privacy much?"

"What?" he asked with a teasing tone. "I've literally been inside you in more than one way and explored every facet of your naked body. What privacy do you need?"

"I'm dyeing my hair."

"Why?"

"Because I love autumn colors."

"Your sarcasm is lacking but caught. Still, why not cast a glamour?"

"It's just…it's hard, and I don't want to screw it up or worry about maintaining it or—"

"Failing?" Bez batted his long lashes. His expression held a playfulness mixed with a sincerity which was vexing. "You need to stop worrying about that and focus on the task at hand."

Bez stepped behind me, squaring my shoulders.

"Easier said than done." I sighed.

"It's not. It's easier done than said. Saying something means explaining and expressing every aspect of how the concept of magic works. It's instinctual. An act of expression. Art." He brushed his shaggy bangs, turning them hot pink. "When you didn't have time to explain your incantations during the break-in for that damned grimoire, you reacted and solved the problem. When you fixated on every step, sigil, and concept, you floundered."

"That's just how I focus."

"Which is fine. But you have to indulge in the freedom magic provides." Bez flaunted his fingernails that had transformed into a polished black. He stuck out his tongue, materializing a piercing from nothingness.

"Hey. You said you were low on mana."

"Hay is for unicorns, who happen to have more Mythic residue coursing through each drop of their blood than an entire mage possesses."

"What about unicorns?" I quirked an eyebrow.

Bez responded by licking my neck. The piercing slid along my skin, making me quake. "It's important to remember glamours are about more than appearance. It's the scent. The texture. The taste. I allow myself to feel the clink of the ring against my teeth. The metallic bite in my spit. So long as you believe in a glamour, others will also believe it."

"That works on humans more than mages. I'd need an advanced glamour."

"Fine. I'm a high-ranked Diabolic housed in a mage host. Change your hair. Only your hair." Bez turned around, facing our tiny room. "Surprise me. See if I'm fooled by whichever color you choose."

I stared at my reflection, checking more to see if Bez peeked, which he didn't. Not sure if it'd matter since I'd fail whether he looked or not. Though, he might just lie to boost my confidence.

"Remember, the best glamours work because it's something you crave. You want the world to see it as the truth because it is true. Your truth." Bez hummed. "Show me your truth, Walter."

I ran my fingers through my curly blond hair, uncertain there was a true color I ever wanted for them. Truthfully, all I wanted was to remove them. My eyes lit up, and I tugged at my curls, smiling at my reflection while imbuing a glamour.

"Okay. I've done it. You can look." I bit my lip, worried it couldn't be this easy. I'd clearly missed a step. Deluded myself. Failed yet again.

"I like it." Bez ran his fingers through my short blond hair. "Have to say, I prefer yanking the curls, but can still make do and run my fingers through this prickly cut."

My smile widened. I hadn't colored my hair. Hadn't cut it either. Yet, Bez felt the short buzz cut on the back and sides of my hair while the top remained long and shaggy. A look I never mastered. In order to straighten my curls, they had to reach a certain length, and it was still too much work. Now, I believed the look, the feel, the everything, and it just was.

"We should celebrate." Bez pulled me away from the bathroom by the loops of my jeans. "You've gotten out of your head and made the top of it completely different. Tomorrow you can change whatever you wish."

"Not sure about that." I blushed.

"You can do anything you set your mind to." Bez unbuttoned my jeans and dropped to his knees. "Right now, I'd like to set your mind to something else."

Oh.

"Oh. Wow. Um." I stood there as Bez pulled my pants down and reached into his pocket, retrieving a tube of red lube. "Did you steal that?"

"It's flavored. Besides, you weren't going to buy it for me." He dapped a few drops on the tip of my dick.

"Cold. Also, stealing is wrong."

"Currency is wrong." Bez licked the flavored lube, taking his time and slowly running his tongue down my shaft before swirling his glamoured piercing around my tip, which felt so real my entire body stiffened. "There isn't one Hell realm that uses money in place of market. It's a bizarre system the mortals have created."

I quivered, running my fingers through Bez's hair as he played with the tip of my cock before deepthroating me, then alternating to create too many sensations for me to keep up with. "That's actually really fascinating because a lot of Mythics associated with the Mythic Council have only accumulated by embracing particular currency demands established by the Collective, and I actually hypothesized some of the Mythics who flat-out rejected aligning themselves with us or dwelling in the world did so because of this factor. Among about a hundred other things. I've also wondered how the Fae—"

Bez stopped. He stood, looking bored and displeased. "You're talking too much, Walter."

"Sorry. I just always have something to say because I have…" I took a deep inhale, wanting desperately for him to continue, but I couldn't find a way to stop talking.

"We'll simply have to find a way to distract your mind and mouth." Bez shoved me onto the squeaky mattress. In a swift motion, his body moved in blurs as he undressed before straddling my chest in a seemingly singular motion. I gasped at the pressure and movement, exhaling everything from my lungs. "Relax."

"I'm relaxed." I adjusted beneath him from his weight.

Bez poured lube on his cock. "It's meat that tastes like candy. You'll love it, promise."

20

Beelzebub

We lay in bed quietly while Wally fidgeted. Desperate to move yet containing himself. His skin practically vibrated against mine and not in a sexy, 'I want to be fucked again' kind of way. No. He was back on his typical bullshit—thinking a thousand things that proved impossible for him to properly contain. Considering how exhausted he was and the amount his muscles strained by the third round, I figured he'd relish the relaxation of simply lying in bed. Even my host body was tired, and my eyelids weighed heavily as I nodded off.

Walter twitched the way he often did in the repository, a way of containing his thoughts that made his body move uncontrollably, offering something to say. This silent behavior was meant not to disturb others, but his rustling startled me into a more awake state. His eyes stared at the water stains on the ceiling, searching for answers to things he wouldn't receive.

I squeezed him tightly, his skin pressed against mine, which should've elicited interest, but his mind craved more than his body. With my chest to his back, I stroked his hair before running my hand delicately down his spine and squeezing his cheek, hoping to elicit a fun distraction once more. Instead, his mind and body drifted. The mattress squeaked as he hopped off the bed and shuffled to the far side of the room. Another reminder that meant we were a temporary fixation.

"What are you doing?" I asked.

"Preparing." Walter unzipped the book bag and retrieved the massive grimoire. "This is important to unraveling what happened at the Magus Estate. I just know it."

He plopped back onto the bed, opening it and flipping through the aged parchment. His hand lingered on the first few pages, wanting to stay on them, studying them thoroughly yet again. If Walter had his way, he'd spend hours, perhaps even days analyzing each passage. I'd watched him decode counterfeit grimoires filled with defective sigils and corrupted incantations merely based on the type of ink used or pressure applied when writing down a spell. He'd determined a Mythic artifact belonging to witches was, in actuality, a repurposed relic from the corpse of a gorgon. A discovery Remington took credit for when returning it to the descendants of Medusa, something of no surprise considering that foul mortal built his career and life on stealing credit from the efforts of others.

Walter wouldn't have the time or resources to fully analyze everything he wanted. Hesitantly, he flipped through the pages doing a quick glance through the entirety of the grimoire.

"What do you hope to find?"

"I've found some fairly clear trails connecting this to the infiltration and archivist regiments. Even the binding of the leather holds high-tier artificer craftsmanship. Nothing here indicates a direct connection to the vanguard regiment, aside from the fact it belonged to a vanguard practitioner. The strangest part is the subtle sentinel coding. It's not standard, but I recognize it, which could imply Chancellor Driscoll used Corvine, his right hand, so to speak, as a way to subvert my mother's regiment." Walter bit his lower lip, unable to contain his continued mutterings. "That wouldn't be good for her. Also, far too improbable to escape her knowledge. Though this is a pretty meticulously detailed plot to sabotage the Collective. It's still unfathomable Chancellor Alden got taken by surprise. She knows everything about everyone, claiming the best thing to protect…"

I huffed, tuning out Walter's rambles as he mused his mother's position and how inconceivable it was she'd been outmaneuvered. It wasn't surprising. This woman had a hold over him, one I'd witnessed in a few short minutes during the tribunal. Her mere presence had a way of breaking his spirit, his confidence. The idea of her fallibility likely rattled his entire outlook, having built her up to be this unstoppable force of power. One that kept him small and breakable his entire life. I frowned. Disgusted by this Chancellor Alden and the way her actions toward her son reminded me of sour memories best left in the Hell realm I abandoned lifetimes ago.

"Holy shit." Walter's jaw dropped, but whatever shock struck him didn't leave him at a loss since he continued scribbling meticulously tiny notes. "This is impossible."

"What?"

"There's an access code to the Archivist Nexus Grimoire in this book. That means there's not only privileged, illegally obtained sigils and spells belonging to various Mythic communities, but there's a backdoor access code to the entire library of every Collective storage system from every archivist regiment across the world." He traced his fingertips along the symbols representing the access code. "They're inverted, too."

"Meaning?"

"Meaning it's likely a one-way doorway, which makes sense.

Corvine wouldn't want others knowing he is looking in on their files and documents and research."

"He was," I corrected with a sly smirk, more and more grateful I'd hurled that mage off the rooftop.

"You really hate mages, don't you?"

"Yup."

"Why?"

"Mages hated me first, so why not?"

"There's more to it." Walter scooted closer to me, fiddling with the grimoire but keeping his gaze locked on mine. "How'd you end up in that orb?"

"Killed a bunch of mages, stumbled into an unfortunate trap, and that pretty much sums it up."

"Why'd you kill them? You killed hundreds."

"It was them or me."

"But you can't die."

I stiffened, reminded how little Walter or anyone knew about Diabolics, my life, my history, and the guise of Beelzebub.

"I know the story. They teach it at every academy." Walter had a curious glimmer in his hazel eyes, the type which expressed that while he confidently understood something, he also believed pieces were missing. "Heck, I knew the story back in high school. You killed Magus Walsh, half his chancellors, and an entire convoy attempting to bridge an alliance with the Fae." Walter's expression softened. The faint light of the moon piercing through the thin drapes reflected off his lens. "The history of that tale paints you as a murderous sadist bent on chaos and carnage. I've seen that side of you, but it felt hollow and forced, unlike other aspects you keep hidden. I'd like to understand the real reason. If there is a real one."

"The Magus wasn't sending a convoy to build an alliance. Their intention was to invade and subjugate the Fae for control of the Dimensional Rifts the Fae hold access to." I sighed, searching for as few words as possible to share a bit of truth because, for some abhorrent reason, I wanted to share the truth with Walter. *My truth.* "I enjoyed my time here. Mora knew so many fun Mythics, less judgmental at times, and then I met a young chancellor who believed the Mythics and mages could be more than tolerant of each other. He dreamed of uniting the Collective, the Mythic Council, and even introducing a Diabolic Embassy."

"You mean, Magus Remington…"

"Yes. Abe. Younger, naïve, but crafty as always. Calculating, too. A silk tongue that weaved a web of lies so easily I fell right into his deceit. I believed I could be something more, which proved incorrect, as it has in the many centuries I've spent in this realm."

Walter leaned closer, listening intently, sympathetically. It was written all over his face. I divulged it all. My friendship with Abe. Our plan to prevent a war. My hope of being seen as a hero as opposed to the eternal villain.

"My desire for acceptance by mortals was something he easily exploited. I think for a time, I even believed killing Magus Walsh was my idea. It took a decade inside that orb before it finally clicked how gullible and pathetic I was for putting trust in Remington."

"It wasn't foolish." Walter rested his head on my shoulder.

A soft, delicate sensation that made me crave him almost as much as the intoxication of his scent. The gentle, quiet empathy he cast lying next to me after closing the grimoire filled with curiosities he likely yearned to explore. Instead, we remained lost in a wordless embrace. I didn't want sweet or understanding words. Somehow, knowing so little of me, Walter understood that much, offering solace through silence.

Hours passed, yet Walter didn't move. The night ached in its long unyielding way. Finally, I flipped through the pages of the grimoire to pique some curiosity from Walter. He resisted, wishing to remain considerate.

"Explore away," I said.

"It's not like I want to read up on this, but there is definitely something I want to work on."

With that, his hands flipped through pages, marking them with a tiny grace of mana before moving to the next. Meticulous and confident, the former a common sight, the latter an unlikely one.

"Why are you saturating it?"

"Practicing, maybe." He shrugged. "Not sure it'll work, anyway. I'm not very good at saturation."

His doubt about his control over the Pentacles of Power often led to his downfall before he even got started. "Okay, but why saturate the grimoire?"

"Saturation can imbue an item with your mana and offer it powers, but it can also help the user retain intel from things they've saturated. Basically, I'll have this information stored in my mind by linking my mana to it; however, the caveat is that knowledge fades once the magic wanes. Once again proving there are no real shortcuts with magic. Just temporary band-aids—"

"Walter. I asked a question, not for a fucking lecture. This isn't the repository. I'm not going to allow you to go on long-winded tangents until my brain rots."

He huffed, practically snarling. The grumpier he got, the more it aroused me. Walter's true nature shimmered beneath that timid boy who feared repercussions, and apparently, there was quite a raging fury beneath, fanned by so much repression.

"I just want the grimoire to remain safe until I figure out the best advantage for using it. But much of what I have planned centers on you."

"Why me?"

"You're basically unstoppable," Walter said, beaming with pride before his natural insecurity overtook him and he cast his eyes downward. "I mean, so long as I'm not around. Which is why we could also wait out the Diabolic bond if you preferred."

"You trust me not to simply take off once it fades?"

"I do. And if you feel better not chancing me as a weakness, I'm okay waiting."

"What is this plan you've got bouncing around that big brain of yours?"

"Track Ian. Catch him in the act of something nefarious. Relay the intel to Al and the chancellors. That's where you come in. You can help force an audience with the chancellors once I hopefully gather evidence. Sort of making parts of this up as I go, which I hate doing."

I sulked, dwelling on my supposed invulnerability. The hubris I'd built around it offered many allowances over the centuries, steering threats away from me. It also led to my downfall and a half-century trapped.

"Sorry." Walter closed the grimoire, tossing it to the floor without a second care. "If you're uncomfortable with my plan, I understand. After all, the last time you followed a mage's plan, you—"

"You are not Remington. You are not like any mage I've met."

"There are better mages than me out there. Kinder ones. Stronger. Smarter."

"Doubtful." The dangers in this plan were worrisome. Trust in Walter clawed at my insides making my skin itch. "I think we should sleep. It's late and with everything you have planned, we'll need to be at our best."

I rolled over, facing away from him while dwelling on what came next. Every outcome seemed far worse than the next, and I had no idea how Walter handled plotting for every possibility. No wonder he defeated himself before any real accomplishments. The anxiety of failure was truly suffocating.

Walter dozed off in a matter of seconds, lightly snoring. I found it difficult to shut off the ocean of thoughts ready to drown me. Walter rolled over, his cool, bare chest pressed against my hot back. His hands hugged my waist, unconsciously tracing his fingers along the hairs of my stomach. I quivered as he nuzzled my neck and scooted closer until his crotch was pressed against my butt. The warmth of my skin called to him, and he wrapped himself tightly around me, spooning me.

Though I didn't require it, I synced my breathing with Walter's, allowing the rhythmic sensation to cradle me into a deep slumber.

A darkness swept over me, flickering flames in the distance. This wasn't a hollow sleep but a haunted one filled with recollections best left dead and buried. Talking with Walter unearthed memories I didn't deign to explore or reexamine. Yet here I stood inside my former Hell realm, forced to observe a past I'd abandoned.

I walked along the black nothingness, struggling to see through this void and view the countless lower demons kept below. Their rotted, festering bodies eternally bound underneath the surface of this dimension. Possibly one of the worst places to dwell in this Hell realm, burning and suffocating as their broken essence fueled the core of this dimension to add to the many lustrous wonders and harsh horrors created. Each step carried a reminder of a hierarchy I despised. Everything here carried a murky glint, making it challenging to wade through the countless shadows. Had centuries away from Hell obscured my memories of this horrid place? Or had my senses dulled from too much time in the mortal realm. Hell possessed infinite differences from the earth, the skies, the stars, the endless void of space. Here in my home world, Hell could be as grand as the Diabolic desired or as bland as a weak mind could conjure.

"Your reign ends here, Beelzebub." The screeching echo of her voice sent a shiver down my spine. Six layered tones, each more venomous than the next.

I examined my hands, paranoid the toxins in her voice had scorched my flesh as they'd done during a thousand court dinners.

Aamon brushed by me, leaving my body undisturbed by her

presence since I was merely a spectator in this memory. She stood tall, digging her eight-needlelike legs into the shadows which crunched beneath her swift spiderlike steps. Her elongated torso, similar to a centipede, coated in gems, cast light in the darkness, reminding me how luminescent Hell could be if one so desired. The gems of every color, from faint pinks to vibrant greens to dark blues and pale yellows, followed my sluggish movements.

I swallowed hard. How impossible it used to be to escape Marquis Aamon's gaze. A part of me wished to remain still, silent, scared as I'd done for far too long in Hell. Another part of me wished to savor the rebellion of ten thousand demon nobles who'd banded together in desperation to strike down the ruler. I smiled fondly, recalling my own fear of death and demise at the time.

This was not a nightmare about my weakness or vulnerability but a reminder of my strength and perseverance. I'd indulge this faded memory for as long as I slept, hopeful to watch the deaths of many treacherous demons, delighted at my own success and the glory of locking them all away for eternity.

Shadows faded, and flames burned white. Each flickering flare held more light than the sun of the world I now dwelled. It burned my vision. I squinted, attempting to make out the blur of demon monarchs who'd come to vanquish the tyrant who reigned as a god-king in this Hell realm. All devils ruled as gods to the peasant demons they'd manifested through sheer will and force and cosmic superiority, but…

"No longer will you terrorize this realm, Beelzebub!" Eligos shouted.

A Great Duke who I still carried fond memories of. One of the few Diabolics I knew who took the time to study the mortal realm, curious of their nature, unraveling their secrets, and predicting futures of wars, which the demons who'd gathered hoped would tip the scales in their favor.

He held a glowing golden lance made of bone and blood and metal of fallen foes. Pieces of their essence he'd snapped off to add to his collection. Flames shimmered against his silver armor. A knightly appearance he was fond of from the fables of mortals. His insides rattled in the suit of armor. Wings and too many limbs contorted within the simple mortal frame he favored. Eligos would've loved the world I'd fled to. Had he survived, I believed I would've enjoyed his company, exploring through his eyes.

"Foolish and feeble, all of you. You come to kill your god as if such weak waste could dare lay siege on me in my home. This entire realm is mine."

I nearly knelt at the sound of such a dreadful voice. One that cast nightmares with a single word. One that reached into a Diabolic's very essence and carved away everything until it took on an image suitable for his entertainment.

"I will destroy you all. Devour your essence. Crush your willpower. Spit you back onto the coals of my world and remold each of you into more obedient subjects."

"Not this day, Beelzebub. Not ever again. Your dishonor ends now and forever." Eligos led a charge, carrying a flock of hundreds of demons to storm the gates of the castle where I lived most of my pathetic eternity.

His final words weren't exactly wrong. I averted my eyes, not wishing to see his demise. The memory swiveled, tilting the entire landscape of the battle, refusing to offer this momentary peace and forcing me to watch the only kind demon I'd ever known meet his end. Mora was a friend through and through, but she was still Morax: a deadly, dangerous, and deceitful demon. Eligos held no cruelty or malice in his Diabolic essence. He rose in strength and rank through honor and kindness, something I didn't believe any demon could do.

In a single blast of black and white fire, Eligos and those foolish demons he led into battle burned to ashes. Barely a trace of their essence remained. Enough for a proper and empowered devil to restore, but this realm no longer had a devil, so I suppose this haunting memory carried a reminder to one of the few nobles in this Hell who ever had a nice word for me. Not that it did Eligos any good.

"This is why you abandoned your realm," Walter said, his voice carrying over the blood-curdling screams and vengeful roars of demons all lunging toward an opponent they could never fathom to match in battle.

"What are you doing here?" I quaked as I asked.

"I don't know. I was, I mean, I am dreaming. Right?" Walter took hesitant steps, frightened by the sight of slaughter. Demons dropped in single blows. Many rushed between us, raging to bring some semblance of peace to a Hell realm that had never known such things.

How'd Walter crawl into my mind? Was he a figment? A remnant of guilt derived from the vulnerability I held back during our conversation? Perhaps I should've told him the truth then, but his plan centered on a lie I'd spun for too long to remember this life that came before.

"Is this real, or am I just overworking my brain?" Walter asked, staring at his glowing fingers. "I've never had a lucid dream before, but those usually give the person control—from what I've read—and this seems very guided and scripted, yet I'm aware. At least, I think I'm aware. Maybe I'm not. Maybe I'm some dream figment cursed with my living selves overthinking, and once he wakes up, I'll forget ever being."

He shuddered at the thought or the many thoughts consuming him and his paranoid brain. I gripped his shoulder, steadying him. The sensation exhausted me, pulling me away from my past and into Walter.

"Motherfucker," I said under my breath. "That makes sense."

"What?"

"It's your saturation," I explained.

He'd practiced it to link to the grimoire, probably worried he'd fail at it. The thoughts likely ate away at him as he slept and with his body latched to mine, he was pouring his mana inside me while we spooned. This offered him an inside view of my past, something he still shouldn't be able to do.

"Did you permit me into your mind? I've heard of mages sharing memories and moments of fondness, but I n-never expected to do something like that."

"It's fine." It wasn't fine. I'd never invited someone into my mind. Not willingly, anyway. In the brief time I'd known Walter, I'd offered my essence to him, twice, craved his happiness above my own, shared my past, and now, I'd invited him into the worst parts of it. This was too much for me. Too much for him. Once he knew how pathetic and weak I was, he'd…he'd… I didn't even know how he'd react.

"This is why you left your realm, because of the betrayal. Betrayed just like you were in our world." Walter half-smiled, empathy shining amidst a battle of death and destruction. "I'm sorry."

"I wasn't betrayed here. I was a worthless no one in Beelzebub's Hell realm." My body stiffened as the words escaped my lips.

Walter remained silent, even stilling his curious eyes.

"I used his downfall to flee and closed the doors behind so none could follow."

"What?" The shock on Walter's face was breathtaking, like a literal weight lifted off my shoulders after centuries of lies atop lies, all to build a persona I never properly filled the shoes of.

"Since you're already here, perhaps I should share the true story of Beelzebub."

Beelzebub, my former god-king, captor, lord and savior, swelled in size, growing larger than I'd ever seen in the long eternity I had spent as his servant. Somewhere deep in the courtyard, my worthless, shackled body quivered in fear. Not fear Beelzebub would win or lose, but of the horrible punishments he'd dole out on a whim because my very presence annoyed him. My weakness. How I wished to savor his downfall again.

"Come, Wally." I looped my arm around his, walking through the demon specters of my mind, each fascinating my little mage beyond belief. "Let us watch the demise of the worst devil who ever reigned."

21

Walter

Bez wasn't Bez. Well, he was. But Bez wasn't Beelzebub. He guided me through hordes of demons barreling toward the true devil. So much to wrap my mind around. Why'd he lie about being a devil? How'd he lie about being a devil? The devil towered high in the sky, greater in scale than most skyscrapers. It left me frightened and awestruck and so curious to unravel the many secret facets of Diabolics, from the devils who reigned to the demons who served.

Golden elkhorns sat atop the devil's head like a crown. He had a sharp jaw lined with teeth protruding in every direction of his long, doglike snout. Four mighty muscled arms, casting magics and swatting away flying demons like gnats. Skin as black as shadows, lined with yellow glowing veins. He flapped his eight wings, each set different from the last. One pair angelic like Bez's. Another set more like something you'd see on a dragonfly. They created a gust, scattering fire and ashes.

"Hell, really does look like the whole fire and brimstone they paint it as, doesn't it?" I gulped, attempting to comprehend the various forms of hundreds of demons.

"Each Hell is what a devil desires it to be. This particular one was far worse than any mortal myths."

I squinted, wishing I had my glasses on as many appeared as blotchy smudges running toward the devil, Beelzebub.

"It's not your eyes lacking, Walter. This is a memory inside my head. Glasses not required." Bez snickered. "You merely lack the inherent skill to fully absorb the glory of this dimension in all its vivid details."

"Meaning?" I cringed as a demon darted through me like a phantom and jumped into the fray. It did little good. Beelzebub, the giant one, waved a hand and shattered dozens of demons into shards of black electrical glass.

"Like the Fae, our Diabolic realms are truly triumphant."

"Cocky."

"It's true. Our realities aren't restricted to trivial things like time, limited dimensional expression, five simple senses, or a multitude of other factors such as energy in constant flux, lost from one form and regained in a new. Honestly, I relish the simplicity of the mortal realm. Fewer concepts to maintain one's station, though those rules on existence are quite burdensome."

Demons skittered along Beelzebub's body, gnawing and clawing at his flesh. Teeth tore off chunks. Talons shredded meat until it transformed into gray vapors. A repulsive sight, but I couldn't look away. Demons swallowed the mist down their gullets, gulping as much as they could. Some exploded instantaneously. Others swelled in size, further tackling the giant devil.

"What's happening? Are they killing the devil?"

"Devils don't die." Bez half-smiled, not the arrogant smirk he had most days. There was a sad joy in his expression. "They constantly recover. The monarchs and nobility formed a legion of followers to each consume enough of the devil's essence to prevent Beelzebub's restoration."

"So they are killing him?"

"No. He'd live inside them. Like mages who perform a Diabolic bond, it's possible for us to take from each other. If one demon devoured too much of Beelzebub's form, he'd simply recover inside their body like a virus, consuming them entirely."

Bez pointed to the demons still exploding, unleashing smoke which whipped through the battlefield, tearing apart demons before returning to the devil's body.

"This is the power of a devil?" It left me awestruck. Such unfathomable power as he struck down thousands of demons. I'd believed Bez to be a devil, his strength an unmatched feat, yet he was merely a demon. The true strength of a devil could shatter our entire world in days.

"Devouring him in this manner allows the demons to divide Beelzebub's consciousness thousands of times over, making it too difficult for him to control or consume those who have sought to overthrow him."

"Couldn't they trap him? Lock him away in some artifact?" The same way Magus Remington had trapped Bez.

"Everything in this realm exists because the devil allows it," Bez explained. "If any of his remains are left unattended, even locked away, they'd simply reform elsewhere in the Hell realm, and he'd kill those who struck him down. No. The best plan was to share in consuming his being entirely, not that it did the hierarchy who'd struck together any good."

"They failed?"

"In a sense."

Bez stared silently at the bloody battle. The devil devoured and destroyed thousands of demons, but finally, his giant form shrank in size. He still towered above us, easily ten to twelve feet in height. Coating his hands in white Diabolic essence, it materialized differently than the talons Bez had summoned. The devil conjured a large double-sided blade in his left hand and a matching white shield in his right. Barreling through the horde, he ruthlessly cut down any opposition.

A group of shackled demons crept from the shadows of some castle. Palace, maybe. It appeared merely as a silhouette in Bez's memory.

One in particular caught my eye. A tall, slender gray-skinned demon crawled ahead of the others. His long, straggly hair covered his face, but his piercing red and pink eyes shimmered. They appeared so hollow and subdued, an expression I'd never expect from Bez. My heart pounded. That was Bez. The real Bez. He looked half-starved and fully broken. Nothing like the confident, muscular, and cocky devil I'd met. He had four horns, three broken off, but the one remaining curled tightly like a ram's horn. His gray wings were closed, scarred, and missing most of his full, lush feathers. His three tails twitched as he abandoned the other shackled demons and crawled over Diabolic corpses toward the warring devil.

"What are you doing?" I asked.

"Winning. It's something that never occurred to me until this moment."

Bez skirted along the field of carnage until he reached a small collection of black mist. The Diabolic essence stabbed at injured demons laying there half dead. They roared in agony. Bez reached out his shackled hands and grabbed the mist. It stabbed at his skin, but he didn't release it. He didn't flinch, either. My entire body wanted to sink deep into the shadows below me, realizing how unfazed Bez was by the pain, like he'd endured so much more, and this simple strike meant nothing.

The misty essence transformed in Bez's hands, becoming a shriveled, bloody heart.

"I wasn't too shocked to find my former devil god-king had such a tiny heart. A ruthless monster who'd made our realm far crueler than most Hells."

"I thought all Hells were like this. Fire, decay, agony."

"Equating Hell to cruelty and horror is a very mortal perspective. A limited one, as well. Hell realms are merely dimensions created by devils and homes to demons," he explained. "Some are quite pleasant, or so I hear. Most, like Mora's, were simply boring and unchanging. She wanted to escape eternity, so she chose to retire in the mortal plane."

"So demons can die in our world but not in your own realms?"

"Yes and no."

"Which part?"

"Demons can and do often die. However, the devil of a realm sets the tone. Rarely do they allow that which they've breathed life into find rest. A demon who dies in Hell is often regenerated by the whim of their devils."

"Why? Why not allow their demons to die? Is that why these ones turned on Beelzebub?"

"They turned on him because he's one of the cruelest devils." Bez stared off at the carnage of his memory. Most demons had died at this point, but more continued fighting and clawing and chipping away at the devil. "To answer your question, devils don't like their numbers to drop because they fear—hmm, fear is the wrong word. Not certain a devil feels in that way. But they wouldn't want another devil to see their realm dwindling numbers as it could be interpreted as weakness. They focus on eternity and eternally maintaining their place in a very bizarre hierarchy of devils. Each a god in their dimension."

A demon lunged at Beelzebub's broken shield, ripping his arm off. The devil hacked the demon in half, then spun his blade until a whirlwind warped the battlefield, and a sparkling blue doorway opened.

"A portal," I said, reminded of the many doorways in the Magus Estate, astonished the devil could fight a sea of demons and muster the magic to tear open the dimensional walls. "What's happening?"

"I was never certain. Perhaps Beelzebub planned on fleeing to the mortal realm to recover or kick a few of the demons out to turn the tide of battle." Bez shrugged, treating this as indifferently as he did so much, but this had to mean something more—this was his most guarded secret. "Didn't stick around long enough to ask. All I remember was seeing his weakness in the moment and making my move."

I waited to witness Bez's attack, unsure how his fragile chained body could compete against a devil who continued slaughtering demons that raced at him from all directions. He squeezed the heart tightly between his hands. Blood dripped down his shackled wrists. Pulling the heart close to his mouth, Bez bit into the heart. His sharklike teeth glistened as he chewed chunks off. Blood gushed, and he continued devouring bite after bite, gulping it down and swallowing. I squirmed as Bez lapped at the blood dripping down his fingers.

"You ate his heart." I scrunched my face. "The whole thing."

"Yes. Taking a potent but less powerful piece ensured I'd maximize my strength without fear of my former god-king overtaking me."

Blood trickled down Bez's gray chin. His body grew, muscles filling out as he resisted the chains which held him. Diabolic essence oozed from his pores, forming needle-like spears which stabbed at the cuffs bound around his wrists, ankles, wings, neck, and torso. The Bez of the memory bellowed furiously while the current one guised in human form cackled. There was a joyful confidence in each of their somber eyes. Stretching his damaged wings wide, the demon Bez soared through the bloody battlefield and crossed through the summoned portal.

Demons screeched and wailed. I covered my ears which did little to silence the overwhelming roar the devil unleashed. As the portal closed, everything fell into darkness. I took a shaky breath once things quieted.

"What happened next?"

"No clue." Bez held a longing gaze at the infinite darkness, then smiled, hiding any emotion other than joy. "I left this Hell and closed the door behind me. For all I know, Beelzebub overpowered them and retook his realm; maybe they're all ruling as a hierarchy, using his power to strengthen their hold on the dimension, or perhaps another devil learned of Beelzebub's precarious position and devoured the dimension along with all its inhabitants. Though, I doubt I'd be that fortuitous with the last possibility."

"So you fled and took Beelzebub's name?"

"He wasn't using it, and the piece of the devil inside me alters my Diabolic essence enough to fool most. Even other demons."

"Why didn't or doesn't he, um, the other Beelzebub, open the portal and take you back or get his heart back?"

"He can't. No one from that world can open its door. Only a complete devil can tear through the dimensional walls surrounding Hell's realms. I took his heart, so no matter if the demon monarchy rules in Beelzebub's stead or the god-king himself restored his power, he'd lack the ability to open a portal while missing a key piece of his essence which I have."

"But demons were ripping him apart, taking his essence the entire battle."

"Yet, they stood in his realm, his very being. A devil encompasses so much more than their form, they shape the reality of Hell, and that reality is an extension of their being. I left Hell. Left with a vital piece and took it outside Beelzebub's domain."

Tactically, that was masterful. Bez not only escaped with his freedom and enhanced his Diabolic power, but he trapped every enemy he had in that realm. Given the satisfaction he took when watching the demon hierarchy obliterated in combat, I gauged he considered them all enemies.

"Couldn't he ask another devil to open a portal?" I mused aloud.

"Unlikely." Bez walked across the shadows, hands in his pockets and a bit of pride in his expression. "Beelzebub, like most devils, doesn't ask or perform favors for his kind. If he managed to reclaim his position, he'd never let the other devils know he'd lost a piece because they'd see his vulnerability. And if the demon lords now rule after vanquishing their devil, they'd do their best to hide that fact from other devils for fear a new devil would claim or consume their world."

"And if another devil found out? Learned you had part of a devil?"

"I doubt they'd care. Most devils refuse to step into this plane of existence. A few, perhaps, over the millennium, to retrieve something trivial they found of interest. Some occasionally send a vanguard of demons to scout, but I've never encountered anything in this world capable of harming a devil."

"There's the orb."

"That contained a Diabolic, not a devil."

"It could." I shrugged.

"It really couldn't."

That explained why Diabolics so rarely ventured in our world. Devils didn't consider our reality of interest, and only they had access to reaching it. Considering how cruel and overwhelming a true devil was, I considered our world fortunate that our presence bored them more than annoyed them.

"Some demons get leave to explore. Sort of like mortal gap years. Only they tend to last a few centuries, so I avoid those demons."

"Because you worry?"

"Because I dislike demons more than I dislike mortals, which is quite a lot." Bez sauntered past me in the shadows of this faded memory. "And to answer your question before you can ask it, I lie about my identity because, as a devil, I invoke more fear. It used to earn me more quiet nights and fewer bouts of violence, yet mages continue to grow bold over the centuries."

"What happened next?" I asked, waiting for the shadows to transform into my world and show the next memory. It didn't happen. We simply stood in this silent void.

"I arrived in the mortal world and dealt with the same bullshit I left the Diabolic realm over." Bez got really quiet, staring off into the distance, lost in his thoughts.

I suppose we were both lost in his thoughts, with my sleeping body nestled against his, pouring mana into his body, saturating a link between our consciousnesses. I chose not to press him for information. Humbled or honored or both that he trusted so much of his history, his secrets with me.

"Not sure how long we're gonna linger in shadows, aware yet unaware. It's weird. Like am I sleeping still, or because I'm aware of my dream state, will I wake up exhausted?"

"I think you'll be fine. And I guess we're here in the shadows until your beeping alarm awakes us."

I fidgeted, looking for the right thing to say. "This changes things."

"How so?"

"My plan sort of relied on your invulnerability, but if you're not really a devil, then you could really die. My link was already a weakness I didn't want to chance. But now—"

"In the centuries I've been here, I've never concerned myself with death. Few have attempted, none have come close, and most assumed I couldn't die. A benefit to living with a devil's name."

"I'm still not okay with it."

Bez meant… Something to me.

I couldn't figure out what that something was. He saw me for who I was. Accepted my flaws. Cherished my weaknesses. He was a monster. Absolutely. One who reveled in chaos, but the more I learned about him, the more I wondered if it came from the harsh reality of his eternity in Beelzebub's Hell realm, the mysteries of his beginning in my realm, or a combination of those factors.

No matter his reasons, his drive, his rage, Bez went out of his way to save me. Protect me. Even when it'd have been easier to let me die. Literally. He could've ripped the remaining bond from my chest and allowed me to die. He hadn't, though. He had saved me.

I wouldn't risk him. Not after that. Maybe it was wrong. Naïve. Weak. I didn't care. I wanted to learn everything he had to offer and prove… I didn't know. Something.

22

Beelzebub

I flew through the sky, wings flapping and Diabolic essence carrying me faster than any eye could detect. As far as any onlookers were concerned, I was merely a dark gust—a shadow cast by a cloud and then quickly carried away by the breeze. Though, I'd tell Walter I used mana to glamour my presence. I certainly didn't want another of his lectures about treading carefully through the city streets he'd sent me out to in order to procure list after list of necessities this week.

The bond linking us had faded and no longer yanked at my chest when I left his side. For some reason, not feeling the tug made my heart pound faster. It made my breathing hitch. I didn't require the air, yet since trusting him in a way I hadn't ever trusted another, I found it impossible not to take wispy breaths when lingering on what it meant. Something to fill these hollow lungs and calm my shaky muscles.

What was it called when a burdensome weight was lifted while simultaneously being consumed by self-doubt? Walter had caused this vexing sensation. I clutched the tank and other magical supplies I'd collected for him on this outing, anxiously determining how he made me feel. Why he made me feel. If I wanted to feel this way. If I wanted to feel.

I'd nearly divulged the truth about my less-than-devil origins to Abe, worried I'd lack the necessary constitution to see our plan through. Turned out best Remington never learned my secret. A pit tightened in my stomach. I couldn't help but question if Walter would truly be different. I believed he would. But I'd believed far too many lies in my long life.

The only other individual who knew my secret was Mora. It most certainly wasn't a confessional. It just so happened she'd passed time with the actual Beelzebub, so when she stumbled across me, having no recollection of her and lacking a few scent signatures she'd been privy to, my lie was discovered. Even then, she'd never seen me. The person behind the façade. The fragile, broken demon serving at a god-king's feet for countless eons. She'd witnessed the brash, misguided soul filling shoes he'd never fit and helped me play a persona to hold my place in the mortal realm. A persona I loved. It offered me a life I never dreamed possible. Free of worries or fear or doubts or anxiety, dread, sorrow, and a hundred other things Walter managed daily. I needed to play the role of the monster for freedom, which I loved being. But I admired how he…how he didn't.

Walter had seen the demon beneath the mask. He cared to protect me. He wanted to learn everything. I saw it in his delicate prying, careful choice of words, and curious eyes. Whether he considered me another thing to research or a person he cared enough to know, I still struggled to determine. Walter was an enigma of compassion and calculations. Also, a blunder of awkward confusion.

I smiled as I landed at the motel, tucking my wings away. It'd take time to sort through my mind and his. Something I truly desired.

Strutting inside, I maintained an aloof grin. "I gathered everything you wanted and then some."

Walter remained on the bed. He hadn't changed, barely shifted since I left this morning, and it didn't look like he'd eaten the provisions he begged me to get him. All the notes he'd started days ago were sprawled across the mattress in a chaotic fashion. Chaotic to a layman's eye, but for Walter, these piles each represented something only his squirrely brain could make sense of.

"How much did you steal today?" He sighed, eyeing my lovely belt buckle.

"I didn't steal this." I traced my fingers along the colorful STUD letters. "Bought it with hard-earned currency."

"I gave you the money."

"Didn't say *I* earned it."

"By the way, a rainbow stud doesn't stand for what you think it does, Bez."

"Really?" I furrowed my brow. "Anyway, I got your favorite candy bar. A Whatchamacallit."

"Snickers?"

"No. Whatchamacallit."

"KitKat?" He raised an eyebrow.

"No, dammit." I held up the candy bar. "A Whatchamacallit."

His glossy eyes lit up, and he practically salivated. "I haven't had one of these in forever."

Forever. Walter, like so many mortals, used the word so casually as if they comprehended the stretch of eternity.

I tossed him the candy bar, which he scarfed down in three massive bites, barely chewing. And he had the nerve to comment on my eating habits.

It'd been eighteen months since he'd had one of these candies. I recalled him muttering about his store discontinuing it for hours, grumbling as he finished someone else's research. For someone who craved a life of adventure, Walter rarely ventured outside his routine. It made sense, though. The city was massive, and he had spent most hours locked inside the repository, with little time to breathe outside of work. Everything he used to do when not in the repository had an incredibly tight routine. The stores closest to his home or job. Calculated with the most affordable prices.

Returning to his notes, he went back to studying the grimoire. A pit grew in my stomach, a gnawing essence that craved mortal sustenance. Something about their food always eased my feelings. Depending on how all this unfolded, he could potentially sink back into such a simple routine. If everything against him was dropped and the devil on his shoulder vanished, of course. Would they simply throw him back into the repository as an eternal apprentice? Would they see the merit he held and offer him the work he deserved? Would they send him on his way with a cleared name but no career within the Collective? I swallowed hard, annoyed at how I dwelled on his well-being when I needed to think about what would happen to me once the dust settled.

We hadn't discussed it. During our late-night conversations, Walter had said he'd ensure everything worked out, but I skirted the topic, dodging the inevitable. This didn't have a happy ending. Nothing in my long eternity ever did.

I held the tank covered in a black cloth. Hopefully, the cloth kept the tiny beast inside settled during our turbulent flight. The last one died of fright before I landed, and I had to tell Walter the pet store was out of what he considered a suitable familiar. "I still think you should've gotten another bird."

"Nope. Can't use a bird for what I'm planning."

"You sure you can control something this deadly?" I set the tank down.

Walter continued scribbling. So much went into planning for everything to go perfectly, he didn't even relish how he'd successfully performed a familiar link with a bird days back to message Alistair. Once things had settled and he knew what to search for, he wanted his brother to track Ian down.

"If you wish to find that cretin of a mage, I could do so quickly."

I still held access to Mora's Diabolic webs. They'd offer swift travel throughout the city, and the nauseating scent of death that clung to Ian would be simple to locate.

"No need. Al's likely been tracking him through his sentinel work schedule."

I sighed. Mortal politics and plotting and planning moved so slowly.

"The only thing Al needs is to catch Ian meeting with someone he shouldn't be, using Agatha's Heart, or literally anything that screams 'I'm behind the attack on the Magus Estate,' which could happen any day. Today. Tomorrow. A week from now. Doubtful. Ian wants to bring the Collective down and free magic to the masses, so it'll be soon. Which means I need to finish the final details on this grimoire."

"If Alistair is retrieving Ian, we should be there to catch him in the act."

"That won't be necessary."

"I simply wish to ensure your brother and his darling sentinels aren't in harm's way against such a vicious misfit mage."

"No. You just want to kill Ian."

"Fair's fair. He tried to kill me first."

"He actually stabbed me."

"Yes, to kill me." I edged closer to the bed, running my black nails along the organized papers Walter had in meticulous stacks. "What if I promised not to kill him? I merely wish to witness just desserts served."

"First, I would say no because our presence might interfere, and this isn't about us."

"It's about clearing your name."

"Which is important, but I just want to prevent a war most didn't ask for."

"Hmmm. You're annoying." I plopped onto the bed, intentionally causing disarray to Walter's many spread notes. "What's the other reason?"

"Oh, that's easy. You're obviously lying—"

"How dare you call my integrity into question. I would never lie."

"Bez, your tails have been out this entire time. Two of them literally crossed."

"Oops. Didn't realize they'd slipped out."

"That's what she said." He chuckled under his breath.

"Who? What'd she say? Was it about me?"

"Never mind. Old joke. Bad joke."

"Don't try to be funny, Walter. It doesn't suit you."

Ignoring me, he dug his hands under my back, grabbing the crinkled papers underneath. I lay there, completely deadweight, and making him put in an extra effort to pry them away without tearing them. His expression wavered between a neurotic desire to preserve the integrity of all his findings and a furious need to smack me for assaulting his research. Bet he missed his laminator or computer or fancy enchanted folders.

"Look, we don't need to deal with Ian. With everything he's behind, the Collective will be spotlighting his case as an example. What we need to do—what I need to do and hopefully with your assistance—is to finish compiling evidence on Ian's inside help. It's all in this grimoire. Well, not all. Enough."

"Ah, yes. Chancellor Driscoll and his wicked ways of working with Mythics and real misfit mages to sow destruction amidst the Collective."

"Yes, the chancellor." Wally furrowed his brow, scribbling furiously to note his findings and avoid conversation. Not sure why he bit his tongue when it came to his discovery on Chancellor Driscoll, but ever since he'd had the revelation, he'd become rather quiet about the subject. Shocked, angry, and determined to tie as much to the chancellor as mortally possible.

I rolled off the other papers to the other end of the tiny bed. My legs dropped to the floor, knees holding me upright while I lay out on my stomach staring at Walter while he returned to work. So painstakingly precise. I remained at his side for hours, observing his detailed work. Dwelling somewhere between curiosity and boredom. Only the slightest murmurings from Walter, the leaky AC unit, and the busy streets outside filled the stiff silence between us.

"I'm over this." I crawled back onto the bed, slowly making my way on all fours toward him. Using a tail, I lifted the pencil he jotted notes with from his grasp.

"Hey."

"I've got some thicker wood for you to hold in your hands." I smirked, carefully crawling over the stack of papers and straddling his waist. "It'll turn that frown upside down, guaranteed."

"You're such a romantic." Walter held a sarcastic edge in his voice, but he grabbed my belt buckle all the same, swiftly unfastening it.

I unbuttoned my shirt and threw it on the floor.

"I aim to please." I shoved the papers off the bed. "Or to be pleased."

"Was that necessary?" He huffed.

"Of course." I ran my hands under his shirt, lifting it. "Unless you wish for cum stains all over the documents you plan on presenting to the Collective."

"I wouldn't present these papers. It's all jumbled nonsense. No, I'm going to have to rewrite all of this properly and—"

"I have a lot of plans for your mouth this evening. Rambling about your research isn't one of them." I removed his glasses and kissed his neck, right in the sweet spot that made him make the cutest, most bizarre sound. Somewhere between a growl and a giggle. Ticklish and aroused. I could spend hours exploring his body.

The motel door burst open, carrying an aroma of blood and death. A wispy trace of citrusy cologne lingered but did nothing to hide the scent. I snarled. Ian panted, clutching the doorframe. Blood and sweat coated the mage's face. His furious eyes tightened.

"You think a few sentinels could really stop what I have planned. Nothing can stop me. Especially not you, Wally."

"Guess I get my wish after all." I fastened my pants. "Didn't even have to blow out Walter's candle."

"You don't frighten me, devil."

"I should." I zipped off the bed in a blur. Walter scrambled to secure the grimoire, then retrieved his glasses. I waited. I wanted him to have a pristine view of me eviscerating this mage that dared lay his hands on my Walter.

"Killing you would've secured my position, certainly. The Collective would've offered trust and acclaim, granting me status to work my way into this flawed system. Years of work and I could've brought it to a halt from the inside." Ian fished a red vial out of his pocket. "But I've found a better solution."

The blood within the vial hummed in my presence, vibrating inside the glass. It called to me. Not blood. It squirmed and wriggled. He'd stolen my essence. How? When? I planted a hand on my chest. The rooftop. My near death. Walter's near death. I fled before securing the terrain.

"If I can't kill the devil, then—"

Fuck that. I lunged forward, everything stilling as I moved in a haze. I'd rip the vial from his grasp along with his arm, then beat him to death with it.

Crimson tendrils sprang from the mage, whipping at my face and defending him from my strike. He'd already consumed my essence. This was merely an act. "When?"

"I took a sip right before stepping inside. Guess the effects work quickly. Good thing, too." Ian chuckled, popping the cork off the vial. "I think commanding a devil will be quite beneficial. Should probably finish this off to ensure you behave."

He guzzled the Diabolic essence. My essence. The bond between us seared my insides as it swelled. This was nothing like the subtle link Walter and I had held.

I had to stop him by any means. My essence would fight to protect him. But it'd take time before he could invoke a command. Coating my arm in Diabolic energy, I prepared to impale his chest and take back my essence, even if it killed me.

"Kneel before me, devil."

My entire body quaked, disregarding my will to fight. I dropped to my knees, obeying his command. I ground my teeth, disdain boiling my blood.

23

Walter

Ian had obtained Bez's essence. That was my fault. Even when he bled in the courtyard, it sizzled and burned away, leaving no trace. The remains on the rooftop lacked the same security measure because he'd prioritized my life above his freedom.

I clutched the grimoire tightly as Ian ran his fingers through Bez's ruffled hair. He grabbed a fistful and yanked Bez's head back, forcing his gaze upward.

"An obedient devil on his knees. I could get used to holding your life in my hands."

Bez growled.

"You look like an angry dog." Ian snickered. "Like a bad dog, you may require some training."

"I am going to kill—"

"Don't speak unless I permit it."

Bez's eyes widened, shocked. He took a heavy, forced breath like exhaling lost words.

"I almost didn't waste my time retrieving the blood spilled during our last encounter. I thought maybe I could use it to track you, kill Wally. You know, if at first you don't succeed, try, try again." Ian's icy expression and smug smile were unlike anything I'd seen from him. "Hidden inside the blood, I noticed the disgusting rot of Diabolic essence. It fed on the blood, becoming more alive. It's fascinating how your kind eats away at this world like a virus."

Bez unveiled his wings, filling the entire room.

"Stop," Ian snapped.

Bez forced himself upright, resisting the pressure of Ian's command. Or perhaps Ian lacked full understanding, much like I had. My heart thumped loudly in my inner ear. Bez overpowered the command and stood tall above Ian.

"I said stop." Ian backed away. "You can't kill me."

"You'd be surprised," Bez grunted, forcing each word through a bloody gurgle.

"No." I trembled. If he attacked Ian, he'd kill him, no doubt about that, and then…and then…

I struggled to catch my breath. Each faster and more shallow than the last. I wanted Bez to kill Ian. I wanted to kill Ian. But not at this price. Not if Bez died in the process.

"Fine." Sigils formed at the flick of Ian's wrists, glowing white until crimson tendrils stabbed the letters, seeping them in a black and scarlet aura. "More than one way to make you heel."

The incantation spun around Bez quickly, but I glimpsed a few key words.

Command. Devil. Beelzebub. Willpower. Obey.

Had he formed a contract to strengthen the Diabolic binding? The idea never even crossed my mind. A cruel concept that made my stomach twist in knots. No wonder Bez despised our bond and my control.

The incantations coiled around Bez locking and sealing around his neck, wrists, bare stomach, and ankles much like the literal chains that bound him in Hell. Bez fell to his knees again, reeling his wings in as the incantation brandings tightened against the skin of his back.

"Lower."

Bez bowed, pressing his head to the floor.

"That's good." Ian pressed his boot on the back of Bez's head. "Unlike Wally, I don't fuck up the things I attempt. In fact, I master them, just as I've mastered this Diabolic binding. Having a devil at my side—or beneath my heel—will hasten everything I've planned for."

"Let him go," I snapped. "Or I'll make you."

"You gonna blunder a spell at me? Fall flat on your face trying to use magic you've had the privilege of your entire life?" Ian snorted. "You're a failure. A failure given too many chances to cast in a world you simply don't deserve. I've mastered more of this world in a year than you could dream of in a lifetime."

Ian's seething hatred for me and the hidden world of magic oozed off him in waves. His shaky, broken mana swelled in the room. Fatigue and exhaustion wouldn't deter him. That, and he had Agatha's Heart tucked away somewhere, drawing on the artifact's reserves.

I flipped pages in the grimoire. Having spent the week analyzing every aspect of this book, I knew a singular spell that would silence Ian's voice and render him incapable of controlling Bez. Keeping a thumb to an earlier passage, I'd have to quickly chant a second incantation and hope I had enough mana to enact it. No. I reached the page I required. No time for doubts. I'd stop Ian and then get Bez and myself as far away from here as possible until I found a proper solution.

"Retrieve the grimoire," Ian said. "I'd like it to be mine."

Bez vanished in a blink, then towered before me. His teeth chattered as he scowled with subdued eyes. An expression I'd only glimpsed when seeing his true demon form in Hell. Bez snatched the book from my hands and returned to Ian's side.

He handed Ian the book.

"Did I say you could stand?" Ian pointed to the floor. "You are my devil, and as such, you should remember your place."

Bez knelt again, taking fuming breaths yet remaining speechless. So much of this must've been traumatizing. I'd done the same to him. Unknowingly. I'd bound us together and made my will his will. Casually making commands to compel control over him. Intentionally and accidentally. It didn't matter. I'd still done it. I balled my fists.

"Surprised you took the book without causing a fatality, Beelzebub." Ian strummed his fingers along the spine of the grimoire. "Must be your feelings for Wally. Do Diabolics have feelings? Was that some compulsion from the bond? Maybe you'll lust for me as I send you to eviscerate the chancellors, beginning with the one who sought to use me as an expendable player in this story."

"You can't." I tensed. Bez was powerful, likely strong enough to hold his own against all the chancellors in a fight. But Ian held him in check through simplistic commands, believing him invulnerable. In the few moments I'd observed, Bez lost his personality and skill in his movements. That'd leave him susceptible.

"Worried about your precious Collective?" Ian smirked, foul and hateful like he'd taken off the final layer of a mask he'd worn since I first met him.

Under that sweet façade was a monster, the complete opposite of Bez, who painted himself a cruel beast but held such longing for more. He hid his compassion because the world offered him none.

I should worry about the Collective. About what he'd make Bez do to Sarai, to Chancellor Belmont, to all the chancellors. Even my mother. How their deaths would ripple through the city, bringing disarray to the regiments. The other regions would rise to squash Ian's pointless plot. Every magical and nonmagical being in the state would end up as collateral to keep the Collective and Mythic Council truce upheld and magic buried from sight. How many would die for Ian's narcissism? A goal he claimed for the betterment of everyone, yet he didn't consider the cost for a second. How long would he keep Bez shackled, fighting for him? How many lives would Bez take before one got lucky and killed the demon disguised as a devil?

I shuddered. How many lives had already been lost because of Ian? Carl's anguished expression flashed, and my chest tightened, thinking about his sentinel jacket covered in blood as he crawled on the floor. My eyes watered. Al and his sentinels had confronted Ian tonight, yet here he stood. Alistair. That could only mean…

No, no, no. Al couldn't be dead. Could he?

I swallowed hard. "I'm going to kill you, Ian."

"Funny. I was going to say the same thing to you." Ian snapped his fingers. "Strike him, devil."

Bez leapt in a blur. I gasped. A heavy punch knocked all the air out of my chest. The only thing dulling the agonizing pit in my stomach was the pain of my back crashing against the wall. I curled into a ball. One punch, and I could barely move. Bez had hit me before, but this was like all my muscles ached at once. The throbbing in my stomach radiated across my entire body.

"Again."

Bez snarled, his face remorseless but his red and pink eyes glossy. He balled a fist and punched me in the face. My glasses cracked. Maybe that was my cheekbone. The shaggy carpet did little to soften the blow when my head ricocheted between the floor and Bez's knuckles. The taste of mildew clung to the roof of my mouth as I wheezed.

"Again."

Bez jerked me up by the collar of my shirt and punched me again. This time something definitely cracked. My vision was red and blurred. Something wet ran down my face. Blood, maybe. I dabbed my head, wincing at the sting. My fingertips were a dark scarlet.

"You barely hit him," Ian said. "Are you holding back, dog? No, that won't do. I need to send Alistair—hell, all the Aldens—a message with this one. He tried to kill me. His mother tried to…" Ian threw the book down.

I jolted at the collision, mistaking it for another impending hit.

"You tried to take my head clean off when we first met," Ian said.

"I should've let him." I spit blood. Had I allowed Bez free reign, none of this would've happened. Had I never tried to catch the damn orb, he'd be free, and Ian would be dead. I'd likely be dead too, but the city would be fine. All Bez really wanted was his freedom, the quiet. I dragged him through this pointless attempt to clear my name and fix a broken system.

Did I think it would make a difference? It wouldn't stop anything. Not really.

"Break something of his," Ian said it so casually, like a mere whim of curiosity. What would Bez break?

I trembled. Bez grabbed my hand and snapped a finger. I screamed, gasping.

"You can surely do better than that. Something bigger."

Bez cracked the bones of my forearm between his grasp so swiftly I didn't feel the agony until my eyes landed on the break. I cradled my broken arm, grinding my teeth so hard I thought they'd crumble as easily as my arm had.

"Better," Ian said. "Another. I want him truly eviscerated when Alistair finds him."

I held onto the fact my brother was alive. He'd find a way to stop Ian. I cried. Between the throbbing pain coursing through every nerve in my body and the idea that if Alistair stopped Ian, it meant Bez died too. I should've told Al everything I was compiling. Should've told him about more than Ian's role in this. Not that it'd make a difference, but if the Collective managed to stop Ian. Stop Bez. They still had a traitor at the top.

Bez rolled me onto my back and pressed his bare foot against my chest. I coughed, choking. Bez was about to crack my ribs open. I couldn't decide if it'd be a mercy to impale my lungs with my ribcage or another slowed and agonizing blow. Part of me knew Bez held back his full brutality to bide time, but another part worried he savored the slow death between us. His life was bound and lost. Why should my end be any less painful than his?

"Stop." Ian had a fuzzy face that looked repulsed between bloody, blurred blinks.

Bez lifted his foot. I choked on each inhale, rolling onto my side, which didn't lessen the agony of breathing.

"This rage is misdirected. I don't want Wally to suffer. So what, his family is horrible, the system he floundered in never made room for anyone else, or he'd rather fuck a devil than meet me for drinks?"

That was a simplification. I'd rather do my job right than meet him for drinks. Gods, if I'd left the manor then, how different would things have turned out? Would Bez have been freed? Would he still be locked away in his orb, hidden with a trove of stolen treasures? Would I be fawning over Ian, pathetic and deluded and ignorant of all the things he did beneath the shadows?

I rolled onto my back again, one arm pinned to my chest because of the pain but dropping the other. I surrendered. None of the what-ifs mattered. I'd die here and now, left to wonder until the end of my days if everyone I cared for died as miserably as I had.

"Kill him quickly. You can scatter his remains afterward. I'm all about presentation."

Bez dropped to his knees. In a swift blur, he jerked my arm off my chest and slammed it to the floor. He growled, backing away and grabbing his own arm.

"What was that?" Ian asked.

I didn't understand why Bez jumped. Had he tried to fight the order?

Bez ignored him, returning to his command. Tracing his fingers along my stomach, I quivered. Such a gentle touch. One meant to remind me he cared, perhaps.

"Stop."

Bez paused.

"Answer me."

"I merely wish to fulfill your command." Bez pressed a firm hand over my heart. His pulse pounded in sync with my heart. "Can't wait to see your face when we all perish."

"Wally still possesses your Diabolic essence?" Ian's face contorted as he caught his breath. "Answer truthfully."

No. The answer was simple. We'd ensured it ran its course because I didn't want to gamble with Bez's life any more than necessary for my foolish desires.

"Yes. He holds a piece of me in his heart." Bez clutched the fabric of my shirt.

He lied. He lied despite a command to speak the truth. It was small and insignificant considering all the horrors which awaited him if he failed to obey Ian's will, yet he resisted it. Enough to spare my life. If Bez could overpower the Diabolic bond even in such a subtle way, maybe there was hope.

"This won't do," Ian said, pacing the confined room. "Can't kill him without risking my own neck. Can't let him walk free without ruining my plans. Beelzebub, detain him, and let us be on our way."

My eyes widened. That was it! I knew how he resisted.

Bez wrapped a hand around my throat. Everything blurred. My throat tightened. I tried to speak but choked on the words. I had to explain to Bez how he'd resisted.

Ian commanded Beelzebub.

I could stop this. I just needed to tell Bez…

…

Everything grew dark.

…

Bez needed to know.

…

I had to tell him. Ian created an incantation to control Beelzebub, not…

… Bez.

24

Beelzebub

I abandoned Walter, tied in a dirty tub, broken and bloody, with no way out. His freedom and survival were as precarious as mine. My wings flapped furiously, wishing to close the distance between myself and Ian, who flew ahead on his broom. The incantations coiled around my wrists and ankles glowed, burning my flesh when I flew too close. The incantations around my chest and back squeezed tight when too much distance fell between us. A constant reminder of my place, obeying Ian's instruction and maintaining proper speed and distance. At this length, the link between us pulled at my neck like a stifling collar. He knew this and relished in it.

How I broke his command earlier, I couldn't decipher. Perhaps it had to do with how I felt for Walter. It was difficult fathoming these feelings. The emotions Walter's mere presence evoked. Joy, excitement, pleasure, serene comfort—all things seemingly impossible for me to obtain, but here I had them all when basking in

Walter. I wanted to protect him. I was prepared to die for him. I would've if I were worth anything. Yet, all I could muster was a weak lie. I said a piece of me remained inside Walter because a part did. A part always would, longing for him. Something I'd surely ruin once I destroyed the Collective at Ian's beck and call. The only grace being some mage might land a killing blow and grant me the peace I should've accepted centuries ago.

Ironic. I'd craved the chance to obliterate every mage in sight, and now, given the opportunity to kill those who reigned in this region, I quaked. My neck itched. Nothing gave me satisfaction. The incantations compelled me, breaking me down the same way Beelzebub had for lifetimes. Ian had shown such mastery over the Diabolic binding. I feared his success more than a failure which resulted in my death. He could use my essence to extend his life for centuries, forcing me with commands until nothing remained. His wrath would break me to create his vision of a future. I'd soon lose myself in this mortal realm as I had in Hell.

It'd taken so long to find myself after being broken down to nothingness for someone else's future, dream, hopes. I couldn't do that again. I couldn't start over and find the missing pieces buried in ash and rubble.

"Keep up, dog." Ian zipped through the sky, swirling through clouds faster than I could follow.

Not faster. Faster than he willed me to move. This dullness in my ability was the most insulting part. I flew as fast as he'd allotted, wishing for death. Mine, his, and everyone else's. Everyone except Walter.

Pointless. He probably bled out. I hit him too hard. I tried not to. I held back everything I could, but my body fought against me with every step.

We reached a warehouse along Puget Sound, landing in a lot with a great view. Waves crashed under the direction of the moon's guidance while merfolk weaved captivating luminescence beneath the water, glamoured by the moon's light and a touch of magic.

If I had a spine, the slightest conviction in my will, I'd snatch Ian and drag him deep into the hidden depths of the ocean. We'd drown together in silence. Maybe we'd even last long enough to reach one of the Atlantean outposts. Their cities were truly a sight unlike any other.

"Don't just stand there gawking." Ian stepped into the warehouse, dragging me with him.

Inside, there was nothing glamorous about the place aside from several sigils drawn on the wall in blood and cloaked by weak glamouring. Clearly, this warehouse served as a hidden meeting place for Ian and his rebels plotting a coup.

"Up on the rafters. Stay silent and hidden unless I call upon you." Ian pointed to the high ceiling.

I wanted to question him but remained speechless as per his instruction. Glaring, I lingered in place as long as possible before my wings flapped of their own accord toward the metal beams. I tucked myself behind them to the best of my ability, awaiting further commands.

After several long minutes with only the subtle creaking of this building to keep my mind from stirring in silent concern for Walter, heavy footsteps shuffled from the opposite direction. The large garage door rattled when opening. Hooves thudded against the concrete, each step easily capable of breaking through the earth itself. A minotaur Mythic with horns larger than mine stomped ahead of a group of others. His body was nearly as big and muscular as my true form, perhaps a bit more on the slender side despite his wide frame.

Of the Mythics who conspired to strike down Magus Remington and declare war against the Collective, this group was not what I expected. Banshees, gorgons, goblins, a phantom latched to the shadow of a sylph, and many other gentler Mythics. Most of these

Mythics belonged to classifications easily accepted in the Mythic Council and approved by the Collective—not that the approval of mages meant much more than they didn't stalk the movements and patterns of friendly species. No. I expected ghouls like the one who attacked Walter. Vampires, Succubi, Weres, and other Mythics which fed upon mortals regularly, draining and killing them to enhance their magical abilities. Creatures among the Mythic community despised almost as much as Diabolics for simply existing as the apex predators they were.

This group consisted mostly of docile Mythics. Perhaps I'd truly missed some grand evolution among the Mythics from my time detained in that fucking orb. Or maybe I never understood these species. It wasn't that I interacted with them often. In passing, perhaps, or observed from a careful distance.

"What is it you've got planned now, misfit mage?" The minotaur's voice bellowed throughout the warehouse.

"This mage has a name." Ian grinned arrogantly, believing too much in his own power and mine. "You'd do well to remember it."

The minotaur snarled, exhaling smoke from his nostrils, fanning the flames which fueled his organs.

"It's time to make our next move. A final gambit which will give you all everything you deserve."

"No," the minotaur said. "Your impetuous actions have already complicated things in this region."

"It's because of me the Collective finally fears you. That fear will turn into respect and will catapult across the world." Ian might hate the hold on magic mages among the Collective had, but his ambition matched that of any trueborn practitioner.

"We were supposed to raid the estate for our possessions. Things rightfully belonging to us which Magus Remington refused to return." The minotaur closed the distance between himself and Ian, towering above the small mortal. "What you did made everything worse."

Of course, Abe refused to return their relics. He painted himself a hero bestowing stolen artifacts when it suited him, but he could've left the vault and repository barren if he truly wished to build bridges with the Mythics. No. Everything that feeble old bastard had done was intentional and meant to strengthen his political hold. Still a real shame I never got to kill him. Maybe we'll cross paths in oblivion, and I could spend my eternal slumber strangling him in the afterlife.

"I gave you a rallying cry. A voice to be heard. Those who went to the estate understood that. Shame only the weakest, most cowardly Mythics survived to reap the benefits."

"Benefits?" The minotaur puffed his chest. "The Collective stalks every corner of our sanctioned communities. Mages have put bans and blockades on travel out of the region and to and from our pocket dimensions. We are hunted for an attack and theft yet have nothing to show for it."

I rolled my eyes. Boo-fucking-hoo. At least they had their precious items.

"Even the vaults with our possessions are still hidden away by you."

Okay. Maybe they didn't.

He jabbed Ian in the chest. My pec flexed at the powerful poke.

"A former ally has your belongings, which I'll be retrieving soon. I simply require your—"

"No. You made promises and spun lies all to manipulate desperate fools to your agenda. No more, misfit mage."

"It was always about freeing magic; those who saw this vision died for the cause. I'm offering you a chance to live. See it through. Tonight, I will end the Collective in Seattle. I'll kill every mage in the state, the region." Ian traipsed past the minotaur, unthreatened by the huge beast. His confident strut caught the eye of a few curious Mythics. "All I ask is once they are gone, once the sentinels and vanguard who keep you in check have perished, you cast openly, sharing Mythic wonder with the world. The infiltration regiment will not glamour away your magic from mortal eyes because they will be felled in one fast swoop."

"You make bold and reckless promises," the minotaur said. "What you suggest is more and more bloodshed until we're all dead."

A few Mythics agreed.

"What if he's right?" asked a banshee. She stepped from the crowd of Mythics. "The only bloodshed I'm hearing is for Collective mages. We could cast freely then."

"And be dragged into a war," a gorgon said.

"I don't require any of you to fight," Ian said. "I'll handle all the regiments myself."

"Lies." The minotaur's words were echoed by many, but the confidence in Ian's stance, the fire in his eyes, and the powerful mana radiating off him captivated some.

"Let me prove it to you. I will burn the Collective down and give you everything. I'll give the world the magic it deserves, in the hands of everyone willing to learn it."

"There are tens of thousands of mortals for every Mythic life in this world," the minotaur said. "Revealing our presence wouldn't offer us freedom or power. It'd force us on the run as it did to the Mythics of the past. Minotaurs thrown in labyrinths to be hunted for sport. Gorgons having their heads decapitated and eyes sold as enchanted gems. Witches burned for daring to rise above mages or humans."

"Our magics can outpower any force of humans," the banshee said.

"But not their weapons. Centuries back, their violent nature was enough to drive us into the shadows. Now they possess tools that can level a nation. What happens when they wage war? If they unite under a single banner to eradicate us?"

"I offer you a future, and you cry at the cost." Ian shook his head disapprovingly. "It's no wonder the Mythic Council bends to the Collective's will. You're pathetic. Weak. Worthless. Most of all, undeserving of the world I'm creating."

"I was about to say the same, misfit mage." The minotaur roared, grabbing Ian by the shirt and lifting him off the ground.

My heart jumped, pattering with dread and excitement. If he were wise, he'd impale Ian with his horn and end this now. The thrill faded when he hurled Ian across the warehouse. His back crashed into the metal garage door, and he sliced his forehead when smacking the ground. Blood dripped down my own forehead, my back aching from our shared pain. I cracked my neck; hopefully, a gorgon would petrify him to stone before he said a word. Or a banshee's wail would silence the sound of his impending command. Perhaps a goblin could rip out his tongue before he spoke.

Ian stood, wiping the blood dripping down his eye. He stared at his bloody hand, chest puffed as he took fuming breaths.

"I should've mentioned…I have a devil under my command now." Ian snapped his fingers. "Kill them all, dog. Quickly and painfully."

I leapt from the rafters in a blur, unveiling my wings to slow my descent, wishing I could resist his commands, but the incantations placed on my flesh itched and added to Ian's control. Unleashing my tails, I strangled the banshee and turned two gorgons to face each other. They petrified one another, and I smashed their stone bodies together. By the time a few other Mythics had called forth their magics, I'd ripped most of them to shreds with my talons, moving through the crowd faster than they could blink.

All that remained was the minotaur leading them. The one who should've killed Ian. I took a bit of satisfaction in snapping off his horns and gutting him with them.

"Not bad." Ian clapped. "Hopefully, you'll have a bit more enthusiasm when you're killing the chancellors and their regiments."

I glared, taking a deep inhale of the blood and death I brought. Each of these lost lives carried traces of Mythic residue released into the atmosphere. It was doubtful he'd allow me to feed on the magic to its fullest and unlikely I'd gain much mana in this act. Still, I hoped for enough magic to cast a spell. Maybe something to break these incantation chains or snap Ian's neck before he ordered me to stop. My essence circulated inside him, reminding me that if I made any attempt to fight, it would defend against me for all our sakes.

If only my essence understood, we were better off dead.

25

Walter

Everything throbbed. I stretched my jaw, moving it side to side, which only added to the pulsing pain coursing down my neck and settling into my chest. All my muscles vibrated, a constant ache as I rocked in this confining tub. My arms were bound in rope, looped together, and knotted around my ankles. Fuck.

I tugged at them, then winced. My arm seized. All the nerves in my broken arm fired off in agony. I clamped my teeth together and took deep breaths through the pain. I had to undo these ropes. They were sturdy. Likely enchanted. But I doubted Ian carried rope on him, so that meant he'd conjured these. Things manifested through an incantation were easy enough to dissolve with magic.

Taking careful breaths, I searched for the elements radiating within my mana. With each exhale, I tried to ignite a flame. I'd seen this done a hundred times. Practiced a thousand times. Surely, when lives were at stake, I could manage to successfully summon one tiny godsdamn flame.

Nothing. Nothing. Nothing.

Finally, a tiny gust carried across the fine fibers of the rope. I kicked my legs against the tub.

"Wrong fucking element," I shouted.

A sizzle popped. Small sparks trailed the gust, burning through the rope. I'd done it. I kicked the lever to the shower nozzle before the flames caught onto my clothing. Cold water beat against my sore body. I shivered, then dragged myself out of the tub.

Cradling my arm, I crawled out of the bathroom on my knees and into the bedroom.

Bez was gone.

The grimoire was gone.

Every hope I had for helping was gone.

I failed. Failed the same way I had a hundred thousand times before. Never in my life had I done anything right. Wincing, I slowly inched across the floor. Just once, I'd like not to screw everything up by constantly falling short.

There was nothing to be done. Bez was bound to Ian. Ian had more magical ability than I could ever muster. On top of that, he had Agatha's Heart to enhance his mana and that Diabolic demon killing blade he stabbed me in the chest with.

"Not that he needs it since…" I paused. It stung when my teeth met my busted open lower lip. Damn habits. "I don't have the grimoire, but I have notes."

I searched the scattered pages strewn about the floor. Countless notes, most trivial, some useless given the circumstances. But I'd jotted a few of those skeleton key spells for further analysis. Something about them reminded me of things I'd learned as a child.

"There it is." I found the notes on hacking pocket portals. Not an actual pocket realm like the Dimensional Atrium, but a tiny holding area mages could create by saturating the air around them and creating a unique incantation. Ian had done that to keep Agatha's Heart and his Demon's Demise blade hidden away. If I could remember the specific symbols he used, I might be able to hack his treasures. "Not that any of that matters."

He'd still kill me or make Bez kill me. Oh, Bez. There was a way to free him from Ian. It had to do with the commands Ian had contracted to Bez. If I reached them, I could tell Bez, let him restrain Ian, then…

"Do something useful?" I groaned, laying back on the floor.

A miserable feeling clouded my thoughts, making it impossible to think clearly. It might've also been the concussion. I probably definitely most likely had one. Staring at the ceiling, the draped glass aquarium Bez had gotten caught my eye. Inside sat a familiar who could fix some of this.

I lifted the black cloth. Motionless, a small emperor scorpion lay. Its black shell was almost as shiny as Bez's talons when coated in Diabolic essence. Opening the top of the tank, I placed my hand inside, patiently waiting while casting trusting energy. Familiar links depended entirely on the aura of a mage. The emotion radiated from mana, which in turn seeped inside the animal. The pigeon I'd connected with to deliver news to Alistair was easier. Less likely to attack, too.

The scorpion backed away, feeling the anxiety I cast in waves. I shook it off. I'd specifically picked an emperor scorpion for their docile nature—they were almost always calm, even when aggressive, they were more likely to pinch than sting. And if this scorpion used his stinger, it wouldn't kill me. Merely a bad bite. Honestly, Bez and Ian had done the worst already, so what would a pinch or sting really matter at this point? Scary looking, perhaps. Dangerous if provoked, sort of. Overall, a friendly familiar which could achieve a lot more stealth than others.

The scorpion skittered onto my palm. His legs lightly tapped, his claws outstretched.

"Ready to come out?" I lifted my hand. "I had a much cooler plan for you. I'd uncovered some things in a dangerous grimoire connecting to a very bad person who put their ambition above the Collective."

A person who threw me into the fire, ensuring blame fell to me. That pissed me off more than anything. Ian had played his part, using and manipulating me, but it was all set in motion by a chancellor who sought to—I didn't know. Provoke a war? Strengthen policies against Mythics? Provide more funding to regiments designed for safety and protection? I ground my teeth. Feeling my rage, the scorpion pitched at the air.

I exhaled. The reasons didn't matter. Not anymore. I set the scorpion on a few pages I'd saturated with mana for a plan which no longer mattered. "It was supposed to be a sophisticated and triumphant win on my part. Guess my life isn't really made for winning."

The scorpion walked along the sigil I created for cloaking, another for tracking, and one to add an extra powerful dose of venom to my familiar's stinger.

"Still, I have some use for your wonder. I hope I can ask this favor of you." The scorpion abandoned the saturated pages I no longer had use of and crawled up onto my leg, crossing over my thigh and laying on my broken arm.

Even without explanation, the scorpion—my scorpion, my familiar—felt the need I had. It knew how I could repurpose the exoskeleton into something durable to mend the break and temporarily heal the injury.

The chitin of his armor was tough, protective, and a flexible fibrous material. I definitely wouldn't hold a candle to anyone in the panacea regiment, but I'd helped Sarai study hundreds of different healing spells, which involved augmenting materials into substitutes for fractured bones, torn flesh, or blood loss. If I were half as skilled as her, I could alter the bed frame. But working with organic living tissue from the scorpion was more at my basic level.

I muttered an incantation, tracing my fingertips along the hard, smooth shell of the arachnid. The polysaccharides and nitrogen would soften and transform. As it dissolved, the scorpion scurried away, left vulnerable and exposed without an exoskeleton. The shell seeped into my pores. I shouted as the fibers burned and crawled under my skin, tearing through muscle and meat to reach the bones.

Taking wispy breaths, I flexed my arm. My body still ached. My finger was still broken. I barely had enough exoskeleton to work with to mend my arm. It would have to do.

"All right, buddy." I scooped the scorpion up and set him inside the tank. I saturated the glass with water, not a lot, just enough to create a more comfortable, humid environment. Grabbing a blank page, I drew a simple incantation for air and placed it inside where the scorpion had hidden himself while molting. "I'm sorry. This is the best I can do for now."

I sat on the bed, letting my arm acclimate to its newly healed form. There was no way I'd actually be able to stop Bez or Ian. There was no way I could actually free Bez from Ian. Free Bez before the Collective killed him. Killed Ian. I stood.

"Doesn't mean I won't try."

I searched through the notes I'd taken, looking for the one which might help hack Ian's artifacts. He'd kill me for sure, but I'd drag him down with me if it was the last thing I did.

Before leaving, I paused and opened a window.

"If I don't return, please, use the seal I placed in your tank to escape once your new exoskeleton hardens." That air sigil would carry him outside the motel window safely. "I wish I could offer more after everything you've given me."

Ian and Bez would reach the Regiment Headquarters before me, and there was no way Ian would delay his attack. He was erratic, fueled by a vendetta, and probably wanted to make the most of his Diabolic binding. Even if I had something to enchant for flight, no way would I beat them. Hell, they could already be there. If he used Bez's speed, he could end up anywhere in the city in a blink.

Wait. Not Bez's speed. Mora's dimensional weaving. She could transport anyone, anywhere, instantaneously. Her place wasn't far. I raced down the street, ignoring the pain in my legs. I needed to reach her so I could save Bez. Save the Collective. The Mythics. The city.

Time to be the misfit mage everyone accused me of being and go kill a real misfit mage.

26

Beelzebub

Ian and I descended, landing across the street from the Regiment Headquarters. The night sky was hidden behind the lights of the city. So bright and sparkling, it was a wonder mortals managed to find rest this late at night. Traffic wasn't thick like when I escaped with Walter, but cars still moved in this busy area. Mana filled the air like thick, sweet humidity. Guess they kept their mages working around the clock since the attack on the Magus Estate.

"It's doubtful the chancellors are here. We'll have to make do killing the regiment fodder assigned here nights." Ian traced incantations in the air, opening a tiny rip in front of him. A hole barely big enough for a finger to fit, yet Mythic residue wafted out, spilling tremendous magical energy which latched itself to Ian. Once imbued, his mana boomed. Even a novice would feel such a massive amount of power.

It came from the witch artifact he'd stolen. Agatha's something. Kidney, liver, lung. No. Heart, maybe. I'd mostly tuned Walter out when he'd cataloged it and the organ looked more like stone than a savory piece of meat.

I considered swaying him, convincing him a morning assault might fare better for his plot. Then I remembered I couldn't speak. Not easily, anyway. When I tried, it was like talking while needles jabbed my throat, claws shredding my vocal cords at the mere attempt of forming a syllable.

"Once we begin, it won't take the chancellors or that wannabe magus long to arrive or bring their best with them." Ian conjured fire in his hands; the flames burned small, tightly swirling inward to remain contained. His veins bulged as he laced the elemental magic with saturation.

Artifact or not, a skill of that level required precision. By pouring his mana into the cast, he ensured the flames would burn hotter and longer. Depending on his capability, he might even be able to control the fire's movements once released. Something few mages mastered.

I scoffed. Just another reason to kill him if the opportunity presented itself, which felt less and less likely with each passing second.

"I want you to destroy everything and everyone." Ian hurled a fireball into the street, knocking a car off course and colliding with a second before both crashed into the sidewalk at the front steps of the Regiment Headquarters. "Tear it all down. The building. The mages. The street. Hell, the whole district. I want your flashiest, strongest magics unleashed before the world. Understand me, devil?"

I nodded reluctantly because I had no choice in any of this. Shame. Killing mortals under any other circumstances would make for an entertaining evening, though even during my flashiest outbursts, I respected the need for discretion. After all, the devil Beelzebub didn't need the entire world aware of his presence.

I conjured electricity from the static in the atmosphere, weaving my Diabolic essence between the tiny sparks and amplifying the jolts a hundredfold. With a swing of my arms, I guided the black lightning onto the street, ripping the concrete apart.

If we survived tonight, we'd have the Collective sweeping up our mess. If Ian achieved the exposure he sought, we'd have the entire world of mortals on our heels. I sighed. This would be an insufferable existence.

It didn't take the mages long to respond. Vanguard dressed in crimson and sentinels wearing their blues flew out, incantations and elements at the ready. Ian hovered above without the assistance of his broom. Impressive use of his sigils. He'd embedded new ones within the fabric of his shirt and the bottoms of his boots. Not only very difficult to do but required incredible coordination as well as massive amounts of mana. The artifact helped on that front. Ian hurled fire at the mages. Sentinels created shields to block his elemental blasts while vanguards prepared to parry with their own elemental strikes.

Mages belonging to the infiltration regiment flitted by, prioritizing glamouring civilians and obscuring the magic at play. Normally, I'd only note their presence to avoid a secretive strike from the shadows, yet I had orders.

Orders. I choked on the word.

I couldn't make this attack broad and seen by the masses if these mages removed the spotlight, so I unleashed telekinesis, lifting them up and into the path of Ian's flames.

Their bodies burned, consumed by the fire, skin crackling down to the bone. Fire like that was on par with a Diabolic's level. That artifact truly held unmatched ability.

Ian laughed, distracted and indulging in the death before him. The level of destruction he released on charred corpses was wasteful and unnecessary. Most importantly, it was boring.

Wave after wave of intense fire turned this street into carnage. Ian's laughter became unhinged as he relished in the deaths. He didn't savor them, instead lapping up the experience in a way I used to. I'd been this hateful and angry once upon a time. Hell, still was most days. It didn't lessen the disdain I held for Ian or the joy his death would bring. But I understood the insatiable drive to burn down every threat. I simply wished not to be the match he used to light the fire.

A few sentinels skirted around the huge flames, their eyes locked on Ian. I unveiled my wings and soared toward the Regiment Headquarters' front door, where the bulk of the defense formed. Ian commanded me to kill everyone. He never commanded me to watch his back, so if his arrogance got him killed, I could live with that.

Well, die with that. Semantics.

Mages gathered in larger numbers, clearly using the portals to swiftly arrive at the headquarters and funnel out the front. Lingering mana in the distance showed they wanted to flank us. Pretty coordinated, given the surprise assault. Though, they probably figured a ruthless and reckless devil like myself would've done this eventually.

I flew at blurring speed, making eye contact with every mage before me, one by one, until I had nearly fifty locked in my nightmarish gaze. Time stilled. The world practically froze as I analyzed their psyches, plucking at the chords of their inner horrors. Magnifying their worst fears, I dropped nearly every vanguard and sentinel mage in seconds.

"No, devil. I want them dead!" Ian snapped, whipping fire at the mages behind him.

I huffed. So much for a sneak attack. Useless fucking mages. Cracking my knuckles, I tightened a fist and pulled Ian's discarded flames into my grasp. Fueling the tiny blazes with my essence, I threw black fire at the immobilized mages.

Water burst from every window of the Regiment Headquarters, creating a huge tidal wave aimed at me. I spun the most brutal waves aside with telekinesis and froze the water, circling me into black ice.

Two of the chancellors from the tribunal descended into the battle, blades in their hands and incantations at the ready. The best of the best from the vanguard and the sentinel regiments.

"Finally." Ian soared past me. "And the one I want dead most is here, too. Fortune favors the bold."

Ugh. Everything out of his mouth was nauseating and trite. Even his movements, while skilled in the swift conjuring of a sword through incantation, lacked elegance when he slashed at the sentinel chancellor and guarded against the newly appointed magus. Ian was so prosaic.

I returned to my commands, harnessing the black flames to melt the ice and kill all my foes. A pink shroud cloaked the immobilized mages. The plump panacea chancellor made her way to the center of fallen comrades, radiating a healing aura. Not only was she working to tend to their injuries—futile considering the psychological depth I'd ripped into—but she coated the pink shroud with the water on the ground. It sizzled against my black flames, unable to smother the blaze but keeping it at bay.

"Chancellor Russo," an injured mage woke from his nightmare, struggling to sit upright. "You can't be here. It's too dangerous."

"I cannot heal the dead," she said, weaving tiny incantations which she whisked through the air, distantly linking to other mages. "Clearly, my assistance is required here."

She kept her eyes locked on mine, mana saturated in her pupils, making it challenging to reach inside and pull her nightmares forward. Quite masterful how she protected herself while also repairing the damage to the psyche I'd caused in others. She'd found the neurons I'd threaded with my Diabolic essence and began to repair them.

Almost as clever as Walter and obviously better at composing herself in a stressful situation. Shame I had to kill her. But orders were orders, and the longer I resisted Ian's commands, the more my body turned in on itself, insides stabbing me for remaining idle. Soon my essence would supersede all my will to obey.

I raced toward Chancellor Russo, talons drawn and ready to tear out her throat. Walls of rock burst from the earth, mixed with concrete and soot from the fiery ashes. The half-healed mages sprang from their nightmares, immediately collaborating to provide the chancellor a buffer from my assault. I groaned, feral and annoyed, the closest word-like thing I could muster.

Slashing at the rocky barriers, I broke through wall after wall. Every wall I tore down was replaced by two more. The healing glow continued radiating further, reviving mages I'd incapacitated, each adding their magic to defend the chancellor, who in turn revitalized their depleted mana. While killing her would render the rest immobilized, it proved rather complicated to reach her through the elemental defenses.

My skin itched, essence squirming under my host, shredding the meat of this body. I grimaced. Every ticking second I went without fulfilling Ian's command caused my body to further betray itself. Flapping my wings, I released a gust of black wind, stealing the air around the mages. I flew close to the ground, evading the walls meant to guard the chancellor, and ripped apart those protecting her.

Chancellor Russo's pink aura continued healing severe wounds, treating deep gashes like they were mere scratches, so I moved into more brutal attacks even the best panacea mage would struggle to reverse.

I kicked in a mage's skull. The crunch beneath my heel sent a tingling shiver up my leg and through my spine. Death lessened the erratic resistance of my essence. I grabbed a second mage, snapping his neck. Quick and simple, yet efficient. The stabbing prickles beneath my skin stopped. In a blur, I impaled two mages, removing their hearts as pink mist sealed the open wound. Not a lot of good it'd do to stop the blood loss since I'd removed the source to pump their blood.

The pain subsided once I slaughtered a few mages. Adrenaline coursed through my veins, heightening the bliss which came from killing, not a satisfactory joy but a calm from obeying commands. Screams flooded me with dopamine as I hacked through fallen mages. Ripping off limbs. Breaking skulls. Shattering spines. Anything and everything too fatal for Chancellor Russo to mend. I continued tearing through the street, eviscerating everyone in my path, mage after mage, until the barriers guarding the chancellor had all but fallen.

There were too many walls to break down, but their placement had thinned, so I darted ahead, flying between the fallen layers. I raised my talons.

"I think not." The artificer chancellor dropped from above, landing squarely between Russo and my claws.

Despite magnifying the essence in my claws, it didn't so much as scratch the metallic shield the old bag held.

"I've been preparing since you ripped through my door during the tribunal."

Insufferable. I slashed at the metal infused with incantations which reinforced the strength. Nothing. The most I managed was catching a whiff of her mana saturated in the enchanted item.

Unable to break through this shield, I zipped back and flew high above. If I couldn't break her crafted tool, I'd stretch past its reach and strike down the panacea chancellor.

"Russo!" the artificer chancellor shouted, shield dropped and eyes darting about the field.

The faintest hint of a moving shadow lingered where Chancellor Russo had stood mere seconds ago. I blinked, and that wispy shadow had vanished. Peculiar.

"What have you done to Russo, devil?" The artificer chancellor rushed toward me, shield in tow bulldozing through the slew of corpses between us.

Me? I hadn't done anything to the damned healer chancellor. Not for lack of effort. Something about that subtle shadow stuck with me as I dodged the old mages barrage.

A sharp sting hit my neck. Simply a light scratch, but enough to pull my focus. Ian. Our link sent his pain my way.

The sentinel chancellor and acting magus sliced through incantations Ian summoned, the pair moving in tandem. Given Alistair had mentioned the two despising each other, they didn't show it in their synchronized strikes. Despite all the magic the artifact offered, Ian struggled to counter or evade the onslaught. A swift slash broke the incantations Ian had conjured for flight. It sent him plummeting to the ground.

I gasped, feeling the air knocked out of my own chest, along with a few cracked ribs. Good. Hope they chopped the bastard's head off next.

"Help me," Ian shouted.

I pivoted, preparing to futilely attack the artificer's unbreakable shield. After all, Ian had demanded I kill everyone I could, so this was *helping*.

"Dammit, devil. Stop them!" Ian's voice carried down the street.

I turned my attention, resisting the command knowing full well it'd offer the artificer a chance to strike me down.

A glint of a shadow dancing atop embers hit my peripheral. In the second it took to turn my attention back to her, she'd vanished entirely—shield left discarded—and the saturation she'd tended to the field quickly dissipated in her absence.

Strange. Mages could manipulate instant transportation through high-tiered incantations and Fae magics, but their movements should still be slow enough to register. These shadows weaved with such ferocity it appeared almost Diabolic, yet I was the only Diabolic here.

Ian's unanswered command burned my muscles, stabbing my insides and twisting my body into obedience.

I soared over the corpses and debris, obeying the newest command. Chancellor Alden flew back at the last moment, abandoning her blade. Not sure if that gave me relief or not. Killing Walter's mother wouldn't please him, yet considering how she treated him, if he survived this slaughter, his life would likely be easier with her dead. All the chancellors, actually.

My claws dug into Chancellor Driscoll's back. Correction, acting Magus Driscoll. Certainly not the magus I longed to kill, but this old prick was pretty annoying the last time we crossed paths.

I gripped his spine, crushing the lowest column and snatching out the entirety of the bone in one quick motion. It snapped from the vertebrae connecting to the skull and cracked away from the ribs, taking a few with it. Blood splattered. The body went limp, collapsing like a deflated doll. A dying gurgle quieted everything else on the battlefield.

Driscoll had made his own bed, conspiring with Ian and framing Walter. And for what? A chance to hold a title? A title that proved as durable as his bones.

Vanguard mages flew toward me in force, disregarding Ian, who continued struggling to catch his breath. The massive surge of mana which spiked earlier had faded, all but vanishing. He must've known the artifact possessed a short lifespan. Still, I would've considered something created by witches to hold more longevity. Agatha's petrified organ was no better than a basic incantation boost.

A vanguard coated in enhancement incantations swept by with lightning in hand. It sizzled and scorched my bare chest, nearly breaking the flesh. I spun around and smacked him with the bloody spine. The three coming to his aid met the same fate as I pummeled them into the scorched earth until the bloody skeleton was covered in more of their blood than Driscoll's.

"That was fucking fantastic." Ian stood. His body buzzed, rejoicing at the bloody sight.

It was something I would've enjoyed more under different circumstances. Perhaps with Walter. No. He'd never accept this type of brutality. He was too kind, too gentle, always thinking of everyone above himself. He likely would've wanted Driscoll spared despite all he'd done to Walter. But Driscoll deserved his fate for framing Walter, sending him on the run, plotting to kill us, and I suppose all the other misdeeds involving conspiring on assault at the Magus Estate. Old prick. Not the magus I wanted dead, but it'd do.

"He was a total asshole." Ian smirked, kicking the dead magus and rolling him onto his back. "Christ, just look how sunken in his face is. Is that what happens when you take out someone's spine? Fuck. You made it look so casual. How'd you do that? No, don't answer. Your voice is grating. Fucking awful sound."

A completely mutual feeling, for certain. How I hated Ian's voice. The joyful lull, mixed with polite confidence, did little to mask his arrogance. Or the deep-seated hatred that seeped from his pores. How I hoped to rip out his tongue as I had the treacherous Driscoll's spine.

Ian knelt, grabbing Driscoll's chin.

"You don't belong here." He mimicked the surly old man's voice. His broken jaw crackled as he wiggled the chin up and down. "Who belongs here now?"

Ian stepped back, conjuring flames. They flickered in and out. He shook his sweaty hands. Frustration squirmed inside me. Insecurity. Paranoia. I scanned the street. Most mages had died, remained too injured to attack, or had fallen back to regroup. I swallowed hard. These weren't my feelings, but those of Ian's in his struggle to manifest his elemental control. His emotions latched until the Diabolic essence coursing inside him, spread to me like a virus eating away at my own.

"He treated me like shit for being some fluke of a human who possessed inherent skills which he claimed belonged to my betters. Mages born and bred and raised in this elusive world. Then, when I wowed every fucking person here, proving I had more strength, skill, potential, power, and destiny than any of them—the old bastard tried to recruit me into his regiment. As if. Of course, when I declined, he whispered lies that I was screwing Chancellor Alden, that her clout was the only reason I succeeded."

I rolled my eyes. Fuck. He was really going to give me his whole damn life story in the midst of battle.

"But I never spent long nights with Victoria for favors. Our discussions veered toward change, not conquest. Chancellor Alden knew old man Remington wasn't leading his mages to the future." Ian burned the corpse of the acting magus. "Though, this is not the change she sought."

Driscoll's body gave off a sweet and putrid aroma, mixing with the smoke of the battle, blood on the ground, and tired sweat caught in the air. This was what living smelled like. Living to be the last one standing. However, it seemed someone else worked to be the last one standing.

"Speak of the devil," Ian said, chuckling at his own lack of humor. "She's almost as wicked as you, dog. Minus the whole Diabolic thing."

Chancellor Alden walked through the rubble alone, carrying an enchanted sword. Water and wind swirled behind her, arching overhead so she could readily defend if Ian or I conjured fire or lightning. Might need to switch to earth. Impressive that she'd pinpointed the elements we favored in such short succession.

My heart pounded. She had set all this in motion.

Chancellor Alden was behind the coup.

My blood boiled. She'd set up Walter, her son. Played on his nature. I panted, a necessity to inhale as much mana as possible. It made sense. Alden ensured the blame fell on her family because of Walter's actions. Actions he'd never taken. I balled my fists, digging my claws into my palms. It did little to settle my rage.

Her goal was probably to have Walter killed during the attack at the Magus Estate, but I messed up that part of her plan. So she pivoted, agreeing with the harshest punishments the tribunal could serve. Even when we escaped, she likely whispered helpful tips to Alistair, knowing he wanted to save his brother and would seek us out. He sent us Driscoll's trail where she'd laid all the evidence in that damn grimoire. A book Walter deciphered and put together a perfect case against Driscoll. She probably had a plan to kill Walter and me after clearing his name and framing Driscoll for the coup where the role of magus landed in his lap.

"I'll admit, I should've killed you the second you'd served your purpose," Alden said. "Would've been less messy."

She didn't predict Ian, though. His hubris bent on bringing down the system she sought to climb to the top of.

"But you didn't. And now, instead of getting that ranking you crave, I'll be getting the world I want."

Chancellor Alden laughed. A small snicker which grew into a chuckle, then her shoulders rocked and she held her stomach, and a powerful cackle erupted. Unhinged and full of delight. This was a woman who didn't appear fazed by Ian's triumphant declaration.

"A world you want? Oh, sweet, tragic boy. The Collective spans the entire world. You know this. We hold magic in check. We dictate law. We create policy. Granted, the shifts in this region have weakened mage authority to offer Mythics elevated voices. A sign of complacency which does no one any good."

"You act like you know everything," Ian snapped. "I've been building alliances this entire time. I saw through your lies. I knew you treated me like a pawn, but I'm a goddamn king."

Admittedly, Ian had gone to great lengths and done his damnedest to ruin Alden's plans for his own agenda. A foolhardy one, most certainly.

"A king? Important, perhaps. Weak, unmistakably." Alden closed the distance, inching closer while lacing the gravel and debris with saturated mana. Quite the stealthy skill. If I hadn't been taking the opportunity to guzzle down as much stray mana in the area, I doubt I'd have caught it. "Your moves were rudimentary, Ian. Basic and barely five steps ahead. And since kings only move one space at a time, it was rather simple to figure out your rendezvous and eliminate any connections that might serve you."

"And yet, here I am," Ian bellowed. "Devil at my side. City in my grasp. World moments from enlightenment."

"Is that what you see? You have no Mythics. You have a bound devil. Artifacts you clearly can't control." Alden shook her head dismissively, in a shameful way I'd wager Walter had seen a thousand times. "You're impetuous, arrogant, entitled, and pathetic. Honestly, finding someone who checked off all those boxes and had some decency in casting without a strong connection was a challenge. Everything you've done since…this couldn't have gone better if I'd planned it."

"Shut up," Ian shouted.

"Truthfully, I accounted for just about everything you'd do. Even crushing on Walter and trying to find an excuse for him to leave, so I made certain Agatha's Heart needed cataloging."

I glared, seething with fury. She was vile.

"Beelzebub was a hiccup I didn't plan on. I will say, devil, you were a wild card I hadn't thought ahead on. Still, your purpose is proving quite beneficial. I can rid the world of this traitor and a Diabolic in one fell swoop."

"Kill her," Ian demanded. "Make it hurt."

I cracked my neck.

She wanted Walter dead. Her own son. She'd conspired and

planned for all of this, taking every precaution to ensure his life ended. Finally, Ian had delivered a command I'd gladly oblige.

I zipped ahead, claws drawn and channeling enough essence to rip through any defensive spells she might attempt. Her death was the last kindness I could offer Walter.

"W-Wal…" My throat tightened, burning and blistering when I attempted to speak.

Walter appeared from nothingness like stepping out of a shadow—it was he who'd conjured them, controlled them, and used them to grab the panacea and artificer chancellors in the midst of battle. How?

I widened my eyes, unable to form words. He swooped between me and his mother, snatching her away in a blink.

How'd he vanish so quickly? Teleportation required portals. Walter was far from strong enough to do that. No mage could. Not on their own. Where had he disappeared to? I needed to talk to him.

Warn him.

The woman he rescued, the one he called mother, had wanted him dead all this time.

27

Walter

Blood covered Bez. His bare torso. His soaked hair. His slick hands, so red it almost hid the black essence of his claws. The shock on his face when I grabbed my mother and disappeared. I clenched my jaw tightly. As much as I worried about him in this situation, I had to keep hoping he'd hold out until I returned.

Agatha's Heart had rooted itself deep inside Ian's desires, and he craved destruction—and while Bez might've hated the hold Ian had over him through Diabolic essence, I doubted the slaughter of so many at the Regiment Headquarters broke his spirits. He'd be fine. It could all be salvaged, too. I could stop Ian. Stop the Collective. The damage brought onto the city could be repaired. Order restored. First, I had to remove my mother.

She fought against my grip as we whipped through the shadowed webs constructed by Mora. Unlike me, her eyes hadn't adjusted to the infinite stretches of darkness in this dimensional void meant for instant transportation. Thankfully, Mora had offered me access—at a hell of a price, too. I'd gladly offer more for this opportunity.

I held my mother by her shoulders, struggling to navigate through this rollercoaster of hazy shadows. The dimensional threads in this void tingled, reaching out like pin prickles meant to guide my body. That made it difficult to navigate, as my body reacted faster than my mind could comprehend a single action.

We must've looped through the length of the city three times over before I recognized the fuzzy glints of light. Unlike a Diabolic, I couldn't shift direction as quickly or properly register everything around. Would've been simpler had Mora joined. She made it very clear this access was temporary, and since I'd planned on dragging other mages into her shadowy sanctum, she'd be tearing the entirety of it down soon to avoid the ire of whatever remnants of the Collective remained.

With any luck, everything would be intact. It all fell to a half-cocked plan I had absolutely no business following. If Alistair were here, he could do it. If I weren't facing someone as talented as Ian, maybe I could. If everything didn't fall to luck, timing, and a whole lot of fucking serendipitous chance, this might work out with Bez and I keeping our heads.

Burying my doubts, I anxiously circled through another layer of webs. Reaching high into the night sky, edging to the furthest point of this void, I pivoted, nearly scraping my back on the sharp shadows' stitching. My gut sank faster than we dropped. Looping between buildings, crossing streets, and barreling through people and cars as nothing more than dusty figments, I finally saw something I recognized.

"There," I shouted.

I pressed my heels firmly against the ground. If someone could call it that. It was slimy and sticky, gripping at the bottom of my shoes to hold us in place. Like everything in this void, it was black.

However, the threads of this web had a brighter sheen compared to the overall shadows of this world. Then again, the brief snippets of the city, while mostly shadowy silhouettes, did hold a grayish hue from the lights. Not that I could make much of it out. Bez's memories of Hell held more detail than this place.

Spinning around a familiar neighborhood four times, I thought I'd puke from the disorienting swirling at rocket speed if I did a fifth lap.

Squeezing my mother tightly, I leapt from the shadows and into the street. She tumbled on top of me, rolling a few times before breaking loose from my grip.

"Get your hands off me!" She stood, brushed away gravel clinging to her ripped jacket, and already half-composed herself in the time it took me to exhale. Her sour expression was darkened by the bright overhead streetlight behind her.

While I didn't like my mother and had found her to be the root of most of my problems and insecurities, I couldn't let her die. She was awful most of the time. Vile, really. But she wasn't evil. Plus, I wouldn't carry the guilt of allowing Bez or Ian to kill her when I had a plan. Something like that would eat away at me for the rest of my life, which I intended on being very long. Of course, it required me to find a way to save Bez from Ian, stop Ian from destroying the city, and avoid the Collective's wrath. No easy feats for my night.

"Where have you taken me?" She raised a hand, already saturating the area in search of nearby dimensional portals to bring her back to the Regiment Headquarters.

I'd dropped her off halfway across the city. It was the best way to ensure she didn't interfere with what came next. Honestly, I had to snatch up every chancellor during Bez's assault and throw them at the furthest corners of Seattle. Bez was too formidable for them. Or he wasn't. I didn't want to find out.

"You're wasting your time," I said.

Thanks to the skeleton key incantation I'd gotten from the grimoire Ian took, I was able to shut down the dimensional portals at the Regiment Headquarters, which meant none of the chancellors would be able to make a quick return. Besides, they'd already accused me of hacking the portal doorways, so I might as well live up to my crimes.

"What have you done? I cannot believe you've given your devil to that hedonistic heretic." She weaved incantations in the air, materializing a broom from dust and dirt in the area.

A flawless transmutation. Swept from the heat of battle, carried through a dimensional void, and thrown into unfamiliar territory. None of it made a difference. Mother rarely missed a beat. Hell, she even managed to toss in a jab blaming me. Guess it beat being scolded for my incompetence.

"To be clear, I didn't give Bez to Ian. He's not property."

"You nicknamed the Diabolic?" She shook her head, disgust in her scowl. "And you allowed it to be taken?"

There it was. I'd let her berate me for hours if it kept her here and away from the Regiment Headquarters, but I didn't have the time to be reprimanded for my shortcomings and reminded of my failures.

"I'm leaving." I backstepped. "Al's six blocks that way. Injured and in serious need of help."

"Alistair? Liar."

I didn't reply, instead focusing on calling out to Mora's essence in the temporal fold.

Alistair was gravely injured. Ian might've had to flee, but only after he stabbed Al in the stomach. His entire squad was half-dead when I found them, thanks to Mora's shadow webs. He shouldn't have been my first stop, but there was no way I'd stop all the bloodshed tonight, the carnage, the death. At the very least, I'd make sure Al wasn't among the casualties.

"You can follow me back to the Regiment Headquarters, or you can check on Alistair."

My sullen expression did the trick, ensuring my mother prioritized his wellbeing instead of the Collective or her position or...

She turned on her heel and flew in Al's direction.

Threads from the dimensional void instinctively reached out. A tingling sensation trailed down my spine, lightly coiling around my limbs. I trembled at the goosebumps. Here, the Diabolic essence held no tangible form, yet I felt it engulfing my entire body.

I'd already collected the other four chancellors, infiltration, artificer, archivist, and panacea. Driscoll was dead, and now Chancellor Alden was on her way to Al instead of directing sentinels. Hopefully, she'd stay put even when she realized I'd already brought Sarai to Al. Chancellor Russo's healing was the best help I could offer my brother and his squad. Besides, everyone at the headquarters had either died or fled at that point.

I leapt into the void. Shadows flung me across the city faster than I could follow. I'd bolted past the Regiment Headquarters before taking my first breath. How the hell did Diabolics navigate this whirlwind maze?

Steering myself back, I took a wide turn skirting over the brightly colored night ocean. Even here, the waters shimmered through the shadows, casting rainbows because of the powerful magics raging beneath the waves.

That was it.

I closed my eyes and sensed the surge of mana. Each weave and jerk whipped me into sticky threads which dragged against my body like skidding across a road. It stung, burning my skin. I ground my teeth, ignoring it, focusing on the most concentrated area of magic in the city. I could do this. I just needed to pinpoint and jump out at the right second.

I sprang out of the shadows and flew through a blaze of flames. Pushing ahead, I balled a fist.

Ian's smug face was the first thing I locked onto once I burst through the smoke and black fire scorching bodies. My body heated. A burning sensation warmed every cell before making its way to my chest and transforming into a powerful pit pumping alongside my heart. This wasn't the fire. It was rage. Fury. A frenzy of resentment I wanted to unleash.

"Ian!" Propelling toward him, I reeled back my fist. Saturation wasn't the most effective way to augment physical strength, but for the life of me, my mind blanked on the thousands of incantations I'd memorized. Any one of them would enhance my muscles and make for a staggering blow—assuming I could manage it.

I seethed with too much anger to weave a spell, so I circulated all the mana into my left fist, sending that pit of rage there, too, hoping it'd break Ian's fucking jaw.

Bez appeared in a blink at Ian's side. I gasped, almost crashing instead of punching. No time to be a fucking failure. I struck Ian, wincing at the loud crack of my knuckles and the jolting pain in the nerves of my broken finger. I should've used my right; no broken fingers. But I'd never really fought. Nothing outside of academy training and a futile scuffle against Bez. I needed to use my dominant hand.

Bez's cheek swelled momentarily to match the hit I'd successfully delivered. Ian fell back, tumbling over himself a few feet and cutting his face on debris. The light cuts on Bez's face indicated that much, though he healed instantly. Bez didn't budge; Diabolic strength kept him planted where he appeared. I trembled at his expression, devoid of his minxy smirk, eyes blank save for the menacing stare. Black veins covered his face and body, unlike anything I'd seen since he first possessed this body. I worried there wasn't enough of the Bez I came to know, to care for, to… How much of him remained intact beneath Ian's control?

Ian had hollowed Bez out, scooped away his personality, which made this all the more devastating. His joy. His wicked charm. All that remained was a dangerous and mightily powerful Diabolic who had conquered Hell and built a legend for himself in our world.

So much of Bez's Diabolic form cracked through the flesh of his host body. His horns, all four, had sprouted. They curled around like a ram, two large and twisting in four loops, and the second set identical in spirals but much smaller. His wings were fully unveiled, gray feathers falling away like stray hairs only to sizzle and create small explosive bursts when landing on the flames. I kept close attention on his drawn claws, ready to strike. The flick of his tails smashed and cracked earth into rubble.

I fell back into the shadows before Bez followed a command to attack. In an instant, I leapt behind Ian. Grabbing him by the collar of his shirt, I tried to yank him back into Mora's void world. He broke away, hurling a fireball at me. Drifting between the shadows, I spun around and tried to grab him again.

Ian swatted my hand away. "You really think you can take me? Not sure what artifact you snatched to pull off the disappearing act, but it doesn't compare."

Good. Ian had no understanding of the Diabolic temporal fold Mora had created. Bez still had access and could've easily jumped in after me, but hopefully wouldn't unless Ian explicitly commanded him to.

"Doesn't compare to what?" I asked, pulling Agatha's Heart from the shadows where I'd stored it.

Ian's eyes widened, raddled and fuming. The more I kept him off balance, the longer Bez would linger without commands until I dealt with Ian.

"How'd you...?"

"You should use better locks for important things," I gloated. "Thought you'd realize I'd taken it once that intense surge of mana faded. Too high on overconfidence, I suppose. This is why I always assume the worst. If you prepare for failure, you don't look like such a fool standing there wide-eyed and slack-jawed."

Honestly, he was so erratic, casting and attacking everyone indiscriminately, I could've slit his throat unseen. I settled for slipping the skeleton key enchantment into his pocket portal and stole back the artifacts.

"Give it back!"

"It's not really yours, though, is it?" I dropped it back into the void. "Not mine either."

And I had no intention of using it since I didn't want to end up as deranged as Ian. Taking Agatha's Heart had slowed his casting assault on Regiment Headquarters. The problem was, Ian still held a lot more proficiency in the Pentacles of Power than I did. I needed to end this quickly. I wouldn't stand a chance in a dragged-out face-to-face fight.

Sweeping in and out of Mora's network, I sprang from every direction faster than Ian registered. A few light punches and kicks helped disorient him. It wasn't enough to land a solid grip, though. Ian was a weaselly prick, slipping away whenever I tried to snatch him into the shadows.

"Hey." I swung a fist, dipping into the shadows before hitting Ian, then swept behind him.

As expected, he braced for the punch, and I grabbed his wrist from the opposite direction.

"Gotcha, bastard." I'd done it. I yanked him toward me, preparing to barrel through the void as far from Bez as the shadows would carry us.

"Stop him!"

Bez snatched my other arm by the wrist. The tight grip nearly broke the bone. He pulled me out of the shadows. I squeezed Ian's wrist hard, hoping to match the throbbing ache in my own arm.

"Get off me." Ian broke free, clutching his pained arm. "Release him."

Bez obeyed. He took heavy breaths, releasing steam with each exhale. His chest swelled in unison with Ian's as they both caught their breath. Breath Bez didn't need yet acted on instinct. *Maybe I was wrong about Bez being able to break free from commands on a technicality.* It didn't matter. My plan didn't involve Bez breaking free. It involved me freeing him, which would be a lot easier if he hadn't posted himself squarely between Ian and me.

"Now, detain Wally." Ian rubbed his wrist. "Nonviolently. I don't need to worry about you ripping off one of his limbs and ending up losing one in the process."

I backed into the shadows before Bez grabbed me. I muttered incantations, but my voice echoed through the void, sending the magic trailing away. *Shit.* Tracing a symbol on my hand, I fixated on the bright glow of mana and magic lighting the darkness.

This wouldn't hurt much but might slow Bez if properly coordinated.

"Come and get me," I shouted as I leapt from a shadow.

By the time Bez had turned, I'd fallen back into the fold and jumped out again behind him. I punched him in the back of the head with my right hand and thought I'd broken another finger. Hitting him was like punching concrete. I continued the surprise barrage attacks a half dozen times.

Seemed more clever in my head. Hit him fast and hard with incantations amplifying the punches and hiding in the void before he could counter, all while waiting for an opening to grab Ian.

All it actually did was annoy Bez and bruise my knuckles and deplete what little mana I had.

"Screw it." I reappeared across the street on the broken steps of the Regiment Headquarters.

It gave enough distance when luring Bez but only afforded me three breaths before he'd raced to me, claws ready to grab me. Back into the void, I continued luring Bez further and further from Ian. Each time I counted the number of breaths between transporting in the Diabolic void, stepping back onto the street, and how long it took Bez to reach me.

Once I'd drawn Bez as far as I could, I went back into the shadows and let them send me barreling toward Ian.

I zipped in close to Ian, almost grabbing him. Bez's claws glimmered in my peripheral. Dammit. He was too fast. I pivoted, backing away before he caught me. One of his claws nicked me, slicing my cheek. Nothing too bad. Ian pressed a hand to his own cheek, searching for a scratch that didn't exist, then turned his gaze to Bez's unmarred face.

"You dirty little liar." Ian dug his nails into his cheek until tiny scratches covered Bez's cheek. "No mercy. Won't be making that mistake again. Kill Walter Alden."

I reached into the shadows, retrieving the Demon's Demise. Ian's second artifact was going to help me release Bez, which I wanted to do as far from Bez as possible. No choice now. I stabbed Ian in the gut, twisting the blade. Crimson tendrils sprang from his stomach, whipping about the same way they'd done when he stabbed me in the chest. Ian dropped to his knees. But Bez shrugged off the injury, holding his stomach until his wound healed.

I backstepped toward the void. Bez darted forward, and I panicked as he dragged me out before the shadows and webs engulfed me. He threw me to the ground. I landed face-first in something awful; rot and charred flesh. I dug my fingers into dirt and ashes, pushing up. Bez kicked me in the spine, dropping me onto my stomach.

I clamped my jaw, biting back screams as he kicked me again.

"Harder," Ian panted the command. "Again, dog."

And Bez obeyed. Kicking me into the broken ground again and again. I couldn't speak. Breathe. Think. Everything hurt. I choked on gravel, burying my face in the debris.

"I said harder. Break his goddamn spine."

The kicks stopped. I tried to drag myself away but was so exhausted. Bez gurgled. Something cracked. Sounded like bones. It wasn't mine. I rolled onto my side, channeling mana for one last push of power. My glasses were cracked beyond repair and covered in soot. I took them off, calling out to the void.

Bez's blurry body contorted, neck twisting and limbs crackling as he resisted Ian's words.

"He can't control you."

Bez pulled back his arm, balling a shaky fist. He wanted to stop. I knew it. He fought the commands because they weren't accurate. Psychosomatic remnants to the actual effect of commands. Orders of obedience in Hell. Orders issued by me when we were linked.

"I saw it at the motel." I wheezed, taking shaky breaths. "You lied. Defied a command because—"

Bez dropped to his knees, grabbing me by the shirt and pulling me close. Our bloody lips were close enough to kiss, but it felt more like he'd rip my throat out with his sharp teeth. I squeezed the Demon's Demise. A dagger meant for killing Diabolics. It'd end Bez here and now. Probably kill Ian. Save me. Save the city. The Collective.

I dropped the blade.

"Kill him now, Beelzebub!" Ian trembled, voice cracking.

Bez held up his free arm, claws at the ready. Our eyes locked. The veins around his crimson eyes faded. The pinks in his eyes watered. His lip trembled, but he didn't—couldn't—speak.

"See. You're resisting. It's because these incantations are meant to compel and control the devil Beelzebub." I spit blood as I spoke, nodding to the bindings covering Bez.

Yes. Ian had Bez's Diabolic essence. Yes. He'd created a perverse contract to force obedience. But…

"But he doesn't know the first thing about the devil. He doesn't know the first thing about you, Bez."

Bez clutched my shirt, his hot breath and bloody lips nearly pressed against mine. Then…

Bez released me. He dropped me and climbed to his feet.

Diabolic essence raged out of him, and he roared. A ferocious shout that shattered all the active magic in the area. His wings flapped, creating a thundering black whirlwind. His three tails whipped about aimlessly. Not aimless. Defensive. Anytime a mage attempted to move in, they struck out. If an incantation or element targeted me or him, the tails blocked them with a crimson cloak.

Ian limped toward us, screaming. His commands fell silent. Either from the chaotic roar carried in the wind cast by Bez or because Bez knew the orders were hollow. The Diabolic link still existed between them, though. I couldn't risk Ian figuring that out until Bez had a chance to breathe. Ian was dangerous. Manipulative. Too intelligent not to discover another way to invoke commands from Bez. Even if he blurted something instinctively like I had, it'd cost me my life and Bez his freedom again.

"I'm going to kill you, mage." Bez glared at Ian.

"No, you're not." I forced myself up, standing in front of Bez, blocking his path. If Bez killed Ian, he'd die too.

"There's no other option, Walter." He shoved me aside.

"I've got another solution." I propelled myself forward with a gust of wind, nearly costing the last of my mana.

It worked, giving me a push ahead of Bez and knocking me into Ian. As I crashed into Ian, I wrapped an arm around the back of his neck. Holding him close to my chest and clutching the blade. With my other hand, I jabbed Ian in his stomach wound. He shouted. Bez stalled. Not long, but long enough for me to drag Ian into the void and finish this before Bez got himself killed.

Ian would pay for what he'd done.

Bez wouldn't. I refused to let him.

I'd fix this.

28

Beelzebub

I soaked in the freedom of the fading commands. One by one, the incantations fell. They peeled off my flesh like sunburnt skin, twinkling brightly as they crumbled to glitter among the ashes on the ground. Embers burned, holding the smallest hints of Ian's magic, kept alive by my Diabolic essence fueling them.

Sucking in a deep breath, I absorbed all my power and the lingering mana on a field of corpses. More potent mana stirred nearby. I grumbled. Mages regrouping. Took them long enough. The faint traces of their magic wouldn't outpower me. For whatever reason, the chancellors had fallen back. Their particular scents had vanished. Killing those who remained would be easy, but there was only one person I wanted dead.

I shook away the last vestiges of Ian's waning magic, allowing the incantations to disappear. He'd overexerted himself, lost his precious artifact, and now he needed to die. Somewhere out there, he held a piece of me and the potential to control my very breathing if demanded. I wouldn't allow it again.

Walter had stolen him. Swept him away. For what purpose, I could only guess. Likely some absurd need for justice. He'd want everything to end so ridiculously delightful. Wait out my essence inside Ian's body. Return him to the Collective for a proper trial. Send me on my way because he pitied my past. Some basic pathetic bullshit I wouldn't allow. Ian would die for what he'd done. What he did to me. Mostly, what he'd done to Walter.

I slipped into Mora's Diabolic web of instant transportation, half expecting her to dwell within. Nothing. Her most recent perfume didn't hit. She hadn't been here in some time, which meant I was right. Some bold move on her part to throw a mage into her laced essence and offer him access to her temporal fold without any understanding of how it worked. Then again, it was Walter. He'd mastered this terrain quite quickly. At least in appearance, he knew the basics.

Kneeling over, I plucked the webs. Each flick of my claw sent a musical melody through this void. It'd help me trail Walter's movements and find him in an instant. No matter how quick a study he was, he'd never grasp the complexities of a Diabolic temporal fold. His path would be easy to follow.

"Son of a bitch." I huffed.

Orange musical notes, the color of Walter's aura, radiated like little stamps all over. He'd gone everywhere in the city with this temporal fold like he was sightseeing or some shit. I continued plucking the webs, uprooting other musical melodies searching for Ian's notes.

"Are you joking?" I furrowed my brow.

A half dozen other colors, representing mages Walter had dragged in here, trailed off in various directions. It'd be impossible to know which one was Ian since memorizing mana auras wasn't a fucking hobby of mine. Where had Walter taken him? How many mages had he dragged in here? And why had he run laps around every inch of this place ten times over?

A deep gash opened below my ribcage. I hissed. Pressing a bloody hand to the wound, I waited until it healed. Light cuts appeared one after another along my stomach, each a shallow slice that healed as quickly as they'd struck. Walter was doing this. It meant Ian fought back against him from wherever they'd landed. Walter aimed for more superficial cuts because he didn't want to kill Ian. But that deranged mage would have no problem killing Walter.

I wouldn't allow that.

Closing my eyes, I zipped through the void along thin webs. I followed each path, weaving crisscrossed circles in search of the tug which connected Ian and myself.

Now that his commands had faded, his obnoxious presence became impossible to feel. Mora had mentioned slack and the sensation. Attaching a connection to Walter had happened inadvertently. It wasn't like I meant to tighten the tether pulling us closer.

Okay. I meant to but didn't realize I meant to. Subconscious curiosity, or however Walter and Mora would mockingly phrase it.

No matter how much I told myself I wanted to find Ian, to tighten the bond connecting us, every thought twisted into an image of Walter. His bloody, impaled chest as I clutched him the night he'd nearly died. I clamped my jaw, furious I'd allowed him to be taken from my grasp and brought to such harm. His primal expression as he'd kissed me, demanded satisfaction. The passing image of his seductive face elicited carnal desires all over again. His curious eyes as he studied my past. It almost brought a smile because there was no judgment in his gaze, in his questions, in his observations.

I frowned, drawn to the memory of his broken face as I beat him in the motel room. But he even turned my failure into a success—his success in the way he fought against Ian and myself amid a field of carnage. His face was brave beyond belief. Everything about Walter consumed my every waking thought.

I had to find him. Apologize. Protect him. End the threat of a murderous misfit mage.

Ian's presence swelled, angry and pained. An instinctual fight for survival fueled me with adrenaline. I burst from the void and chased the tether. Not to live. Ian was feral and would do anything to escape, which wouldn't happen.

Flapping my wings, I soared swiftly in the direction my heart pulled me.

A deep searing pain dug into my stomach, rooting around my insides, carving almost methodically. I could feel the way a blade sliced around my organs. Around Ian's. Nothing which would severely impair me or him. Light nicks followed. I flew faster, desperately, as the link faded.

It was still there, a light, slow-moving pulse, so I chased the rhythmic sensation because I had to reach Ian and rescue Walter. The entire flight, my insides were ripped and torn apart. I winced from the deep incisions around my ribcage, followed by swift slices along the outside of my heart muscles. A sharp stabbing sensation ran through my chest, pressing against my lung and wriggling.

It took everything I had to ignore it and fly faster. If Walter was dying, he put up a hell of a fight. Literally. I'd seen demons dish out less damage before being overwhelmed.

If Walter was overpowered, harmed beyond repair, I might not be able to resist Ian's next command. My throat tightened, a heavy pressure weighing on my Adam's apple.

What if Walter was already dead?

The streets grew darker—fewer streetlights, fewer mortal homes illuminated. It was an isolated location. Only the moon and stars lit this desolate area. I turned the corner of an abandoned building and found Walter and Ian entangled in combat outside.

Hovering above them, I raised a brow at the perplexing sight.

Walter straddled Ian while holding a bloody blade. He kept a hand firmly pressed to Ian's throat. Crimson tendrils thrashed between the pair. Eight shoestring thin threads of essence attempting to repair the damage dealt from that Diabolic killing artifact.

What was happening? Walter was bloody and bruised, clutching the hilt with the same hand I'd broken a finger of. There was no essence inside him, not that I thought Mora would offer any, but his arm had healed. The lengths he'd gone and skills he'd accomplished were a sight unlike any other. Pure determination, unfettered by anxiety. Even now as he sat on Ian's hips, his body pained, he didn't tremble. His hands were steady, his breathing calm. The way Ian quaked beneath him and Walter's eyes followed the tendrils, it was like watching a viper. Beautiful and deadly. Violent and vicious, but only when provoked.

"Do you know why it's called the Demon's Demise?" Walter asked, carrying a wicked lilt in his whisper. "You were right about the name being silly."

My body trembled at the way his words slithered into my eardrums. This wasn't an effect of the essence linking me to Ian. No. The wisps of essence which remained fervently fought off Walter— unsuccessfully at that.

"But you were wrong about its use." Walter sliced two tendrils, wrapping them around the blade like noodles on a utensil. I expected him to lap them up, heal his injuries, and reunite our bodies.

Instead, he delicately dropped them next to him onto a pile of my discarded essence. Blood and essence pooled together in a tight, spongy ball.

"You see, this particular blade is curved almost for scooping." He giggled to himself as he dug the tip into Ian's exposed, bloody stomach. He plucked another tendril and continued his lecture. Oh, how he loved to share his wealth of knowledge. "The Mythics which created it likely believed it could be used to remove Diabolic essence—which is true, as we can both see—but it was ceremonial. Meant to reverse possessions. You don't know much about that. Don't feel bad. Neither did I. Turns out, once a Diabolic possesses a host, there's not really anything to salvage. These models were quickly discarded, considered incapable of undoing possessions."

Ian's eyes locked onto mine. Frantic and frightened. "Beelzebub, I demand you s—"

Walter pressed the blade inside Ian's mouth.

Blood gushed from my mouth, and the tip of the knife stabbed into Ian, slit my tongue in half. I smiled, licking the blood on my lips as my tongue healed and Ian's remained forked.

"What's the matter?" Walter grinned. "Devil got your tongue?" He laughed. The freest sound I'd ever heard come from Walter. It radiated around him, casting waves of devilish delight which sent a shudder through every cell of my body—a truly intoxicating sensation I wanted to savor.

I descended, yet he kept his wide eyes locked on Ian. "What are you doing, Walter?"

"Freeing you." He plucked the final strings which linked me to that bastard beneath him. "I wanted to fix this my way."

"Your way is quite unexpected." I approached, kneeling in front of him. "Have you accessed that witch artifact? You mentioned complications with the effects on the mind."

He shook his head. "This is all me."

"You certain?" I brushed away the damp curls that clung to his forehead.

"Yes." Walter pressed the tip of the blade just below Ian's left eye, settling the mage who'd begun to squirm as we spoke. Perhaps he deluded himself into thinking it an opportune time to plan his escape. "Besides, I don't have Agatha's Heart."

"What happened to it?"

"Mora wanted it as a fair exchange of goods and services. Better in the hands of a witch anyway. She said it belonged to Kell's coven."

Of course, Mora used this dire situation to acquire a gift of power for her beloved. Mora was so annoyingly selfish.

Walter nicked Ian's cheek. My cheek twitched, instinctually bracing for the cut as Ian yelped.

"Just wanted to double-check." Walter leaned over, kissing my unblemished cheek. "Couldn't risk your well-being for what comes next."

He licked his lips, cherishing the taste of my skin. Gods. How seductive and destructive he looked under the moon's light, blade in hand, blood covering him, and straddling Ian's half-conscious soon-to-be corpse.

"You don't need to do this, Wally."

He paused, half-smiling. "I want to."

What came next was required. I'd never let Ian walk away. But taking a life, a mortal one… "This is a permanent change. Let me handle ending this mage's life."

"I understand that. And I doubt I could enjoy taking lives the same way as you. There are too many variables and reasons and calculations and considerations to take into account. Still, I want this. Everything he did to me. The lives he took at the Magus Estate. The lives he manipulated."

"I've done worse."

"You've also done better." Wally tilted his head. "This isn't about morality. It's simple revenge. What he did to you was cruel, and I could never allow something like that to happen without a response."

Wally. Sweet, considerate Wally wished to avenge what he considered wrongdoing?

I extended a hand, ready to grab the hilt of his blade. "Are you sure?"

"Absolutely." He had a calm sincerity I never thought possible.

"I feel free. Happy. Glad you're safe. But mostly angry, which I don't like."

I smirked. "You're cute when you're mad."

"I don't like it." He lifted the blade, ready to end Ian's worthless life.

I moved in close behind Wally, straddling Ian's thighs as he trembled beneath us, and pressed my chest against Wally's back. Despite the shaky mage, Wally kept his posture straight and position steady. I guided his wrist, bringing the blade to his palm.

"What are you doing?" he asked.

I cut open his palm and pressed the same hand which accidentally connected us in the beginning to my essence pooled beside us.

"Stop. I don't want to control you."

"You won't. I trust you." I kissed his nape.

"I don't want my mistakes to cost you again." He shivered, biting his lower lip. "I love you, Bez."

"Nothing you do is a mistake." My heart pounded rhythmically with his, safely indicating my essence was once more bound to him, ensuring I'd always be able to protect him. "Besides, I'm happier knowing a piece of me is inside you."

"There's a joke there."

"There are no jokes in how I feel for you, Wally." I brought his face closer and kissed him. My lips burned from the abrasions and cuts we shared linked together. The taste of iron from trickling blood added to the sweetness of his lips, the passion in his tongue, the bite of his teeth. Every sensation hollowed me, refueled me, completed me. "I love you, too."

His ears burned bright red.

"Shall we begin?" I whispered.

The heat of my breath hit his ear, and our skin tingled in sync with each other. Wally slowly slid the blade down Ian's face, who winced from the cool blade, shuddering beneath us as the blade reached the tender flesh of his stomach. He sputtered something incomprehensible due to his slashed tongue.

Wally pushed back against me, the essence inside him pulling at my every fiber gently yet demanding. It craved my control and satisfaction.

"Let me." I wrapped my hand around Wally's, guiding it up Ian's quivering body and resting the tip of the blade a hair below the tough bone of the sternum.

I probably should've thanked Ian for his nefarious plot. It brought Wally and I together. Had this meddling mage not attempted to slaughter the entire Collective of Seattle, I doubted I'd have the fortune of truly crossing paths with Wally and having him in my life.

Instead, I led Wally's hand forward, cutting deep into Ian's chest and puncturing his heart in one swift, fluid motion. His breathing wheezed as his chest tightened; the life left the mage's eyes.

We ended Ian's life. While I would've most certainly preferred extending the mage's death, dragging it out for days or weeks—years—I considered myself content in this momentous moment with Wally, one I'd relish forever.

Forever with him, if he allowed it.

29

Walter

I buzzed with a euphoric pleasure wrapped in Bez's warm embrace. He kept his firm biceps tightly wrapped across my chest and stomach, my back pressed against him, and his tails holding my legs at length with his during the flight. I lost myself in his comfort, but there was so much to consider as we flew back to the motel, so much more than what I'd just done.

Bez wanted to escape the city, which would be wise, but I had affairs to settle. I wanted us to lay low until we could resolve things with the Collective and leave Seattle once and for all. I needed to check on my familiar. Needed to visit Al. Needed to resolve the last remnants of Ian's treachery and all the fallout tied to it, from stolen artifacts to dead mages all the way to a treacherous chancellor. I couldn't resign myself to think about Ian.

Ian.

It was strange how I didn't dwell on it. Not really. Guilt didn't consume me like I'd expected. I prepared for it, anticipated it, and weighed the outcomes of living with the guilt of killing him, but I knew full-well in the end that I couldn't allow him to walk away after everything he'd done. Where I expected remorse to strike, I only found a calm clarity as we soared through the night sky. It was peaceful, taking in the crisp night air as we zipped by the illuminated city. A part of me knew I should've let him go into the Collective's custody, let them dole out their punishment which, given everything he'd caused, would've surely been death. I couldn't, though. Not after what he did to Bez.

My Bez.

"Where's your head?" Bez asked as we descended to the motel, landing in front of our room door.

"Nowhere," I said, immediately rushing inside and checking on my recovering familiar. He'd need a name. A name befitting an emperor scorpion, a friend, a protector who'd helped me when I was at my most desperate.

"That little beehive of a mind is swirling; I can see it in your eyes."

"It's nothing." I adjusted my heavy shirt, sticky with sweat, grime, and blood. My blood. Ian's blood. "Do you think I'm a bad person?"

"The absolute worst. Never in my long existence have I met one as bad as you." Bez grinned; the soot and blood on his face didn't take away from the cute curl in his lips or the minxy mischief in his eyes.

"This is serious," I said. "You don't think I'm going to start killing people regularly, do you? Because that wasn't my intention. I'm not like a sociopath or anything. Although, I suppose if I were, I would say I wasn't, right? But I'm not. Someone doesn't just wake up a murderous sociopath. It doesn't work that way." I bit my lip, wondering if I'd need to read up on this, what the healthy reaction to murder was, if such a thing existed. "What if there's some subtle allure to murder, which creates an addiction, and I've gone and—"

Bez stepped in close, a single clawed finger lifted as if to tell me to hush both in words and my squirrely mind. His bare muscles were covered in as much filth as my tattered shirt. "I assure you, you're the furthest thing from a cold-blooded killer."

"And I'm not okay with you killing indiscriminately either. Just want to throw that out there. I'm not saying sometimes your reasons aren't justified…hmm, wrong word. Valid? No. I don't want to endorse killing. It's just—"

Bez chuckled, rubbing his hands up and down my arms. "I rarely slaughter without cause. Though, my whims may occasionally be fickle." He paused, inspecting my face, which had scrunched. "But I'm a work in progress. Moving forward, I'll be more discerning with my kills."

"Or maybe not kill people moving forward."

"Might as well ask the sun not to shine, Walter."

"I'm serious," I said. "You act all nonchalant about brutality and murder and violence in general, and honestly, there's probably some cathartic pleasure that comes with that, but I don't want my base nature to be murderous or yours. I know you're more than the devil who delights in destruction the world paints you as."

"I don't take joy in murder. I take satisfaction in it. Carnage and agony were all I knew in Hell. Pain and death were the first things I was graciously introduced to when I arrived in this world."

I tensed, arms flexing in Bez's hold. He hadn't shared what happened to him when he first arrived in our world, but I knew there must've been some devastation behind it, as with so much in his sordid past. I didn't want that for him anymore. No more pain, no judgment, no closing himself off from others. All I wanted to give him was what he deserved—which was everything.

"If you desire me to be more discreet and display more reservations when handling obstacles, I will." Bez ran a hand up my arm, rested it momentarily against my shoulder, and then raised my chin until our eyes met. I lost myself in his gaze; crimson irises illuminated the beautiful pinks of his eyes. "But know this, Wally, I will never let harm come to you. If someone threatens you, I will end them. If someone wrongs you, I will end them. If someone hurts you, I will savor their death because you mean the world to me."

I kissed him, incapable of holding back a second longer. A salty, metallic taste hit as our lips smacked, mixed with dirt, but I didn't care. I wanted the taste of *him*, to tell him a thousand things, but mostly to feel him.

I pulled away, pressing my forehead against his. "There are still things I need to do, prepare for, finish."

Bez frowned. A silly little pouty face of disappointment.

"Maybe we could take this into the shower," I said. "I'm in desperate need of one."

Bez gripped my wrists, holding me in place. "I like your scent as is."

"I'm filthy."

"Yes, you are." Bez licked my neck.

"Shower, Bez."

He nibbled on my sticky, sweaty skin until I moaned.

Dammit.

I found myself unbuttoning his pants as he ripped my tattered shirt off, his aggressive hands running over my entire body as we kissed, consumed in a fiery passion. He ran his fingers through my hair, pushing me down to my knees, which I gladly obeyed. My body tingled from his slightest touch. I was his, however he wanted me, whenever he wanted me, for as long as he wanted me.

The two of us covered in blood and sweat and grime, exhausted from a battle at the Regiment Headquarters—none of it mattered. There was only this primal desire to satisfy him.

Bez immediately thrusted his hips, demanding I get to work, which I eagerly obliged. When I gagged, he slowed so my throat could adjust to the entirety of his cock. Not an easy feat. My eyes watered, but I continued, throbbing with every muffled grunt Bez released. As I choked, Bez attempted to backstep, but I didn't allow it, wrapping my hands at the back of his hips and squeezing his firm butt, keeping him planted so I could please him and feel the pure gratification in his pleasure.

"Off." Bez stared down, fully erect and rubbing the tip against my lips teasingly.

Before I could say a thing, he'd dropped to his knees in a blur and taken off my jeans, flipping me onto my stomach.

Pinned to the carpeted floor, I arched my back as Bez kissed my shoulder blades. He fish hooked his fingers in my mouth, and I sucked on them. Slowly, he worked his way down the column of my spine, kissing each vertebrae with tenderness. With a gentle suddenness, he removed his fingers from my mouth and smacked my butt with a spit-covered hand, then licked lower and lower until I quivered, practically convulsing from his hungry and keen tongue work.

Bez pressed his knuckles to my lower back, remaining wordless behind me, but his demands rang clear. I arched further, allowing his hands to guide me as he entered me. I whimpered when the head pushed through, and he took slow, steady strokes until I adjusted to the length of his shaft.

I lay my head on the carpet, taking jagged, irregular breaths as he pounded harder, running his clawed hands up and down my back. When I panted between moans, he rested his hands on my rising shoulders, massaging them while holding me in place.

My cock had pulsated with every thrust of his hips. Not sure if it was because of how precisely each stroke hit or if the essence coursing between us created this masterful dual sensation. It amplified every nerve ending in my body. Our bodies.

Bez fucked me for hours in the motel room. On the floor. In the shower. The bed. The floor again. Against the paper-thin walls.

He threw me into position after position to further satisfy his cravings. On my back so he could kiss me and bite me with each stroke. Pinned and standing so my tired muscles would beg for his completion. Riding him so he could run his hands over my sweaty body while I commanded the pace with the thrust of my hips.

Days blurred, and we barely slept as he drove his cock into me nearly every waking hour. However, he did hold back slightly. I hadn't noticed it at first, but the longer I focused on the essence inside me, the more I understood the essence coursing through him. Perhaps he was concerned I couldn't handle his Diabolic nature. I very much intended to prove I could, but as the days drew further, I had to pull myself away.

Truthfully, I could lie next to him forever, satisfying his insatiable stamina.

But I needed to ensure things properly unfolded after the fallout of Ian's attack, so I slid off the bed and threw on an outfit then returned to my notes.

"Toss them in a suitcase. We can sort it all later," Bez said, remaining sprawled across the mattress. "After we leave."

"Can't go just yet."

"Mm." Bez tickled the back of my ear with a tail, teasing and sensual. "Craving me again, already? Vixen."

"No." My ears burned, and I swatted his tail away. "Not even close."

"Your body would disagree." His gaze rested on my erection where all the blood flow seemed to travel, but I very much needed that flow to go to a different head so I could focus.

"I have to finish things."

"What's there to finish? The misfit's dead, the Collective is scrambling, we're both alive and well. I say we leave before the chancellors have time to launch a futile strike, and I'm forced to kill what remains of their regiments."

"Bez," I whined.

"Kidding," he said with a flirty smirk but the crinkle in his brow suggested he would very much slaughter the lot of them if they made a counterassault against us.

"I need to check on Alistair, see that he's recovering, and then there's my mother." I bit my lip.

"She's vile. Horrid. Skillful yet sadistic. Under different circumstances I'd admire such tenacity." Bez huffed, then hesitated. His expression softened, losing its natural minxy charm. "I digress. But you should know…" His shoulders slumped and his eyes drifted anywhere except for on me. After a long pause, he sat up and straightened. "She's the reason—"

"I know."

"What? How? When?"

"Since we got the grimoire." I rocked my head, contemplating the specifics. "Well, not exactly. More like a few days into evaluating the contents. I wanted to sort out a plan before getting into all the sordid details, which is why I sent you to retrieve those spell items. But then we were attacked here in the motel, and everything just sort of got complicated."

"An understatement." Bez shifted, scooting to the edge of the bed where he pulled me into his arms. "What are you planning?"

"I'll tell you everything because it's actually a really cool plan. But also, I sort of need your help with part of it."

I explained it all to Bez, watching his eyes gloss over my more detailed portions since he obviously didn't find the intricacies of my plan as fascinating as I did, but he didn't protest them—much. Once we'd set everything in motion, I left the motel and buzzed the entire trip through the city. Though, that might've had more to do with the lust fueled by Bez, and not the magics I balanced in my core.

I returned to the Regiment Headquarters. The excitement twisted and turned into dread once I stepped through the doors. I lingered in the foyer, wishing I'd stayed in bed with Bez. Burying my thoughts of him, I sat with the anxiety this place gave me.

News of Alistair's recovery was on everyone's lips, then quickly turned quiet once I stepped inside. All eyes landed on me, whispers abundant, yet not one person spoke directly to me. There was so much I needed to do before bidding farewell to the Collective and Seattle. Seeing Alistair was at the top of my list, but it wouldn't be easy considering all the sentinel security posted during his recovery. Then again, I managed to walk in here without alerting suspicion. I gulped. So far.

A week had hardly settled the dust, but everything had mostly calmed in the city since Ian's death. Mages worked to glamour exposures, removing memories and footage of the carnage. The chancellors followed the trail to Ian's body and uncovered details in his home connecting him to other Mythics and mages involved in the attack on the Magus Estate. Most of them turned up dead, too. Guess Ian's partner didn't want any loose ends, which didn't bode well for me as a very much alive loose end.

It was business as usual for a lot of mages who rushed past me with not so much as a second glance. I made my way to the Sentinel Chancellor's office because she needed to be dealt with before I permanently walked away from the Collective. Not that I expected them to take me back with open arms. My name might've been cleared of conspiracy, but they'd definitely consider me a threat if they learned I continued my Diabolic bond with Bez.

Diabolic bond. I needed a better name than that. What we had went far beyond a simple bond, an exchange of power or connection.

I paused at the door leading to my mother's office. Was I really about to do this? Her actions more than warranted it and if left unchecked, who knew the horrors she'd bring down on the Collective to achieve her goals. Still…

Releasing a breath and as much trepidation as humanly possible, I stepped inside. Before I could form a word, my mother stepped from her desk and took strong strides to reach me. She wrapped her arms around me, squeezing tightly. I nearly collapsed in her embrace. She hadn't hugged me like this since I was six. No. Five and eight months. I remembered it. Counting down and crossing off the days, thinking it meant she'd buy me that archivist toolkit I wanted so badly for my birthday. She didn't, though. Said it was a waste of time. When I cried, she blew out my candles and said wishes were for the weak.

Now, I let all that wash away. Years of resentment. Years of rage. Hate. Longing for the same affection my siblings got. Whether it was because she loved them more or they simply fell in line with her expectations better. That wasn't it. I guessed this hug was what I needed after so many years of waiting for her approval. Sort of the perfect goodbye.

"I'm so happy to see you've fully recovered." She released me, and I lingered in the calm her kindness had left me with. "Chancellor Russo made your injuries sound more dire, as usual. Incompetent girl knows so little considering her title."

"There were some severe breaks."

"Please, that rat bastard, low-bred, social climber, misfit could never beat you. Remember that." She caressed my face in a way I'd seen her do to Alistair a thousand times yet never once felt myself. It was pleasant, awkwardly comforting. A bizarre show of affection I'd never understood before. Made me almost regret why I'd come here.

"It's good you're here, though," she said. "The Collective will be sending representatives from other regions to inspect our standing. They're going to look for any chinks in the armor. I need your charm to ensure they don't."

"I'm sure whoever they're sending won't be swayed by a little charm."

"Please, Alistair." She patted my shoulder comfortingly, believing it to be my brother's. "You'll have them wrapped around your finger."

I gave a weak smile, attempting my brother's softest, most charming smirk. No way could I pull off his big, full smile of confidence; I'd need more than a glamour for that. Still, she hadn't seen through the illusion, which meant my casting had improved tremendously.

"Are you okay, sweetheart?" She eyed my shaky cheeks.

"Yeah. Just not feeling a hundred percent."

"Of course." She stepped away, making her way back to her desk chair. "I'll give you talking points to stick with, keep their attention away from Diabolic discussions and more on misfits and Mythics."

Something I was grateful for, given that I didn't need Collective oversight finding trails on Bez.

"We'll have to find that devil," she said.

"Pretty sure he's dead, considering how the mage controlling him turned up." I made a crude dead expression with my tongue sticking out. It was the closest thing I could picture Al doing.

"No. Ian is dead. Autopsy shows he was carved up by a fucking de-possession blade."

Ugh. One, I should've burned the body. Two, Demon's Demise. How hard of a name was that to remember? Whatever.

"And your brother's out there with it."

"The blade?" I shrugged. "Unlikely."

"No. That devil. It's very probable. Knowing him, he's plotting. Planning something against us."

"Why would he be planning something against us?" I attempted to laugh it off.

She wasn't wrong. I was plotting against her. Keyword—*her*. Not

Al. Not my sisters. Not the other chancellors or any mage in the regiments. Just her.

"I know you love Walter, but he's always had his issues. His selfish needs. This drive to put himself ahead of family at every turn."

I ground my teeth. Selfish. Forcing a smile, I nodded, still seeking her awful approval. "I doubt he's plotting anything. What would he even do?"

"Bring that devil down upon us, for starters. No. I've been trying divination around the clock with practitioners, but that Diabolic energy makes it difficult to pinpoint."

I huffed. That explained how Bez and I avoided tracking for as long as we did.

"Maybe Walter's out of range." I shrugged. Divination only ever worked within a few miles, and that span lessened based on experience.

"No." She squinted, tilting her head. There was a long silence between us, and then my mother pursed her lips and continued, "There's Diabolic essence circulating the city. A lesser mage wouldn't note it, but I feel his presence. The devil's presence. We have to act before he brings ruin to everyone."

Congratulations. I bit my lip. She'd figured out there was Diabolic essence lingering throughout the city. I should tell Mora her concerns about being noticed weren't unwarranted. Pretty certain she was dismantling her void as we spoke.

"You can't actually think he'd come for us," I said.

"I do." Her expression darkened, affection in her eyes lost, and the typical hardened stare emerged. "I worry he'll attempt something sinister. Try to kill me. You. Others. With Agatha's Heart and a devil at his beck and call, he could do more damage than Ian ever attempted."

I couldn't believe she'd think I'd actually kill her. Sure, I'd come here, guised as Al, attempting to put an end to her threats. She fully deserved that. But kill her?

"He wouldn't kill you. He has no reason."

"Walter doesn't need a reason. He's got insurmountable resources, and he's crafty. A dangerous combination."

Impressive she'd considered me such a threat. A bigger threat than Ian. What could she possibly think I wanted? She was probably concerned Bez told me of her involvement, which he had. But like I'd explained to Bez, I'd pieced together her involvement while analyzing the grimoire we acquired which was intended to frame Chancellor Driscoll. Something I planned on telling him sooner, but then Ian kicked in the motel door and… I balled my fists, squeezing them tight until Ian's memory faded. The intricate detail put in place to set up the vanguard for a coup would've worked too. It almost did. Anyone else would've missed the subtle markers of sentinel sabotage.

It was practically missed by me.

"What would Walter even want?" I asked, wondering if she'd confide the truth to Al. She trusted him so much more than me, than anyone, but even he didn't see behind all the masks she wore, creating the Alden façade.

"I think he'd…" She paused. Silence stirred until she filled it with a slow applause. "You've gotten better, Walter."

"Excuse me?" My heart hitched.

"Walter. Walter, Walter, Walter." She stood, hands firmly planted on her desk, already saturating everything in her office, claiming this space and fueling her magic to attack. "I can't believe I didn't see it sooner."

"Fuck." I grimaced. "Al calls me Wally. Everyone, really. Except you. And Bez. Fucking Bez. He threw off my mojo. This would've worked if it hadn't been the name thing, right?"

"Nothing you do works." Her face scrunched, eyes almost

breaking contact to investigate the mild pain that had hit her hand. Instead, she swatted the air, keeping her glare trained on me.

"Well, that worked." I approached, delicately walking my fingers along her desk until they reached her hands.

Only then did she break eye contact and look at the pinprick on the back of her hand. A tiny, red bump.

"Don't worry. Less lethal than a bee sting. Despite the name, emperor scorpions aren't the monarchs of destruction humans are." The scorpion that'd saved my life crawled onto my hand and up my arm as the saturated cloak fell away. "They're quite docile, friendly even in a quiet way. Perfect balance for Bez since he's so loud."

"How dare you." My mother balled a fist. Weapons lining the walls of her office rattled.

"The first thing I learned becoming an archivist was to investigate without assumptions. Never delve into your research believing you already have the answer."

"What have you done to me?" she asked, realizing the incantations secured around her office waned, not registering or attaching to her mana.

"I almost made that mistake when analyzing the grimoire found on Vanguard Corvine," I explained, ignoring her question. "You see, Al believed it was connected to proof about Chancellor Driscoll's involvement, and I believed Al. I suppose *acting* Magus Driscoll since he died before the ink dried and all that. Point is, it filled a preconceived idea and connected dots in the weirdest way."

She rushed to the wall, grabbing the first weapon she could pry off a mounted display. I flicked my wrist, accessing the telekinesis embedded in the essence offered to me by Bez. The axe flew from my mother's hands and into a neighboring wall.

"Once I threw out my preconceived notions, the pieces fit together so much better," I continued, more for myself than her. As per usual, she'd rather see me dead than listen to what I had to say.

This was a pretty triumphant moment, and she didn't care. Bez didn't either. He didn't even listen when I explained the intricacies of my plan, claiming killing her would be easier.

"The grimoire was too perfectly connected to Driscoll. A fake enemy you allowed to rise above you as acting Magus so you could lay the blame at his feet. If anyone other than me had gotten their hands on the grimoire, I doubt they'd have made the connections. Yes. It belonged to an elite vanguard mage. Yes. It had the fine binding craftsmanship of the artificer regiment. Yes. It held access to the Nexus Grimoire, something only an archivist should have. And all those keys and codes pointed to the secrecy of the infiltration regiment. If I'd had a few more days, I'd probably have found a link to the panacea regiment, too."

She seethed with rage, refusing to acknowledge a single word I'd uttered. Her eyes scanned me, searching for incantations or tech meant to record her complicit actions. As if I'd be so pedestrian.

"Chancellor Victoria Alden always taught us as children in order to be the best defenders, it's important for sentinels to know how all regiments work." I smiled. "Your way of guiding us to protect the Collective from outside threats and those within."

Her obsession with awe-inspired names for her children came from her own name, given to her by her grandfather, a tradition from his father before him and down many generations of powerful Alden's dating back to the founding of the Collective.

Victoria meant victory, something she believed fated to her at every encounter.

Victory didn't lie in her future anymore. She held her hands close together, creating the tiniest spark of lightning. An attempt almost as tragic as every practitioner exam I'd shown up to.

"It won't work. I've stunned your mana."

She glared.

"It's temporary." I shrugged, treating this complex siphon of her magic like a trivial casting when in actuality, it required all five Pentacles of Power. First, I needed the Mythic toxin from the glands of a basilisk. Another request from Mora and a debt I was certain she'd collect one day. I had to channel water through it to funnel away the deadliest aspects, then use incantations to alter the numbing agents to specifically target the nerve receivers which channeled mana. After that, I needed a familiar to administer the toxin, which I had to calmly saturate, and finally glamour to sneak inside.

It was a really amazing process. She wouldn't want to hear it. Bez rolled his eyes the entire time I explained my plan, claiming that it was too many steps. Sure, killing her would've been quicker, but I wanted her to live with this. Feel how her ego and ambition destroyed a legacy she claimed I was never fit to inherit.

"You should get used to not having access to your magic. Trust me, it sucks." I snickered at the reversal of fortunes in our casting. "Once Chancellor Russo sifts through the evidence I've provided and finds the long list of stolen items from the archives in your home, I'm sure the other chancellors will have you brought before the Collective to properly bind your magic or simply lock you away in some dungeon for the rest of your days."

Both truly abhorrent acts, each kinder than what she'd planned for me.

My mother threw things from her desk, hurling items and profanities at me in equal measure. I left her, taking my final leave from the Regiment Headquarters, the Collective, and the Alden legacy.

Once outside, I hopped on a broom someone had left unattended. Saturating the sigils with my mana, I levitated high above the streets, cloaking my presence with a glamour. I soared freely through the city, allowing the wind to carry away my anxiety.

30

Beelzebub

Mora rummaged through the treasure of artifacts I'd brought from the Alden Manor, treating them like baubles. Wally wanted to allow the Collective to keep most as evidence to use against his mother. Killing her would've been quicker. Quieter too. Bet she wailed and cried at his spells. It was a sophisticated measure he'd developed to bind her casting. I listened to him prattle about it for hours, explaining the history of each step. How most had been lost or remained unknown since whoever didn't share whatever with whomever or something.

"So, I'm meant to discreetly unload all these trinkets on my own time?" Mora asked, feigning irritation—if she were really annoyed, she'd have simply avoided me.

"Yes. Think of it as a way to improve relations while you maintain a lower presence."

"Because your audacious arrival has put a spotlight on all things

Diabolic." She picked up some elven hand mirror, studying the fine craftsmanship while primping her hair. "I'm not just handing them out. I'll do my best to make a modest profit off this junk."

"I really don't care." I rolled my eyes as she delicately set the mirror back onto the table, being extra careful with the so-called *junk*.

The few things Wally sent me to pilfer from his family home were items he believed would end up lost in bureaucratic red tape for the better part of a century.

"All that matters is you pawn it off to Mythics, not mages," I said since that remained one of Wally's only stipulations.

"Fine. But your mage owes me."

"He owes you nothing." I zipped before her, flexing my muscles and glaring. "Consider yourself grateful I don't kill you for interfering just enough to steal Agatha's Kidney."

"It's a heart, Bezzy." She patted my chest, unthreatened.

"I hate you so much."

"Aw. I'll miss you, too."

"You survived fifty years without me," I scoffed. "You'll be fine when I'm gone."

She hooked her fingers into the loops of my pants, pulling my hips against hers. "So, you're really leaving the city for good?"

"I despise this place. Too big. Too rainy. Too loud. Plus, Wall…" I bit my tongue. "Ter is over it, so au revoir or some shit."

Mora ruffled my bangs, parting them. They'd become impossible since my horns burst through this balloon of a host. "Tu vas me manquer, mon diable préféré."

"I'm the only devil you like."

"Still my favorite." Mora released me, kissing each of my cheeks before sauntering into the kitchen. "Hope you return for my hundredth with Kell. I know, I should be planning my fifty-third, but that's done. I just love the celebrations of love. I'm already planning a smashing event for this year. Literally. I'm going to smash something into pieces. Currently undecided. Maybe that loud bitch in 3C. Seriously, I will break every one of his fingers if he strums 'Wake Me Up When September Ends' on his guitar one more time."

"Fine. I'll attend your trivial anniversaries so long as you attend mine." I swallowed hard like it'd bury the words I'd blurted.

"Oh? Planning ahead?" Mora grinned, retrieving two glasses and a cocktail shaker. "Bezzy, you're so adorable."

"Whatever. It's unlikely to last. One of us will kill the other in a year or so." I forced myself to downplay it. It wasn't like I'd intended to tell her; it just sort of happened. Mora managed to drag out all my confessionals and then use them against me in the future.

As much as I doubted Wally would stay with me, I hoped for the best. A chance to prove I could… I didn't know. Be something with him. Not better. Not sure he wanted that. Be me, maybe? Myself. All of me and every piece I'd buried or lost or forgotten or burned away to dust. Be the parts of myself I never had a chance to explore. I didn't want to change, which I believed he was fine with.

Truthfully, I'd stay at Wally's side for as long as he'd have me. I wanted to see everything through his eyes.

Standing here, thinking about everything I wanted. Everything I could have. Everything possible moving forward. It made my skin itch in the worst way. Mora's horrible hovel became even stuffier. Impossible to breathe or think or feel. Gods, I needed air.

"Don't just storm out," Mora shouted as I slammed the door. "I was making us drinks."

I darted out of her apartment complex and flew high in the sky, back to the motel where Wally waited.

Only he didn't wait.

He still hadn't arrived. His presence lightly yanked from far off. Likely still tying up loose ends with his mother in a complicated and polite mortal manner.

I took the time to clean this ratty room. The fragrance spray Wally had bought did little more than ooze a sludgy, overly sweet smell above the stale mold. I exited, breathing in the fresh air and squinting at the bright sunlight. I could've grabbed my sunglasses, but I grew bored with blending in. I went to the check-in office in search of real cleaning supplies.

The bell chimed as I entered.

"Whoa." The man at the front desk stared wide-eyed. "What's with the ComiCon get up?"

I didn't understand this slur, but my horns and wings were not comical.

"Silence, mortal." I locked him in a tiny nightmare and went in search of supplies.

Since my battle with the mages, I'd shredded most of this host body. I couldn't retract my wings or horns or claws. Wally urged me to use a Diabolic haze to maintain a low profile until we left, but that was tedious, and I had no intention of lingering long in this city. He claimed we'd leave soon enough, anyway. I'd dwelled here enough. It was time to put Seattle behind me. Behind us, hopefully.

Using my tails, I raided the cabinets, only finding canned foods, musty towels, and other useless things. Walking down the halls, I eventually found an abandoned cart with half-empty spray bottles. They were a grimy brown, holding strong cleaning scents mixed with each other. I hated this cheap place. I needed more currency moving forward. I'd assumed the mortal obsession with it was a passing fad, yet it remained strong, stronger in fact, than when I'd arrived in this realm. If Wally and I were truly setting off, we'd need nice things.

And since he complained when I stole things, I'd need to steal currency instead so I could properly buy things. It seemed very mortal.

I returned to the motel room, occupying my time thoroughly cleaning everything in sight. Ammonia killed the grime, even erasing the musk of mine and Wally's sweating bodies. The sun set, and he still hadn't returned. I'd scrubbed every inch of the room three times over to occupy my time.

Nothing bad had happened to him. While I kept the tether connecting us loose, I felt the slightest tug of the slack. He moved throughout the city all over. My heart hastened, wondering if he avoided returning. Maybe the hours away from me had offered clarity. Perhaps he'd contemplated returning. Doubted leaving with me.

"Fuck." I huffed.

I went to the nightstand, grabbing his notebook and scribbling additional destinations. If he didn't want to join me, he wouldn't have to. I'd make my own adventure. I didn't need Wally. I didn't need anyone.

I gulped, swallowing the lie hard. What if I'd been too pushy about how he should handle his vile mother? What if killing Ian changed him? Made him question his life? What if he didn't want to walk away from the Collective? Especially now that he'd easily pass the practitioner exam, surpassing all the pathetic mages who'd always been beneath him.

My heart pounded, practically jumping out of my chest.

It took careful breathing to realize this was the tether, not anxiety. Mostly.

His mana surged outside the room. I rushed to the door, almost opening it as he fumbled outside. The knob turned, and I returned to the bed, ignoring him in favor of my notes.

"I texted you four times," he said, holding a dozen plastic bags in one hand and his tiny pet in the other. "What's the point of getting you a phone if you don't use it?"

"I didn't ask for a telephone," I grumbled.

"It's not a telephone. It's a phone. You text, you call, you video chat. Add apps. You'd probably enjoy them."

"Telephones were not made for letter writing. I hated writing letters when they were standard."

"Bez, it's not letter writing. It's quick, conversational, and to the point." He placed the scorpion in the tank.

"If you wished to check in, you should've called."

"I tried. Straight to voicemail."

That was because I'd already broken the damned thing. The glass was fragile, and the telephone kept turning my words into incomprehensible sentences. Who says 'ducking'? Piece of shit device deserved the death I'd served it, transforming my charm into illogical, poorly strung-together notes.

"What is all this?" I nodded to the bags he set on the floor.

"Gotta eat, right?" He pulled out a container of fried chicken. "I also got you a few things. Not a lot but hopefully enough to last a few days."

"What'd you buy?" I peeked inside a bag of raw steaks, sweet pickles, and a tub of cool whip.

"I tried to think of the most horrifying taste combos and just grabbed everything I could carry."

There were so many delectable treats inside.

"It'll tide you over while we figure out our first destination, which is fine because it'll take a few days for me to find a cheap car, find the best routes, decide on—"

"How'd you buy all this?" I licked my lips. "Did you steal for me?"

"No. Al might've given me something from his trust. Sort of a farewell."

"Why does he have a trust and you don't?"

"Oh, I lost my trust fund years ago when I switched from the sentinel regiment to the archivist." His voice became deeper, his face stern. "An Alden who does not hold up the legacy cannot reap from its history."

So brave, even when at his most timid, Wally always upheld his belief in himself and his goals. If he hadn't been bold enough to go on his own then, our paths would've never crossed.

"Not much of a legacy to uphold now." He chuckled.

I grabbed his arm and pulled him close. He stared at my horns, studying the intricate ridges as he ran the fingers of his free hand along them.

"Not that I have a problem with them, but you're going to have to do something about your Diabolic features before we head out."

"This body's busted. I'll just put a haze up."

Wally twisted his lips. "Liar."

"I've been absolutely discreet."

"I saw the clerk."

"He called me a clown."

"Maybe we can find you a misfit mage before we leave."

I strummed my claws against the small of his back, ready to rip through the cotton and denim which separated our bodies. "There's only one misfit mage I want to be inside right now."

"If you're not going to get a new host, then I'll have to glamour away some of these." He locked his gaze on mine, staring deep into my crimson eyes.

Moving his hands from my horns, he gently traced his fingertips along the black veins where my essence circulated. He hadn't made comments or shown concern since the changes appeared. Honestly, I thought he was overcome with the rush of killing and the freedom of leaving the Collective. Or the regret of both actions.

I hesitated, studying his reactions.

His expression didn't show either of those. Nor did his words. Tone. Body language.

Everything about Wally screamed blissful freedom.

"I rather like the Diabolic additions, but I prefer my dashing devil a little less dashing"—he yanked my tie, loosening it—"and a lot more naked."

He lifted the tie but hadn't loosened it enough to go over my head, so it got stuck at my forehead below my horns and covered my eyes.

"Wally, let me—"

I fumbled with the knot.

"No, let me." His knees hit the shag carpet hard, and he'd unfastened my belt and pulled my pants down to my knees by the time I'd unsnagged the tie.

"Well, well, well." I played with his hair as he swirled his tongue around my tip.

Getting a firm grip on his hair, I let the motion of his head guide my hand. It didn't take long for the muscles of his throat to adjust, and he swallowed the entirety of my cock.

I took a sharp inhale, holding all the air in the room inside my lungs while also keeping his head firmly in place. He gagged, lips gasping around the base of my cock. Realizing his struggle, I released his head. But he didn't move. In fact, despite the involuntary jerk of his body seeking air, he grabbed my hips with his hands, holding steady for a few more blissful seconds. His throat was warm and wet and tight.

Finally, he backed up, taking in hasty breaths. "Please stop treating me like I'm breakable."

"Didn't want to choke you," I wheezed, missing the feel of his mouth. He'd made his desires clear from the first time we'd screwed, and while I got carried away from time to time, I did hold back sometimes.

"I don't mind choking." Wally stood, his arms swaying back and forth, casting wind throughout the room.

A light breeze circled our bodies. Wally used the current to lift himself before wrapping his thighs tightly around my hips. We fell back onto the bed. He kept a hand pressed against my chest, ripping through the buttons of my shirt one by one as he eased onto my cock. I took slow thrusts, allowing him to adjust. My chest warmed, and he leaned in close, pressing his cool skin against mine.

"Not that I don't enjoy this." He continued grinding on top of me. "But I prefer it when you show me what a devil's capable of."

I released a primal roar, rolling us onto my side and taking faster strokes. Wally buried his face into my neck, moaning as I sped up. His throbbing dick hit my stomach with every thrust of my hips. He bit down on my shoulder hard. So fucking hard. I pounded into him faster. Using my tails, I finished undressing so I could properly maneuver on this small bed.

I released him, then threw him further up the bed, stripping off his clothes. His eyes lit up at the assertive way I tossed him. I turned Wally over, burying his face in the mattress and raising his hips. Moving my hand down to the small of his back, I pressed my claws ever so. He arched further, obeying the light instruction. How I relished his desire to serve. I slapped his ass; a claw scratched him. He moaned, and I paused, backing away. I kissed the red mark on his cheek.

He remained as he was, his body aching for mine. The tether connecting us pulled at my heart. I returned to my position.

For the next quarter hour, the only sounds were Wally's groans and our skin slapping together as I rammed him. I leaned in, pressing my chest to his back, pinning him, and continuing to thrust deep inside him. He turned his head, lips searching for mine. I kissed him, soft and delicate. My tongue ring massaging his tongue. Then I slid an arm under his, wrapping a hand around his throat.

His face turned red; hazel eyes glossed over in a haze of delirious ecstasy. Kissing him again, I resumed ramming further into him. I released his neck as he jerked up, then buried his face into a pillow. Yanking his hair, I pulled his head back up. I wanted to see his expression as I continued. His brow wrinkled, and his face contorted involuntarily as his muscles spasmed beneath me.

"Bez, I'm…" He released a muffled grunt as he came.

He lay there, breathless, but I continued. "I'm not done with you yet, little mage."

I kept his head pressed deep into the mattress with a hand pressed to the back of his head. His soft whimpers fueled me as I kept thrusting with a rhythmic pace matching his panting. Licking my palm, I reached my hand around to grab his flaccid cock. Stroking slowly at first, I gave him time to stiffen before moving at a blurred speed. My palm vibrated around his throbbing erection.

The second time he came, I couldn't hold back. I pushed all the way to the base of my cock and growled. A long feral noise followed by jagged, irregular breaths.

Rolling off him, I scooted further up the bed, pressing my back against the wall.

Wally lay on his stomach, ass exposed with the covers just below his cheeks. He rested his head on the pillow, taking steady breaths which helped ease my own. I traced my claws down his back, indulging the subtle shiver of my own spine as he giggled. Minutes of still silence passed. I relished this gentle moment with him. I'd have to wear him out like this more often if I wanted a bit of quiet.

"What's this?" Wally grabbed my notes off the nightstand, placing them on the pillow in front of him.

I rolled my eyes. Clearly, nothing tired him out enough to prevent curious studying. Propping himself on his elbows, he squinted as he read.

"You should get new glasses before we leave."

"I'll be fine. It's just a little fuzzy. Probably has more to do with your chicken scratch than my vision."

"My penmanship is exquisite."

"Your cursive is sloppy."

"At least I can write in cursive." I scowled.

Wally ignored me, smiling as he read through the list. "Is this like a destination road trip?"

"I wasn't going to aimlessly wander this tiny world." I maintained a scowl, resisting the smile his joy brought me.

"You made a plan." He rubbed my leg, fingertips tickling the hairs of my inner thigh, and stopped short of reaching my cock. "You nerd."

"Hey!" I snatched the paper from him. "Since you're going to mock it, I'll just tear the dumb thing up."

"No. I love it. Actually, a lot of the places are spots I have always wanted to go. Not for the sights. Not that there aren't a ton of things to see. It's just there's so much history in the places you picked. Mythic, mage, even—"

"Mortal, I know."

These were all destinations Wally dreamed of visiting. I wouldn't be able to get him access to the Collective archives in these places he craved to see. He'd spent years gushing about them while working in the repository. There were other things I could show him, wonders he'd never heard about, which he'd love even more. Of course, that meant I'd have to listen to him blather on for hours.

"Okay, so if we take a…" The rambling had already commenced.

Wally typed furiously on his phone, planning every minute of the first destination. Sights to see. Places to eat. Rooms to stay. An itinerary that'd fill every waking minute of our travels.

"Did you pick these places because of me?" He bit his lower lip.

"No. I'm following the migration patterns of unicorns. They're delicious and nutritious."

"You know unicorns are dangerous, right?" Wally shuddered. "They eat children."

"I know. That's what makes their magic so potent." I snapped my teeth. "Their rainbows are fueled by the hopes and dreams of their prey."

"That's not true. Is it?" His hand twitched, practically itching to scribble the note for further study.

"I'm going to show you a whole world of Mythics the mages have barely scratched the surface of."

Wally pounced on top of me, legs wrapped around my hips and

hands firmly planted on my shoulders. I reached out, brushing his parted lips. He kept his eyes locked on mine, pupils dilating. His mana mixed with my essence casting such a radiant glow around his aura. The pleasure of his company was as comforting as it was arousing.

Wally's heartbeat thumped faster, hastened by my own excitement. I could feel him syncing to my emotions the same way I'd linked to his. Our muscles and minds held this rhythmic unison. Still uniquely our own, simply with a subtle afterglow of the other's presence on a constant loop. A blissful existence I could get used to.

"Before you show me the world," he whispered, nibbling my ear. "Think you can show me that vibrating thing you did with your hand one more time?"

"You're insatiable." I rolled over, pinning him beneath me.

I licked my palm, then softly trailed my claws down his ribcage. Using my tails, I bound his arms together above his head and wrapped each of his ankles, spreading his legs wide.

Delicately, I kissed his neck, then chest, then stomach, savoring the sweet taste of his skin with each light smack of my lips.

He let out the lightest moan as my palm rubbed his crotch. The simple sound of his voice made me fully erect.

"Maybe I'll show you the things I can do with this tongue ring."

Quivering, he held back the convulsive pleasure, which sent a tingling sensation down my back. I stretched my wings wide as I went down on Wally.

THE END

ACKNOWLEDGMENTS

Thank you! Thank you! Thank you! I'm grateful to everyone who's taken a chance on *The Misfit Mage and His Dashing Devil*. This story was such a rollercoaster to draft and an absolute delight from beginning to end. This was the first book I wrote purely for myself though I hope others will love it as much as I do. I usually struggle getting out of my own head and trying to find the purpose of a story I'm working on. That didn't happen with Wally and Bez. I did ultimately find the purpose, the journey each of the main characters needed to have, but this really was just a fun ride for me.

If you enjoyed the story (or even if you didn't) please consider leaving a rating and/or review on your thoughts. It means the world to me that you gave my story a chance and every rating/review really helps boost a book's visibility for other readers. No pressure though because I'm already grateful you picked up this book to begin with.

I'd like to give a huge shout out to my amazing editor, Charlie Knight. Their continued support has tremendously helped elevate the books I share with readers. I'd also like to thank all my early readers, from those who have critiqued all my stories (even the ones

I haven't shared with the world) to the folks who thought an enemies to lovers fantasy adventure between a mage and devil sounded fun.

There are more journeys ahead for Wally and Bez and I hope you'll return to join them in the next installment of the Diabolic Romance Book Series. If you're interested in learning more, consider checking out my author website (mnbennet.com). Feel free to subscribe to my newsletter where I offer monthly updates and some sneak peeks. I've got a few projects planned for 2024 and can't wait to share more with readers.

325

AUTHOR BIO

MN Bennet is a high school teacher, writer, and reader. He lives in the Midwest, still adjusting to the cold after being born and raised in the South.

He enjoys writing paranormal and fantasy stories with huge worlds (sometimes too big), loveable romances (with so much angst and banter), and Happily Ever Afters (once he's dragged his characters through some emotional turmoil).

When he's not balancing classes, writing, or reading, he can be found binge watching anime or replaying Dragon Age II for the millionth time.

Author website: https://www.mnbennet.com

Amazon page:
https://www.amazon.com/stores/MN-Bennet/author/B0BLJJK5NF

Goodreads page
https://www.goodreads.com/author/show/23017668.M_N_Bennet

www.ingramcontent.com/pod-product-compliance
Lightning Source LLC
Chambersburg PA
CBHW030138310726
48970CB00005B/1490